Stories From the Center of the World

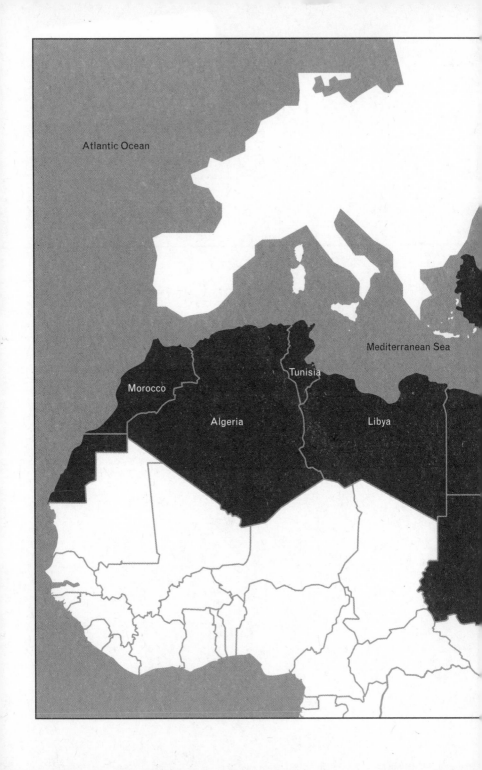

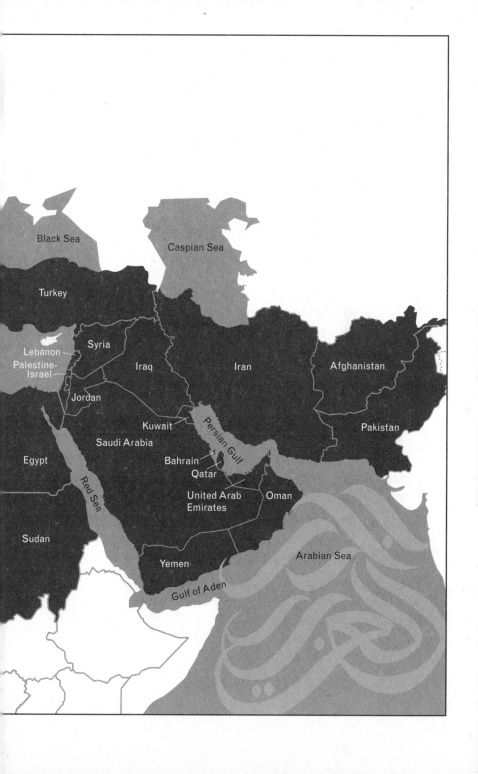

"This remarkable collection of short stories showcases the vast diversity of what has come to be called the 'Middle East,' as well as the diasporas that have sprung from this constellation of cultures. Provocative and subtle, nuanced and surprising, these stories are hard to categorize — for how does one categorize such a vast region except through unfortunate stereotypes? Together these stories demonstrate how this complicated and rich region might best be approached — through the power of literature, wielded so well by a host of established and new writers."

    — VIET THANH NGUYEN, author of *The Committed*

"A truly ambitious mix of established and emerging literary stars from a region of the world too often viewed through the lens of religion and politics. The stories collected by Elgrably reflect almost every corner of the mosaic that is the modern Middle East, giving practically everyone a voice and serving as a reminder of our common humanity. A timely and necessary collection for anyone who loves good stories."

    — REZA ASLAN, author of *An American Martyr in Persia*

"It seems like short fiction by Middle Eastern writers, writing in English or in translation, has taken an evolutionary leap in the last few years. *Stories from the Center of the World* is the latest entry in this renaissance. This volume is loaded with two dozen stories of exile, love, and magical realism. The characters that populate them are a patchwork of ethnic identities, as it is the case in the "center of the world." What is impressive about this collection is how culturally informed and varied it is. The languages and settings referenced stretch across the globe, from Las Vegas to Beirut. These riveting and original tales range from a story about an Egyptian in exile looking for a place to pray in Las Vegas to a story about an ambitious writer who accidentally lands on the devil's waitlist. I highly recommend that readers of this rich anthology take time to rinse their palate between each story."

— ZEIN EL-AMINE, author of *Is This How You Eat a Watermelon?*

"Iconoclastic, intimate and powerful, this ample collection gathers unforgettable short stories from just-emerging diasporic writers as well as the region's stars, covering a wide range of experiences from Edward Said's 'exiles, emigrés and refugees.' A balm for our time, when much of what the world hears about the Middle East has to do with numbers and political ideologies. In this collection, we hear intelligent, distinctive voices, expressing joy, humor, pain and irony in stories about love, exodus, renewal and assimilation."

— MONA SIMPSON, author of *Commitment*

Stories From the Center of the World

New Middle East Fiction

Edited by Jordan Elgrably

CITY LIGHTS BOOKS — SAN FRANCISCO

Cover design by em dash

Text design by Patrick Barber
SWANA map illustration on pages ii–iii by Maece Seirafi

Library of Congress Cataloging-in-Publication Data

Names: Elgrably, Jordan, 1958– editor.
Title: Stories from the center of the world : new fiction from the Markaz
    Review / Jordan Elgrably, editor.
Description: San Francisco : City Lights Books, 2024.
Identifiers: LCCN 2023053548 | ISBN 9780872869073 (paperback) | ISBN
    9780872869080 (ebook)
Subjects: LCSH: Short stories, Arabic—Translations into English. |
    Arabic fiction—21st century—Translations into English. | LCGFT:
    Short stories.
Classification: LCC PJ7694.E8 S76 2024 | DDC 892.7/3708—dc23/
    eng/20240205
LC record available at https://lccn.loc.gov/2023053548

City Lights Books are published at the City Lights Bookstore
261 Columbus Avenue, San Francisco, CA 94133
citylights.com

Table of Contents

III The Roots of Heaven

Introduction

THE CENTER OF THE WORLD, WHERE RECORDED CIVILIZATION got its start over 7,000 years ago, can be found in southwestern Asia, in ancient Mesopotamia. It can be found in *The Epic of Gilgamesh*, in the Torah and the Talmud, in *The Odyssey* and *The Iliad* of Homer; in Zoroastrianism, which predated the Qu'ran by over 2,000 years; in *A Thousand and One Nights* and in the literature of 20th-century poets and writers, among them Khalil Gibran and Naguib Mahfouz, Hanan Al-Shaykh, Ahdaf Souief, Nizar Qabbani, Ghassan Kanafani, Mahmood Darwish, Forugh Farrokhzad, Amin Maalouf, Edward Said, Hisham Matar, Assia Djebar, Kateb Yacine and too many more to name.

Eventually nationalism took root, as it did in Europe, and the ancient civilizations became identified as Iran, Iraq, Syria, Egypt and the many other countries, small and large, that stretch from the Mashriq to the Maghreb – from Pakistan and Afghanistan in the east to Morocco in the west.

But in 1902, American naval historian and retired admiral Alfred Thayer Mahan expressed a hegemonic vision of the world in a paper he published in the *National Review*. In "The Persian Gulf and International Relations," Mahan described the western Asian region from the Gulf to the Mediterranean as "the Middle East," suggesting that whichever navy controlled that part of the world would hold the key to world domination. After World War I, Europeans jumped into the fray with the secret Sykes-Picot Agreement, which divvied up the region after the fall of the Ottoman Empire, with several countries coming under British or French influence. The domino effect of outsiders meddling in the affairs of west Asian nations led to the Balfour Declaration, the San Remo Conference, the partition of Palestine, the creation of Trans-Jordan (a British protectorate for 25 years), the division of Greater Syria into Syria and Lebanon, then the end of Palestine and the establishment of Israel . . . right up to the year 1953, when the CIA with the machinations of MI6, succeeded in fomenting the overthrow of Iran's democratically elected leader, Mohammad Mossadegh, which would lead to the anti-Shah uprising 26 years later that became known as the Iranian or Islamic Revolution.

All of this to say that the "Middle East" or the "Near East" are akin to exonyms, terms used by outsiders to define others as they often do not define themselves; they are convenient catch phrases that continue to cause consternation today among those of us who are from the center of the world. Lebanese poet and translator Huda Fakhreddine calls the "Middle East" a trap – "a made-up thing, a construct of history and treacherous geography, the Middle East as an American trope, a stage for identity politics."

To be sure, neither Rear Admiral Mahan nor Lord Balfour, much less Mark Sykes, François Georges-Picot, or any of the other many thousands of Western politicians, secret agents, generals, businessmen and other meddlers have ever given much thought or exhibited empathy when it comes to what it means to be Iraqi or Syrian or Iranian or Egyptian, or Palestinian. Geopolitics has been capitalism's overlord and nationalism's emperor, serving agendas that have little to do with the needs of real people.

It is a given that governments prefer borders and passports, shored up by flags and patriotism, while people will always find a way to relate to one another, in spite of their nationalities. Personally, I prefer the metaphor of the mosaic or the salad when it comes to parsing identity: just as it takes several colors to create a mosaic, and a salad contains diverse ingredients, we are all the sum of multiple parts, and each of us is much more than our national identity card.

●

I became closer to my own North African roots as a result of living in Spain in the lead-up to the 1992 Quincentennial, when there was a lot of talk about the Spanish Muslims and Jews who were effectively exiled as a result of the Inquisition in 1492. They left a powerful imprint on the soul of the country, as Marie Rosa Menocal so elegantly describes in her classic work, *The Ornament of the World: How Muslims, Jews, and Christians Created a Culture of Tolerance in Medieval Spain* (2002). But the *convivencia* that Menocal described was not merely a period of Spanish history; this cultural entente was innate to southwest Asian societies, which had long been comprised of a mix of religious, cultural and ethnic communities. In the aftermath of the post–World War II reconfiguration, the Nakba, the Islamic Revolution and the Iraq War, however, the region has lost much of its organic diversity, and current economic strife and climate devastation continue what Western meddlers started over a hundred years ago.

Not all is doom and gloom when it comes to the center of the world today, however, because despite the failures of the Green Movement, the Arab Spring and the Syrian civil war, "what has not changed is West Asia's geopolitical centrality," as Chas Freeman has written. "It is where Africa, Asia, and Europe and the routes that connect them meet. The region's cultures cast a deep shadow across northern Africa, Central, South and Southeast Asia, and the Mediterranean. It is the epicenter of Judaism, Christianity and Islam, the three 'Abrahamic religions' that together shape the faiths and moral standards of over three-fifths of humankind. This gives the region global reach."

This is the time for the original voices of people from the region to be heard – for Arabs, Iranians, Kurds, Middle Eastern Jews, Armenians, Turks, Afghans, Pakistanis, the Amazigh and Kabyl peoples, Druze, Assyrians, Copts, Yezidis et alia to speak up, and speak out.

•

Here we have a collection of 25 short stories selected from *The Markaz Review* (TMR), an online journal of culture and the arts that seeks to transcend boundaries and highlight connections throughout the global Arab/Muslim world, elevating a cultural voice that is often misrepresented and misunderstood. This selection of the best fiction published in TMR from 2020 to 2023, and features authors with roots in Egypt, Greece, Iran, Jordan, Kuwait, Lebanon, Libya, Palestine, Morocco, Pakistan and Sudan. The stories are divided into three sections, loosely themed around immigration, love and family, and death and immortality. Many of the writers live outside the countries where they were born and often write about. As a result, I think of them as exquisite insider-outsiders – the natural condition of all writers, I would argue, is to be both within and from the world of which we write, and yet hovering at its edge, almost as if we don't quite belong.

Hanif Kureishi takes up the cause of outsiders in "Asha and Haaji" who become unrooted when war or disaster strikes and they flee for safe haven. Asha, who describes himself as a harmless bookworm with no religion, notes that "no terrorist ever found inspiration in Kafka," and seduces the younger, whiter Haaji with his erudition. He reminds us that "the foreigner has been suspect from the beginning of time," and we are not surprised when Asha realizes that in polite London society, he is a pariah, an outcast.

In "The Salamander," the young Lebanese American writer Sarah AlKahly-Mills champions women and girls, who want to escape abusive men and poverty. The salamander becomes a metaphor for regeneration, and as a result, hope for a better tomorrow. In "The Suffering Mother of the Whole World" by Amany Kamal Eldin, Nadia El Sha'er returns to Cairo to visit her retired father and weary grandmother, but knows that she feels far more at home in her American life. Unmarried, she exults in her freedom and exhibits no desire to move back to Cairo. For Nadia, having become an American, being Egyptian now is a matter of nostalgia.

In Ahmed Naji's "Godshow.com," another Egyptian exile searches for a place in Las Vegas to pray, but one feels that the exercise will be in vain, that the search is just for show, for appearances. "All I had wanted was to visit a mosque, not send my children to an Islamic brainwashing laundromat." In muscular prose, translated from Arabic by Rana Asfour, Naji winks at the reader, inviting us to experience life in his skin, albeit with just the right dose of irony. We are at once inside the character's experience, and outside with the writer, enjoying his sharp-eyed observations.

In "Nadira of Tlemcen," things take a more serious turn with Abdellah Taïa's story about a young Algerian named Samir, whose father always understood that his son was different from other children, but it isn't until Samir can escape to Paris that he will begin to become his true self. In "The Afghan and the Persian," a literature professor from Kabul has no choice but to become a *harrag*, and finds himself in France following a shipwreck. "Why have I come here? I washed up on your shores as a man who loves books and words and libraries and ideas. I thought by coming here, I could save myself."

Often the men, women and children in these stories have no choice but to flee their troubled countries, but in Malu Halasa's "A Dog in the Woods," an Arab patriarch remembers how he became an educator in Ohio, and raised his children to be more American than Arab; he had little desire to look back, and successfully assimilated, but his children do not seem quite so assured in their identity.

With the second part of the book, "The Question of Love," writers recount divergent tales of love and loss, strained family relations, and dashed dreams. Farah Ahamed's innovative love story, "Anarkali, or Six Early Deaths in Lahore," upends expectations as it recounts events from the end to the beginning, and the poor street sweeper known as Anarkali (not her real name) is a surprisingly articulate narrator. In Alireza Iranmehr's "Buenos Aires of Her Eyes," translated from Persian by novelist Salar Abdoh, a love story between an octogenarian and a much younger woman strikes us as both inevitably tragic and absurd, but also touching and inspirational. The old man — an Iranian transplanted to Switzerland, who is said to have been in love only twice in his life — instructs his children that "Each person lives in their own special universe. A place no one else can know and yet is not impossible to imagine." Iranmehr's story, like the others in this anthology, invites the reader into the special universes of a diverse cast of characters who are each fallible, vulnerable, and yet incredibly strong at the same time, fortified by the experience of having started life over in a new country, often in a new language, braving rejection, and sometimes persecution, as they slowly adjust to their new lives.

We find reliable narrators in the stories by Nektaria Anastasiadou, MK Harb, Leila Aboulela, Danial Haghighi and Natasha Tynes, which all take place among people who have not had to leave their country, yet confront situations in which love itself is a questionable unguent or adhesive. Love may not be enough, it might not solve all problems, but clearly we are better off living with it, as ugly as things can get.

In Anastasiadou's "The Location of the Soul According to Benyamin Alhadeff," two students in Istanbul issued from different classes — and religions that have often been at odds with one another — believe they can overcome all obstacles. In Harb's story, "Counter Strike," we're invited to empathize with queer love among Beiruti adolescents, yet we may find ourselves scoffing internally at Al-Naas' heteronormative character in "The Cactus." Aboulela's "Raise Your Head High" features a sympathetic narrator, who loves her sister Dunia (married to a creep) but is hounded by her Tante Walaa. She ultimately seems like a very lonely soul, right up to the moment that the Egyptian uprising erupts, on January 25, 2011. In Haghighi's "Here, Freedom," an arranged marriage turns out not to be quite what it seems, right when Iran is going through another series of protests. And in "The Agency," Natasha Tynes invites us to experience traditional Amman, as men and women look for their ideal mate via a dating agency that has developed its own peculiar classification for what passes for a virtuous woman (the men are under no such scrutiny).

Finally, in the last section, "The Roots of Heaven," Salar Abdoh invites us into the world of former militants, fighters who fought ISIS or Daesh in Iraq and Syria, who are having a hard time readjusting to civilian life. There is glory in being a martyr, but not everyone makes the cut. In Mai Al-Nakib's "The Burden of Inheritance," a departed husband's death turns out to be the beginning of a calvary, as his wife discovers that art can become a wearisome housemate. Do we best remember our loved ones via their words, or the work they leave behind?

Karim Kattan, a native of Bethlehem who writes in both French and English, tells an unexpected Palestinian story, almost haunting in its detail, in which the usual bogeymen – Israeli occupation forces – are mostly absent, while another malevolent force seems to overtake an unsuspecting family. The brother in "Eleazar" is both an innocent and a potential suspect, and his sister Mariam, who narrates, seems out of her depth.

The young Lebanese American writer May Haddad takes readers on an outer space journey in their speculative fiction, "Ride on, Shooting Star," in which Carna' is an unconventional heroine, to say the least. Here, the future seems inconsequential, while the present looms as large as the known universe. There are, of course, no pat answers, but we are somehow with this young cosmic courier all the way, dreaming with Carna' that she will find her utopia. In Tariq Mehmood's "The Settlement," the oldest and tallest tree in the world is at the center of a controversy in which a jailed mystery woman resists interrogation. And in Sahar Mustafah's "The Peacock," a Palestinian woman who has become an internal migrant to escape her futureless existence, finds her power unleashed when she decides to risk everything.

Omar El Akkad's "The Icarist" is a coming-of-age story, yes, but it's much more than that. It is about the encounter that inevitably occurs between the haves and the have-nots, the underworld in which illegal immigrants are forced to live, and what happens when one dares to break away. A quintessential outsider, El Akkad's thirteen-year-old Mo'min Abdelwahad is dimly aware that his future in Dubai is limited, yet he remains unilluminated for decades, until the moment he risks death.

We come to the end of our adventures with Ahmed Salah Al-Mahdi's story about a mediocre writer who imagines that he might just be able to escape his destiny, challenge what is *maktub*, if only he can make a deal with the devil. In "The Devil's Waiting List," Mansi takes the initiative, but begins to feel that he is a fool – not unlike the way one feels buying a lottery ticket.

Taken together, these 25 stories represent an orchestra, playing a complex collective composition that radiates out from the center of the world. Clearly, we all have a lot of work to do to agree on our common dignity and humanity, and with a deeper understanding of our center, we can better move forward as one.

— JORDAN ELGRABLY

MONTPELLIER, FRANCE, JANUARY 2024

PART ONE

Exiles, Émigrés, Refugees

"Modern Western culture is in large part the work of exiles, émigrés, refugees."

EDWARD SAID
Reflections on Exile and Other Essays

Asha and Haaji

HANIF KUREISHI

CALL ME EZRA. CALL ME MICHAEL OR THOMAS. CALL ME ABU, Dedan, Ahmed. Call me Er, Asha, Trash or Shit. Call me whatever or no one or nothing. You already have more than enough names for me.

In this place my identity and even my nature changes from day to day. It is an effort for me to remember who I am. Like a child rehearsing his alphabet, when I wake up I have to reacquaint myself with my history. That is because I am not recognized. I have no reflection here. Except in her eyes. When she sees me I come to life, if life is the accurate word, which it probably isn't.

Wearing my only shirt, in the small shabby hotel room which we are forced to leave, I jerk about on my toes waiting for her. I see that I am very thin now: near-death has something to say for it. It is a very odd thing, living every day in fear. At least you get to practice renunciation, but I am, I have to say, a reluctant ascetic. At home I never went to bed with less than five pillows.

My few pathetic possessions, along with my sacred books – Hegel, Dostoevsky, Kafka, Kierkegaard – are in canvas bags. I hope they send a limousine because I am not sure how much further I can walk. Something tragic has happened to my nervous system which makes me twitchy. My head is too heavy and my body scarcely obedient. I'd have been better off as a cat.

She was lucky to find a job as a maid here. For two weeks she has been hiding me in her tiny room. We took turns to sleep on the plank of a bed until I made an unavoidable mistake. I had a terrible dream, screamed, and was discovered. Here, even your nightmares can betray you. In the future – and I also use this word with a laugh – I will sleep with tape over my mouth.

She and I must get out again. Who knows where. They suggested I am some kind of security risk, or terrorist, and that it would be no trouble to them to report me to the police, who will interrogate me again. She begged them not to bother since I have no religion and, I have to admit, no acknowledged beliefs. I am only a harmless bookworm as soft in the head as ice-cream. No terrorist ever found inspiration in Kafka. And I'm far too lazy to start killing people. I don't give a damn for invasions or wars; I expect nothing less of humanity. But all this, what has happened, is an inconvenience too far.

●

In my city far away I ran a coffee shop.

●

She is angry. She has had enough. And she is all I have. I like to believe she would never abandon me. She must know I will not survive. This strange life is too much for me and my mind is a madhouse. I wait for her. In two minutes everything could become different. I will know from her face.

Haaji is ten years younger than I am and not as dark. As soon as she arrived she stopped covering her modern hair. She is not regarded with the suspicion us men are. She could pass as a "normal" person. I'd never touched a body so white.

For a few weeks I became her savant. She had never met anyone like me, and my view of the world became hers. She risked her life to protect me, though I am not sure if she will continue to do so. We will see what I am for her.

My town in my country was destroyed. I fled and traveled here to the land where the Enlightenment originated, to the democracy where I became an outcast overnight. I woke up to find I'd turned into someone else.

The foreigner has been suspect from the beginning of time. But let us not forget: we are all potential foreigners. One day you too could be turned over from the white side of life to the black. It takes a moment.

Others will notice you do not belong; you will disgust them; they will fear you.

My close pal from the coffeeshop, One-Arm, was relatively organized. I'm aware this is unusual in a poet. We escaped our country together and the first few weeks were chaotic and rough. But he had connections here. He guided me.

With him, two months after I arrived, I got a job, as did many others like me, working for Bain, the king of miles of wedding cake mansions and magazine apartments, whose work was to secure empty houses and apartments in the great city. And so, after the terrible journey, things began to look up for me. I was even excited to see Europe again, the buildings, libraries and landscapes, though last time, when I was a student, I had with me a tourist guide, camera and a cheerful curiosity. This new perspective – think of a man viewing the world from inside a litter bin – is, let us say, less exotic. It is more informative to be at the mercy of others.

Bain could do anything he liked to us. We swarm of new nomads walking in history whether we like it or not, are the new slaves. We were compelled to obey and even admire him, which he seemed to enjoy. We shadow people have no tourist guides or even meaning. Strike us if you want to. Take advantage. No one complains.

We were inside the most beautiful houses and apartments in the world, places I'd never seen except on television, and certainly never set foot in before. Empty of life and people, we could enjoy these properties more than the owners – bankers, money launderers and criminals, princes and dirty politicians – who lived in Beijing, or Dubai, Moscow or New York, and who might have forgotten about them altogether.

I can tell you: emptiness doesn't come cheap. I'd never seen so much light in a building before.

Things that were not dirty, that had never been used, had to be maintained. That was our job: cleaning the clean. Working all day every day, we cared for deserted swimming pools, plump new beds, steam rooms, saunas. Acres of wooden floors and yards of blinds, walls, garages, and gardens had to be attended to. The repainting was continuous. People get less attention but they are worth less.

Our team went from house to house. Sometimes the places were close together, in the same block. Other times we were driven around in a van. People like me, we so-called talkers and intellectuals, those of us who live by abstract things like ideas, words and beauty, are of not much use in the world. I wondered how long I could last in this job. However, in one remarkable house, I was assigned to the garden, clearing leaves, pruning, digging.

It was in this house, under an elegant staircase, almost resembling the one in my favorite movie – and Hitchcock's best – *Notorious*, that I discovered a small room with sloping walls containing an old armchair. I guessed the billionaire owner had not only never used this space or seen the armchair; he didn't know it existed. What would he care that when I sat in it, and rigged up a light, I was comfortable at his expense? Perhaps he was kind and would have been happy for me. Why not?

Just two months before this, when the shelling started in our city, and we finally recognized the truth – that our lives as we'd known them were finished forever – we had to clear out. I gathered clothes and as much money as I could get hold of. Then I stood and stared into nothingness: even while my companions waited for me, something kept me back.

•

My books. You might find this odd, but they were my main concern even then. There's nothing like displacement to give you time to read. Kafka, Beckett, Hegel, Nietzsche, Montaigne. My father had passed them on to me. They were my mind and treasure, my single resource.

When it was time to flee, and everything was falling down, I rushed to the back of my café, which also functioned as a library and bookshop, pulling down whatever I could carry, filling my hold-all, other bags and my pockets.

In the new city Haaji and I had found ourselves working in the same house. Bain mostly employed women but he needed men for some work. At first I barely noticed her. She seemed quiet and humble, with her head bowed, wisely keeping out of trouble. None of us spoke much. This assembly of ghosts was in shock. Our mouths were shut.

When I saw her looking at me, I wondered whether she had seen me talking to myself.

Late one evening, when we had finished work and were yet to be taken back to our accommodations, there was a rap on my cupboard door. I was inside, in my armchair, reading. At this noise in my secret place I was terrified. Was it now I'd be punished and dismissed?

Hearing her soft but urgent voice – "Asha, Asha, it's Haaji" – I opened the door. She stepped past me and sat on a stool, opposite my chair. Her intrusion seemed brave. I was puzzled. I waited for her to speak.

"What's in that book?" she said at last. She pointed. "And in that one? And that one?"

"What do you think? Why do you ask?"

She was able to admit that she wanted to talk to me, this small girl in her white work coat and white shoes. Two scared people sitting together in a cupboard. She asked me to say something about what I was reading. Would I explain it? I could tell she was clever and even educated, but only up to a certain level. Perhaps she had had problems at school or with her family. She was thin and frail, yet with some determination to her.

These visits were repeated over many nights. I saw that I had to clarify and simplify my thoughts. There's only so much most people would want to know about Hegel. But she was fascinated to hear about the master-slave relationship, the interdependence of the owner and the servant, leader and follower, creditor and debtor. How they are bound together. The eternal impossible reflection.

I was surprised; I became enthusiastic. I wanted her to know what I saw in this stuff, why I said it was more important than money. More important than most things people valued.

"You're so kind, you can be my teacher," she said.

I enjoyed that. It was invigorating to be of use again at last. What did we need? Better words. Fresher ideas for her circumstances. The new vocabulary gave her an enhanced angle. She could see more clearly from the adjusted position. What you think you're doing under the official description you're not doing under another. Like sinning, for instance. Suddenly it can appear under love.

What a discovery. Modesty has its limits. Let me say that at this time, with her, I found myself liking myself very much. I had a function. She made me into a person.

Like me, like all of us here, she was afraid and running from something. But unlike me, she was running towards something. A new life: hope, the future. It was good to see.

Haaji and I, as new companions, could consider ourselves privileged as we went from house to house carrying cleaning equipment. We got to see good furniture, art, sculpture. Only the richest people could afford Warhols, usually the Mao. There were eerie deserted swimming pools and kitchens with no food in them bigger than apartments. We washed down sheer walls of glass overlooking the city.

At night, when I was sometimes the watchman in these houses and all was quiet as a monastery – the beautiful quiet of a city – we sat with our feet up, compelled by the ever-changing night landscapes. In our way we could share the privilege. We could walk on the most beautiful carpets and eat on tables made of Carrara marble. We slipped into their swimming pools and floated on our backs in our pants. What a wrongdoing it was. How we violated them, living their dream. And how childish it made us.

In this panopticon, permanently under the unfeeling eye of some nebulous authority, Haaji and I did a dangerous thing. Our eyes lit up when we saw one another. Something was starting between us; luckily it wasn't what you think.

We began to play games. We knew where the cameras were. No one looked; Bain and his men rarely glanced at them. There was nothing to see. I'm not sure if any of us stole anything. We were searched all the time.

•

Haaji and I liked to pretend we actually owned these houses of the rich where we served. During these games we could be wealthy and royal.

We strode about with authority, shouting orders. We discussed how difficult the builders were and how severely our lawyers would treat them. We wondered about lunches and lovers. I asked her which suit she preferred me in, and which tie and shoes looked best. We speculated about whether we would go to Venice or Nice for our holidays, if we would have sea bass or veal, champagne or vodka.

It was an empty exhilaration. One-Arm came to me with a warning. We had to be more secretive. The others had noticed. There were several black men working with us, mostly doing building work and deliveries. They were dirty, licentious, argumentative, threatening. Their language was incomprehensible and none of them had read a book. Forgive me, please. I hear you. But to each his own foreigner. Can't I hate arbitrarily too? Is that another privilege I have to forsake? Sometimes hating tastes better than eating. You know what I'm talking about.

One-Arm said the blacks were gossiping about us and they liked the girl. Why would these others want us to be happy when they were not?

In my city I ran a coffee shop ...

•

In our familiar closet, bent under the sloping walls and in our armchair, Haaji and I talked harder by candlelight. Democracy, love, dreams, gender, virtue, childhood, racism: we had it all out. The sensation of infinity and no one else in the world.

She tried to show me her body, a madness I couldn't sanction. I looked away and told her about my coffee shop. To keep the café alive I'd describe the families, smiles and jokes of my friends there, now scattered who knows where.

In my city I ran a coffee shop. These beautiful words I recite each morning, like a prayer or affirmation.

I consider myself middle-class. With a hesitating, timid manner, I've have always feared mirrors. I was never much to look at, with bald patches, a heavy, duck-like walk, and shortness of breath. I have had two lovers, but I was always scared of women and never keen to copulate. What is a man before a woman who is having an orgasm? Is there anything more terrible? I don't believe most people really like sex. Certainly, I found so-called sex physically intrusive if not obscene. It seemed unbelievable that people could want to put their tongues in one another's mouths. Now, I loved motorbikes. A Ducati is a thing of glorious beauty.

Socrates said, I can only think of Eros. I take this to mean: how does one relate passion to the rest of one's life? Some people look for God, but I look for my own god of Eros in everything and not only bodies. I see it in coffee and sentences. So I go along with St. Augustine: I may have remembered it wrongly, but I like to think he said that having a penis was God's hilarious punishment for being a man. Your dick goes up and down randomly, particularly when you're young, and you can't control it by willing. In church, I found, it went up with inconvenient regularity. Then, when you're finally in bed with Cindy Crawford and she is murmuring your name, you know you're not going to make it. Forget penis envy, I'm all for castration. That is why I hide my penis in books. I'd rather read about it than live it.

There, before, in my town, with my routine, I was dedicated to my work and liked to serve. It was an honor; I was proud of the little place. Making an Americano, offering pastries and newspapers, talking to my customers, seeing if I could charm them, this was my vocation.

My 1200cc motorcycle was outside where I could appreciate it, large and classic as I wiped the tables down and swept the floor. There were pictures and photographs on the walls – works I bought from local artists to encourage them. In the back of the café were books on architecture and comfortable chairs. My clientele consisted of fine dissenters a blink away from prison: human rights lawyers, academics, blasphemous writers, singers, anarchists, troublemakers. I made sure to know them all by name. Sometimes I was invited to their houses. I imagined a band of aliens, bohemians and originals. Like Paris after 1946: Richard Wright and Gertrude Stein chatting.

Now, suppose some dictator takes the guns the West sold him and blows up your coffee shop. Not only that. The street, in fact the whole town, everything and everyone there, is, one day, obliterated in a surging fire. Suppose you look out at your neighborhood one morning and everything you know is gone. Behind the conflagration there is only filth, ruin, smoke. The people you saw every day – shopkeepers, neighbors, children – are dead, injured or running. And no one recalls why making this hell was necessary or what good cause it served.

*

Civilization is a veneer. Underneath we are incontinent beasts. Who doesn't know this? Yet it is not true. If we are savages it is because we are commanded to be so. Because we are followers. Because we are obedient.

People: I am coming at you with my strange ways. Like many others, I scrabbled to the city of the enlightenment. At first I slept on benches and beneath dustbins. I shat in your parks and wiped my ass on your leaves. It was dangerous. Strangers roughed me up. I took that as an affront, having never seen victimization as a natural part of my condition.

Almost as soon as I arrived, my papers were stolen as I slept. Later, I got new papers. I had been warned, but I was forced to go to Bain. You should have seen the approval on his face. He had predicted I would have to ask him humbly for help. He had done it a hundred times with others and made sure it cost me. His friends grabbed all the money I had brought with me, and Bain took his cut. Then I worked to pay him back. I would never pay him back. Like the others, in exchange for some safety, I was the devil's forever.

You must think me careless. I got new papers. Then I lost them. Really, it was then that I lost everything. This is how.

You walk along a quiet street in a normal city with your friend, One-Arm the poet. It is a part of the city which considers itself civilized. You see a woman in a café reading a book. Attractive people talk of Michelangelo. You see galleries and museums with people strolling and looking. There are new buildings with fabulous curves. You want to go in. You tell One-Arm that even Ulysses went home.

You approach a bar. For you, the ordinary citizen, it is nothing but a bar. But to me, for whom the normal was a long time ago, it is a danger point. From where I see things, you might call "the normal" a façade or window-dressing, just as the dying might think the healthy inhabit a stupid illusion.

Outside the bar a man is drinking. He looks up and his eyes take you in. Here, in the heart of paradise, an explosion takes place inside him. Your being outrages him. At the same time he is filled with a peculiar pleasure: this is satisfaction anticipated. I should say: madness is the mainstream now. Haaji calls it the new normal. For thirty years I was a free man. Now I am a dangerous dog in someone's path.

You grab your poeticizing friend by his one good arm and you shuffle away. You have recognized definite danger.

As you feared, the man comes, with others. They are always nearby and they are quick. These are productive times for vigilantes, the protectors of decency.

Nihilism doesn't dress well. You wouldn't want to discuss poetry with them. They have shaved heads. They wear leather and have tattoos. They have clubs and knuckle-dusters.

One look at us is all it takes for them to know civilization is at stake. We raggeds with our awful belongings and need are a threat to their security and stability.

I have no doubt: it is dangerous for us here in Europe. I am paranoid, I know that. I hear interrogations and arguments in my head. I expect people to have a low view of me. We are already humiliated. Not that there isn't much for us to be paranoid about. If we are on the street, just walking, they stare and often they turn their backs. They spit. They want us to know we are peculiar to them, unwanted. They talk about choice and individuality, but it amazes me how conformist and homogenous everyone is.

We, the reduced, the primitives, savages and filthy drifting blacks are terrorized. We, I say. We are not even a we. We are still a "them." The cause of all their problems. Everything bad stems from us. I needn't enumerate their accusations. I don't have much time.

We flee, One-Arm and I. We run as we've never run before. A blur of limbs, a streak of terror.

They catch us. They beat me so badly I can't open my eyes. I can barely hear. The police are indifferent, of course. The fewer of us the better.

One-Arm was murdered that night but saviors came before I died. Haaji persuaded Bain to let me stay while she wrapped me in her pale love. What use was a wrecked man to him? She convinced him I would soon be back on my feet. I wonder how she really persuaded him, particularly after he said he would have her skin made into a pretty handbag for one of his employers? It wasn't entirely a joke. He was selling the women in other ways. Our bodies have their uses.

Haaji must have been in love, or at least devoted at that time because her kindness was unlimited. This will surprise you, but she had been uplifted by my optimism. These are dark days in a dark world for us dark people. And perhaps I'm some kind of holy fool. Yet I never stopped telling her that I believe in the possibility of collaboration and exchange. People can, I maintain even now, do creative things together. I'd seen it in the coffee shop where good things were said. If there were only destruction, there'd be no life at all on this planet. Hear me: let us try some equality. Equality is such an interesting idea. Why is it the most difficult thing?

◆

After the attack nothing was right with me. Bain had his group, and he had seen that Haaji was susceptible. There are many men keen to run cults, and many devotees who will join them if they believe they will be eventually rewarded. The cult generally, whether religious or political, patriarchal or matriarchal, has not stopped being the modern form of belonging.

There were those who saw him as a liberator. He was Schindler, protecting and hiding those of us threatened with extinction. Unfortunately he had his theories and preferred belching words to listening. After work, in a millionaire's mansion, I can see him pacing up and down like an imam or preacher, on a priceless wooden floor, while we slumbered at his feet.

Humor is usually humiliating and tyrants don't encourage such instant deconstructions. My mumbled quip about the price of disenfranchisement being the necessity of enduring hurricanes of hot air didn't boost my attractiveness. Unluckily for me, I'm an enthusiast and skeptic rather than a follower. In a properly efficient tyranny – the only ones worth considering – someone like me doesn't last five minutes.

Despite my desire to remain cheerful if not cynical, the world was making me bitter. If you think literature is weird, try reality. I had always been an admirer of Beckett. As I giggled through his prose in my coffee shop and wrote his quotes on postcards to send to friends, it never occurred to me that I'd be buried up to my neck in manure. Unfortunately, the fictionists I admire give no instructions and require no sacrifices. That is their virtue and failure.

With nothing to lose, I had a good idea.

Since the attack, toothache had taken me over. My teeth were giving me unforgettable trouble. How could someone like me afford a doctor or dentist? The pain was too much and I wanted to strike out at the world. Why can't people be nice? That's a good question, isn't it? Kindness has no politics and there wasn't enough of it in the world. I would introduce some. So I became keen to murder Bain.

He was rarely alone but came out into the garden of the mansion to smoke one night. He had his back to me: the part of him I most preferred. I was sitting behind a tree at twilight, reading by the light of a small torch. I noticed a branch nearby and it occurred to me to relieve Bain of his brains. I thought: aren't I really a murderer dreaming I'm a respectable man? By sparing the world an evil force I would receive both satisfaction and moral fulfilment. If you ask me, it is the sadists and perverts who cause trouble, being overly concerned with what others are doing. Didn't I want to be good?

He turned away.

I thought: I can still catch up with him, and strike him. There is time. Millions have murdered. Many liked it. Didn't they seem to live on, unworried, continuing to enjoy TV and discounts at their local supermarkets? But I was weak. We are all Hamlet's brothers, and killing wasn't a breeze for me. Why should it be? I let the moment go. As he disappeared along a path, I picked up the branch and knocked it in regret against my knee. The log disintegrated.

I wasn't able to do the work Bain demanded. I was limping and weak. I had no rights and no money. There were rumors he was selling the organs of recalcitrant workers. Not that he would get much for mine. I asked her to leave with me.

It was touch and go. I had to tell her that the protection she sought was an illusion. There's never any shortage of tyrants and their self-interest was catastrophic. She had found the wrong master in Bain, and I couldn't be a master at all.

We escaped at night, taking backways and hiding in woods, washing in petrol stations.

We were settled in a small town which is worse for us than the city. The residents are restive and nervous. There have been bombings and attacks throughout the country by maniacs, religionists and politicos. There was a shooting not far from here. The politicians hurry down like housewives at a sale. After each tragedy, the people hold vigils and light their candles. They link hands, weep, and swear they will never forget. But they do forget when there is another and then another incident.

They insist that they are being forced to put their values of decency and tolerance aside. They must protect themselves against outsiders. We are not the saints they thought our suffering obliged us to be. We have let them down with our banal humanity.

And here we are now. Haaji got a job in the hotel and smuggled me into her room. We didn't talk. I had no mystery left. I'd taught her everything I knew and it wasn't enough. After a time I saw what was wrong: I didn't know what to ask of her.

I lay there for days. The room became a kind of tomb. It was a good opportunity for me to think about death. Socrates, after all, wanted to die in his own way, when he was ready. It was not suicide: death was not a "must-have" for him. Nor was it despair. Rather, it is a question of whether there is any profit in living. People want to live too long now. Considering my own death certainly changed a lot in me. I lost a lot of fear.

Late at night, if the coast was clear, she and I would sometimes sneak out together, through the backdoor. She walked ahead, wearing lipstick. I had to go behind, tattered, making sure not to lose sight of her. Our distance was essential. A woman like her, with a man of my color, we could never hold hands. They already believe we copulate more than anyone deserves.

At the harbor we'd sit apart, on different benches, joined by our eyes, signaling to one another. I have come to like, if not admire, ordinariness. Along with an empty head, it is the loveliest privilege.

One night, when the weather was wild and the sea a frothy cauldron, I caught sight of many other boats on the horizon, bringing hundreds more of us aliens with upraised hands, shouting "freedom, freedom!" Meanwhile there was a hubbub in the harbor. Some wanted to watch them drown. For others, human values had to persist. While they fought amongst themselves some of the boats went down.

Now I hear a noise. It is her footsteps. She comes in. She barely looks at me. She is different.

She gathers her things and walks out into the street. She is ahead of me as always. She knows how weak I am, but she is walking fast, too fast for me to follow. She knows where she wants to go. It is raining. I hurry along. But it is hopeless.

I call after her. I want a last glimpse and a memory. "Here, take them. You will need them."

She stops.

One day everything will be borne away in a great fire, all the evil and all the good, and the political organizations and the culture and the churches. In the meantime there is this.

I hand her my bag of books. They are inside me now. Let it go.

The Salamander

SARAH ALKAHLY-MILLS

Zahra

IN ONLY A DAY'S TIME, ZAHRA WILL FIND HERSELF SWIMMING across a sea, and the grueling journey will be infinitely preferable to what she will leave behind. Anything, anything at all to escape. She will formulate her plan, if flinging oneself headfirst into the Mediterranean with nary a belonging but a good luck charm may be called such, in between blows from Kareem, the generous. For now, she sits in a café in Bsharre with the old woman they call Humbaba on account of her obsession with guarding the last cedar tree, and they wait for their coffee to arrive.

"They want to put me in a 'home,'" Humbaba says of her adult children. She refuses to budge. A sentinel does not give up her post. "If they call that a 'home,' then what is a prison?"

Zahra looks across the way to an ancient limestone house, its red tile roof missing shingles like a grin its front teeth, its walls enclosed with something like a police perimeter. *Traditional Lebanese house!* Reads a sign with an arrow pointing to the crumbling edifice, designating its purpose as an attraction for the tragedy tourists who flock to see the ruins.

"Tell me the story of Warda," Zahra implores.

"Warda, ya Warda. Warda was born before the Blasts, before even the Wars! A long time ago, fi qadim al-zaman, when you could eat pine nuts and drink from the streams of the Qadisha Valley and buy things you didn't need!"

When she talks about the Golden Age, Humbaba's cloudy eyes

smoulder with dignified, martyrish resignation. She scrapes mind-lessly at dry scales on her hands. Her short white hair branches out in peaks and slopes like thorns. She puts Zahra in mind of a mother she never knew.

"She picked wild berries, chased down kibbeh nayyeh with arak, listened to vinyl records of Fairuz, wore full skirts and sunglasses, drove her own Beetle, and her purse was never empty of Lucky Strikes!"

"Yes, Humbaba, but tell me the part when she kills her husband," Zahra says.

Humbaba looks behind her to the etiolated cedar. Coffee arrives at the hands of a handsome waiter. A tourist snaps two photographs: one of the house and one of them.

•

Zahra hitches a furtive ride back to Beirut on a small bus overflowing with bodies. *Warda*, she says to herself like a spell, and it snaps its fingers – gone! The sounds of snorting, wheezing, cursing; the smells of exhaust, sweat, chemical aftermaths, brine. She grips the ladder with one hand and stretches the other out into the wind, leaning with the bus as it slides like a puck down its winding road, smiling, feeling as though something grand were on the brink of birth. She knows the story more intimately than the sound of Kareem's weight as he steps on that loose tile between kitchen and living room. She became en-amored with Warda immediately after Humbaba told her the wom-an's story, which was after Kareem had let loose his German shepherd, Zelda, on her black cat. She had named him Najmi for his coat, dark as a star-studded city night after the grid collapsed, but Kareem had named him Haram because whenever he would bully the creature with a stomp of his foot and laughter that barked like his hound, Zahra would say, *Haram! Mish haram? Isn't it a sin to torment an innocent creature?* All that had remained of the innocent creature was gore, a memory she painted over with vermillion thoughts of revenge set to Kareem's words: *Such is nature.*

It is only Warda she sees now, standing over her felled husband, engorged a translucent pop-ready purple with a poisoned morsel caught in his throat. He died the way he lived, swollen with greed. Zahra laughs with self-pity. The humid air leaches the last of the spell's bliss from her mind. *Where would I even get poison?*

•

Home is a stilt house near Ground Zero, one of several spread out over the seawater that rose like a prophecy and washed away the Mövenpick Hotel, many cafés and restaurants, and the last of a generation. She pays the taxi boat driver with a promise and takes measured steps along a creaky boardwalk with handrails made of rope. He waits where the water laps at a stilt.

"I need to pay the taxi," she says to an empty home. "Kareem?"

The house rocks and shifts with the waves. The searchlights of foreign government vessels on the lookout for people-smugglers illuminate the dark living room at intervals, landing on wet eyes that glow a ghoulish green. Zelda guards Kareem's stash: wads of worthless cash, bags upon bags of salaam, and all the scraps he's collected from those desperate for the hallucinogen, bartering away the last of their valuables in exchange for a moment of peace. A moment of salaam. She's never tried the drug, but they say it makes a person rise far above their body into the sky and meet their idea of home.

Nothing leaves or enters the cage where Zelda and her master's cache are kept, not without his knowledge. A gleam at the edge of the enclosure catches her eye. Within her reach, a piece of green porcelain shaped like a hook, something that looks as though it were broken off a larger body. Zelda snarls as Zahra extends her hand slowly and snatches it away quickly, pocketing the piece before hearing the loose tile move.

"Stealing from me, ya kalbe?"

A searchlight finds Kareem and lingers on him, and Zahra, dread be damned, plucks a moment of wicked pleasure from the knowledge that nothing but his deception and her despair could have ever bound them together, so undesirable he was by each and every metric. He had had to lie his way into her, a woman made pliable by all the dead ends she'd rammed her panicked beak into. Cracks in his façade had begun to show not a moment after he'd no longer had any reason to pretend, and he had steadily decayed over the years, chain-and-padlocking her into an old manor of a man, crumbling brickwork, mold-eaten walls, gates off their hinges, ghosts who whispered into his ear, commanding him to hoard, as his only guests.

"I need to pay the taxi," she says.

"Give him the only thing you have, then. And swim next time if you don't like the arrangement."

A violent blow unlike any wave to have ever made their house sway now makes it spasm. Below, Taxi Man bellows with an axe in his hands, ready to deliver another hit to their weathered stilts: "My payment or you sleep in the sea tonight!"

Zahra walks past her husband. He grabs her wrist. "Where is it?"

◆

How Kareem could have ever spotted such an inconspicuous trifle missing from his reserve is a mystery to Zahra. She wants to ask him, *Is it an artifact? Are you hoping to sell it to the British Museum?* But he had laid into her for less.

Now, as Kareem extracts vows from her to never so much as look at the cage again, Taxi Man pronounces his sharp threats, the house shudders, and the latch comes unlatched, displacing some of the stash and freeing the dog, who stands over them while Zahra struggles under her opponent, cheering on the wrestling match as though she'd placed bets on it, bits of her frothing spit landing on Zahra's cheek. Kareem bears down on her neck and carbon dioxide accumulates in her body and a single thought forms in her mind with striking lucidity given the circumstances: Would she look like Warda's husband, purple and ready to pop? Fear fuels her last act of resistance, and she feels around her body for the green hook. The house cedes to a final blow from Taxi Man's axe and collapses just as Kareem howls and his hands shoot up to cover his left eye, where she pierced him with the hook's fighting edge.

The fall lasts forever and for only a fraction of a second.

Below the water, Zelda dances in slow motion, twisting among the thick debris to propel herself to the surface. Above, it rains paper money, along with clouds of salaam that gently float down and meet the scream in Zahra's throat, coating her lungs and stretching fingers up to her brain, where they curl onto themselves and hold. She clings to the floating cage and sees Taxi Man fighting to keep sure footing in his ramshackle vehicle as he snatches at the air for falling bills.

"Satisfied now?" she asks him, turning onto her back to look up at the night sky and seeing herself instead, in sunglasses, with a cigarette poised between fore and middle finger.

"Warda, ya Warda, the One Who Pushes Through Cracks in Concrete. So you did it!" Humbaba says, floating next to her on the rocking chair where Kareem would sit and survey his day's gains – a butane gas lighter, a titanium tooth implant, a bicycle wheel. On her lap is dear little Najmi with sparkling stars in his fur.

"I can't be here anymore," Zahra says to her.

"*Lakan* – leave!"

"Come with me. I'll carry you across my back, and we'll cross the sea to the other side. What are you even doing for that sorry old tree?"

Behind Humbaba, unending acres of lush green cedars and a mezze table as long as the coastal highway.

When Zahra comes to, it is morning. Kareem lies belly up on the front door of their ruined house, Zelda's jaws working through his entrails, pulling up her prize – his *ghammeh* – and snapping away at it.

"Such is nature," she says. She remembers her plan, flashes of her body cutting westward through seawater like a dolphin as Kareem squeezed strobing visions into her oxygen-starved mind. "So, this is what we leave behind?"

A sinking ship. Stalwart Humbaba and her melancholy tree.

The green hook calls to her with a well-timed wink of sunlight as it floats by. She pockets it for good luck.

◆

Zahra registers with mild surprise the texture of something other than water beneath her fingertips. The sea crawls over her body and pulls, begging her to come back. *Do you think I am as easy as the rocks you've battered down to grains? I've killed, you know!* She drags herself further up the shore. She hears the voice of a child.

"*Zikra, c'est une sirène!*"

The crunch of sand beneath boots.

"*C'est juste une femme,*" Zikra says. "But please, Arabic, Barakah."

Barakah

"*Qu'as-tu dans ta main?*"

At first, they feigned kindness when they asked.

"Won't you show us what you've got in your hand, little one?"

All patronizing grins and stooped shoulders in the way of adults who imagined they could swap sincerity with saccharine sweetness and go undetected by the children they hoped to dupe.

"Show us, girl."

The Merciful Sisters of the Adoration of Perpetual Crises, Barakah thought, might have been more accurately named the Intrusive Sisters or the Meddlesome Sisters or the Inquisitory Sisters. They hated that she guarded something from them.

They had begun to scheme on how to obtain the secret Barakah held in her hand, preferably through non-violence so as not to rouse the suspicion of the many money-*mahshi* voluntourists at the orphanage. *Bless us with more children*, read the wrought-iron sign over its entry gate, a prayer answered abundantly, a cup overflowing.

"Why won't you show us? Is it because you know you are holding something evil? Something dangerous maybe?"

Smiles into sneers into threats, but Barakah's small hand remained a mighty fist, one they eventually tried to pry open with force, receiving bites that bled in the process.

"You will never be adopted," one sister pronounced gleefully, dousing her injured hand with antiseptic.

Barakah marveled at their ugliness, which adults refused to see. They never came close enough to the sisters to see them for who they really were and thus never saw the fault lines in their patchwork papyrus skin, taut hermetic-tight over brickly bone. They never saw them from the necessary vantage point, heads at their hip-level and looking up into black nostrils crowded with spiderwebs and loose folds of flesh stitched back under their chins to not belie their decline. They never saw how, at night, they hung rightside wrong and huddled together from the rafters, bats in black habits and wimples.

But all their grotesqueness mattered little to Barakah because she could retreat into her secret.

It had come to her by pigeon beak on a breezy morning. She had been banished to an empty dormitory as they all performed Sunday worship. For so slight an infraction as a growl during prayer, imagine. The sisters had thought it punishment, oblivious to the effervescent delight Barakah kept hidden behind pressed lips and blank eyes, little left fist by her side like she was gearing for a fight. Alone, she'd stared out the window to a playfield of tires and pipes and scaffolding and shell casings and traced her mind's fingers over a fading memory of her father's face, blurring at the edges evermore with passing time. He was tall and kind of smile, and he would fashion meals and toys from scraps and his own ingenuity, a golden dusting of improbability that breathed magic into the mundane and taught her that beauty was the banal seen through clever, playful eyes.

"Carry a message for me," she told the wind as it touched a hand to her forehead, reminding her of when Baba would feel her for fever, "Tell him I miss him." It did as she said and changed directions towards the port, lifting her hair as though tempting her to join it, and it was in that moment she saw the pigeon, struggling against its flow, carrying something unwieldly between maxillary and mandibular rostra. It drew closer and closer until it reached her window and landed on the ledge, tucking its wings in and disappearing on scaly foot off to the side.

Barakah stuck her head out and followed the bird with her eyes. It deposited the thing like an offering into a spacious nest where a mother waited over eggs, warming them with her body, and where other objects were collected off to the side like gifts at the foot of a

Christmas tree – flowers stolen from graves, a diamond tennis bracelet, a pin badge in the shape of a shield. This latest addition was a piece of green porcelain with small protrusions and sharp edges on either side, as though it were once part of a whole, perhaps the handle to an amphora.

Already, she knew it was hers. She didn't like to steal, but mustn't the pigeon have stolen it from somewhere too?

"Plus," she told the feathered couple as they watched her apprehensively, "it has sharp edges. It won't be good for your little ones. And God help you if the sisters should see it shine like that. They'll take it, you know, and destroy your home for the fun of it."

She hid her secret under the closed lid of a toilet tank, third stall from the door, and kept a red herring balled into her left hand ever since. If they suspected something there, they wouldn't look for it elsewhere.

One night, a sister came for her.

"It seems you've made an impression," she sneered, baring tiny sharp teeth.

Barakah followed the sister down the coffin-shaped corridor that led to an office she had never been called to before but knew was where prospective parents went to discuss serious matters, all the time wondering whom she had impressed and how.

And that's when she saw the woman she would leave with before the end of the year. Wild black mane marbled with white, a long grey overcoat that obscured her body, a spyglass at her hip, an unmoving glass eye, and the shiny skin of a burn wound on the side of her forehead above it and her cheek below it. She never once asked what Barakah pretended to hold in her fist, and she never bent down to talk to her.

"What should I call you?" Barakah asked her.

"Zikra," she said, sounding very sad.

They were alone in the playfield under a muggy, mottled sky when Zikra said in her soft, breathless voice: "I need your help. I've been tasked with a very important mission, and I like the way you guard what's important to you."

"Why can't you do it yourself?"

"I'm dying."

"What's in it for me?" Barakah asked, watching the dormitory window as the new parents carried cracked eggshells away from their nest.

"A chance to get away from here."

When they readied to leave, the woman looked at her and asked, "Haven't you anything to bring with you?"

Barakah asked if she could keep a secret. Zikra nodded.

"And what is special about this?" she asked, examining the green porcelain, turning it over between her fingers.

"It was mine when I had nothing."

"And so it shall remain yours. Say fare poorly to the sisters."

Barakah turned back into the orphanage for a final time and stood in front of the committee. Smiling, she held her fist out and opened it, empty palm facing vaulted ceiling. Her victory, their gnawing disappointment in the space between. An eruption of new wings from the dormitory window.

◆

"Did you know that a salamander can regenerate its limbs?" Zikra says as they walk by the river in front of her estate.

It drains into the Mediterranean, she had said of that sinuous waterway on Barakah's first day on the island.

The mermaid who calls herself Warda lies on a lawn chair, watching them from behind her sunglasses and puffing on a cigarette. She looks different than the day she showed up on their shore. Healthier, with the arrogance of the accomplished. She is unmoved by their undertaking, sceptical of its value and success.

Barakah has begun to see the animal everywhere, in the scurry of field mice and lizards, in the flutter of birds fleeing their footsteps. In the fantasy landscapes of her waking reveries and in the vespertine layers of deep dreams, Zikra's fixation seeping into her pores and settling behind her eyelids, ready to pounce at every stimulus.

It is one of a kind, Zikra told her. *No one has captured it before, but it is as real as the ground you walk on, Barakah, and one minute spent looking into its eyes is enough to bless you with a feeling of home that lasts forever.*

"Alas," she mutters under her breath, looking to the figure atop the hill behind the estate, "you are too big to be a salamander."

Under the dimming sky, a silhouette. The magnetism of something more than chance pooling the incongruous together into meaning.

"Such activity on this island as I've never seen," says Zikra, squinting at the stranger through her spyglass.

Zikra

A young man. When he walks, his ornaments herald his presence: the rainstick shake of beads from bracelets at his ankles and wrists, the whisper of fabrics touching and parting. He holds his hand to an azure turban. Cape and pantaloons billow with the breeze like sails. A heavy pendant at his chest, a ring on every finger.

The details of his person shift into focus as he approaches them, and Zikra is reminded of all the things she mistook for her salamander, the many mirages induced by poor eyesight and distance, formidable shadows cast by small branches, smiling and scowling faces in the most unlikely places.

"Who are you?" Zikra asks him.

"I am Amir," Amir says.

Wrapped around his head, a United Nations T-shirt, its globe and laurel wreath positioned in the space between his black eyes. At his ankles and wrists, obsolete, hole-punched coins threaded through with zip ties. His cape is a bedsheet, his rings beer and soda bottle caps, his pendant the porcelain head of what looks to be a snake.

●

"I was never supposed to see them," Amir says as they sit around the fire pit and he recounts the story of how he came to be a fugitive.

"But how can you tell one day from the next until it is different? It was a day like any other day, and as such, I hiked through the hills and valleys of rubbish in search of something I could fashion into fashion, art from the discarded, use from the abandoned."

It was how he found the sequins that now adorn his vest, the empty Coke bottles from which he built his raft to sail to the island.

"The others made fun of me. For them, it was a useless pursuit. But what is more useless than waiting for something better to come to you? I might be wearing rubbish, but you tell me whether, for a moment, you did not mistake me for a prince!"

No one argues.

"I was outside Parliament when I saw it in one of the windows." He touches his fingers to the colubrine head. "It looked so real. Alive. And it was staring at me like a prisoner crying for help with those mesmerizing mirrorball eyes that drew light to them and multiplied it millionfold. I was bewitched. Most of the security had been diverted to the other end of the city because of a riot, so I took my chances and went inside and got it." He holds up his pendant proudly. "And there they were."

The president, the speaker, the party leaders, all filling the seats as though they were still locked in talks, but over the hall reigned a thick, static silence and the ancient smell of an undisturbed crypt.

"At first, I thought they might have been puppets, dummy mummies. But as soon as I touched the president, he fell forward and shattered like a sandcastle against the desk, sending up dust into my eyes and nose. And that's when I started to sneeze. I outran the drones that came for me, but why should I have to hide forever when I've done nothing wrong? Unless it's this they're after,' he looked down to the pendant at his sternum again.

"The living are an inconvenient presence in the realm of the dead," Warda says, falling back into her unbothered state.

"Who oversees the country then, if they are all dead? Whose drones followed you?" Barakah asks.

Amir looks at her sadly, a red-winged, yellow-bodied bird dancing between them and on the reflective surface of his pendant. Zikra has seen the shape of that tapered head before, its colorful kaleidoscopic eyes.

•

Zikra remembers little besides the beautiful stories of Backhome, a place she could see from the island, a place that sent up chemical vapors like a factory's smokestacks, that whistled and rattled with unrest yet beckoned to her with the pull of a terrible drug. She remembers having a mother and father who told her those stories, planting germs of yearning inside her that would steadily bloom into stalks and multiply into fields until her body grew too small to contain all that desire for a place she'd never really known but would try nonetheless to recreate on her island, populating it with rescued relics of the past – vinyl records, photographs, books, a reminder in every architectural detail of the estate, a fingerprint in its *mashrabiya* and arcade windows, exhumed semiotic signifiers to create a sense of place in the displaced. Of all the stories, though – of forests and beaches and mountain slopes and valleys and barbecues and crystalline brooks and ancient ruins and dazzling cities and glorious food and shahs and emirs – that of the salamander was the most excruciatingly enduring one, fermenting into an obsession that bordered on the malignant, bubbling just barely under her skin and erupting with every disappointment. She would find it, or she would die trying. And nearly died she almost had, scrambling after some slinky amphibian to the edge of a volcanic crater, liquid sulphur seeping from its cracks, and rushing into a sudden plume of blue fire that took her eye, the soft skin above and beneath it, and years of her life. Illusion after illusion, encounters with danger built upon dangerous encounters until her body became a storybook of consequences, ripe for reaping, alveoli steadily deflating, bronchioles brittle. Breathing, that industry that in others asked for nothing in return, demanded of her a formidable attention. Such was nature: always up for a duel so it could beat you.

She lied to herself that Barakah would be more even-tempered, more slow-and-steady-wins-the-race, when she knew from the moment she saw her at the orphanage that the girl was all potential, wild determination in every excitable cell of her. Zikra was almost sorry to recruit her into that carnivore's life, so much energy expended in empty pursuit of such a light-footed thing as a dream, always leaping out of reach.

"I won't be here for long, but I'll be watching from wherever I go afterwards," she had slurred one evening, unstopping a decanter of liqueur she had just stopped up, chest-deep in a pit of insecurity, hope a flickering thing in a cold corner of her ribcage.

"You don't need to threaten me," Barakah had said. "I want to find it too."

"The others say it doesn't exist. For them, it is a useless enterprise."

"What is useless is sitting around ridiculing others for chasing their dreams instead of finding their own."

•

The newcomer mourns at night, cape trailing behind him as he circles the estate in slow, measured steps like a ghost condemned to a moment on eternal repeat. During the day, he strategizes on how to de-patriate all the people he has left behind and bring them to the island, casualties of his reckless promises to remember them when he reached paradise.

"You know what the diplotourists would say to us?" Amir says. Every so often, he pauses to indulge his anger. "They would say, 'Look how you can see the stars now with no light pollution!' And we would look into that uncaring sky and wish for the warm glow of home, of civilization, of a kitchen or living room lit up with something other than foreign searchlights!"

When at last he sleeps, when it is almost morning, Zikra creeps into his room and finds the pendant on the commode by the window. Then, she goes to Barakah's room, where the girl's secret lies bare and trusting in a nest of discarded clothing. Warda's good luck charm too is defenseless, heaped in together with a pile of curios – a vintage poster for the Hotel Riviera, a stamp with Emir Bashir Shihab II's face on it, a red-white-and-green lighter with a map showing Tripoli, Fakeha, Byblos, Baalbeck, Zahle, Beit-Eddine, Jeita, Anjar, the Moussa Castle, and Tyre.

"How cruel," Zikra whispers once she has assembled the pieces. She sits at a table under the gazebo where yesterday Warda played casse-tête and stares at the porcelain likeness of her salamander, divided against itself, head-body-tail. Alone as night lifts and its chilled air sinks to the river, she weeps for all the time siphoned from her. A million ways to keep alive a legend was all she would ever know — drawings, etchings, oral histories, near-sightings. "How cruel to pass a sickness on to your children."

She rests her head onto the mist-damp wooden table and sleeps.

The Salamander

It is a glorious thing to be whole again. It takes me a second to find my footing, but once I do, I dart into the tall wet grass by the bank and scuttle through it before dropping into the water — and she after me. For less than a moment, we look at each other, suspended in that quiet limpid world. Her eyes are wide, and her striated hair swells around her. I am sorry to go, but she asks too great a sacrifice of me to stay and offer myself up for study. Ah, the adventures I went on though, the phenomena I saw, the way I was loved! I could not ask for more. I leave all this behind, unafraid.

It is known that salamanders swim far better, faster, and farther than humans. I plan to reach the sea within the day, and from there, who knows? Byblos, Tripoli, Tyre, Beirut . . .

The Suffering Mother of the Whole World

AMANY KAMAL ELDIN

WHATEVER GREATNESS COULD HAVE BEEN ASCRIBED TO THE
El Sha'er family at one time – and clearly, to rise above the dusty poverty of Egypt required some talent – was no longer apparent. On the
contrary, the family legacy that had been passed down from older generations had been abandoned or cheapened, like the French boudoir
table blurred by so many coats of paint, its hinges rendered immobile;
or the chipped portrait of a handsome, slender relative at the turn of
the century, with silk cravat and elegant fez, his pale face staring out of
the darkness. Perhaps, as the Arab philosopher maintained, a family's
downfall is inevitable.

The El Sha'ers had made their fortunes as merchants and lawyers. They claimed the requisite legitimacies: descent from one of the
Islamic caliphs, Turkish blood. They rose to prominence as ministers
under kings. Whenever you visited the El Sha'ers, in this apartment
or that, at the beach or in the country, their things sat around in dis-
repair gathering dust. They fought each other tooth and claw for land
and objects, even in front of the servants, who mumbled audibly that
money only caused trouble between people.

One elderly Sha'er, recently returned from the United States after
three decades as an insurance executive, bought an airy apartment
overlooking the Nile. He had long since lost his American wife, such
that the closest relative left to him was his daughter, Nadia, who was in

graduate school in Boston. Being a dutiful son, he installed his mother in the flat with him.

Adnan had returned to Egypt to retire, to sit on his balcony overlooking the Nile with his childhood friends, drinking whiskey or beer, nibbling on cucumbers and carrots. They would talk about the good old days before the 1952 revolution, and before nationalization, with such fresh enthusiasm the events might have happened yesterday. One man had ridden in the motorcade of the king, another had joined in his pigeon shooting. Life was elegant in those days.

When Adnan wasn't on the balcony, or reading in the study, he was at the club, walking around the racecourse and chatting with his friends under the jacaranda trees. Through most of it he fingered his sibha, a habit he had only indulged, in private, abroad.

Adnan had retired mentally long before he had retired physically. The new bridge spanning the club playing fields, the brazen behavior of the youth, the gaudy fashions of the club members left little imprint on his perceptions, were powerless to offend his sense of propriety, nor even moved him to expressions of impotent annoyance.

Adnan's ability to retreat from modern Cairo was helped by his home environment. The flat was filled with his mother's graceless furniture: a carelessly gathered hodgepodge of English Victorian, French Art Deco and badly copied Louis XV. Red velvet curtains were hung to shut out the sun and dust, the same material that covered most of the furniture. Adnan's quarters were separate from his mother's, so he was not bothered by her visitors, most of them supplicant, poorer relatives; or her screaming fights with the servants; or the occasional squawk from a scrawny chicken being weighed on scales at her feet.

In the early summer of 1980, Adnan sat in his brown study, sipping a cup of Arabic coffee out of a chipped demitasse cup and reading a letter from Nadia. She was coming to Cairo for the entire summer, not just the usual two weeks. His daughter was in need of a period of recuperation after a year of serious study and serious drinking. Nadia having been born to him at an advanced age, Adnan had developed a relationship of camaraderie and tolerated her speaking openly to him.

Still, he felt a twinge of worry at her coming. He enjoyed the apathy in which he existed, and which was shared by most of the populace that year. She tended to stir the air when she passed into a room. He wondered how she would fit against a background of somber furniture and velvet plush. Still, he also looked forward to her arrival, to having her sit late with him on the breezy balcony watching the city lights, laughing at the comic plays broadcast on television.

When he told his mother over tea that afternoon (she had the curious habit of always insisting that he eat a pastry with his tea), she suggested that they once again look for a husband for her. Adnan: "You know, mother, she has a Western mentality. In Amreeka girls choose their own husbands, after a long period of knowing them."

"Nevertheless, there is nothing wrong if she falls in love with an Egyptian and marries him. When she was going to the American University at Cairo she had many Egyptian boys as friends. At any rate I want her near me in Cairo. We could furnish her an apartment, with everything . . . a refrigerator, a washing machine . . . and we could buy her a car. She could work if she wants . . ."

"Mother, don't start again. You know these things wouldn't work for Nadia. She has her own mentality."

"That's your fault, Adnan. You married an American."

Adnan calmly stood up and left the room. As he walked through the silent, dark apartment, his bedroom slippers padding on Persian carpets, he realized he no longer had the energy to get into any of these facile arguments . . . about marrying outside his culture, leaving his family and country. None of that mattered anymore. They were no longer issues. He remembered why he had had to leave. And now, when he opened the door to the balcony and looked at the river, most beautiful before sunset, under diffused light, with a few scattered felucca sails billowing, he knew why he had returned. It was for no logical reason . . . just that his skin did not grate against the air here and deeply buried memories rendered him familiar with most of what he now saw and heard. The heat and the dust of this place had been woven into the fabric of his body in his youth so that he felt comfortable nowhere else.

Adnan thanked God for the view and for having rid him of his half formed ambitions, his myriad illusions. And he thanked God for having spared him the misfortunes that had befallen Egypt in the last decades.

●

Nadia sauntered into Cairo Airport late one June night, in jeans, a loose overhanging shirt, and sneakers, tossing her head to get the bangs out of her eyes. She barely recognized her father, standing near some soldiers with olive complexions, dark eyes and jungle green fatigues. Military uniforms used to be desert beige but then someone had decided that the locus of military activities would change. Policemen, who would one day quarrel with their military counterparts, wore summer whites.

Nadia had never felt comfortable in the ramshackle chaos and milling uniforms of the airport reception halls. Her father's tired smile did little to reassure her. The frailty she sensed in him prompted her to refuse his offer to carry her shoulder bag, her only baggage. As he drove her through Heliopolis, asking her questions about school, she fought back her tugging doubts about his possible mortality. When they reached the square near the Sheraton and the young men weaving through the cars selling flower garlands, she asked for a string of jasmine. Adnan bargained with a young man, all dressed in white and holding wreaths of blossoms, to one-third his asking price and handed the jasmine gingerly to Nadia. She cupped it in her hands and inhaled the reassuring smell. One of her earliest memories was of a string of blossoms hanging from a car mirror.

Nadia awoke the next morning to street and construction sounds. It was already blistering, the sun high in the sky, and the household had been awake for hours. Adnan was at the other end of the flat, sitting on the balcony drinking a cup of Nescafé. A strong breeze tugged at the newspaper he was reading. Nadia walked onto the balcony: "This place is like a morgue," she said.

Adnan: "Good morning Nadia, what would you like for breakfast."

Nadia: "Ful with white cheese and olive oil, please, and Nescafé."

"Ya Mohammed," Adnan called to a young man. Wearing green trousers, fitted white shirt and platform-heeled shoes, Mohammed appeared, smiling. He greeted Nadia with a deep handshake and more smiles. Adnan told him what Nadia wanted and he left for the kitchen.

Nadia: "What kind of salary do you give that man?"

"Officially, he's paid thirty pounds a month, but I give him an extra fifteen behind your grandmother's back."

"Is she still as bad with the servants as she used to be?"

"I don't know. I don't think so. How are you? How are you feeling — tired?"

Nadia squinted to look over the brilliant surface of the water. "No." She noticed buildings under construction everywhere and asked her father about them. They were mostly hotels.

"Is the Carlton still a whorehouse?"

"They've made some changes at the Hilton . . . very nice . . ."

Nadia's restless mind rebelled at seeing Egypt through her father's eyes. She had resolved to feel the country's pulse this summer, not look at it in terms of new Cairene hotels or imports in the shops. If she had any responsibility to Egypt, it was that, to determine its mood. She expected to sense that mood, the almost tangible frustration level, from the city streets — surely not from the countryside, which was another world after all, another age. It wasn't true, Nadia deliberated silently, that the Egyptian peasants had always accepted everything and endured. There had been rebellions, armed insurrections. It seemed to Nadia that the countryside was always receding behind a shimmering hot veil that blurred one's vision and clogged one's hearing.

Adnan interrupted her thoughts: "Your gramma is anxious to see you."

"I'm anxious to see her," Nadia replied, wanting to seem polite.

"She has become a little hard of hearing, so you'll have to speak loudly to her."

"Why doesn't she get a hearing aid?"

"She doesn't want one."

"Well, how is her health?"

"Better. Her rheumatism is still bad but she didn't suffer as much this winter as last. I bought her a new car, a Fiat, because her old one kept breaking down. Without a car she has no mobility."

For as long as Nadia could remember, her grandmother had had no mobility. She had always known her as overweight and slow moving, shuffling when she walked. But with the years her legs had gotten worse, with poor circulation, pain in the knees, forcing her to bend over and use a cane. Nadia had blamed this on her grandmother's fondness for starchy foods, which had rendered her overweight since her early widowhood. She was convinced that eating had been her main pleasure in life.

Nadia had barely finished her breakfast of fava beans and white cheese when Mohammed appeared. "Ya Sit Hanem, your grandmother is asking you to come to her room." This with a smile and a bow. Nadia knew that she'd get a long, close hug, like being pulled into a sponge, as her mother used to say.

Nadia found her grandmother sitting upright on the edge of her bed in front of a small, French boudoir table. On the table were a mirror and brush, lemon cologne, a worn novella and masses of keys. When she was a child Nadia would come into her grandmother's room to find her opening and inspecting closets, bureau drawers and steel boxes. Nadia was never interested in their contents. As far as she could see, these locked treasures consisted of bolts of cloth, embroidered linen, plastic combs, sequined coin purses, bottles of perfume that would eventually lose their scent.

Her grandmother looked up at her with a smile that was sincere if a bit distracted. She had cut her hair short and no longer bothered to dye it black. She had also acquired a pair of glasses. Nadia bent down to be hugged.

"I am very, very happy to see you. This time you will stay longer. Your father told me you will live with us now."

"No, gramma, I have to go back to Amreeka to finish my degree."

"What degree? You've already finished one degree. When you were asked in marriage four years ago we explained that you had two more years to finish your degree. Now you are working on another degree? Why do you need all these degrees?"

"I need them to teach, gramma. Anyway, you didn't encourage that marriage. Now, I'm in love with someone in Amreeka," she lied.

Nadia sat in a wide bamboo chair facing her grandmother. The old woman gave two resounding claps, upon which a spare, middle-aged woman in a soiled and faded cotton shift and cotton scarf tightly tying back her hair tentatively poked her head around the door. She didn't smile. Nadia didn't recognize her.

"Sharshira, bring us coffee." To Nadia: "Do you want some ice cream?"

"No thank you, I just had breakfast."

"How about some pastry, baklava?"

"No thank you, I had a heavy breakfast."

Her grandmother dismissed the woman with a lugubrious wave of the hand and a "go bring two coffees and two plates and two knives." She then turned to a little cabinet at her side, fiddled with some keys until she found the one that worked, and brought out a plate of unappetizing fruit. Nadia found this new habit vaguely worrisome.

After half an hour of shouting answers to her grandmother's questions, mostly about this fictional character in Amreeka (how many houses does he have, how many cars, what kind . . . that proves nothing) Nadia pleaded jet lag and the need for a nap. Her conversation with her grandmother had deteriorated in the last few years. They used to chat . . . easily. They had both been younger then. When she wanted to go traveling her grandmother supported her, against everyone, particularly the male members of the family. She gave Nadia the keys to her flat in Alexandria. She offered her cigarettes in public, to the consternation of her father. She even financed and organized a party for Nadia at the family farm, and moved her hulking shape there for the day, sitting on a straight-backed chair in a closed courtyard while Nadia's friends moved about the lawn.

In earlier times Nadia used to love to sit and listen to her grandmother talk about the past. Her estranged father had sent her a piano when she was made to quit school at puberty... her husband had been kind ... Adnan's Saudi friend had treated her royally when she went to perform the pilgrimage ... Nadia knew what was essential about her grandmother, which was never alluded to: that she had always wielded power over the family, through her money and force of character.

Nadia didn't care, since she didn't need her money. Relatives used to be jealous of Nadia's relationship with her grandmother and couldn't understand it. After all, Nadia was unmannered, ingenuous and a mere female. Her grandmother chose Nadia to accompany her on official outings – a wedding in the mansion of a family from Mansoura, her visit to the wife of an imprisoned minister. On these occasions Nadia could barely contain her impatience with the formalistic, empty chatter. When men asked for Nadia's hand in marriage as a result of these public forays, she and her grandmother use to sit and giggle at each overture.

Whatever comfort and camaraderie Nadia had provided her grandmother for a short time would not endure during her last years. While Nadia was away at graduate school her grandmother fell sick several times. She then consented to live with her son. Her hearing weakened. She yelled at the servants more. When she visited, Nadia saw at first hand how relatives started visiting more frequently, sometimes stopping in the kitchen to help themselves to fruit in the refrigerator. If Nadia's things disappeared from her room, she didn't know if it was because of the servants, the relatives or because her grandmother had locked it away for safekeeping. Her father would admit to none of this, even if he noticed it.

Nadia began to feel a foreboding when she visited. She knew that people were trying to marry her father off, marry her off, and convince him to adopt a son and heir. Even her grandmother started encouraging her to marry, so that she would stay in Egypt. Nadia saw the deterioration of the city mirrored in her family. How could she justify this loss of faith in her Egyptian heritage, which had once seemed so glorious, this dread she felt as witness of decline?

Nadia's late morning slumber was interrupted by a knock. Mohammed was apologetic behind the door: "Would Sit Hanem like to join her father and grandmother for lunch?" Nadia got up, frowning because of a headache, blaming herself for sleeping in the heat. She washed her face, brushed her hair, took two aspirin and walked to the dining room. The dining room was dark, the curtains drawn, an air conditioner whirring. The three of them took up one quarter of the table. Mohammed served. There wasn't much conversation while they were eating. Roast chicken, mouloukhiya, rice and salad were served on unmatched crockery, parts of elegant sets long since decimated. Nadia wouldn't look up from her plate. She now avoided the sight of her grandmother eating – the slurping of the soup, the dripping of shiny liquids down the chin, the masticating of the bread. Nadia wondered if she looked like that, and why was it customary for people to eat together, in company. Why wasn't eating one of the private functions?

Adnan: "How are you feeling Nadia? Still tired?"

"No, I'm all right. I must be jet lagging."

"Ustaz Mounir called. He's coming to see you tonight."

"Oh good." Ustaz Mounir was her old oud teacher. He used to give her lessons years ago and they had remained friends.

Adnan: "Your grandmother thought that you would like to go to the farm this afternoon. You'll be back in time for Ustaz Mounir."

"Yes, I would."

"We'll go at five. The driver will be here then."

Grandmother: "Nadia, have some dessert, some konafa."

"No thank you, gramma. I'm no longer hungry."

The grandmother started to fiddle with her keys and was going to ask Mohammed to go and get fruits from her room when Adnan stopped her: "Mother, you must rest. The driver is coming soon." And to Nadia: "Ask Mohammed to make you some coffee." They lumbered away, Adnan supporting his mother as she shuffled out of the dining room.

Nadia went into the air-conditioned study. The white walls were smudged, the bureau dust covered. She decided not to have coffee because of the feeling of queasiness in her stomach. It was undoubtedly the water; it always took some time to get used to the water. She would drink a lot of lemonade. It would be good to see Ustaz Mounir again, although he was always telling her to settle down. Her fondest memory of him was of his coming off the dusty streets as the sun was setting after a scorching day. He was wearing his usual dark grey suit, his seasonless garb. She couldn't figure out how he made it from the popular quarter where he lived, Sayedna Zeinab, to the fashionable quarter where her father lived. He had no car and the buses were so crowded with people stuffed inside and hanging out, that they were moving death traps. On that day, he smiled his toothy smile: "A beautiful breeze is starting to blow off the Nile. The Nile is the gift of Egypt and Egypt is the mother of the world." Nadia remembered thinking that Ustaz was like a cool breeze himself.

They had never spent much time on the oud lessons. They sat with the balcony doors flung open. He would offer her hashish and improvise musical pieces, dedicating them to her. They wouldn't turn on the lights as the dusk gathered, but wait for the lights to go on outside, on the bridges, the mosques, the hotels. It was at times like this, with the onset of a Cairene night and under the enchantment of the hashish, the music and the softening light, that Nadia managed to share Ustaz Mounir's languid vision of life.

While they worked at the music, nobody bothered them. Dusk was a quiet time in the apartment. Eventually, Nadia would turn on a light, go to the kitchen to get some refreshments and they would chat. Ustaz Mounir had a mistress in Sayedna Zeinab . . . a man had to have a woman. A person couldn't live without emotions.

Nadia got up from the dusty couch. It was too cold in the study. She walked into the living room and pulled back a velvet curtain, leaving a second, gauzy curtain to filter the light. It was still too hot, although the afternoon was advanced. Soon it would be time to ask Mohammed to make tea for her father and her grandmother, their waking up ritual. Mohammed was himself napping. This was Nadia's favorite time of day, when silence reigned both inside and outside the apartment, and only she walked around. She could feel her skin dampening slightly. It was a familiar sensation. Soon she would hear the plaintive chant of the muezzin.

*

The trip out to the farm was slower than usual. First one had to get the grandmother to the elevator, down the majestic and cruelly numerous steps from the lobby to the street. Then, as they were reaching the outskirts of Cairo, a traffic jam was created by a horse unable to pull his cart up an incline. When finally they reached the pocked and bumpy road leading to the farm, they were preceded by heaped garbage carts pulled by donkeys and driven by children perched on top of the garbage. But when they turned off this road it suddenly became country, green with palms, women washing clothes along a canal.

The gates to the property were unlocked, as were the gates to the garden of the villa. Servants ran out, rickety lawn chairs were placed on the grass, tea was ordered. Nadia accompanied her grandmother along a stone pathway to a chair, her grandmother leaning heavily against her. As always, it was quiet and cool here. Some ancestor had shortened the garden wall in one corner to reveal a vista of rippling green alfalfa fields and swaying palms. Peasants on donkeys could look into the garden at that point. They provided a moving tableau for those looking out.

Nadia told her grandmother and Adnan that she was going for a walk and bounded over the fence. There was the canal with the bridge and the whistling tree. Bordering the canal on both sides were footpaths and across the canal, fields dotted with ibis, considered inviolate since pharaonic times. Off to the left were the pigeon coops, resembling the turrets of a miniature castle. To the right a young woman walked along the canal footpath, her loose, brilliantly colored shift molded against her body by the breezes. She walked upright, a clay water jug balanced on her head. Nadia started to make her way along the footpath to the left.

Adnan watched her walk away. He hoped that being at the farm would calm her. When she was younger she had urged him to take over the farm, reconstruct the villa. She had pointed out the rich, dark topsoil to him, saying it was well known that one could grow anything in it. He had carefully explained that the revenue from the land, now rented out to peasants, would not pay for the renovation of the villa. In any case, the ownership of the villa and adjoining workers' quarters was being disputed by several relatives who wouldn't spend a piaster on the grounds. They didn't even subsidize the tea and sugar they demanded when they came to sit in the garden and left carrying baskets of fruit.

It was her father who paid for the man who guarded the orchard. He paid for the medicine needed by the aging, ailing caretaker, who had seen better times. He couldn't be expected to sink money into a disputed property. But surely, Nadia had insisted, there was room for negotiation; with the relatives, with the peasants. How about preserving his heritage, or honoring the care with which someone had planted the twin royal palms, laid down the tiles around the fountain in the Andalusian-style courtyard, built the large aviary. Yes, he would answer, but that was a different time and he wasn't going to throw his money away in quicksand for sentimental reasons.

Still, her father had to admit, earlier it might have been possible to buy out other interests. Now it was impossible. Earlier it might have been possible to restore the villa. Now it was literally sinking. Amazing how quickly something could fall into ruin. He didn't mind the tiles buckling because of tree roots, or the birdcage empty of exotic birds. But he felt helpless in front of the mildewing living room wall.

Adnan wondered how Nadia would have felt if she had seen the farm in its heyday, with his uncle still alive. The villa had had crackling fires in the chimneys, shining parquet floors and elegant furniture. His uncle had set up a modern clinic for the peasants. He had imported Dutch cows. The garden and orchard had been laid out in consultation with an agrarian engineer. When Nadia was a baby and Adnan had been visiting with her and his wife, his uncle had given her a jasmine garland. But she was too young to remember.

Nadia would be coming back for tea soon. Adnan resolved to find a way of keeping her out of the villa, one room of which was full of chicks – the project of some relative. Under the overhang in the inner courtyard another relative, an old woman, sat on a straw mat with a clay water jug at hand.

When they got back to the apartment, Ustaz Mounir was waiting for them. He was sipping Arabic coffee in the harshly lit living room. He rose to his feet when they entered. He looked the same to Nadia, ageless, his smile as wide as ever and his body as thin. She couldn't tell if he was wearing the same grey suit of earlier years or another one. Her father retired to the study and grandmother to her bedroom. Nadia took Ustaz Mounir out onto the balcony. The first few minutes were spent exchanging niceties. They were clearly delighted to see each other. Ustaz Mounir then remarked on the splendid view. Nadia brought a chilled bottle of white wine onto the balcony and poured out two glasses.

Ustaz Mounir: "Are you back in Egypt for good?"

Nadia: "No, in fact I think this will be the last time that I come to Egypt."

Ustaz Mounir sat upright in his bamboo chair: "God give me strength. What a thing to say. You who have so much here; people who love you and are willing to give you everything." Ustaz Mounir squinted into the living room, where the chandelier glow rendered the Louis Farouk furniture gaudier than necessary.

Nadia: "Every time I come here it is dirtier."

Ustaz Mounir: "It is dirty everywhere."

Nadia: "No, not to this extent."

Ustaz Mounir: "If you were married, with children, you would be happy here."

Nadia: "What do you expect me to do, Ustaz Mounir, live in this apartment and have children? And then what? Anyway, you never had children."

Ustaz Mounir: "I didn't find the woman who suited me."

Nadia: "Ustaz Mounir, when my grandmother dies she will be the last relative I can stand, and if anything happens to my father, the relatives will descend on me like vultures because I have no brother."

Ustaz Mounir looked back into the living room, at the tapestry worked by the grandmother, at the dark portraits. "Your husband will protect you."

"Marriage with an Egyptian would be like a business contract. I cannot live here, Ustaz Mounir. It upsets me to even visit."

Ustaz Mounir looked down at his veined hands, at a loss for words. Then he looked up, or rather perked up and with a wide sweep of his arm at the river said:

"Nadia, look at this view. Where else in the world can you find it? Egypt is the gift of the Nile and Egypt is . . ."

Nadia interrupted him: "I know, Ustaz Mounir, Egypt is the suffering mother of the whole world."

Godshow.com

AHMED NAJI

Translated from the Arabic by Rana Asfour

1.

LAS VEGAS WAS BRIMMING WITH MOSQUES. AS SOON AS I'D
typed "mosque near me" into the Google Maps search, myriad red
dots displayed themselves all at once on my screen.

The Al-Hamada mosque, one of the first Las Vegas mosques
founded in the Seventies, and winner of a five-star rating, boasted
a review claiming that its writer had "felt at peace" as soon as he'd
crossed over the threshold. Another described how its congregation
had helped "during the family's short stay in Las Vegas" and that "*God
is Great.*" A perusal of the mosque's online images seemed to indicate
that the building itself occupied a tight space, with no dome or minaret. Most of its visitors appeared to be dark-skinned, which meant the
congregation were most likely followers of the Nation of Islam.

I scratched it off my list.

I had no plans to attend an American Salafi mosque. I hadn't left
the shortened robes, the *miswak*, the scent of musk and the bushy
beards in Egypt, only to come here for much of the same. At times, I'd
come across them in West Las Vegas as they approached cars stopped
at the traffic light, hawking their literature for *$10 my brother*. One of
them honed in on me while I was in my car. Cornered, I lied that I had
no cash. *No problem, brother*, he replied, undeterred as he presented
me with a card reader attached to his mobile phone. After I'd paid, I
browsed the magazine and found that it mostly contained news of the
leaders of the brotherhood.

I quickly moved on to click the link to the second mosque on the list. There, on their website (in the third line to be exact), was a message explicitly indicating that they were open to all races, nationalities, and sects. The recurrent usage of words like "race" and "color" seemed to imply that they did not belong to the Nation of Islam. It appeared that they belonged to the Las Vegas Islamic Center, which was founded in the Eighties.

A further online search came up with the Al Omariya, a mosque as well as an Islamic school. The images portrayed girls as young as ten in their hijab. This website was loaded with proselytization on sound education, proper morals, and the preservation of the nascent Muslim youth. Off the list it came. All I had wanted was to visit a mosque, not send my children to an Islamic brainwashing laundromat. Yet another mosque's website displayed a picture with a caption titled *Bless you, Oh Hussain!* declaring its Shiite affiliation. Al-Hikma, on the other hand, had received comments regarding the quality of the food.

Just then, as the waitress came round to clear my now empty beer bottle and to ask if I wanted a second one, Jose Al----- appeared. I stood up to shake his hand and he hugged me and took a seat across from me. He asked me the usual questions about work and family and I answered, albeit distracted, and then proceeded to mechanically ask him much of the same. Once I had a new frothy beer at the table in front of me, I duly announced my plans to visit a mosque.

– *Don't you have a mosque you go to already?* he asked.

– *No*, I replied.

With seven years between us, Jose was still in his twenties. Sleepy-eyed and huge, his large, impressive, and tightly wound muscular bulk was covered in tattoos. He was a bartender at the same hotel where I worked as a purchasing director, in charge of quality control and food storage. But that was before we were both laid off. We met by chance at a work gathering that brought together employees from the various departments to listen to the "motivational" spiel of their managers. In that first encounter, he brought up poetry, and I let on that I not only read it but wrote some myself. Immediately, he extended his hand for me to shake and introduced himself as a poet. And so, we became friends. But we didn't really talk much about poetry, as his interest and expertise centered mainly on American poetry and a little Mexican, while I read exclusively in Arabic. I confess that I hadn't read a single poem in English before I'd met him. As one who claimed to write for immigrants like himself, his English poetry was duly peppered with Spanish. *Southern poetry. It's all about fiery, passionate words my friend. Do you get what I'm saying?* he'd ask.

When Covid-19 struck, Jose was among the first batch to be laid off. For a while, he scraped by on unemployment benefits and food delivery gigs in his old Kia, until he managed to find work at a large warehouse that imported cheap goods and auto parts from China that were resold in the US.

I fail to recall now how Jose met Phil, whom he brought to our second meeting. Since then, he's become the third in our triumvirate that communes weekly for beer drinking. I remember, back then, how he'd plunked his solemn, imposing self down, asked for his beer and once it had arrived, remained silent the entire time, listening as I explained to Jose the difference between Friday prayers and Sunday church service.

I confessed to Jose that I hadn't once been to Friday prayers since I'd arrived in the United States. At that, he reached into his pocket and retrieved a black hair tie, gathered his hair between his fingers, and launched into an extensive monologue about the importance of going to the mosque and to Friday service. Even if I wasn't particularly religious, it was the best way for me to get to know my community, especially since an immigrant could, at any given day, find himself in need of help or support. Generally speaking, he extrapolated, religious people, regardless of their faith, were always eager to help, believing this would bring them closer to God.

I conceded that I hadn't considered any of this. All I'd been searching for was a clean mosque that I could attend for the afternoon prayers where the ceiling fan dials would be turned to the fastest speed. Preferably, an empty mosque with very few – one or maybe even two – worshippers, reading the Qur'an in a barely audible voice. I wanted to reclaim the time when, as a child, I'd visit the mosque to lay down on its carpeted floor, close my eyes, and let all my worries and troubles spirit themselves away.

Phil piped in that he understood me completely, and that although he himself was an atheist, he could still understand how places of worship could be repositories of energy, able to evoke and withhold soothing communal memories for their congregants. It was a cave in the Valley of Fire State Park that did it for Phil – a place where early inhabitants of the valley had worshipped and prayed. On every visit, without fail, he felt the energy coursing through the place, despite the centuries that had passed.

Phil was five years older than me. I've never understood exactly what he does. All I knew was that he was born in Las Vegas, had a big family, and owned a house and a car. Phil, who worked in the deserts of Vegas and Arizona, looked upon his work – shooting documentaries for PBS – as something closer to a hobby in which he went on long expeditions exploring nature, delving into the history of the deserts' inhabitants, and unearthing extinct civilizations. His theory was that life in the Vegas Valley went through expansive cycles every four or five centuries, during which the valley would flourish, attracting people to settle down and build. Two to four centuries later, depending on the extent of that civilization's depletion of nature, another drought would strike the valley, forcing its residents to abandon their parched lands, leaving the dust from the heels of their forced exodus to wipe away the urbanization they left behind.

– *I don't get where the problem is*, said Phil, interrupting my thoughts. *Aren't there any mosques in Vegas?*

I unlocked my phone and showed him my screen displaying the last mosque I'd been researching on my browser.

– *On the contrary*, I said. *I'm spoilt for choice at the number of mosques here. But, I'm at a loss over which one to choose.*

2.

I hadn't yet made up my mind regarding the mosque situation. That is, until I picked up a woman and her two children. She asked me if I was from Turkey because of my name, and when I said I wasn't, she asked me if I was Muslim. After a quick glance at the children, and a few more seconds of hesitation, I replied.

— *Sometimes.*

She smiled.

— *Why not always?* she asked.

I smiled back at her through the rearview mirror before I turned my eyes to the road without saying anything more. As we drove to their destination we passed the Al-Isra Mosque, and my three passengers disembarked two blocks later. I switched off my GPS, turned around, and drove back to the mosque with half an hour to spare before the noon prayers.

Al-Isra Mosque is adorned with a minaret and a dome painted in bright yellow. It was plain to see that its architects had ambitiously hoped to replicate Jerusalem's venerable Dome of the Rock, only to fall well below their aspirations. The entrance to the mosque was crowded with signs written in English, Arabic, and Urdu, as well as a donation poster for an organization caring for Muslim orphans in East Asia, and another for digging wells in Africa. Below these were stacked FBI-produced leaflets with their messages bold and clear, printed with the customary grammatical and linguistic errors; *If you see something, report something* or *I live in this society, inform and protect our society*.

I refuse to believe that the American government and its agencies are devoid in their entirety of people who can speak and write proper Arabic. I believe, rather, that it is a special form of communication that arrogantly displays its mistakes as a sign of their utter disregard for any need to camouflage themselves among "authentic" Arabs, seeing them as part of an insurgent plan to establish autonomy and identity within ﺟ — a form of westernized Arabic, if you will, perfected by the supposedly omniscient FBI, which resists the need to comprehend Arabic, and the Arabs alike.

I became aware of a man in a fluorescent yellow jacket, standing just outside the mosque, devouring a green apple with his gaze entirely fixated on my every move. I took off my shoes, placed them on the allotted shelf, and entered the mosque. The prayer hall was spacious with green thick-carpeted floors and a high ceiling. The names of God were inscribed in gold on green ribbon that ran along the walls of the hall.

Soon, worshippers began to trickle in and I was relieved to note, mainly from how they were dressed, that they were of diverse racial and cultural backgrounds. As it was still midday prayers, many had come in their work clothes. I noted a few construction workers, nurses, one HVAC worker, and a Pakistani dressed in a shalwar kameez.

As soon as I entered the bathroom, I was assaulted by the familiar smell of sodium hypochlorite, the requisite odor of all mosque bathrooms it seems, regardless of their location. I was delighted to note that they had bidets in there too. I urinated, and completed my ablutions before catching up with the prayers. Finishing two *Sunnah Rak'ahs* I remained in place while the majority of the worshippers started to retreat back to where they had come from. I closed my eyes, trying to evoke the expectant grace that washes over one in moments of serenity. But, none of that shit happened. All that ran through my mind was how, as an Uber driver, I had wasted so much time that could have been better used to lock in two or three more rides.

Immediately after I'd stepped out of the mosque gates, the man in the yellow jacket came up to me. He had a wide mouth, green eyes, dripping wet shoulder-length hair, and nails that were long but clean. He addressed me in a language foreign to my ears.

I must have looked askance because he switched to English to let me know that *Asr* prayers were for the weary, even though he didn't pray himself. I thanked him, after which he advised that should I ever be in need of anything, I am to consult with Dr. Burhan, the man who had built the mosque as well as the adjacent Islamic Center. *A good man*, he called him, who helped the likes of him, even though he was a non-Muslim because, he added for good measure, *God loves us all.*

– *Who are you?* I interrupted before he could go on.

He straightened himself up to his full height, spread the palm of one hand on his chest, while pointing with the other to a camera hanging above the mosque's gate.

— *Security.*

He then launched into a full-on monologue that began with praising the neighbors and the neighborhood. How "bad" guys were everywhere; the drunk and the angry who created trouble. How although the mosque sometimes received bomb threats or other violent threats, the police were there to protect them by sending two cars for Friday prayers and during Eid holiday prayers.

He was now well into his speech, moving his hands in every which direction assuring me that he'd always be there to make sure everyone was safe. As he went on, I took in my surroundings, and saw, at the opposite side of the street, behind a low wall, a row of run-down homes. It was only after I finally thanked the man, and walked away, that I remembered that I had forgotten to ask his name.

On the way to the car, I noticed that behind the mosque was a junkyard, filled mostly with broken yachts and boats of various sizes; they all looked sad and dead. Another "only in Vegas" site: a yacht graveyard in the middle of the desert. They were most likely brought in at one point by owners to sail on Lake Mead. Now instead they lay on their sides like giant boulders that even God had forgotten about. In fact, the lake's water level had begun to decrease, heralding a new wave of climate change scaremongers, who felt that the disgruntled climate would wipe out Las Vegas within the next fifty years. But at that moment, all I could see on the horizon was the clear blue Vegas skies and the mountains that surrounded our valley.

3.

I returned home after midnight to find the bedroom door locked, which meant that my wife and the two boys had finally gone to sleep. The mess of toys and other debris was scattered everywhere and plates were piled high in the kitchen sink. I checked the mouse traps distributed in the house. All clear, no mice — today.

We moved into this house a month ago, the third since our relocation to America. At first, we rejoiced at the extra space, as we both held on to high hopes that we were headed towards a new chapter, one in which we could reclaim our love and zest for life. Now we are Henderson residents, part of the upper-middle-class echelon of Las Vegas.

My wife and I first met seven years ago in Dubai. She was working in an advertising and marketing firm, and I was managing a grand hotel. Over there, we lived our years immersed in fleeting pleasures, working hard and spending all what we'd earned on leisure and travel. We eventually got married, giving the idea of children not the slightest thought. But everything changed the day she came to me with a hesitant smile and a positive pregnancy test. I was so happy. We hugged and danced. That evening, she told me that we should plan to have the child in America so that it would have a shot at a real passport, just like her nephew. We both knew that up until then we'd been living a life of false stability, for without the guarantee of a path to citizenship, we'd have no choice but to return to Egypt.

A former colleague of mine worked at one of the big hotels in Vegas, and he suggested that we come check it out. Samira loved Vegas, and found the city similar to Dubai – *déjà vu* at every corner. With the help of this colleague, I landed my first job with a substantially bigger salary than the one I'd been earning in Dubai, and with far better working conditions that did not include excessive censorship and the constant dread of deportation hanging over my head.

Instead of one child, we had twins. We entered an inferno that we have yet to come out of. The stress hit us hard. Samira and I turned from lovers to parents burdened with responsibilities, exploding in each other's faces because we knew no one whom we could offload on in the city. We thought about going back to Dubai, but the pandemic decimated our exit plans. Airports and borders closed down. The hotel I worked in reduced my wages before I was eventually laid off in the second wave, and we had to move to a house that was hardly bigger than the tiniest room.

That year, our life became a living nightmare in which we struggled day after day to lift our heads off the pillow just to meet the needs of our two boys. My colleague, the only Arab I knew in town, had up and left for Florida, while we remained stuck in the city that the pandemic had forced into darkness, the howls of solitary slot machines pining for players echoing through its deserted streets as they bounced off the walls of abandoned luxury hotels.

I hear a sound coming from the kitchen, so I get up and look around, wondering if it's a mouse or simply my imagination.

After the vaccination campaigns, the city began to recover, and I was able to secure an administrative job at a famous restaurant in addition to my work as an Uber driver for food delivery gigs. We moved to this larger house with a back garden and two rooms and I spotted a mouse making a run for it behind the kitchen fridge. I bought a bunch of mousetraps to distribute around the house after I made sure to smear a lick of peanut butter onto each one.

We caught the mouse the next day. But it was Jose who told me that one mouse in the house meant there were two, and that two meant a family of them and that we should expect them to appear one by one. There are times, during the night when we can hear them and on more than two occasions, I've found traces of their feces in the corners of the house.

I open the bedroom door, and in the glow of the pale light seeping in from the hallway, I see Samira's body sandwiched in between the two boys. I lift each one to his bed then brush my teeth, undress and lie down in bed in my boxers and an old T-shirt. Samira turns around and, for the briefest moment, she opens her eyes and closes them again, pulls the covers tighter around herself and turns around, giving me her back.

We still love one another, but where has the desire gone? When will the exhaustion and endless worry end?

A few months ago, I passed a family of three near a public park. The father, mother, and child were living in their car. I didn't tell Samira about what I saw but since then, all I see is our family sliding down that slope, eventually ending without a home. Such fears are no longer the stuff of nightmares, but a reality that thousands face each and every day. For a time, we too had perched on the brink of the tipping point.

Lately, I've been failing to recognize my own feelings. My heart has started to beat to the rhythms of stress and anxiety. I've realized that I no longer laugh. I try to watch my favorite comedies. I just can't find the time. I bought a joint and smoked it with Samira. By the end we hugged and passed out on the sofa. In the past, one puff was all it took for us to drown in a sea of hysterical laughter.

I still love Samira, but love isn't everything when even in its presence I turn my back to her. I shed the covers and sleep naked. After pregnancy and childbirth, Samira's body has transformed into a new, alien one, that I don't recognize. She, too, has become ashamed of it, refusing to let me get into the bath with her, and asking me to turn off the lights if, by chance, every two months we decide to strip naked and go for it.

Sleep refuses to come, and I think about jerking off out of despair and boredom, but I imagine, for a fleeting moment, that I hear something in our darkened room. I sit up straight and wonder, *could there be a mouse in the room?*

4.

I returned to the Isra mosque for another visit. This time I arrived just in time for the last *Rak'ah* of the *Maghreb* prayers. Again, after completing my prayer, I remained in place until most of the worshippers had departed. I stretched out my legs in front of me, and in the stillness, I closed my eyes and tried searching for what had gone missing inside me. I was pulled out of my meditation when a hand patted my shoulder. A man with white hair and brown skin, wearing brown cotton trousers and a summer shirt, asked if I was okay. He didn't leave even when I confirmed that I was and instead sat down, extended his arm out to me, and introduced himself.

— *Your brother, Dr. Burhan.*

— *Ahlan Wa Sahlan.*

I shook his hand, and he asked again about my condition. He said that he hadn't intended to interrupt my devotion, but had merely wanted to introduce himself, and to get to know me seeing it was the first time he'd seen me around.

I was cagey in my initial dealings with him, and opted to withhold giving too much away, including my name. Instead, I nodded as he was describing the lovely community they have here and told me I was welcome to reach out to him or anyone in the mosque's administration if ever I was in need. *For every problem God has created, there is a solution.*

I thanked him for his love and assured him I would take him up on his offer, should the need arise. I left the prayer hall and stood at the mosque entrance, where the worshippers' shoes were stacked. An advertisement for a center offering psychological and counseling services tailored to Muslims caught my eye. *You're certainly looking for a psychological expert who understands your cultural background and the nature of your local community . . .* There was that word again, I thought. Community.

I photographed the ad and smiled as I imagined Samira's reaction if I suggested that she book an appointment or that we do so together. Maybe our salvation lay there.

In complete contrast to me, Samira had nothing positive to associate with Islam. And I don't blame her. She lived in Egypt with a father who insisted on interfering in her life — even after he divorced her mother on the pretext of religion — and what he considered halal or haram. She hadn't been able to break free until she'd moved to Dubai.

The security guard was waiting for me when I stepped out of the mosque gates. I greeted him from afar and headed to my car, but he ran towards me and asked if I had spoken with Dr. Burhan.

— *Yes. Thank you,* I replied.

He explained that he'd told Dr. Burhan about me. In amazement I inquired what he'd had to say, seeing he knew nothing about me. He'd worried that I might've been a Islamist fundamentalist.

— *An extremist? Is that what you're accusing me of?*

– *Yes,* he said. *I watched you examining the mosque from the inside and out and staying long after the worshippers had left. Don't blame me but the country's in peril with whites killing Blacks and the Latinos collecting and storing weapons. America is going to hell and a civil war is brewing! Would you believe it if I told you that just last year a group of Iraqis — Shiites — came looking for trouble because Dr. Burhan agreed to host a betrothal ceremony between a young Sunni man and a Shiite woman from their community? Why are you looking at me like that? I'm not even Muslim. I'm a Christian Turk. I haven't been to Turkey in years, nor to church for that matter. Dr. Burhan offered me this job and the community is helping me out ...*

There was that word again, I thought. Community.

5.

Then Phil asked me if I'd found what I was looking for in the mosques of Las Vegas. I told him that what I was looking for was most likely not found at the mosque, and that nonetheless I'd been to the Isra mosque. I offered up the address when he asked me and he explained that this neighborhood had previously been an industrial site crammed with workshops and factories. I described the boat cemetery behind the mosque, and he confirmed my hunch and told me that although it may seem strange now, there was a time when a thriving Las Vegas was famous for manufacturing boats and yachts, and that Lake Mead had not only been a booming nautical tourism destination, but a sought-after place for business meetings, remotely tucked away, far from the prying surveillance of security services.

– *What language are the prayers and the Imam's preachings conducted in?* he reiterated.

– *I've not been to Friday prayer there, but I do know that the sermon's in English while the prayers are in Arabic.*

With his usual hesitancy, Phil asked timidly, if he could one day accompany me to Friday service.

– *Why?*

–*I've never been inside a mosque before.*

I made a quick mental rundown of all the topics that could come up in a Friday sermon. In Egypt, for example, part of every Friday sermon is dedicated to prayers damning the infidels — those who have strayed from the faith.

A quick sweep of the Al-Isra website on my cell phone revealed that the upcoming Friday prayer would be followed by a celebration to commemorate the *Isra* and *Miraj*, with free sweets for the children. I figured the sermon would surely be dedicated to retelling the story of the night Prophet Muhammed journeyed from Mecca to Jerusalem and then to heaven. An entertaining story full of adventures with, *Alhamdulillah*, no place for hate speech or contempt for other groups.

— *Next Friday should be fine,* I informed Phil.

That Friday afternoon was promising to be another scorcher of a Las Vegas day when I drove to pick up Phil. He was dressed appropriately, in blue jeans and a white and blue checkered shirt. On the way there, he questioned me about the meaning behind the name of the mosque.

— *It means "night journey."*

I proceeded with a brief explanation, peppered with my own scientific twist to the tale, about how the name dates back to a legendary journey undertaken by the Prophet Muhammad called *al-Isra wal Miraj*. The Prophet's tribe, or what we would now refer to as "community," I pointedly explained to Phil, in a show of power besieged him for daring to step outside their traditions and the norms of the commune. Things became tough after his first wife and uncle-cum-guardian passed away in the same year. He was sad, frustrated, and probably depressed. To cheer him up God sent Buraq, a heavenly creature with wings, smaller than a horse but larger than a donkey, who flew Muhammad from Mecca to Jerusalem, where he met and prayed with all the prophets who had come before him. Then, the angel Gabriel — with whom Phil indicated he was familiar — took him to the farthest reaches of the seventh heaven, to *Sidra Al-Muntaha* or the lote tree, where he received his instructions from God to pray five times a day.

In a flash, he was back in his bed in Mecca, before the mattress had gone even slightly cold.

– *Whoa. What a story. Was the Buraq an animal or an angel* –

– *A mythical animal.* But Muslims believe in its existence. I explained to Phil that, for Muslims, this was in no way a fictional tale. Each Muslim was obligated to believe that this journey was an actual miracle bestowed on the Prophet in which time and place succumbed to God's command and will, making the journey possible. *Very much like that movie* Interstellar, *you know?*

I parked in the mosque's parking lot, and no sooner had we started walking towards the building than the security guard ran towards us, with a disconcerting smile and an enthusiasm that seemed slightly out of the ordinary.

– *You're late*, he said. *Everyone's finished the prayer and gone to the show. Come here, follow me.*

The mosque door was closed, so Phil and I followed the guard towards the yacht graveyard. He pointed to the corner at what appeared to be a large storage shed and said:

– *Everyone is there. Hurry or you'll miss the miracle.*

Phil and I crossed the dusty, unpaved yard until we reached the half-open door. Inside we saw a stage, half a meter high, in front of which rows of chairs were occupied by women, men and children, some of whom were enjoying unicorn-shaped candy. Phil and I chose two chairs in the back row.

It was clear we'd arrived in the middle of the show because, above the stage a screen was already playing panoramic views of the Nevada desert. We had no clue what was going on when suddenly out of the right corner of the stage, a Black child emerged, wearing a long robe, leaning on a walking stick, and speaking through a headset. He spoke in English.

– *Finally, the Night Journey ended, and the Prophet Muhammad, May God Bless Him and Grant Him Peace, returned, with a gift for all Muslims. The five daily prayers.*

A small chorus of children and teenagers appeared behind him on the stage and broke out into a short song about the rituals of prayer. Phil looked at me in confusion, so I leaned in and whispered.

— *I'm not really sure what's going on either. This is certainly not Friday prayer, which I think we must've missed. This is a celebration marking the Isra and Miraj.*

The choir wrapped up their performance and diligently withdrew from the stage, while the child in the robe remained. He opened his arms wide and addressed the audience.

— *But, Brothers and Sisters, what happened to the Buraq after that trip?*

— *We certainly don't know, Omar, that's for sure.*

It was Dr. Burhan, who had suddenly appeared on the left side of the stage and was making his way towards its center. There, he turned to face the audience.

— *However, we are truly fortunate because, here in the blessed land of Nevada, where all signs indicate that the Buraq's blessed hooves once trod, is proof that the message of our Prophet, the message of Islam, was able to reach every place on earth.*

Dr. Burhan broke off into Arabic to quote a verse from the Qur'an — *We sent Thee as good tidings* — before continuing in English.

— *The Buraq dynasty inhabited the valleys of Nevada and were known to the indigenous people of the land, who adopted their principled morals. But sadly, they were chased away, persecuted, and finally exterminated by the settlers. Today, in memory of this miraculous journey, we are proud to host the last of the surviving Buraqs.*

A montage of images of caves in the Vegas mountains popped up on the screen. Some scenes portrayed hunting creatures with multiple arms and legs. At that moment, Dr. Burhan's voice rose dramatically as he shouted,

— *Ladies and gentlemen, feast your eyes on ...*

The room went dark save for the flickering light emanating from the screen, which now displayed an image of an abstract drawing on a cave wall of what appeared to be a winged animal with four legs.

Suddenly the screen came crashing down and as the lights gradually returned, there before us stood what appeared to be a beast that was longer than a donkey, wider than a horse, with a silver tail and mane. On its head lay a crown studded with red jewels. The thing was draped in a red cape adorned with golden stripes, its eyes as wide as a bull's.

Complete silence reigned in the room, before, as if all at once, it shattered into a million voices calling out, *Allahu Akbar* and *Glory Be to God*.

The Buraq spread its silver wings, shook its head, and snorted. And then with a gentle flap of its wings, it lifted itself off the ground to hover over the stage.

The room erupted with further *takbeers* and ululations. The children were visibly stunned, the mothers and fathers moved to tears.

The Buraq continued its ascent upward until it reached the roof of the storehouse, its wings fully spread out, the silver feathers turning to gold. The Buraq glowed like a celestial planet lit up by the blessed tree from the heavens.

I turned to Phil and he was stunned, his mouth hanging open. When he could finally speak, he was breathless.

– *Bro! What a show, I've never seen a unicorn in my life.*

I admit, I was not only taken aback by what we had just witnessed, but felt something akin to a communal familiarity, despite the strangeness all around me. A pride I couldn't restrain had crept into my tone as I answered Phil.

– *Not a unicorn. See, no horn. It's Buraq.*

I reveled in the look of bewilderment on his face as he pretended to grasp what I was saying, all while Buraq flapped its radiant wings, as golden as if they'd been spun from the sun itself. A heady scent of musk and jasmine infused the room. I tried to make sense of what was happening in front of me, applying logic and reason to explain it all. But my mind refused to see it as anything but a miracle. A sign of future good tidings.

The Buraq folded in its wings and began its descent as the voice of Egyptian singer Hisham Abbas chanting the revered 99 names of God rose from the speakers. I smiled, but soon found that I was struggling to suppress bubbling laughter that was threatening to burst forth and disturb the revered peace that was now reigning over the room with the Buraq's majestic descent.

It had all been going very well for me and I'd been willing to eat it all up, but Hisham Abbas's song managed to topple down the dream, pulling the mask away from this farcical charade and exposing it for what it was – a joke.

Lodged in my memory is that same chant, usually played as an opening number at weddings or parties to let invitees know that the real party was about to begin with its sashaying, grinding revelers and belly dancers, flowing beer, rolled up joints and *shishas* dipped in hashish. In that context, the euphoric magnanimity of the moment was lost on me despite being surrounded by a theater packed with a captivated audience swaying to the hymns of Hisham Abbas. When the singer chanted "the Manifest, the Hidden, the Exalted" the audience raced towards the Buraq to be blessed.

Chaos ensued, and Dr. Burhan's voice could be heard bellowing at the crowd to return to their seats. Leaving Phil behind, I took the opportunity to head outside, with my hand still over my mouth, hoping to suppress my laughter until I was at least out the door. Standing in the boat cemetery, I experienced a joy I hadn't felt in years. I took out my cellphone to call Samira and to share with her what I'd just witnessed. Before I could do that, a Jesus-like figure with loose hair down to his shoulders and a long white robe approached me holding a set of what looked to be promotional cards in his hand.

– *Did you enjoy the show?*

– *It was magnificent. Out of this world.*

At that, he handed me one of the cards.

– *I'm pleased to hear that. Our company specializes in religious and educational entertainment shows. We cover five religions and have package deals that you can view on our website, the Godshow dot com.*

No sooner had I grabbed the card than I was seized by another fit of laughter. Undeterred, he continued, explaining that they were a local business with plans to build a theater in Blue Diamond, a small town about a twenty-minute drive from Vegas in the heart of the Red Rock Mountains. Although he agreed that the location might be remote for some, he also felt it worked best given the nature of the shows they offered.

— *Besides, most ancient religions first appeared in the desert and the mountains. We have us here magnificent nature we can use to support religious tourism in Vegas, don't you agree?* he asked.

— *Wonderful my man. Really wonderful, I nodded.*

My laughing had escalated to include an embarrassing snort, for which I quickly tried to apologize.

— *Please excuse me, but the show has me under some kind of spiritual spell, in which my whole body is brimming with joy and laughter. I haven't laughed this much in so long. I can't begin to explain how happy I am right now.*

— *That's exactly the sort of thing we hope to bring to our audiences. I'll have to go now to help my colleagues shut down and pack up the drones in the unicorn's body. I hope to catch you at other shows.*

He left. I stood there, alone in the boat cemetery, laughing and chortling, under the glare of the relentless Vegas sun.

Nadira of Tlemcen

ABDELLAH TAÏA

Translated from the French by Jordan Elgrably

I MISS YOU, BABA! I MISS YOU! I'LL BE THERE. WAIT FOR ME. I'M coming. I'm sick of this place, this world, the cold, the wind, the grayness! I'm coming. I'm coming, Baba. You've been there, alone, for so long. Since I left Algeria in 1990. I've been talking to you. I'm talking to you. I call you. I see you whenever I want. And we remake the world as before, when I was still close to you in Tlemcen. The house. Ed-Dar. Darni. Your little boy, Baba ... Baba ...

The others ... We left them aside, the others, we forgot them, the others, the mother, the brothers, the sisters, the neighbors' stares and we played you and me ... They're napping ... ? They're napping ... I'm coming ... ? Come, my son ... You say: Don't go with people in the streets, don't accept their sweets, little gifts, love apples, *karantika*, *nouba*. It's not for you. You attract them in spite of yourself, my son, but they're too mean out there, on the streets, on the roads, in this life. They'll hurt you. Make you dirty and throw you away. Keep your head down in the streets, in the neighborhood. My son, my light, my Samir. You're so beautiful, so white, so Kabyle and your hair so long, so soft. Hide it under the cap. Hide everything about yourself and come here with me when you want to be you. In our home. In our home. Our world. I'm the father. I give you what they'll never give you. I am the father. I allow you to be a little girl here, within our walls. With me. On my lap. Be you the way you feel. Be you even if I don't understand everything. I see you, you're mine, you're mine and I want to follow you, to see what comes out of you ...

71

Take this bag. Take it. Open it. Do you see what it is? It's for you
... Put on these young girl's clothes whenever you want, when I'm
here and when I'm not ... Samir, my son, I bless you and protect you
... Samir, my daughter, I love you and I'm fond of you ... I've spoken
to your mom. She won't bother you anymore. And if she does, I trust
you: you're eleven now, you know, you understand, you'll know what to
say to the mother, you'll know how to play the bad guy too. Changing
words, words to prevent others from hurting you. Words to drive a
wedge between you and them. Harsh words. Harsh. I've seen you do it,
say it, those words. I've seen you with a different face too. Being mean,
meaner than all the others. Smarter than them. You are what you are.
I am the law here. And I give you again and again all my love. All my
blessings.

I don't know the future. What awaits you later and where. But I
know that with you, I melt, I can never be the one to kill you. You're
alive. You'll be more alive. Put these clothes on. Put them on and show
me. Come on, Samir! Come on, Samir! Be free in front of your father!

At Orly airport, I wasn't afraid. France! I took bus number 65 to the
Place des Invalides. That's when I panicked. I had to take the metro to
Pigalle. Just when I had to go down the stairs into the underground,
I couldn't. I'd never done that before. I couldn't do it. To go underground, into a gigantic tomb. I didn't understand the meaning of it.
Burying yourself alive. I had just arrived in Paris. I was barely 17. And
dying was out of the question. Not now. Not now. So, instead of taking
the damned subway, I looked for a cab. I had 500 francs. I could afford
it. Kamal, my favorite customer in Tlemcen, had given them to me. A
farewell present! I could pay for more than a cab.

*

In Pigalle. At the address of Sabriya, the girlfriend of an Algerian girlfriend, nobody (Sabriya had moved). In front of her door, I sat on the
stairs and waited and waited. Then Hayat arrived. She lived next door,
next to the other one who'd disappeared, Sabriya. Hayat looked like a
real Arab man, and looking at him I could never have imagined that he
was like me too. He was like me. Like us. Hayat was called Badr-Eddine

by day and, by night, she became the terror of the neighborhood, the policeman, the protector, the mother, the father, the big sister, the big brother, the biggest whore of us all, the bravest, the most suicidal . . . All at once . . .

He let me into his house, gave me a drink: cold milk and cheap madeleines, I still remember. He went into his bedroom. He came out in Hayat. I can't believe it! Incredible! Incredible! Incredible! A beautiful woman. Strange and beautiful. Tall. So tall. Another face. Her real face. Very sad. I threw myself into his arms and cried. It didn't last long. Hayat never wanted us to let ourselves go. No pampering. No weakness. Enjoy. Enjoy. Fuck. Steal. Take everything they've got, yes. But without getting weak. "Never weak. Stronger than the whole world." That was her motto. Her mask. Her song. And I quickly adopted it too. Bigger and stronger than life itself.

Hayat took me to the *hôtel des copines*, the girlfriends' hotel, in the Algerian quarter. Not far from the Place de Clichy metro station. A whole hotel. All boys, boys and girls from Algeria. A whole world. Hayat sought out Sabriya, introduced me to her and summoned the others to celebrate my arrival in Paris. Six hours later, close to midnight, I was with the girls working at Porte de Clichy. Sabriya had dressed me. With nothing at all, she made me a woman. She gave me a red one-piece swimsuit, an extra-large black leather jacket and gold pumps. I put them all on. It's perfect, for starters, Sabriya said. She made me up, not much. She said I was lucky: my hair was long and beautiful: no need for a wig. She said I already had the essentials to transform this body into a woman. But, as of tomorrow, you'll start taking hormones. I know a chemist who sells them over the counter.

Do you agree, Samir?

I agree.

Samir . . . No . . . We'll call you Samira . . .

No, no . . . I've already got my woman's name . . . My father gave it to me . . . Nadira.

You're Nadira.

I'm Nadira.

The first evening, the first night, I was already working. Hayat used to say that the Bois de Boulogne was for those who weren't afraid. It was too dark. No lights. Only tough guys and drug dealers. You should stay at Porte de Clichy. I took his advice and every time someone wanted to hurt me, I said: I'm Hayat's girlfriend. That was enough. Everyone knew her and everyone was afraid of her.

•

I lived at night. Only at night. From 1990 to 2011. From time to time I dared to go to the Bois. But not too much. Anyway, there was no shortage of customers back then. The whole of Paris came. I knew it all and did it all, with the powerful and the working class. Stars and drug dealers. Arabs, blacks, Asians, rich people from the Gulf States, unfaithful husbands from Chartres and Orléans. Professors from Paris' *grandes écoles*. Those from the 5th arrondissement, the 6th, the 7th and even those not far from the Élysée. They came too, of course. They needed it. They paid well. I was one of the best. I played the game perfectly. And I raised my rates as I went.

The golden age. From 1990 to 2011. A shower of money. A shower of adventures. A shower of transformations. Lives. Of tragedies. From Pigalle to Clichy. Paris, under my feet, in my hands. And Algeria, in the fire, further and further away. Far away . . . I went through a film, writing about it every day. An Egyptian film, of course, not a French one. A tragic and flamboyant melodrama, in which I knew so well how to play the heroine who rises, who falls, who flees, who sleeps, who cries, who cries again, who sacrifices herself but never gives up . . . Never . . . In this Paris by night, I was like Nadia Lotfi, like Hind Roustoum, like Magda . . . Like Isabelle Adjani, the first Algerian. Like Isabelle Adjani, the first Arab, the first Kabyle . . . Our star . . . The pure face of what we are here on this earth, between the borders of this country . . . The tormented, haunted soul of what the world and France have made of us.

From the second day, I went to the police and cried, so hard, so sincere, so well. I lost my passport. I have nothing left. I've lost everything. Everything has been taken from me. Everything taken . . . Help me, please . . . Please . . . I was lying so well . . . But I had no other options

. . . I had to find a way to stay in this country. They gave me a lost ID card. When the police arrested me and did what they wanted with me, I gave them this paper. When they made me wait several days in the police depot near the Châtelet metro station, I gave them this paper . . . In this paper, I had told them anything so they wouldn't know which country to deport me to . . . Just in case . . . My real passport, I had sent it by registered mail to Algeria.

I walked in Paris, I prospered in Paris, I built a family, I sold myself in Paris, I became what I am in Paris, without papers. For years without papers. For years eaten, exploited, gradually destroyed. And, in the end, never free. Never free.

I knew that one day I'd have to put my affairs in order. Take stock. That day came six years ago.

●

I had to relearn everything. All at once. Live in another country. The day. Living in the daytime after having lived most of my life at night . . . Walking like everyone else. During the day. Doing the same things as everyone else at the same time as everyone else. Endure the yellow or gray light of day. Running after I don't know what goal like everyone else . . . I pretended for a year . . . I discovered another France for a year . . . But it's not for me, the day. It's not for my soul and even less for my body.

The silicone in my butt exploded. Then in my breasts. And my thighs. By the time I realized it, it was too late. The doctors removed what they could. The silicone had mixed with my skin itself. They're so mixed, so blended, that the doctors can't do anything. Today, when I go before the management of the Altaïr association, I make an effort. I came without a wheelchair. But the people in charge know. I'm *une personne vulnerable* and they know.

I'm doomed.

They're waiting for me to die.

They won't be able to expel me from this association. They already feel guilty, too much so.

They gave me a small studio set up like a hospital room, like giving alms to the beggar who's been cold for years at the entrance to the Blanche metro station.

With nothing, I rebuilt the night, my night, in this studio. My other country.

I'm far from everything. I'm leaving. I'm leaving. I leave. I disappear. I'm fading. Tomorrow. At dawn. Not in France. Not in Algeria.

I'll be joining my father soon.

Baba . . . Baba . . . Baba . . .

My Rebellious Feet

DIARY MARIF

MY FATHER MEASURED MY FEET WITH A THICK THREAD AND quickly went to catch the pickup truck that waited for him. He put his *Jammana*, a checkered scarf worn as a turban, under his right arm and looked back.

"If you herd the calves, I will bring you shoes," he called out to me.

That was great news. Having new shoes was one of my aspirations because I had hardly ever worn good shoes. Yummy food, warm clothes, and good shoes were all the things I ever wanted. With my five siblings, we watched the car until it was out of sight, and then went to herd the calves.

My feet were chapped and both palms were blistered. It was difficult and painful to walk in my shabby, patched shoes. My father had promised to buy new shoes, and that was one of the most exciting things I'd heard in my childhood. I knew when my father said he would do something, he wouldn't break his word.

It was a warm summer afternoon in 1992. It was only one year after my family had returned to Bardabal, our village, which had been ravaged by Saddam Hussein's regime in 1979. A few families had returned empty-handed these twelve years later. There were no shops, no power, no public amenities, but the families were so thrilled to start their new lives with nothing but hope guiding them forward. Bardabal is located in a remote area of Sulemani province in northern Iraq, near the Iranian border.

The road to the village was rough and unpaved. A few times a week, a car or two would show up, and the people could catch a ride into the town of Saidsadiq, around ten miles away, where they would do their shopping. My father had to walk home with a heavy load if he was not lucky enough to find a car to bring him.

I wished he would come back soon, so I could see what the shoes looked like. For weeks, I'd had no appropriate shoes. The shoes I was wearing were patched so heavily that there was no space for new patches. Some spots were double-patched. My feet sometimes bled, and thorns would pierce the shoes, pricking my feet and adding to my blisters.

I was happy herding the calves as I imagined my new shoes. The color, the size, how they would fit snugly around my feet. I wished he would bring Adidas shoes. I thought how great it would feel to brag about them to my cousin.

That evening, my father returned. Luckily, he'd found a car that was going to the neighboring village, Qalbaza, which was a gunshot away from ours. He brought with him two large bags. He had bound both with his *Pshtween* (sash), put them on either side of his shoulders, and carried them home panting and drenched in sweat.

I tried to take one of the bags from him, but it was too heavy. I did not dare to ask if he had brought the shoes until he had rested and my mother had handed him a mug of fresh water from the nearby spring.

"Please ask father if he brought my shoes," I begged her as she made black tea at the pit fire. My mother was my refuge.

"I brought the shoes," my father said. "Give me a large sewing needle to open the holes for the laces."

Wonderful! I pushed my mother's hand to quickly find a large needle. My father had already found one, and started opening the holes. To my deep disappointment, the shoes were not Adidas. They were a brand called Plasko, which were not popular. I do not know why they were called Plasko and where the name came from, but elderly people used to wear them. If children wore them, they were ridiculed.

I looked at my father's spray of wrinkles running down his face. My fingers trembled and my voice was resigned.

"I don't like them," I said.

He responded, "Try them now. Do not kick the ground. Do not lose them."

I put them on, but they were too big for my feet.

He had kept the thread that measured my feet. He took it out of his pocket and measured my feet again. He knew when he knotted the thread, his thick fingers took the thread larger than the true measure of my feet. He used the thread for measuring my feet as he was illiterate and did not know how to write the numbers and, in any case, we did not have paper and pen in the first place.

I asked him to change the shoes.

"I am not sure when I will go to the shop, maybe next month," he said. He was in the process of building our first mudstone house by himself. He had started working on the Iranian border to provide for the family. My mother, on the other hand, was a housewife. So, I had to wait another month for new shoes or suffer wearing my ugly big shoes.

I wore them.

Oh, the plan of showing off in front of my cousins turned into shame. The shoes were extremely hot in the summer. I put some clothes inside the shoes in order to make them fit me. I wore them without socks which made them produce fart-like sounds. As usual, I complained about the shoes to my mother, and she told my father my concerns. But my father's response was dismissive.

"When I was your age, I had nothing to wear on my feet," he'd say.

That was true. Until the age of eight, he had never worn a pair of shoes. But times had changed, and we had enough money to buy me comfortable shoes.

I somehow lost one, but I did not dare to tell my father I had lost the left shoe. When I saw him, I would hide my foot with some clothes or weeds. After two days, my mother told him of my lost shoe.

"I will not buy another new pair unless these ones completely tear," he warned me. I sobbed behind the shed for a while, but he did not show any empathy. My father is a very realistic person. He was not worried about money at all, but he wanted my siblings and I to be more respectful of the things we had. I was half-barefoot for days and my left foot was filthy and black, while the other was protected.

It was unfair. One foot was protected while the other was hurt and suffered. For me, this symbolized the extreme realities of human injustice. Some have everything, a high-end lifestyle and happiness, while the others struggle and risk a lot just to live.

For my next pair, my father measured my feet again and brought me another new pair of shoes. I wished he'd bring me the same Adidas shoes as my cousins had. My father never bought me the things that I liked. He just bought what he thought was appropriate without any consultation.

This time he brought out the shoes in a plastic bag. "Wear these ones. Do not ask me to change them," he sternly cautioned me.

The shoes were too small!

I kicked the ground to try to force them to fit. "They do not fit me," I sadly mumbled and looked at him. He knew he was not good at choosing shoes and the other things I wanted, but all he said was, "It is what it is."

He asked my mother to serve him another tray of black tea with cubed sugar. He was dismissive, which was his usual way of handling situations where things had gone wrong which he did not want to discuss.

I had to wear small shoes. My feet were squeezed and turned red and chapped. When I took them off, I needed to fan my feet because they were too hot, with uncomfortable dents on my skin from the tightness of the shoes. I did not complain. I wished for the old, loose shoes. My uncomfortable shoes sometimes reminded me of the Iraqi politicians. Everyone was upset with the new regime and wished for the old Saddam Hussein era. During Saddam Hussein's regime, everyone complained about him, but then he was overthrown, and some new, corrupt politicians took power.

I had many sad days and was traumatized by the small shoes. When I went to school, I thought about how to wear them on cold days when they were frozen or how to walk and sit for several hours in class without noticing the discomfort and pain. The more I felt pain in my feet, the more it affected my body and mind. I could not breathe well and I talked loudly.

My father bought me new shoes more than two years later, but they were uncomfortable and undesirable shoes. I strategized about how to rebel and demand for better shoes and clothes. My life needed to change, and I had to find a way to fight for it. I deliberately tore my shoes and told my father it was because they were too small. Although he did not trust me, he kept quiet.

I begged my mother to buy me shoes. She listened to me as she always did with my four sisters. Traditionally, fathers brought their sons' necessary items, as mothers did for their daughters. Until that time, I was the only one on my father's side because my elder brother, Ary, bought his own necessities while my mother did for my sisters. My mother's team was lucky. She conversed with my sisters before going shopping. They all decided what they needed. I thought of defecting to my mother's team since there was freedom of choice there.

I told her I would not wear any shoes or clothes if my father bought them. It was a coup against my father. I had to do it, I absolutely needed to. My father is so kind and deeply loves his children, but he never expresses love with words but rather with action. Money was never the issue, he just bought things without much consideration.

My mother promised to bring me Maradona shoes when she next visited the doctor in Sulaymaniyah. Maradona shoes were named after the Argentinian soccer legend Diego Maradona. It was a new shoe brand that many children and teens were crazy about. My mother could not come back the same day she visited the doctor due to lack of transportation, and therefore she needed to stay at a relative's home either in Sulaymaniyah or Saidsadiq.

I patiently waited for my lovely Maradona shoes. I waited a day and a night. I told all my classmates and friends. I envisioned them and the other things she had said she would bring, sweets like *luqma qazi*, and Kurdish donuts. I became more alert as the clock ticked away. It is one of the strongest memories of my childhood, that time waiting for my mother to return. I waited for something I had been assured would happen. I was sure of the success of my little strategic coup and was looking forward to showing my father how my mother did great things for me.

Waiting to end the unpleasant days of uncomfortable shoes, I imagined how my mother would go to the shops and bargain for shoes and would tell the shopkeeper about my deep passion for Maradona shoes. Finally, she came back and brought a lot of things in huge bags. I waited in anticipation. Words cannot express how excited I was. I ran and hugged her and inhaled the wonderful smell of *mekhak* (clove) on her chest.

"I brought Maradona shoes," she triumphantly announced.

I joyfully jumped around her. The thick laces, the solid heel of the shoes, and the big holes on the sides of the laces made me so delighted. I tightened the laces as I put the shoes on. It was time to boast to my friends and cousins. I felt as strong and confident as a steel gate.

The Maradona shoes were also a little bit big, and I suffered on cold days because it was freezing that winter. But I still loved my Maradona shoes. It is a nice sensation when you love something or someone, so even if you suffer, you feel okay, as though it's worth it. I kept the Maradona shoes in a safe place in case someone tried to steal them. When I went swimming at pools, I covered them with leaves. My shoes inspired me and gave me a sense of independence. It was my first step toward making my own decisions and fighting for my rights. I learned that no changes you want can come to pass unless you do something about it or pay a price. This most definitely applies to government systems. Without struggles, reforms never come to light.

My journey from unsuitable shoes to standing up against a broken system has taught me that change is only possible when we dare to step up and speak out.

The Afghan and the Persian

JORDAN ELGRABLY

THIRTY-EIGHT CLANDESTINE MIGRANTS, INCLUDING NINE-teen children, died one Saturday night when their vessel came apart off the coast of Italy near a seaside resort just outside Vintimille, where dozens of bodies were found strewn on a beach. Another eighty *harragas* on the same vessel survived when the *gület*, a Turkish wooden ship, hit the rocks in bad weather. The ship was smashed to splinters, and debris was found along 500 meters of Italian coastline, only a few kilometers from the border with France. Many of the survivors were from Afghanistan, Pakistan, and Iran, and there were migrants from Sudan and Somalia on board. Almost all the survivors were adults, while many of the missing and those found drowned on the beach were children. During triage, Italian authorities, aghast, lined up the little corpses but did not have enough body bags of the right size to go around.

The next day Tamim, a *harrag* and a lover of words and dogs, washed up dirty and disheveled on the beach a few kilometers from Narbonne, having survived the shipwreck that nearly cost him his life. The robust but shaken migrant, age thirty-five, was then lucky to find refuge in nearby Montpellier, where Afghans, Syrians, and migrants from Africa were able to gain a foothold.

A woman named Romy, with a tanned face and long exquisite fingers, working at the offices of sos Méditerranée, recorded his full name, date of birth, nationality, and other vitals. He spoke through an interpreter in a mix of Dari and English, while drinking chai that he

83

nervously stopped to stir counterclockwise, as if he wished he could slow time or turn back the clock altogether.

•

Three weeks earlier he had crossed the border into Turkey in the back of a refrigerated meat truck, he and ten other men protected with nothing more than blankets and a determination to escape death sentences. From Kabul he had caught a ride hidden in the trunk of a family car that took him to Herat, and from there he'd found a bus that dropped him off in Isfahan. Another bus took him to the frontier with Iraq, and then there was the treacherous journey to Aleppo in which the truck he was riding in took three sniper bullets before miraculously escaping into the night. It was in Aleppo that he found smugglers who sold Tamim the last space in the meat truck carrying them into Turkey. But before they reached the border between Azaz and Kilis, two of the Syrians boxed him into the corner of the truck farthest from the driver, one holding a knife to his gut and the other saying, in English, *where is your money, give it to us, brother.* At that very moment the truck must have hit a large pothole, because the three of them lurched backwards and Tamim threw his blanket over the Syrian with the knife and kicked him viciously in the head. The other man had rolled away to where two fellow Afghans took hold of him, but before any of them had long to consider what to do next, the truck stopped, the doors flew open, and they were all ordered out. *From here you walk, imshi!*

•

Romy recorded as much of his story as she could, and then asked: "Why are you applying for asylum?"

"You know, the Taliban took over the country and the Americans left, and during the chaos that ensued . . . they . . . killed my wife. They . . . killed my daughter . . . Women are no longer permitted to get an education, or even to work . . . I was a professor of literature at Kabul University, where I met my wife . . . her name is Rohina Rahimzai . . . there she met her end. They beat her to death with sticks in front of the library. You would like to know why? Yes, I want to know why, too. Do you think that they required a reason? Who would put those thugs and murderers on trial? Shall I tell you how my daughter Mojdeh, only six years old, perished? I am certain you would like to know, but I'm not prepared to talk about that now. I fled the country because people like me who ask questions, who ask too many questions, who aren't necessarily good Muslims, who don't revere the Qur'an above life itself, those of us readers . . . we are more likely to be killed than ordinary Afghans, who would prefer to live politely and quietly. Why France? Why have I come here? I washed up on your shores as a man who loves books and words and libraries and ideas. I thought by coming here, I could save myself."

As much as he wanted to resume working as a literature professor, Tamim could not teach in Dari or Farsi in Montpellier, nor was his French more than rudimentary; but he spoke English well enough, with a pleasant accent that the French found easy to comprehend, and he was therefore able to make his way about the city. It wasn't long before they found him a shelter and a bed, and from there he went to daily French classes along with other immigrants and refugees. During the evenings, he pored over a much-used copy of Norwegian writer Åsne Seierstad's *The Bookseller of Kabul*, remembering that the subject of her story, Shah Muhammad Rais, had attempted to sue her for defamation, and lost.

Despite being a man absorbed by words and books in Dari, Farsi, and English, Tamim wasn't beyond taking matters into his own hands – and, indeed, working *with* his hands. He informed Romy at SOS Méditerranée that he was, in addition to his former university position, a man of all trades, a handyman with experience in carpentry, masonry, and many household projects that required speed and ingenuity. In other words, *bricolage*. She began to field him small jobs here and there, and after being in the city for only two full moons, he obtained a cheap cell phone. Soon afterwards he learned that he would be granted asylum, though the process would take much longer than even he could have predicted.

Maxime del Fiol, a client of his who had benefited from Tamim's handy use of carpentry tools and who was a monthly donor to SOS

Méditerranée, knew the *propriétaire* of a building in the city center only a short jaunt from the Préfecture, who had a studio apartment for rent.

Madame Gallimidi was a stout brunette in her retirement years. She sat the two men down in her large flat overlooking some of the oldest buildings in town. Finding Maxime and Tamim agreeable company, she served them Moroccan mint tea, and while beginning to slowly fill out the lease, she chattered about her late husband and how she had inherited his family's apartment building, which had infuriated his two brothers and sister. While Madame Gallimidi regaled them with stories she had no doubt recounted a hundred times to anyone who would listen, Tamim looked about the flat, noticing the antique furniture that looked straight out of *Madame Bovary*, the Art Deco gilded mirror that ran from floor to ceiling, the shelves of old hardbound books, the musty smell of time and tobacco, and the bric-a-brac that revealed an eccentric's penchant for collecting. Out of the corner of his eye, Tamim saw a white blur dash behind the sofa on which they were sitting. Madame Gallimidi perked up.

"Don't mind him," she said. "That's just my dead husband, who's come back to spy on me." The large Persian poked his head out from behind the sofa, as if he understood that he was now the subject of conversation.

"Madame," said Maxime, "I am going to be Tamim's *garant*, as he's new in our country and we have to support those who deserve asylum."

The three of them signed the paperwork and Madame Gallimidi handed over a set of keys to her small, furnished studio on the top floor, which came with a mini-fridge, hot plate and microwave, for just 450 euros per month. Maxime wrote a check for the deposit, and the two of them thanked their host. Moments later, downstairs in the street, as Maxime was leaving, he said Tamim had a year to repay him.

About to part ways, Tamim thought of his dead wife and daughter and felt his heart tearing up his chest, but nonetheless experienced a spasmodic moment of joy and relief. Tamim was a six-foot man with coffee-colored skin and slightly Asian eyes, what Americans call "a person of color." He wanted to seem strong but he could not stop his tears. "I can't thank you enough, I'm in your debt. Don't worry, I'll repay you."

Maxime fidgeted, uncomfortably put off by the man's weeping, and finally blurted: "It's nothing, nothing at all! You would do the same for me were the situation reversed, I know it."

"I don't know what I would do, because it's hard to know who I am after all that I have experienced these last months, but I hope you are correct, Maxime, *j'espère que vous avez raison* . . . I would like to be a good person. I have not killed anyone, I was, after all, a literature professor and a writer, not a soldier; but after what they did to my family and my country, there are people I would like to kill. Yes, I would, and in fact—maybe I shouldn't admit this to anyone—I often think about the ways I would like to strangle or stab or suffocate the men who took my family from me . . . I am sorry if I sound angry," he said.

"Vengeance is in your heart," Maxime replied. He paused for further consideration. "I can understand that you would think about it; it doesn't make you crazy, or criminal. I would feel the same." Maxime regarded his newly-minted friend and shook his hand sternly before rushing away down the cobblestoned street.

◆

Tamim began to receive more and more calls on his new cellphone, which at first was a challenge, as all the callers began by speaking in French, but then switched to English, sometimes good English, and sometimes quite shaky and difficult to understand. After a while he had begun to build up a roster of regular clients who needed his handyman services, so he was often away from his flat during the day, working at jobs that had to be paid via a complex system organized between SOS Méditerranée and the Préfecture; but at least it had the veneer of legality, and he did not fear deportation, which was the usual way migrants inhabited Montpellier — always wondering how long their idyll would last.

One day, Tamim noticed a beautiful dog that was stopping to sniff up people seated at the café where he was taking his morning coffee.

He wondered about the breed, as the dog was of medium size with brindle coloring and light brown eyes. The animal was quite striking, reminding Tamim of a small lion in majesty and coloring. Tamim noticed that the dog had a collar, and he decided to call to the animal, which he did in a quiet voice. "Here, here," he said, emitting a low whistle. The dog turned his head, scanned him for a moment, and then appeared to walk away, but then turned around and trotted back over and slowly approached him. "Hello, *bonjour*, what's your name?" Tamim asked, holding out his bunched-up fist so the dog could smell him, which he did for a moment; then the animal licked the outside of his hand. Without any sudden movement, Tamim reached to examine the dog's collar, and tried to read the tag on it. *Si vous me trouvez, c'est que je suis perdu ; appelez la SPA, 04 67 27 73 78.*

How odd; whose dog was this? Tamim looked up the SPA on his phone and decided to take the dog to the shelter himself. He went inside the café and asked the barista for a piece of string or cord. The dog was still waiting at his table when he returned.

Later the following day, after it became evident that the dog had no owner, and careful to avoid his landlady and any of the other tenants in his building, Tamim brought his new companion home. The studio would be cramped for the two of them, but the building's inner courtyard featured quite a large garden with trees, bushes, flowers, and a bench on which to idle away the day. He had already spent more than one afternoon sunning himself out there with *The Bookseller of Kabul*. Now, with the addition of the dog, which he decided to call "Ardeshir," he would be spending much more time outdoors. He soon found himself taking Ardeshir for several daily walks around the neighborhood, which mainly comprised old stone buildings, and let him play in the garden. He also took him for long walks around the Promenade du Peyrou.

At first, as a new tenant, Tamim did his utmost to hide Ardeshir's existence, as he had rented the studio as a quiet widower. Madame Gallimidi would likely not have been happy had he rented the place with an animal — a 30-kilo mixed-breed dog with a large head that could frighten almost anyone. But very quickly, people in the building took notice of Tamim walking his pet, and word soon drifted up to Madame, who lived on the third floor below his attic studio. She rapped at his door one morning, shortly after he had returned from walking Ardeshir around the neighborhood and down by La Panacée museum.

"Monsieur Ansary, you did not mention that you were the owner of a canine, but as a pet lover myself, I'm not going to let myself be upset with you."

"Madame, I only rescued him ten days ago; I didn't know of him at all when we signed the papers here, I promise you. He needed a home and a good daily meal. His name is Ardeshir, because he looks a bit like a lion . . ."

"Regardless, you should have consulted me. Now that this is a *fait accompli*, let me warn you to keep your dog away from my cat! You may not have noticed, but he is large and fearsome, and I daresay your boy would have his eyes scratched out if he tries anything funny, should they ever happen to meet. Try not to let that happen."

Tamim felt grateful and relieved that he could keep his furry new friend, though he was surprised that Madame Gallimidi had made no remark about how on earth the two of them could possibly cohabit in such a constricted space, a single room of only 25 square meters. She couldn't know that it was four times the size of the prison cell he had shared briefly in Kabul with eight other men, crammed in together for days with hardly anything to eat, and nothing but a hole in the concrete in which to do one's business. The nearly airless cell carried a stench – the filth was beyond imagination – and they had had to take turns sleeping, twenty minutes apiece, while the others remained standing. By such standards, his Montpellier studio was a princely home; and besides, Ardeshir had been living on the street, and now the two were sheltered and warm.

One day after idling on the bench with a book, Tamim decided to venture out to the Monoprix to pick up some groceries, leaving his companion to wander the garden without him. The dog tried to follow him out into the courtyard, but he held up a palm to stop him. "You'll be just fine here, Ardeshir, I'll be back shortly. You stay ... stay," he said.

A short while later, bearing a bag packed with purchases, he let himself in to fetch the dog when he noticed Ardeshir tearing around the garden like a mad fiend. There was something black in his mouth, a large object that was a blur as he tore through the undergrowth and emerged from one bush only to vanish into another. Tamim whistled to the dog, and Ardeshir trotted out of a bush and cautiously approached. At last, he dropped the black object in front of Tamim, who could see with horror that it was a cat. The cat was not moving. Instinctively, he glanced up at Madame Gallimidi's courtyard window, relieved that the lifeless animal wasn't hers.

He struggled to get the dog, the cat, and the bag of groceries up the stairs. Once inside, he scolded Ardeshir and commanded him to sit: "You're lucky we didn't run into anyone on the stairs, you bad, horrible dog!" Tamim turned his attention to the cat's corpse, and in that moment he realized that the animal was covered in black mud. Shaking his head, dreading the worst, he washed the cat off in the sink, and sure enough, its white fur was revealed. The cat was certainly dead, and must have belonged to Madame Gallimidi. He looked at Ardeshir as if to ask, *why did you kill it?* He remembered her quip about the cat being her dead husband returned to spy on her, and began to feel superstitious, as if he were being watched by the evil eye. This gnawed at him: he thought himself a modern man, a university-educated Afghan, not a person who would ever affix an amulet to his door or mutter preventive sayings to ward off maledictions.

Late that evening, shortly before midnight, noticing the moon was quite nearly full, Tamim stole down the stairs and deposited the dead Persian on the landlady's welcome mat. The following morning he left shortly after dawn on a job, filled with fear that Ardeshir's kill would cost him his asylum — or, at the very least, put him on the street.

That afternoon when he returned home, he noticed an ambulance pulling away from the apartment building. Two neighbors, a man and a woman whom he had previously acknowledged in the stairwell, were conversing in loud voices. "*Bonjour*," Tamim said. "What's going on?"

The man spoke and the woman shook her head sadly. "They've just taken Madame Gallimidi to the emergency room at Lapeyronie; she's had a heart attack," he said.

Tamim froze, as if he were paralyzed.

"The poor woman was going out to check the mail, but when she opened her door, she found her dead cat on the doorstep. Apparently, the cat had died three days ago, and her son had buried it for her in the garden."

•

The woman from the first floor was shaking her head, and Tamim had no words. Reflexively, he glanced up at the lone window of his studio at the top of the building, angry with Ardeshir, but still unable to move. "Do you suppose she'll be all right?" he said. The two neighbors bore sad, uncertain looks, and the woman shrugged as if to say that the old woman was doomed.

He found himself walking aimlessly around the quarter, unable to go home or decide on what to do next. After hours of wandering, Tamim found himself standing at the Louis Blanc tram stop and realized that he had to go visit Madame Gallimidi in the hospital. When he arrived at the Urgences, he was asked to produce his identification and *carte vitale*, but he said, in broken French: "I came to see Madame Gallimidi, she was brought here with a bad heart earlier. Please . . ."

"Are you a relative?" the woman behind the counter asked. Tamim shook his head. "I live in her building. Is there anyone else here to visit her, perhaps I could talk to them?"

The woman had no idea, and was of no further assistance. Tamim found a seat in the large waiting room and lost track of time, not knowing what he was doing there. After a while he realized that he could slip in past the guard desk when no one was nearby, and he wandered into the long, cold hallway, searching for Madame Gallimidi; but with four floors and kilometers of hallways and rooms, one after the other, he was unable to locate her. Several times, hospital personnel stopped to ask where he was going. Tamim failed to reply, and eventually a security man showed him the exit.

When he got home, he was a wreck, overcome with fatigue, weighed down by voices and ghosts. He had no idea whether Madame Gallimidi was alive or dead, nor whether he could be held responsible. The light seemed to dim, the walls were dark, and the dog lay quietly by the door, staring at Tamim with what appeared to be sad eyes. Without realizing what he was doing, Tamim kneeled down in front of Ardeshir and wrapped his hands around the animal's throat, squeezing furiously, and the dog struggled for breath, kicking all four legs, eyes staring at his master's darkened face as Tamim took the life out of him.

•

That very week, the *Midi Libre* reported that a thirty-seven-year-old man in the Tarn was being questioned about the death of his dog, a five-year-old Malinois that starved to death in his apartment just east of Albi. Placed under arrest, he was charged with "serious abuse and cruelty to a domestic animal." He faces five years in prison and a fine of 75,000 euros.

A Dog in the Woods

MALU HALASA

HE LET THE DOG OUT AND WAITED BEHIND THE PLATE-GLASS patio door. The day was crisp, the sun peeking through thick winter clouds, but it was too cold to go out. Melted ice covered the deck, along with snow that had frozen over again. The last thing he needed, with his bad knees, was to fall.

The dog ran through the trees, down towards the barn – the roof of which was visible through the pines he'd planted forty years earlier. He kept beehives in the barn, but in the spring worker bees abandoned their queen, and the larvae and unhatched eggs died. He kept the barn door permanently open even in the winter, and when the dog was out she usually meandered in for a sniff, or relief from the cold. The old man, holding onto a kitchen chair by the glass door, watched from the house. The dog belonged to Emily, his youngest daughter, who had come from New York to Ohio for the holidays. She had lived with him during the Covid pandemic, and had gotten a rambunctious puppy that was now an adult. This afternoon Emily was driving back from Detroit with one of her cousins. They had gone to visit family there, and the dog had been left in his care. He slid open the patio door a crack and called out: "Zouzou!"

He could see the dog through the lower bare branches of the trees in the partially snow-filled clearing by the barn. Maybe it was his voice, or the wind; Zouzou stopped suddenly, head cocked. He shouted her name again to make sure, and just as she seemed poised to turn back and run towards the house, a deer caught her eye. The chase was on. Deer and dog ran straight into the woods.

"Damn," the old man muttered.

Against his better judgment, he opened the patio door wider and stepped outside with great care. He wasn't dressed for the weather: thin cotton pants, no sweater. Slowly, he made his way across the deck, holding onto the long wooden picnic table his family no longer used. The kids he'd had with his wife had grown up and moved away, and the kids he'd had in secret with another woman he rarely mentioned were finally old enough to start families of their own. Emily, now 27, was the last of these.

As a teenager, she had believed that the old man and his wife were her adoptive parents. It came as a shock to their conservative Arab relations that Emily, her sister Nora, and her brother Bobby were also all his children, along with another boy still, with a different woman. His older kids, by then middle-aged women, had been pragmatic about their suddenly enlarged family; they were grateful that the truth had emerged only after their mother's death.

Of all his children, Emily was the most devoted to him. She phoned every day from her job in New York City, and took care of him when she came home to visit – despite his fierce independence. In his early nineties, he still got up at sunrise and drove seven miles through the Ohio countryside for coffee at the nearest McDonald's.

In a loud voice, he yelled again for the dog. The sound resonated in the deep, empty spaces between the trees in the woods at the back of the house – but no dog materialized. Zouzou could have gone anywhere: the back or the front of the house, the rolling fields belonging to his neighbors. The deer were brazen; they went all over the place. He just hoped the dog hadn't followed the one she'd spotted under the bridge, onto the Interstate.

He retraced his steps cautiously across the frozen, slippery deck and went back into the kitchen. There he exchanged his shoes for boots and pulled on a sweater, then a jacket. He swept up his car keys from the table and was about to descend into the basement, but changed direction and went down the hall towards the front door instead. He thought twice about locking it and left it a bit ajar, just in case – the dog was familiar with this way into and out of the house. He returned to the kitchen and focused his attention on the stairs leading down, one step at a time. In the basement was a bar where he had once entertained his cronies. Now the room was a home gym filled with a stationary cycle and rowing machine, which he used most days. On the other side of a door waited a garage large enough for two cars. He really had no choice. He had to go out and find that dog.

●

Many of the housing developments in the more suburbanized area of this township were newly constructed. Along the county line where he lived, however, stood older, rundown, wooden houses, between the larger estates that belonged to families that had inherited acreage or, like him, had bought undeveloped farmland whenever it became free. The old man drove a couple of miles away to a family whose property abutted his at the back. A track on their land went into the woods. But before he had a chance to stop at the house, his phone rang. It was Emily. She could see him in his jacket behind the steering wheel through the car's camera.

"Hi, Dad. You and Zouzou going somewhere?"

"Honey, can't talk now. I'll call you back."

"Okay," she said. "Me and Leila are on the highway. We just crossed the Michigan state line." She signed off: "Love you."

The old man had known Dave, the owner of the neighboring house, ever since he had been a classmate of his eldest daughter in high school. Estranged from his own father, Dave would come over and have heart-to-heart talks with the old man. Dave became an adult, and had married a few times. He maintained the same taste in women: usually blonde, petite, lovers of the countryside. His current wife answered the front door. She knew animals, and was sympathetic to the old man's predicament.

"Gee," she said, her hands aloft as she considered the weather, "can't say how good the track is back there. We've only been as far as the barn, 'cause of the snow. But feel free. You want me to tag along?"

"No, I'll be okay." The old man waved as he climbed back inside his car.

"If I don't hear your car coming out, we'll send in the plow!" She meant it only half in jest.

Behind the spacious ranch house, the once-muddied track showed deep impressions left by the plow's industrial-size tires. The mounds of gray snow that had been pushed to either side had frozen, thawed, and mixed with mud; a recent snowfall had frozen them again. In some parts, the mounds were spotted a murky yellow: even in freezing temperatures, foxes, raccoons, and feral cats urinated. The terrain had a wrung-out, damp, sullied, uninviting look. The last low rays of the failing afternoon sun made a final retreat behind a low bank of foreboding clouds. The track petered out behind the barn, which housed the tractor plow. By a fence, a couple of horses in coats shivered. He inched the car further along and then stopped. As the trees thickened around him, he grew unsure which part of the leftover snow and grassy tufts belonged to the track.

He used the open door to pull himself out, and stood next to the car. The temperature was dropping. It was going to start snowing. The old man didn't want the dog or himself to become trapped in the woods. He slapped his bare hands together for warmth, put them to his mouth, and hollered, "*Zouzou!*" In amongst the trees, his voice sounded closer, more contained. He turned and faced another direction. The dog's name was shouted again when the phone rang. It was Emily.

"Now where are you?" she asked.

He sighed. He was going to have to tell her. "Well, honey, Zouzou ran into the woods after a deer."

"She knows to come back." There wasn't a speck of worry in his daughter's young voice.

He never liked correcting her. "This time she didn't."

In the few seconds it took for the news to sink in, he added quickly, "I'm in the woods behind Dave's house. I thought she might be back here."

"You're *where*?" Emily's voice rose suddenly. He could tell she was anxious. "That's all I need," she scolded. "Go home. You'll fall down and hurt yourself. And who's going to come out and rescue you? *Daaad . . .*" She sounded like a little girl again.

"I'm okay." He always became annoyed whenever his kids thought him weaker than he was.

"Just passed Cincinnati," he overheard his niece Leila announce, while driving. She was a solid, calming presence against the white noise of whooshing cars and trucks on the busy expressway. Emily's words slightly slurred when she told him, "Okay, I'll get off now." There was no *love you* as she hung up. He could picture her face, screwed up. If she hadn't started crying, she was about to.

*

Leila, at the wheel, kept an eye on the semi overtaking them in the lane to their right. She felt around for the box of tissues she kept near the driver's seat. Grabbing hold of it, she shoved it towards Emily. Leila often broke down in the car when life's difficulties became too much to bear. But the one thing she could say in her favor was that she'd never once cried over a dog. She was about to console her cousin, but Emily was already on her phone.

"Yep." Bobby sounded somewhat annoyed when he answered. He was definitely coming down with something. It was winter, and he and his wife and their four kids – the three that were his and Theresa's and BB, a cute Vietnamese baby girl they'd adopted – were always getting sick. The family had survived Covid, but their antibodies hadn't been strong enough to ward off the virulent strain of flu that was making the rounds of the homeschooled kids who met a couple of days a week at the local library.

He could immediately tell Emily was upset. With their mother's two older children, he, Nora and Emily – because of their father – had become a unit within a unit. Still, Bobby tried not to let his two sisters intrude on what had become an incredibly busy life. Between work, the children, and his studies, he didn't have much time to do what he loved best: make music.

"Okay," he said impatiently. "Stop worrying." He leaned his guitar back against the wall, downed a couple of aspirins, and got ready. In his winter coat and rubber boots, a warm hat, scarf, and gloves, he stood by the doorway of the bedroom and told Theresa his reason for going out. Two of the kids were in bed with their mother; the other two were down the hall, tucked up in their cots. The way he felt, it was only a matter of time before he joined them. But maybe by then they would be up and about, and he could bring his miniature keyboard to bed with him.

"Take a flashlight," Theresa – wan and sick-looking – called out from the bed.

"I have the light on my phone."

Theresa nodded wearily. "Phones break. Take a flashlight, for my peace of mind."

Bobby smiled. How did this slip of girl he'd met at church become such a pragmatic matriarch? "Get some sleep," he said, and his voice softened as he added, "By the time you and the kids wake up, I'll be back." He tiptoed through the silent house and left through the garage door.

Nora, Emily's sister, answered a FaceTime call at the One-Minute Walk-In Medical Clinic in Memphis, where she worked as a nurse. "Okay, calm down," Nora said, peering into her phone. The connection was a little blurry, but she could see that Emily was distressed. "I remember something about lost dogs because my neighbor lost hers. Wait, let me look." Nora swiped Emily's image on her phone to access the Internet. Emily could hear the beeping of medical equipment, and what sounded like a crowd of people clamoring in the clinic.

Nora said to one of the other nurses: "Give me another five. I'll be right out." She whispered into the phone: "Because of the flu, it's nuts around here." Emily felt bad. On FaceTime, she could see that her sister was sitting in a cubicle, a mask under her chin as she sipped a quick cup of coffee. Nora tapped in Zouzou's details: the color, gray and white; the breed, labradoodle. "How old's Zouzou?" she asked.

"Three." Emily stiffened. She had been good at holding back her tears, but at any moment they were going to erupt.

"Shush!" Nora typed in their father's address. "All done. An email alert from www.mydogismissing.com has gone out to two hundred addresses within a five-mile radius of Dad's house. Someone's bound to see Zouzou and bring her home. Got to go—" With that, she cut Emily off.

Before Nora left the cubicle, she speed-dialed their mother's number and told her Zouzou was lost in the woods, and that Emily was on her way back from Detroit, nervous and upset. Over the past six months, Nora and Emily hadn't spoken much with their mother; the relationship had soured over something stupid. It had been more than a few years since Shirley had communicated with Emily's father, but that didn't matter when her children or their pets needed her. Shirley loved children and dogs. After getting off the phone with Nora, she put together an emergency care package of food, bottled water, dog kibble, and a small, warm blanket, and placed it in her car.

Emily began sobbing. The cousins' trip to Detroit had been a washout. She and their other cousin had let Leila sleep in, and she'd missed going with them to yoga class. That had caused a nasty argument. Now Zouzou's disappearance had compounded an already awkward situation. Leila glanced over at her passenger and said, "I've forgotten; in your twenties, you really feel things."

Emily looked over through her tears. "What do you mean by that?"

"To be so worried about a dog . . ."

"Zouzou's not just a dog." Emily shook her head in utter disbelief. "She's family." *My family,* she thought to herself. But how could she expect anyone else to understand? Leila came from a close-knit family. She had grown up in the same house with her sisters; she had known her parents her whole life. Even though Emily's family secrets had been revealed to all, it didn't mean that everything was all right between, say, her and Bobby – although Nora had always been a solid older sister – or, worse yet, her parents. Zouzou had come into Emily's life during lockdown, and had been a constant presence. She was there

99

for Emily when Emily thought some of the people who should be, weren't.

Bobby, meanwhile, called his father.

The old man picked up. "Hello, son! Emmie call you?"

"You bet," Bobby said, matter-of-factly. "Dad, any luck?"

"Been driving around the neighborhood. Haven't seen Zouzou yet."

"I'm at the house. Thought I better call now. Who knows, the reception in the woods. You might think about coming home. I don't want you to get sick."

The old man bristled again. "Will you kids stop badgering me?"

The two got off the phone and Bobby stepped out of his car. Darkness came early. He was cold and felt like crap. It was just like Emily to lose her dog in the middle of winter. When they were kids, she had gone to live in the big house with Dad and his wife, and had grown up there. Bobby and Nora stayed at their mother's. Dad regularly visited, and invited them over to play with Emily, but none of the kids knew he was their father. They thought he was a family friend who showed up with groceries whenever he visited their mother's house. As they grew older, he intervened in a decisive way and made sure they went to college; but Bobby and Nora hadn't been afforded the opportunities lavished on Emily.

Bobby's adolescence had been troubled. Learning the identity of his father so late in life could have had long-lasting repercussions, but Theresa had changed all of that. Having his own children had given him a different perspective. Sometimes dads did what they were only able to do, and sometimes that had to be enough. If only his sisters would cut their mother the same slack.

Bobby walked past the barn. Tiny sleeting bits of ice crystals stung his eyes. He could feel them stiffen his hipster beard, which all his male friends in their early thirties were growing. He had known the woods since he was a little boy, although he didn't let his own kids play there. The tall, long grass between the trees crunched beneath his feet. Further in, he realized that no one looking for him would be able to find him. He was going to have to follow his footprints back out, and pray that it didn't snow; he was a useless Hansel for not trailing bread-crumbs, as in the story he read to his children. The ground, squishy underfoot in some places, was frozen, rock-solid ice in others. It made him glad he was wearing his thick rubber boots.

Forty minutes later, another car stopped in front of the big house. Whatever Shirley thought she might feel seeing it for the first time in years was pushed aside by her worry for Zouzou. Down by the garage, Bobby's car was parked in one of the spaces near the pond. Before she got out of hers, she called his number, but it went to voicemail. She arranged the provisions she had brought by the open front door, al-though she knew better than to call to anybody who might be inside. Before she got back into her car to leave, she walked down the drive-way beside the house and glimpsed the long beam from a flashlight, combing the woods on the other side of the barn.

*

The old man decided he had wasted enough time driving around on country lanes, and stopped in the driveways of neighbors he knew, along with newcomers to the neighborhood whom he didn't. Each time he rang the front doorbell, he asked the same thing: "We lost our dog, have you seen it?" All of them said "no" except for another wiz-ened grandfather like the old man, who suggested: "Don't forget to check the camp."

The old man nodded. He had forgotten Camp Francis of Assisi. Rented out for religious conferences, school sleepovers, and nature events, it was on the edge of the woods that started at the bottom of his yard and fanned out for miles behind his house. His car followed the roads leading to the camp, and he pulled up in a clearing surrounded by log cabins. He remembered the last time he was there. He had been looking for another lost dog. He and his wife and his second daughter, then 11, had two German shepherds, Tipsy and King. Whenever they weren't on the leash, they ran away.

He had probably spent years of his life searching for lost dogs, and the thought suddenly weighed heavily upon him – like fatigue. Instead of leaving of his car, he remained in his seat and peered out the front windshield. He hit the switch to roll down the passenger-side window. Once satisfied that nothing was there, he slowly pushed open the door on his side and continued to take a good look around, without getting out. Absolutely nobody had been in the camp since the big snow had melted and frozen again. Only his tires had left marks in the snow still on the ground. All the log cabins were shut up. There wasn't a soul for miles around.

"Zouzou!" he called through the open door. But he was tired, his voice weak. When he could, he stood up on the icy ground and held onto the roof of the car as he made his way to the trunk. He pressed the smart key and the lid flipped open. From inside he retrieved a Cleveland Browns scarf (he'd supported the team until the quarter-back was accused of sexual misconduct) and a thick pair of winter gloves he only wore in times of emergencies. He never used to feel the cold, and as a younger man had prided himself on never needing a coat even during the worst winters. But everything, it seems, changes in your nineties. He also took out a small plastic bottle of water from a case of 50 he kept in the trunk, a habit from when he ran marathons. The nearly icy water soothed his aching throat. He called out the dog's name again, but his increasingly hoarse voice wavered. He grabbed onto the trunk to catch his breath.

The last time Tipsy and King ran away, he had driven to Camp Francis of Assisi and had almost run into a pickup truck turning into the road leading to the camp. The two vehicles came to a stop nose to nose, inches from each other. The other driver, the camp's mainte-nance man, got out, but the old man – then in his forties – just leaned out his window. It was summertime, when the evenings were long, bright, and full of promise.

"Man," scolded the maintenance man, "what're you doing here?"

"I lost my dogs."

The maintenance man motioned for him to get out of his car and follow him. Behind a mesh at the back of a truck stood a sleek German shepherd. It was Tipsy. Once she was home, King returned as well, looking like he had missed her. Some twenty years later, when Emmie was growing up, the family had another German Shepherd, named Princess. He didn't know why Zouzou hadn't been given a generic name like the others. How did his youngest know about Zouzou, a character from the Egyptian film *Khalli balak min Zouzou!* (*Watch out for Zouzou!*) – which is what he'd been doing since that pesky dog had run away. The film had been popular in the 1970s. It was about a reformed belly dancer who forgoes the family profession in entertainment and focuses on her studies after falling in love with her college professor. It wasn't exactly a rags-to-riches story, but something almost as important in the Middle East – respectability: a girl saved from the gutter of immorality by love.

The old man sat back in his car, rolled up the passenger-side window and realized that Zouzou's name said everything about his experience as an Arab immigrant to America. He had hid his ethnicity even from his dogs. Emmie had been the one in the family keen to celebrate it. The old man shook his head. There had been too many runaway dogs. Princess took off and never came home. Emmie had cried so hard, he was sure she would be scarred by the incident for life.

Zouzou wasn't at the camp; nor was she by any of the fancy new housing developments across the street from the extensive lawn surrounding the mansion belonging to LeBron James. The old man pulled up on the side of the road in front of the mansion, got out and stood by the car. People driving by must have thought he was another crazed basketball fan.

With a heavy heart, he stamped his feet to get the gravel and snow off his boots before climbing back inside the car. He wended his way back home and turned into the driveway. Before he had paid to get the long driveway properly concreted and paved, it had been almost impossible to make it up the graveled track to the house in wintertime. He thought of the night he and his wife had returned from a trip to South America to visit her family. With absolutely no traction in the heavy snow, the car slid backwards down to the road. Luckily, it had been past midnight, and nobody else was around. They left the car there and struggled through the knee-high snow with their suitcases up to the house. Back then winter was winter, not this hybrid mess of cold, wet, frozen slush that seesawed between mud and dangerous ice on account of climate change. That night his wife had been wearing a pair of boots she had gotten made for herself in Buenos Aires. In the snow, one got sucked off. She left it behind in the dark and walked to the house, one boot on, one boot off and one stockinged foot. The boot was never found, even after the snows melted in springtime.

Because of those years, the old man was in the habit of inching the car up the driveway in the winter. He was surprised. In the headlights there seemed to be more tire tracks in the smattering of snow than when he had left three hours ago – and some footprints, too.

Midway, he caught sight of a couple walking down the drive towards him. He stopped the car, and waited for them to reach him.

Eventually, a woman peered in through the driver's side window, which he had lowered. "Are you the man with the lost dog?" she asked.

He nodded.

She continued, "My husband and I came out to look for it."

They were in their thirties. *Hell,* thought the old man, *only a young couple without a care in the world would come out looking for a stranger's dog.*

"How did you know?" he asked. "Did one of the neighbors tell you our dog was missing?"

The young woman said, "I received a text on my phone."

The man with her was obviously her husband, not her lover. The old man could tell by the way they stood close, comfortably together in front of someone they didn't know. The husband started to explain that the two of them had grown up nearby and had worked elsewhere, but had recently moved back. The old man didn't recognize them, but thought that even so, there was a good chance that they had "borrowed" his driveway when they were courting. In another decade, when he used to come home at midnight after spending the evening with the mother of his younger children, he'd sometimes surprise a couple of high school students necking in a parked car, far enough away from the road and just out of sight of the house. He never blamed young people in love, and always gave them enough time to make themselves presentable as he drove up slowly behind them, stopped his car at a suitable distance and yelled out in a friendly voice – lest they panic – that they should turn around at the top by the house. It was time for them, and for him, to go home.

"You lost one dog or two?" the woman asked him.

"Just one," said the old man.

The woman exclaimed to her husband, "I told you I saw it." Her deep blue eyes regarded the old man. She was earnest, kindly, and Midwestern. "It went into the house."

"It did?" He took off his gloves. Through the open car window, he shook hands first with the young woman and then with her husband. He added, "Thanks for all the trouble you've taken," although he didn't quite believe that the dog had made it back by herself. Before he drove off, he watched the couple in his rearview mirror as they walked hand-in-hand towards the road. That's how he had been when he had gotten married: optimistic, attentive – until the rot set in. He and his wife met when they were foreign students. But America had too many temptations. By the time he had assimilated, so had his libido. He wondered whether or not he would do everything the same way again if he had known then that his actions would cause so much hurt and resentment.

At the top of the driveway, the exterior sensor lights came on, and the vista revealed the large, gracious, six-bedroom home that he and his wife had built, perfectly situated behind an elegant turning circle. He stopped the car at the front of the house and got out. The sidewalk, still snow-covered, needed salting. Down by the pond, he saw Bobby's car. On the porch behind the columns, someone had left a dog bowl, a bottle of water, a bag of dog food, and a blanket in a box. The front door was open wider than when he had left. He trudged inside.

"Zouzou!" he cried out. The house was as silent as the grave.

". . . Zouzou!"

Still nothing.

He looked downstairs, starting in the dining room overfilled with glass cabinets of cut crystal and Wedgwood china. His wife had loved fine things, and he lived in the lavish home she'd created. Before her death, she changed all the appliances in the houses and made sure they were under warranty. She had tried growing orchids in a special window installed above the kitchen sink, but the weather in Ohio was too cold for tropical plants from the Amazon. He would have been the first to admit that his treatment of her hadn't been honorable or great, but she had been smarter than he was, and he was sure she'd known what he'd been up to. They never spoke about it, although, as she drew closer to death, there was an unmistakable tone in her voice that didn't disguise the deep anger and disdain she felt towards him.

He turned down the short hallway that led to Emmie's old bedroom, which she occupied whenever she came home. He peered inside, saw nothing untoward, and retraced his steps down the hallway to the kitchen and open-plan living room, and the extension and new bedroom his wife had built. Still no dog. He was back by the open front door, at the bottom of the staircase leading to the second floor of the house. His knees usually stopped him from going up there, except to do his taxes, which he worked on every year in the study.

Using the banister, he pulled himself up. He had a strong upper body from all those hours spent rowing. It was the cartilage in both knees that was gone, because of the marathons. In the excitement of looking for the dog, he had forgotten about that. At the top of the stairs he entered his eldest daughter's bedroom, which housed the same gold-trimmed white French provincial furniture from when the family first moved into the house. His eldest had been a moody girl who'd left home as soon as she was able to. He walked through the adjoining bathroom into his second daughter's bedroom. Here, Emmie's collection of American Girl dolls – which she refused to give to Bobby's little girls – peered out from within a glass-fronted cabinet. Out through another door, he paused in the hallway.

On the walls were his and his wife's framed college degrees and PhDs. He could almost see his wife instructing Shirley, the housekeeper, as they were being arranged. Next to them, someone had taped a black-and-white snapshot that showed him as a wiry, young, athletic man. *Such a charming bastard*, he nodded to himself. He had a smile women couldn't resist. The door to the guest room was open. He went inside.

There, on the bed, Zouzou was sleeping.

He sank onto the wooden chest at the foot of the bed. His thoughts went back to someone else who had gone missing. It was when he and wife had switched cars because one of them had to go to the garage for repairs. She went grocery shopping and left their youngest daughter in the car. His wife came out of the store with her shopping bags and couldn't find the car or the child. The police were notified, and they called him at work. This was before mobile phones. Without saying a word to anyone, he ran out of the lab, thinking, *if it's that easy to lose a child, we should take precautions and make sure we have more than just one or two, in case any went missing.*

It didn't occur to him that his wife had been looking for the wrong car until he drove hers to the shopping center and spotted his own car among those parked. He stopped behind it, and could still see the surprise on his daughter's face as she looked up from the book she was reading and rolled down the window. Stubborn and sullen in her parents' arms, she was exhausted by their hugs and kisses. In a voice older than her years, she complained: "What's all the fuss about? You people panic!"

He gazed deeply at the reflection in the mirror on the dresser. He hardly acknowledged Zouzou on the bed behind him, exhausted from her exertions. An old man in a jacket, Cleveland Browns scarf, and boots, his thin hair completely white, stared back at him.

"You stupid dog," was all the figure in the mirror said.

PART TWO

The Question of Love

"Words should not seek to please, to hide the wounds in our bodies, or the shameful moments in our lives. They may hurt, give us pain, but they can also provoke us to question what we have accepted for thousands of years."

NAWAL EL SAADAWI,
Walking Through Fire

"Love is like death, like illness, always arriving when we least expect it, at the most peculiar times and places. Love makes us behave like irrational children. Why can't they just invent a vaccine against it?"

MALIKA MOUSTADRAF,
Something Strange, Like Hunger

Anarkali, or Six Early Deaths in Lahore

FARAH AHAMED

The Sixth and Final One, Anarkali

THE END.

Through the open window, the smell of strong spices from the dhabas intermingles with the stench rising from open sewers and fills my small room. It was raining earlier, and the mist has cleared, but now the drains are overflowing with muck. In the flat next door, a qawwali is being played too loud on the radio. I lie on my bed, without a cover, listening.

I go down, knowing it is late for a single woman to be outside on her own, walking the narrow alleys.

In my pocket I have the envelope with Jameel's last letter. I hear his calm voice in my head, reciting the words of Faiz's poetry.

> *Surud-e-shabana — Nim shab, chand, khud faramoshi*
> *Midnight, the moon and self-forgetfulness*

He and I had wandered down these lanes together, many times. Ancient, dilapidated buildings on either side. Each had been allotted an area of dug-out earth, more than three hundred years ago. Now the buildings are in ruins; windows boarded up, signboards of defunct shops hanging lopsidedly and balconies curtained by tangled-up skeins of dead wires.

Shapes move without making any sound in doorways. Shadowy

forms are coming closer. A man in uniform is looking down at me. It's Khan, he's waving his baton, and speaking in a loud voice.

What is he trying to tell me? If only I understood his gestures, then there might be just one thing I'd be able to rescue from all of this.

I feel a sharp blow at the back of my head. His figure fades. I can't see him, no matter how hard I try. A grey haze descends over Lahore.

Silence wraps all.

The First One: Jameel

This is what Lahore calls its fifth season: every November the city is oppressed by smog, which shrouds it in a haze. The people complain of a choking sensation in their throats, stinging eyes and an acrid burning smell.

That evening the fog was especially thick. Jameel and I had arranged to meet Rob for the last time. I imagined Rob already sitting at a table in the corner of the roof terrace of Koko's, sipping his cardamom tea and contemplating the Badshahi Mosque through the mist. I stood in the doorway of the old apartment building, my suitcases packed and ready for Jameel to take to his place. We'd decided we should get it done before meeting Rob. The azaan echoed through the walls of the city.

Jameel was late. I checked my mobile but there was no message, which was unusual for him. He was always fastidious that way. In the distance, I could make out the silhouettes of black birds circling the mosque minarets as though participating in a joyous sacred ritual. Further down the alley from where I was standing, kiosks had lit their colored lanterns. The trousers of my pink salwar kameez flapped in the gentle breeze as I waited. I pulled my dupatta closer around my shoulders. The evening would be tense, but I had every reason to be optimistic. To my relief, a rickshaw drew up outside and honked. But it was Rob who alighted.

"Where's Jameel?" he asked.

"I've been waiting for him here," I replied. "I thought he might be with you."

I stepped aside to let him pass, then followed him to the flat. He went straight to the bedroom. I left my cases by the front door and joined him. He removed his shoes and lay down on the bed. I sat by his feet and took off my dupatta.

"Where can he be?" I said.

Rob leaned his head back against the pillow and closed his eyes.

*

One Year Earlier

The Anarkali book market was busy, as it always was on Sundays at noon. Shopkeepers in brown kurtas covering large paunches stood in the shop entrances or lounged on charpoys, drinking tea, smoking bheedis and discussing politics. Women and children huddled in groups round the books, choosing which to buy. It was like any other Sunday. I had noticed him searching through the volumes laid out on the pavement, taking his time with each one. There was nothing special about him; foreigners often came to the market. He was of medium height, and his brown hair was flecked with grey. His clothes were casual – jeans, a red sweater, a striped scarf around his neck. I wondered where he was from. He gathered up a pile of books from the plastic sheet and began haggling with the seller. I was squatting on the pavement with my brush. I saw him cast a look in my direction, as though he sensed I was watching him. I covered my head with my scarf and carried on clearing the sidewalk of leaves.

Each time I looked up he was observing me. I pretended to be busy but kept glancing at him until he finished buying the books. Then I picked up my brush and pan and went to sit under the old banyan at the end of the street. I saw him approaching.

"May I please buy you a cup of tea?" he asked, in surprisingly clear Urdu. "My name's Rob, and I'd like to talk to you." He raised his arm. "We could go over there to the Tea House."

"I'm not that sort of woman."

"I was going to have some tea myself, that's all. I didn't mean to trouble you."

I'm used to refusing invitations from all sorts of men. But this was

113

the first time I'd ever spoken to a foreigner – a white person – and I was curious.

"Why do you want to talk to me?"

He was walking away. "Nothing important," he called over his shoulder. "Forget it."

"Wait," I said. "Give me a minute." I hid my brush behind the tree, and followed him.

"Oi chura, where do you think you're going?"

I turned to see Nazir, my supervisor, shouting at me.

"It's two o'clock," I replied, pointing towards the clock tower opposite. "I'm off duty."

"Don't think I didn't see you were late this morning."

"Did you notice I was early yesterday?"

A couple of shopkeepers came out to see what the shouting was about.

"You need to keep her in check," one of them told Nazir.

I followed Rob to the Pak Tea House. As we entered, the waiter stopped me. "What do you want?" he said.

"She's with me," Rob said. He led me to a table at the back and we sat down opposite each other.

I had never been inside the Tea House before. On the walls there was only a row of black and white portraits. From the street it always looked so enticing, I'd expected it to be much fancier.

"Those are Lahore's most famous writers," Rob said. "They used to come here to discuss their ideas. He pointed first to one photo, then another. "Look, that's Manto. And that's the poet Faiz."

I looked down at my hands in my lap.

"People like me don't learn to read," I said. "We have no money for books."

He didn't reply. The place was crowded, and the chatter from the other tables made the silence less awkward.

"What would you like to eat?" he said.

"I don't know. Whatever you decide."

He asked the waiter to bring a plate of biriyani and two cups of tea.

The young men at the next table were smiling at me.

"Good catch," one of them said. "The gora looks like he has money."

"Pay no attention to them," Rob said.

The food came, and he placed the plate in front of me.

"Please, help yourself," he said.

I wouldn't normally let a stranger buy me food, but I was there of my own free will and I was hungry. I picked up the spoon.

"So what did you want to talk about?" I asked.

"Right," he said. "I'll get straight to the point. I'm a visiting professor at the university here in Lahore."

"Where are you from?"

"London. But I've been in Lahore about a year now. I'm doing research into the Punjabi Christians, and I was wondering if I could ask you a few questions."

"What kind of questions? How do you know I'm a Christian?"

"I could be wrong, but most sweepers and cleaners in Lahore are."

I put down my spoon and stood up. "I must leave now."

"Why? You haven't even told me your name."

"I've heard about you foreign journalists," I said. "You'll do an interview and take my photo, and the next minute I'll be in the newspapers, accused of blasphemy or saying something against the government."

"No," he said. "I'm not a journalist. Please stay, and at least have some tea."

I sat down.

"Let's eat," he said. "The food's getting cold."

We ate and drank in silence. When we'd finished, he said, "Allow me to explain. Do you remember the bombings of the All Saints church in Peshawar in 2013, and the Roman Catholic church in 2015?"

"How could we ever forget?"

"You see, my research is around those incidents. I'm investigating what actually happened there and what led to the attacks."

"I'm twenty years old," I said. "I was an innocent girl then. And now,

I work. I come to the market every morning, sweep the streets and go home. That's my life. I only know what I hear on the news, like everyone else. How could I know anything about a bombing?"

"Of course," he said. "Not directly. My research involves talking to Christians from all backgrounds. I want to understand."

"What makes you think I can help?"

"Well, it was your community that was targeted."

He told me he would pay me for what he called "the interview." It was more than a month's wages.

"It's too risky," I said. "I shouldn't have agreed to come here with you."

"I'll pay you double," he said. "You won't be in any danger, I promise. I don't need to know your real name."

I sat looking around, my thoughts interrupted by laughter from the well-dressed women at the next table.

"My family needs the money," I said. "So I'll do it. I just pray I can trust you."

"You can," he said. "Thank you. Shall we meet here again, next Sunday at two? And how about I call you Anarkali?"

"If you like," I said. "But only the one meeting."

We fell into a pattern. After I'd finished my shift I'd make my way to a group of trees to the side of the Tea House, where he'd be waiting for me. We'd sit at the same table, and he would order tea and food. Then he'd take out his notebook. Initially his questions were broad: Where was I born, where did I live, how often did I go to church? Then they became more probing: Which church did I attend, who was the pastor, how big was the congregation? Was I, or my family, involved in any church activities? Did we receive any assistance from the church?

"I don't think I should tell you," I said.

"I simply want to understand," he said. "I'm a Christian myself, a Catholic."

After our fourth meeting, I took him to my church and introduced him to Father Stephen. I explained Rob was a visiting professor from the UK doing research at the local university.

."Leave the past alone," Father Stephen said, wiping the sweat from the back of his neck with his handkerchief. "What happened was God's will."

Rob persisted. Why did Father Stephen think those particular churches were targeted? Did he suspect insider help?

"You're a firangi," Father Stephen said. "Foreigners can't understand." He shook his handkerchief at me. "And you stay away from that business, too."

Afterwards, I told Rob, "I've helped you all I can. I should be free to go."

"You've been a huge help," he said, handing me an envelope. "Inside you'll find what I owe you and something extra."

"Thank you," I said. "I'd better go then."

"Could we meet next Sunday?" he said. "No questions, just for tea."

"Why?"

"Because I like talking to you."

We continued to meet every week at the Pak Tea House. Then one Sunday, after a walk in Lawrence Gardens, Rob said he needed to pick up some books from his flat before he went to work. He led me to an alley just behind Badshahi Masjid, and as we reached the entrance to his building, it began to rain.

"I'll wait for you here," I said.

"You'll get soaked," he said. "Come on in."

"No, I'm fine, really."

"Don't be silly, Anarkali. I won't eat you."

Rob's flat was large, with separate rooms for sleeping, cooking, watching television and reading. He showed me around and pointed out all the different "treasures" he'd discovered in the old city; antique furniture, and books.

"Have you read all of these?" I asked, looking along the shelves which lined two walls of the living room.

"Almost." He took my hand and looked down at my dirty, broken fingernails. I pulled away.

"You don't have to sweep the streets anymore, Anarkali."

"You've given me enough already," I said, "and helped my family."

"Stay here with me. I could teach you to read."

●

Rob opened his eyes and turned his head towards me.

"Anarkali," he said softly. "What will happen when you go away?" He reached out his arm and pulled the pins from my hair so that it fell around my shoulders. Please, lie down with me one last time."

"I can't," I said.

"I was so sure you'd never leave me. I tried to give you everything." He switched on the lamp, casting a dull glow over the room and onto his face, making it appear younger and more open. In that moment, I felt I could believe anything he said, just like a year ago.

"Where's Jameel?" I said. "We have to find him."

"Your hair smells of roses," Rob said. "Please stay with me."

"It's not right," I said, as I got up and went into the living room.

●

I'd known Jameel for three months. Rob brought him to the flat one evening, and after introducing us, went out to a meeting.

"I'll leave you in Anarkali's safe hands," he said, gesturing to Jameel to sit down in the armchair. "Make yourself comfortable. I'll see you later."

"Anarkali,' Jameel said. "That's an interesting name." He was tall and athletic-looking.

"I'll make some tea," I said, and went into the kitchen.

When I returned, Jameel was leaning back, seeming at ease. I sat down on the sofa and poured the tea.

"I think you know," he said, scratching his dark stubble. "I'm working with Rob on his research."

"Yes, he told me."

"But what I like to do most is study poetry."

"I don't know much about it," I said. "Rob pointed out a photo in the Pak Tea House, of Faiz I think."

"He's the finest."

"Rob's taught me to read in Urdu a little," I said. "But I'm not up to poetry yet, and he's always busy."

"You don't have to read it," Jameel said. "You just have to hear it, and it will stay in your mind. Listen.

> *Surud-e-shabana — Nim shab, chand, khud faramoshi*
> *Midnight, the moon and self-forgetfulness*
> *The past and present are faded; afar,*
> *A supplication shapes the stillness,*
> *Dimmed is the sad assembly of stars.*
> *Silence wraps all . . .*

"Do you really think I could learn to recite it?" I said.

"Of course," he said.

"Can you teach me?"

When Rob came back, Jameel got up straight away.

"I'd better be going, Prof," he said. "Thank you for putting up with me, Anarkali."

"What did you talk about?" Rob asked, after Jameel had left.

"Poetry mostly," I said.

"Ah, yes. Jameel's a dreamer. I'm glad you had a good evening."

"How was your meeting," I asked.

"Long. I think I'll go straight to bed."

•

The hours passed, and there was still no word from Jameel. Rob came into the living room, where I was sitting on the sofa.

"Did you speak to Jameel at all today?" I asked.

"No. The last time was a few days ago, when he told me your plans. He said you'd be moving out today and we should have dinner together."

"He wants to marry me," I said.

"His family will never accept you, Anarkali, they're very strict Muslims."

"Jameel doesn't care about that."

"His father owns a textile business, he's the only son. They've probably arranged for a suitable girl for him."

"Jameel says we will be happy."

"Of course you will."

I checked my phone. "Why hasn't he sent a message?"

"I told you. I haven't been in touch with him today."

"He'd never be this late without letting us know."

"Don't worry, he'll come."

I went to the window and drew back the curtain. Through the thick mist, the yellow street lights appeared blurry. In the alley, figures disappeared through narrow doorways.

"I wish I were Jameel," Rob said quietly.

I turned from the window. "Why?"

"He has youth." He picked up his notebook and pen from the coffee table and sat down. "And now he has you."

There was a knock at the door.

"Thank god," I said. I hurried to open it, brushing against a vase of wilting gladioli, scattering dried orange petals on to the floor.

I was faced by a tall, thickset man with a grey beard.

"Asaalam alaiykum," he greeted me. "I'm from the Central Police Station."

"What does he want?" Rob called out.

"Who lives here?" the policeman asked, looking past me.

Rob came and stood beside me.

"What's going on?" he said. "Why are you here?"

"I'm afraid I'm going to have to ask you both to accompany me to the station."

"I'm not going," I said. "I'm waiting for Jameel."

"You're both required."

"What for?" Rob said.

"I'm only following orders. I was sent by Inspector Khan to fetch whoever lives at this flat." He showed us the chit.

"But what if Jameel comes?" I said.

"There's no use arguing," Rob said, putting on his shoes.

"We have to go," the policeman said. "Now."

Rob could have given him a few thousand rupees to report that he had been to the address and found no one there. It would have given us time. But Rob, as he always insisted, would never do anything like that.

The policeman pointed to my suitcases. "Does she live here?"

"She used to," Rob said.

*

When I'd first told my family I was moving in with Rob, they tried to change my mind, and my older sister Ruksana insisted on meeting him. I introduced her to him at the Tea House.

"You see, I knew you'd like him," I said afterwards.

"I don't trust him," she said. "How can you be sure he'll divorce his wife?"

"He's promised he will."

"But does that mean anything? How do you know he's not taking advantage of you? This research could just be an excuse. He's running away from something."

"He loves me," I said.

"Love? What's he prepared to sacrifice to be with you?"

Whenever I asked Rob if he'd heard from his wife, it was the same answer.

"These things take time."

I always knew when she telephoned because he would go into the bedroom and shut the door. Then when he came out he'd give me a hug.

"You know I love you, Anarkali."

*

At the station, we were taken straight to the Inspector's office. He was overweight, and looked morose.

"I'm Inspector Khan," he said, stubbing his cigarette out in the full ashtray. He beckoned to the two chairs in front of him. "Please, sit."

"I'm expecting one of my students at my flat," Rob said. "So if you don't mind, could we make this quick?"

"I would like to question both of you, separately," Khan said.

"We're together," Rob said. "And we have a right to know why you've brought us here."

"How long have you two been married?" Khan asked.

I looked down and twisted the ends of my scarf between my fingers.

"I am married," Rob said. "But not to her. My wife's in the UK."

"I see." Khan pointed his pen at me. "Then who is she to you?"

"She's engaged to one of my students," Rob said. "Jameel, the one we were waiting for at the flat."

"That's your flat? And she's living there? Why?"

"That's none of your business."

"We asked your neighbors and they told us she's been with you for almost a year."

"So you've been spying on us?" Rob said.

Khan sat back and chewed the end of his pen. "Tell me Professor Saheb, how much do you pay her?"

"You've no right to ask me that."

"You can stop acting," Khan said to me. "I recognize your type."

"What are you implying?" Rob said. "She's helping me with my research."

"What kind of research?"

"What do you think, Inspector? Academic, obviously."

"So she's living with you," Khan said, "and she's engaged to your student?" He tapped his pen on the desk. "Rather puzzling, wouldn't you agree?"

"Inspector Khan," Rob said. "You can see how distressing this is for her. Jameel's been missing for several hours."

"Professor, I should tell you, our police force is well-qualified to handle missing persons. It is our specialty."

"My cousin Zahid's never been found," I said. People went missing all the time, it was nothing new. Zahid was picked up and taken to the police station for questioning. When my uncle went there, he was informed Zahid had been released. I told myself it would be different for Jameel. He was not a Christian.

"Professor," Khan continued. "Why did you both go for the same girl? There's no shortage of temptation in Lahore."

"I told you, Inspector, I'm married – separated, actually. But we're going round in circles." Rob pushed back his chair and got up. "We've got nothing more to say."

"Kindly sit down,' Khan said. "This is serious and no one's going anywhere until I've finished." He took a pack of cigarettes from the drawer and lit one. "Now, Professor, I'm told you're very well connected, so maybe you can tell me what's happened to your student?"

"If you're suggesting . . ."

"Please answer the question." Khan pushed his ashtray aside.

"They were meant to join me at Koko's for tea," Rob said. "When they didn't show up, I went home and found her waiting on her own. Neither of us has heard from Jameel."

Khan turned to me. "Are you sure you don't know where he is?"

•

Jameel often came to the flat in the evenings to drop off papers or show his work to Rob. Sometimes he'd come before Rob was back, and he and I would talk. Then Rob would persuade him to stay for supper. The three of us would listen to music during the meal, then they'd discuss their research.

One evening, Rob and Jameel argued.

"I want to meet Father Stephen," Jameel said. "I want talk to him myself."

"That's not a good idea," Rob said. "He already feels I've asked him too much."

"Just once," Jameel said.

"No Jameel, I won't allow it."

"I won't push him."

"I said no. Your personal involvement would be unwise."

The following day, Jameel phoned me from the library in the Lawrence Gardens, where he was studying.

"I finish in an hour. Would you like to meet for a walk?"

After that, we began seeing each other often. We would sit in the shade of the old banyan behind the library, where no one could see us. Jameel would read poems he'd written for me, or something by Faiz.

"It's a betrayal," I said.

Jameel pulled me on to the grass, lay down and rested his head on my lap.

"It's nobody's fault," he said. "You'll just have to explain to Rob, you hadn't planned on falling in love with me."

"He's helping my family."

"With me you can have marriage and a future," Jameel said. "Rob can't offer you that." He stroked my cheek.

"He can," I said. "He's promised. He just needs time to sort his divorce out."

"He's been saying that for months. He's a Catholic, remember."

"It's hard," I said.

"Love's never easy. Faiz could tell you that. Listen."

I rested my head against the banyan's trunk, trying to forget all but Jameel's voice, and the verse.

•

The policeman who had escorted us to the station came in with three cups of tea and a packet of biscuits. Khan tore off the wrapper, pushed a cup in front of me and offered me the packet. "Help yourself." I shook my head.

"You haven't told us why we're here," Rob said.

Khan crammed his mouth with biscuits. His phone rang and he ignored it.

"I want to know where Jameel is," Rob said.

"What makes you think I know, Professor?" Khan replied.

"Something's happened to him, hasn't it?" I said.

Khan looked straight at me. "Tell me where he is."

"She knows nothing," Rob said.

"Why aren't they telling us what happened?" I said to Rob.

Khan looked at me. "What's her name, Professor?"

"Anarkali," Rob said. "That's all I know."

"And what was *Anarkali* doing before she started helping you with your so-called research?"

"What are you accusing me of, Inspector?" Rob said. "Whatever it is, it won't work."

"Jameel was seen near Bhatti Gate at twelve-thirty today," Khan said. "If you know anything, you'd better come clean."

"Don't be ridiculous," Rob said. "Why don't you tell us what's happened?"

Khan leaned forward in his chair. "Very well," he said. "But it's not what you want to hear. He was found in an alley near your block. He'd been stabbed. I'm afraid the ambulance arrived too late."

I stared at the chipped cup in front of me. "Jameel," I said.

"Do you know who did it?" Khan asked Rob.

Rob put his head in his hands. "I tried to stop him getting mixed up in the whole church business. I told him, stick to your research."

"If I may speak frankly," Khan said. "We've had our eye on him for a while now, and he had it coming. Those church bombing incidents, Professor, you should have left them alone. Your academic investigations are actually state security matters. And now you see the consequences of your meddling. You firangi never seem to understand."

"Enough," Rob said, raising his hand. "May god protect us from the guilty."

"The guilty, Professor?"

"Jameel was, in his own way," Rob said. "It's you who don't understand. Everything was mixed up in his head, he thought he had uncovered a conspiracy in the church."

"No one's innocent," Khan said. "That will be enough for now, but we may need to talk to you again. You are free to go, but first, can I ask you to accompany me to the hospital to identify the body?"

"I must see him," I said. The only thing going through my mind was Jameel's voice reciting Faiz. If Jameel was really dead, was it my fault? I had warned him to stay away. Could I have done more?

"No, Inspector," Rob said. "There's no point in upsetting ourselves any further. I assume you'll be informing Jameel's family."

A month earlier, Jameel and I had met in the Lawrence Gardens. We sat on a bench and Jameel told me he'd been to see Father Stephen.

"But Rob warned you not to," I said. "You mustn't keep going back and asking questions. You can't trust Father Stephen – or anybody."

"How can I keep quiet about what I know?"

I rested my head on his shoulder. "Don't believe everything you hear."

"Why would Father Stephen lie to me?"

"I don't know," I said. "But please don't see him again. Leave Rob to ask the questions."

"But the victims' families, they deserve answers."

"My father always says there are many truths, Jameel."

"But what if it happened again, and you were in church that day?"

"There's nothing you can do."

In the west, the sky had turned a deep orange with streaks of black. Kites circled above us. We walked around the gardens, and stopped beneath the canopy of my favorite tree. We looked up through the leaves at the sun filtering down. Then we bought roasted peanuts and returned to our bench to watch the moon rising from behind the clouds.

Jameel held me close and whispered,

"*Surud-e-shabana – Nim shab, chand, khud faramoshi; Midnight, the moon and self-forgetfulness.*"

A few days later, Father Stephen had phoned me.

"You fool, what have you got yourself into?"

"I don't know what you mean," I said.

"Do you realize the trouble I took to secure that patch of pavement in the market for your family? I had to beg my friend at the government office for it. But you showed no gratitude. You gave it up for a gora. You didn't care, you thought you were above sweeping leaves. You were told to keep him away. But did you listen?"

"Please, Father," I said. "He's a Catholic."

"First him, then his student, pestering me with questions. Do you think life's a game?"

"I've done nothing wrong."

"One minute you're living with a gora, the next you're messing with a Musla, bringing shame to the church. There's a special name for be-sharam women like you."

"He's going to marry me."

"That remains to be seen," Father Stephen said.

"I haven't committed any crime," I said. "And neither has Jameel."

"You've no idea what you've done."

●

Neither Rob nor I spoke when we got back from the Police Station.

The next morning I rose early after a sleepless night, and was sitting on the sofa when he came into the living room, looking weary. He put his notepad and pencil down on the coffee table, then went to the door and picked up my suitcases.

"You can unpack these later, Anarkali." He took them into the bedroom.

When he came back, I poured some cardamom tea into a cup and passed it to him. Then I cleared away the wilted and fading gladioli petals from the coffee table.

The Second, my cousin Zahid

My uncle was woken up by a banging on the door to his flat. He hadn't really been asleep, but just lying on his bed wondering about Zahid. He'd checked every police station and hospital. Had the boy eloped? Had he fallen under Father Stephen's influence? The boy was a fool and always getting into trouble.

My uncle went to see who it was. It was his neighbor, Pawan Singh.

"Sat Sri Akal," Pawan said, "you need to come with me."

My uncle knew it had to be about Zahid. "Is he dead?"

"I'm not saying anything, just come with me."

My uncle got dressed and followed Pawan to his house, where his wife answered the door.

Pawan's father, Kharak Singh, was also there, sitting by the window, wearing a white kurta pajama and a blue turban. He was the high priest at Gurdwara Darbar Sahib in Karatarpur.

"Where's my son?" my uncle said, looking around. "Is Zahid here?"

Kharak stroked his beard. "Give him the letter," he said.

Pawan passed my uncle the envelope which was lying on the side table.

Father,

I'm going after those bastards who bombed our churches. Father Stephen was right. This is Christ's work, if we don't stop them, who will?

The police found me, and locked me up. I was there, when you came, I could hear you begging. I managed to escape, but I can't tell you where I am. Those fuckers want us to die, but they won't get me.

Zahid

Pawan's wife called from the kitchen. "I told Pawan not to let him stay at the gurudwara. But he wouldn't listen. It's not a place for mischief makers."

"Be quiet," Pawan said. "Helping a person in trouble is worship. Maybe that's something you'll never understand."

"Worship which brings suffering in my own house?" she said. "What's there to understand?"

"Where is he?" my uncle said.

"There's nothing anyone can do," Kharak said, standing up. "Nothing."

"Exactly," Pawan's wife said coming to join them. "Nothing, that's what we should have done." She looked at my uncle, her husband, and her father-in-law. "You're all responsible." She pointed her chopping knife at my uncle. "You especially."

"Is he alive?" my uncle said.

"Who else can we blame?" she said. "Can we leave Lahore? And where will we go? And what for? All because of a useless Christian boy."

"Bus karo, enough," Kharak said. "Humanity is one."

"But she's right," Pawan said. "It's terrible."

His father pulled his beard and sat down. "A tragedy."

"Why won't you tell me what's happened?" my uncle said. "You're talking as if he's dead."

"He got what he deserved," Pawan's wife said.

"He was my best friend," Pawan said. "But he was confused."

"He's my son," my uncle said. "His heart's in the right place.'

"Maybe," Kharak said, "but only what's up here, counts." He tapped the side of his forehead with his finger.

"Tell that to your son," Pawan's wife said. "Maybe next time he'll use his brain."

"If a man can't assess the consequences of his actions," Kharak said, "he may as well be shot, because otherwise he'll end up causing more harm."

"You don't know what you're saying," my uncle said. "Who are you to decide?"

"It's up to you," Kharak said. "But what's happened is very bad."

"Bad is an understatement," Pawan said.

"You're forgetting," Pawan's wife said, "because of him we could've all been arrested."

"But where is he?" my uncle said.

"We cremated him yesterday," Kharak said. His voice was flat. "Zahid escaped from jail, the police were after him and he came to Pawan for help. They ended up at the gurdwara in Kartarpur. We hid Zahid in the kitchen of the langar hall, but the police managed to track him down and insisted on doing a search. Zahid heard them and fled through the window. We saw him running along the electric fence, down the Kartarpur Corridor, towards India. The security guards switched on the floodlights, and shouted over the loudspeaker for him to stop and surrender, but Zahid kept going, like a madman, as if India was his salvation."

"Of course they shot him," Pawan's wife said. "They couldn't know he wasn't a terrorist, but a raving lunatic."

"The Indian army," Pawan was weeping. "Zahid reached the border gates, shouting he was Christ, he was innocent. But the Indian guards pointed their rifles at him and kept firing. I saw him falling, he fell backwards."

My uncle said, "Jesus."

"The police told us to keep quiet," Kharak said, "to stop it exploding into a political fiasco with India. They said they'd record him as a missing person."

Pawan covered his head with his arms. "His face was a bloody mess, you couldn't even recognize him."

"He gave Pawan the letter the day he died," Kharak said.

My uncle said, "Zahid didn't want to die."

The Third: Father Stephen

Father Stephen must have driven the truck gently along the road. He had found a black cloth mask lying on the seat and put it on. With the dark glasses he was sure no one would recognize him. He negotiated one corner, then another. No one would think of checking the church truck for a dead body. He'd done many things he wasn't proud of, but this must be the worst. He'd warned Jameel, but the boy was stupid, and hadn't listened. He kept asking interfering questions, taking notes, looking for evidence, about the church bombings. It had made those higher-ups nervous. Over the long bridge, he turned right and then along a bumpy road for half an hour. Then stopped at the farm house with a high metal gate.

When he'd parked the truck, the boys must have come out to meet him.

"Do you know Bhatti Gate?" Father Stephen must have asked.

A boy was there with four pigeons in a cage. He drew nearer.

"No one's free," Father Stephen said, looking at the birds.

The boy told Father Stephen the names he'd given the birds. "Matthew, Mark, Luke and John."

"What's your name?" Father Stephen said.

"Let's set the birds free," the boy said. "They belong in the sky." The boy held up the cage.

"Maybe the sky isn't safe. Maybe, when you're out there roaming the blue, you miss the safety of the cage."

"So you're on the bird's side?"

"I suppose so."

"Then you're meaner than I thought. You should help the bird be a bird." The boy waited for Father Stephen to release the catch on the cage, but he didn't.

Father Stephen asked two of the other boys to dump Jameel's body in an alley. "But check his pockets first."

The boys dragged the body from the back of the truck and searched it. In one pocket they found a pistol, in another, a wallet and a dirty envelope. Inside was a chit of paper.

> *Beloved Anarkali,*
> *Surud-e-shabana – Nim shab,*
> *Chand, khud faramoshi*
> *Midnight, the moon and self-forgetfulness . . .*

Father Stephen read the note and gave it to the boy. "Look, because of a besharam woman, a man is dead."

"What should I do with it?" The boy stared at the crumpled page in his hands.

"Let it be a reminder," Father Stephen said. "There's always a price to pay."

"Father." The boy looked at Father Stephen with a serious face. "They told me about the bad things you do."

The sound of crows, smell of diesel leaking from the truck and the stink from Jameel's body.

Father Stephen said, "He died for nothing." He was remembering the stillness behind the church after the scuffle. He'd tipped them off, they'd been waiting for Jameel.

It was getting dark.

Father Stephen asked the boys to load the truck. They hoisted Jameel's body into it. One of the boys started the truck and reversed.

They would return in an hour without the body. A vendor selling pink candy floss would find it in the alley and alert the police.

They found Father Stephen dead the next morning. He was lying on his bedroom floor. Jameel's pistol had been fired two rounds.

The boy released the pigeons from the cage. Some days later, he managed to find me and give me Jameel's letter.

The Fourth, my sister Ruksana

The two of them were inside a chai kiosk.

"When he warned Jameel," Rob leaned back in his chair. "I wondered."

He stopped, as tears welled up in Ruksana's eyes. "Please," she said, "tell him to leave me alone." She wore a yellow salwar khameez with a white dupatta. Her hair was tied in a low ponytail. "You know, you can't just speak to people, and ask them anything. That's not how things work in Lahore." She wiped her eyes.

"Father Stephen doesn't scare me."

"I hope you didn't tell my sister?"

"Don't worry," Rob said. "Anarkali doesn't know we've met."

"Excuse me," the chaiwallah, standing behind the counter, said. "There are rules. You can't sit here without ordering anything."

Rob asked for two tandoori chais.

Ruksana started getting up. "I shouldn't have come. If Father Stephen knew I was talking to you . . ."

"I'll take care of it, Ruksana," Rob said. "I've promised Anarkali I'll help you all. Now, tell me exactly."

She sat down. "One of the choir boys told me. He said he wasn't the first. There's a secret farmhouse where Father Stephen hides the boys . . ."

"For Christ's sake."

Her face was covered in tears. "When Father Stephen found out I knew, he threatened to tear my body into pieces if I ever spoke about it."

A man with thick arms appeared through the door. He was wearing a black kurta and black face mask.

"Get out of my way," he said to Rob. "Let's go, kutiyaa." He grabbed Ruksana by the arm. "You were warned to keep your trap shut."

"Hey, what's the problem?" the chaiwallah said.

"Let her go." Rob pushed the man's chest. "Who the hell are you, anyway?"

The man released Ruksana. "Sid," he said. "Just call me Sid."

"I don't care who you are," the chaiwallah looked from Sid to Rob. "We don't allow fights in here. This is a respectable establishment."

"I'll show you who's boss, chutiya." Sid grabbed the chaiwallah, and lifted him from the ground. At a half run, he went for the door and heaved him through.

Rob went after Sid, took his shoulder and gave him a wallop. "Keep away from her," Rob said.

Sid bent over groaning. "Madharchod. I won't leave you now."

The chaiwallah returned. His face was bruised and cut from the pavement where he'd landed. "Who is she?" he said to Rob. "I'm calling the police."

Ruksana was crying.

Sid pulled a gun from his pocket and waved it in the air. "Shut the fuck up, bhenchod."

"Put down the gun," Rob said, his voice firm.

Sid pointed it at him. "Father said don't kill the gora, but I've got nothing to lose."

The chaiwallah was on his knees, blubbering. "Please, I've done nothing."

"Fucking chutiya." Sid pointed the gun at him and fired.

Ruksana took the chance and gave the plastic table a hard push. It overturned, spilling tea everywhere. She dashed through the door into the street.

Sid gave a shout.

The first shot missed her shoulder. She turned to look back, her face lit up with anger, and a car coming at full speed knocked her over.

She tumbled down with a loud cry, and fell heavily on her side. Rob ran to her.

She died instantly.

Sid ran. Down the first alley, onto the next street, a right turn, a left, onto another street, and another alley. He was young and fit so he made it away.

The Fifth, Rob

This is how it must've been.

Rob couldn't sleep. He'd tried to read, but couldn't make sense of anything. He sat on the sofa, where I'd always sat with Jameel.

Images floated around in his head, and he couldn't piece them together. He thought if he had some whisky, or took some medication, it would help him think clearly.

He poured himself a glass of Jack Daniels.

Persia's poet, Hakim Nizami, was renowned for his romantic tale of Layla and Majnun. Majnun was mad for Layla. But fate had destined to keep them apart, so Majnun roamed the forests, a tormented lover.

When Layla's marriage was arranged to someone else, Majnun sent her a note:

"Even though you're with another, remember there's a man whose body, even if torn to pieces, would call only one name, and that's yours, Layla."

She'd replied with a letter.

"Now I have to endure spending my life with one man, when my soul belongs to another."

Rob must have thought, that's how it is for me. Anarkali never loved me. Her soul always belonged to Jameel.

I'm alone, like Majnun, wandering around lost, in the wilderness of Lahore.

•

I found Rob slouched on the sofa, his head drooped.

"Rob," I said, and shook his shoulder. "Wake up."

134

Saliva dribbled from the side of his mouth. There was whisky leaking from a bottle near his feet, a glass about to slip from his limp fingers.

On the coffee table was an empty box of Valium diazepam and a notepad with one line written in pencil.

"There's a man who will call only one name, Anarkali."

Buenos Aires of Her Eyes

ALIREZA IRANMEHR

Translated from the Persian by Salar Abdoh

UNTIL HE WAS EIGHTY YEARS OLD AND DOCTORS WERE SERI-ously considering amputating his left leg, my father had never been unfaithful. His mother had saved for a lifetime so that at twenty-three he could walk away with a degree in Philosophy from Leipzig. He was a slender young man back then with a pencil-thin moustache, who could probably go on about Kantian epistemology a lot more easily than exchanging a couple of words with the German girls he saw at the university. And not just any Germans, but one, or ones whose eyes were apparently the color of dawn over Buenos Aires. He'd admitted as much to my mother, even though he had barely spent more than a week of his life in Buenos Aires, and only because he was working for a Swiss bank at the time and was on an assignment to South America.

That had been fifteen years before I was born.

Often, I've wondered what it was that made my father connect the sky over Buenos Aires to a pair of eyes back in Europe? What was it that he'd left behind in Leipzig? I never asked. Or else, maybe those memories came from Geneva or Paris, cities where he'd also studied mathematics and management and lived in and worked later on.

"Your father fell in love only twice," my mother would say many years later.

I think it's debatable if it was actually twice or three times. The first time it was at an Armenian pastry shop up in Tajrish where his-soon-to-be wife, my mother, happened to be eating a peach melba dessert. My father was just back from Germany with his philosophy degree; a month later they were married. Seventeen years afterwards he was sent on a project by the treasury department – this time to the city of Shiraz. I was only two years old then and from what my mother tells us, he was slotted to stay down south for forty-five days. But he'd come running back to Tehran after only two weeks and wouldn't leave his room. After the third day he came into the kitchen and held my mother's hands.

"I've never been unfaithful to you," he declared to her in a trembling voice.

Then he confessed that he'd seen a young woman in Shiraz who had made him feel like he was being thrown off a cliff. She was no more than twenty-one years old and her fingers were blue from the ink of the typewriter ribbon. She was the secretary to that office where my father was supposed to have worked at for a full forty-five days. He could not last more than two weeks. The storm inside him was too much. He had to leave everything and come back to Tehran.

●

On a gloomy and rather humid day in Geneva, I realized it was time to bring my parents back home for a visit after their twenty-seven-year sojourn in Switzerland. The window to the hospital room where my father lay looked over at the shimmering surface of the lake and the doctor was telling us it was not impossible that they'd have to amputate eventually. Mother sat beside him on the bed gazing at her husband's hands. Six years earlier she'd had a stroke and would try to talk only when absolutely necessary. I asked the doctor what was the best thing I could do for my father. His was a body riddled by illness now. Diabetes just happened to be the more pressing issue. But then he began to get better without the doctors having to take extreme measures just yet, and so I put my parents on a plane and brought them back home.

My father hated being confined to our large living room couch. The entire twenty-one days that they stayed in Tehran, his seat of choice was a Polish chair by the dining table. From nine in the morning till two in the afternoon he'd drink his unsweetened tea and accept visitors on that chair – mostly former students of his and senior managers who had once been trained by him. On a late afternoon as he bent over trying to clip his toenails, I finally decided I needed to do something "real" for this man, something he had never been guilty of but also had never stopped thinking about since that decisive week of his life in the city of Buenos Aires. And I had to do this before the diabetes or some other disease finally staked a claim on him and left him in darkness.

He had always said, "Each person lives in their own special universe. A place no one else can know and yet is not impossible to imagine." I was imagining an alternate life for him. Or, at least, a holiday from the only life he'd known.

That life had been one of austerity, marrying my mother quickly after returning from Germany and never once veering from the straight path except for the one time when tears welled in his eyes for a girl from Shiraz with blue ink on her fingertips. His entire world was summed up in his devotion to his kids and his wife. Never had he allowed himself to gaze deeply into another pair of eyes, a luxury he always refused to accept as a possibility for a responsible man.

I'd been divorced for a couple of years and was living with Fariba. It was Fariba who turned my unusual idea into reality. She had someone in mind who would write love letters to my father.

She had soft eyes, honey-colored eyes and all she had to do was pretend she preferred the friendship of an older man like my father.

"Her name's Sonia. She and I used to go to high school together. Back then she probably wrote hundreds of love letters for all the girls in our school."

"And?" I asked.

And Fariba's old classmate turned out to have a pair of eyes there was no escaping from. Fariba noted that of all the love letters Sonia had composed, several ended in marriages. One turned into a suicide. And three eventually ran away with their lovers.

Two days before my parents were set to return to Geneva, I put together a small goodbye party and invited Sonia. I asked her to meet me at my office the day before. She certainly had soft eyes, honey-colored, and she was working as a secretary in a music school. I offered her three times what she was making and told her there was no need to quit her regular job. All she had to do was pretend she preferred the friendship of an older man like my father. "Stare into his eyes. And once they return to Geneva, write him a letter once in a while."

At the goodbye party my father was naturally mesmerized by Sonia. I too could hardly believe that this woman who'd been so business-like the day before could as quickly turn into a seasoned actress. She took my father's hands in her own and led him into the kitchen where she carefully sliced a pear and set it on his plate. Here was an image of happiness I hadn't seen in my father in years, perhaps ever. The old man was leaning against the kitchen counter, eating the pear slices, telling jokes and laughing. I left them there and went upstairs where my mother was quietly packing their suitcases. I embraced her and kissed her on the forehead. Her head still had that scent of the medicinal plants of my childhood. I had not asked myself if she would ever be curious about the letters my father was going to be receiving and, naturally, hiding from her. She would be very curious, of course. But she would never ask. That was not her way. And what did that make me for even instigating all of what happened next?

In the following months, the news from Geneva was ideal. Every time my older brother called, he'd say that some kind of a miracle had happened. Our father was eating only healthy food, for once in his life. No sweets, no pastry. He was taking care of himself and was neither unhappy nor irritable. "He goes to the lake every day for walks, with mother. It's as if he is another person."

My generous monthly checks to Sonia did not stop. A year passed that way and then one day I caught sight of her sitting behind the wheel of a silver BMW, at the light before the Jahan-Koodak intersection. It should have been a revelatory moment; I should have realized right there and then that even the best of intentions and realized fantasies can slip, fish-like, out of one's hands.

I wanted to call Sonia to ask about my father but kept putting it off. Two weeks after having seen her in that car my brother called again. His voice was shaking. "The old man left a note saying he is running off to Hawaii!" According to my brother, our dad was not unlike an el-ephant who feels death upon itself and goes off to die somewhere far off from the herd. "Two days straight I've been calling every hotel in Hawaii. Not a sight of him anywhere."

Son, why should a young woman with eyes like hers fall in love with me, of all people?

Of course, our father was not in Hawaii because three days later I found him in Tehran's Grand Hotel. One of my colleagues had called and said he'd spotted the old man in the lobby of the place. I refused to believe it until I was actually sitting across from him in that same lobby and he was confessing to me. His hands trembled and his eyes were bloodshot from crying and lack of sleep. He could barely bring the coffee cup to his lips without spilling it.

The first thing he said to me was, "Son, I've come to find out the truth." The chair I sat on felt like it was on fire. I watched my dad star-ing at the huge chandeliers above his head, dreamy and confused. "I mean, why should a young woman with eyes like hers fall in love with me, of all people?"

It turned out that two months earlier he'd invited Sonia to leave Iran and come to Geneva, where he had reserved a suite for her. He wanted to tell her about Nietzsche's love for Salomé and talk about his own feelings for her. But after a week together, where he'd leave the house in the morning and not return till late at night, he was even less sure of anything. Here was a man who had never lied in his life and now he was lying all the time. So he'd upped and come to Tehran to fig-ure out if he was truly loved or not.

The two of them seemed to have had a good time together these past few days. She'd taken him all over the city, even on the mountain cable lifts to the "Roof of Tehran." At first the old man had imagined that all this attention might be for the sake of money. But, he wanted to find out, could money be the only reality there was? Could it be the cause of all these sensations? Time and again he asked me if it was possible that a feeling could be so overpowering as to make one day-dream around the clock. He insisted that unrequited love could not possibly exist. Our poets were liars, he kept saying. Love carried responsibility, but all that our classical poets had wanted to do was shun the obligation that loving entailed by complaining about the lover's fickleness.

"You know son, one should never ascribe one's own disappointments on another's lack of devotion. It makes me sick when people do that."

He had become a philosopher again. I took him north of the city where I knew a restaurant that served a menu without oil and salt and sugar but its food was still, almost, edible. As I watched him put a slice of fish into his mouth, suddenly I saw him as he had been forty years earlier – a time when he had been a god for me, and faultless.

He met my eyes with the fatigue of eighty years and said, "Sonia says she doesn't want to get too close to me. Says she's afraid she might hurt me. But there's something off in this logic, son. I might not be good for her. That, I can understand. But *she* cannot be bad for me. Think about it: if she didn't really care for me, would she even be worried about hurting me?"

The logic he'd learned in Germany sounded plausible, but it wasn't helping us here. I tried to convince him not to be hasty. I told him that maybe his initial hunch that she only wanted him for his money was right after all.

"What does that even matter? Do you know of anyone on this earth who doesn't think about money? I've already given this girl everything she can dream of. She could have run off by now and done whatever she wants. Instead, she still likes to talk to me every day."

I thought about confessing everything to the old man, how the whole thing had started and who had started it – me! But then I noticed with what zest he was talking and eating what looked to me like a perfectly tasteless lettuce leaf and I backed out.

He said, "The other day when we were sitting on that lift going up the mountainside, I noticed she was gazing at me as if she were laughing inside. My heart sank. Was she laughing at us? Maybe she was laughing at our situation, because what's there not to laugh about, really! But then I saw in her eyes a sense of satisfaction too. I can't really explain it. I honestly don't know what she thinks about me. But I'm convinced there's nothing in life that one can't fathom; all you have to do is think hard enough."

The old man meant to stay in Tehran for two weeks and I hadn't a clue how I was going bring relief to my mother and brother over in Geneva, not to mention my other brothers in Tehran, without giving away his whereabouts. It took several phone calls and asking favors of friends of friends until I found somebody who actually lived in Hawaii and agreed to send a message to Geneva, telling them the old man was doing fine and just needed to be by himself for a while.

The much harder part to all of this was to convince my father not to take the girl's so-called love for him too seriously.

His reply when I broached the subject was, "Can you appreciate how it feels to suddenly have everything you ever dreamed of but could never mention to anyone?"

That did it. I would have to pay Sonia a visit.

•

"I never asked anything of your father."

"You take me for stupid?"

"I never asked for money."

"I don't care if you did or didn't. Our deal is done. Finished. You can speak to my dad while he's in Tehran. After that, you're forbidden to stay in touch with him."

She didn't argue. Soon my father returned to Geneva. But it took no more than twenty-three days before I had another desperate call from my brother; the poor man could barely talk. "Our father lost his mind in Hawaii! He's no longer himself. Won't recognize anyone. Mutters all the time. Won't sleep at nights. Sits in front of the window staring at the water and crying nonstop."

Back to Sonia.

This time I offered to pay her twice what I'd paid her before, if she only restarted her love letters. I had no guarantee that things wouldn't go wrong again. They did, of course. In late autumn when I answered the phone, my brother blurted, "Father has a lover!"

The old man's half dozen maladies, including the possibility of an amputation, had returned with a vengeance. Now he was reconsidering his final will and testament for the substantial assets he owned. Until now I had kept my brothers in Tehran in the dark. But our father's new will, with the name of another woman besides our mother's in it, finally was going to let the secret out. I had made a mess of it all.

No one had the courage to ask our father for an explanation about the new clause in that will. Only our mother could do that. But telling her about the situation needed another kind of courage that none of us had. The lot finally fell on the brother in Geneva. We had expected every kind of response from our matriarch except boredom. In the end she took a piece of paper and wrote on it: *I had guessed something like this since a year ago. Why do all of you want to make your father's life more difficult? If you really want to do something, find me a picture of this woman so I can see what her eyes look like.*

The collective decision now was to find "the woman" and threaten her with the force of an entire family of means. This was on me; I was the real culprit. I had started this thing, and I had to put an end to it, right away.

I asked the family to give me a little more time and sent a message to Sonia to meet me.

As soon as she appeared in my office, I forgot everything I'd prepared to throw at her. She didn't give me a chance. She reached into her handbag, fished out an official document that she'd signed and had stamped at a notary, and pushed it toward me on my desk. The piece of paper witnessed that she wanted no part of my father's inheritance and forfeited any claim to it in perpetuity. I sat there stunned. Was this document real? Could she go back on her word? I didn't know. What I knew was that I had to take her with me to the best photography studio in town and have them take a picture of her that was for the ages — a photo of someone whom my mother could accept as worthy competition for her husband's love.

Thirty-seven days later the old man was back in Tehran. This time he didn't have to hide anything. He had decided to take Sonia to every one of his old haunts of some half a century ago. She was happy to humor him. But his stay in Tehran came to a sudden end; seventeen days after his arrival, on a sunny winter day when he'd had Sonia take him back to the mountains, my father died. Sonia mentioned that despite the clear day, a crisp wind was blowing in those heights. He'd wanted to walk to the edge of a cliff to get a better glimpse of the city below them. He never made it.

And I never found out if the old man ever truly realized the answers he was looking for. Just three days before his death, we were at a restaurant downtown when he admitted, "There's nothing more awful than love. It is like being Alice in Wonderland. You are bewildered every moment. I have a feeling this girl lies to me sometimes. Though I can't call it lies. More like, she doesn't reveal certain things."

He had made her promise to get on with her life, if and when she found someone. So, she'd let on she might marry her boss's brother. This exchange had taken place exactly one week before he died. He was fuming and regretful that night. He kept pacing around my house and repeating the same refrain: "It's impossible. She can't have just met this guy. This was her plan all along. It's all lies. She has been lying to me."

"You really think so?" I asked.

"No. I think I'm just trying to make myself feel better. You know, whenever I've done something really nice for her, something big, she just looks at me and smiles and says 'thank you.' Other times she'll cry over the smallest of my kindnesses. How can this be? Do you think if she didn't love me, she'd go out of her way to lie to me so much?"

•

After the funeral, I only spoke to Sonia one more time. She sent the last photograph she had of the two of them together and then she called me. She was about to get married in a month, she said.

"I can send you some money if you like," I offered.

"No need. He gave me enough money to buy a house. He was upset, but he still insisted on giving me the money when I said I might get married. I'd been thinking about marriage for a year, but couldn't make up my mind while your father was alive." Her voice shook as she talked. I could tell none of this was easy for her and I wasn't sure why it wasn't easy. She said she felt guilty about having told my father she was getting married. "Listen, I'm no longer sure if I told him the truth because I had a hunch he would want to buy me something, like a house, once he knew. Or if I told him because I was being loyal and took his words seriously when he said I should get on with my life. Maybe if I hadn't said anything, he'd ... "

She'd asked a passerby to take that last photo of them. Just a few seconds earlier he'd been telling her about Buenos Aires, she said. About dawn in that city. His dream was to take her there so that they could look out the window of a hotel room together as the sky changed and matched the color of her eyes.

There's a background of snow in this photo. It's another dawn, or perhaps dusk, in Tehran. The old man and Sonia are sitting on a park bench and one can see a tinge of red on their noses from the cold. Yet my father holds a chocolate ice cream cone in his hand – enough sugar to kill him a few times over. He looks like he's just woken up from a dream, laughing, and maybe trying to recall what the dream was about. The young woman is holding his free hand in her own and my father leans ever so slightly toward her.

The Location of the Soul According to Benyamin Alhadeff

NEKTARIA ANASTASIADOU

THE BOSPORUS, NORMALLY COBALT BLUE, WENT ELECTRIC turquoise that weekend. Some thought there had been a pollution spill. Others said the change had something to do with the earth-quake that had shaken the Aegean on Monday afternoon. The truth, Benyamin had written in a Ladino piece for *Neşama News*, was that there had been a surge in beneficial *Emiliania huxleyi* plankton across the Black Sea. Nevertheless, Benyamin couldn't help wondering if the Bosporus had turned the same otherworldly color when, according to legend, the witch Medea had thrown poison into its waters.

The week before, Chloe had agreed to move in with him. He'd searched for piano transport companies, visited them personally, and settled on a firm based in Kadıköy, on the Asian side of Istanbul. Their rates were more than he could afford, but the safe transference of Chloe's 1898 Bösendorfer grand piano forte to their new apartment was his knightly quest, the proof of his undying *amor*. Madame Eva, her mother, hadn't objected when Chloe announced that she was leaving, nor did she say a word when her daughter added that, apart from clothes, books, and personal items, she would also be taking the Bösendorfer.

Benyamin turned his back to the Bosporus quay and faced the crane. He watched the main hoist rotate. The telescope extended, and the boom reached over the high stone wall of the clapboard *yalı* mansion, where three brawny movers were rolling the dolly-perched, legless piano onto a balcony. What if something went wrong? What would happen if a strap broke, or if they moved the piano too fast and it slipped out of its hammock and through Chloe's roof, or worse, through the roof and floors of the neighboring yalı? Benyamin would be to blame.

The hoist line lowered. The men wrapped the heavy-duty yellow straps around the sideways piano and attached them to the crane's hook. Chloe stepped onto the balcony. The Etesian winds tangled her black hair. Benyamin was too far away to see the expression on her face, but he knew she was worried. He waved to reassure her.

•

When they met in September of their senior year at Istanbul University, Benyamin Alhadeff hadn't understood that Chloe Stefanopoulos was on different footing in life than he was. The disparity in their religions might have been a red light half a century ago, but now, with so few Jews and Rum Orthodox Christians left, they could almost be lumped together into one group: non-Muslim. When Chloe said she lived in Tarabya, Benyamin didn't guess that her family owned a vast Ottoman yalı built in 1869 for Nurbanu Hanım, the daughter of Sultan Abdülaziz's dentist. Nor did he think much when Chloe described her garden's highlight, an ancient plane tree, because he wouldn't learn until much later that it had been planted by Nurbanu Hanım herself. He didn't even pay attention when Chloe raved about her flower beds, which hosted wisteria and tulips in spring, hydrangeas and roses in summer, and chrysanthemums in autumn. For Benyamin supposed that Chloe lived in one of the rundown shacks remaining from the time when Tarabya was a Rum fishing village. Besides, Benyamin's late mother – *alav ashalom*, peace upon her – had also grown flowers on their back balcony, mostly geraniums on which the neighborhood tomcats tended to urinate. Benyamin didn't understand that there was still a great divide between beds and pots, even if the gap between Jews and Christians had narrowed.

The following spring, while walking with his father in their working-class neighborhood of Kurtuluş, he said in Ladino, "Papa, will you disown me if I marry a Christian?"

It was Orthodox Easter Sunday, just two days after the end of Pesach. Across the avenue, the municipality had hung banners that read "Happy Holidays to our Christian Brothers." Bakeries still displayed sealed boxes of "Kosher for Pesach" matzah in their windows, and the warm mastic and mahleb perfume of *tsoureki* Easter bread sailed through every bakery door into the chilly street. That was what Benyamin loved about Kurtuluş: despite its graceless cement blocks and dodgy newcomers, it was the last interreligious neighborhood in Istanbul.

Sammy Alhadeff, sidestepping an Armenian woman's pavement display of illegally imported vodka and Russian sausage, said, "Is the question theoretical or practical?"

"Practical," said Benyamin.

"If it's really *amor*," said Sammy, "you shouldn't be asking."

Just then a man standing outside a semi-basement shop – in a confidential tone more suited to a bordello keeper pushing his whores than to a merchant trying to unload made-in-China tops – murmured to Benyamin in Turkish: "Everything on sale for ten liras." The advertisement unsettled Benyamin: it was almost as if the man had intimated that even amor would sell for ten liras. But of course, he didn't understand Ladino.

Benyamin shook off the false impression and asked, "What would mama say if she were alive?"

Sammy turned the thin wedding band on his right pinky. "*Deskoje mujer y vakas de tu civdad.*" Choose a woman and cows from your city.

"She's from my city, but . . ."

"In my opinion, Benya," Sammy continued, "you should be announcing rather than asking for permission. Love means sending everything to hell with one kick."

"But what would that make our children?"

Sammy stopped short. An Iraqi refugee – judging from the cross around his neck and the Arabic he was speaking into his phone – walked straight into Sammy. That was the problem in Kurtuluş Avenue. The sidewalks weren't even a tenth of the width necessary for the neighborhood's pedestrians, and everybody used the main avenue to avoid the steep up-and-down streets surrounding it.

When the Iraqi had passed, Sammy looked Benyamin in the eye and said, "Our ancestors came to Istanbul from Galicia in 1492. We stayed Jewish even though plenty of others converted. We gave you your grandfather's name instead of a modern Turkish one, and we taught you Ladino even though everybody else stopped speaking it decades ago. But only you can decide what's right for you. *Haberes buenos.*"

Good news. But did his father use the expression to confirm good news or to ward off bad news? That was the problem with *haberes buenos*: it could be used for both.

*

Chloe's mother, Madame Eva, was another matter. During the week, Chloe was not allowed on dates with Benyamin. Madame Eva ostensibly knew he spent some weekends in her yalı, while she was absent at their summer house in Burgazada or traveling in Europe; during the week, however, she did everything in her power to keep the lovers apart. Nevertheless, Benyamin was determined. In freezing rain and snow, he had made the trip from Kurtuluş to Tarabya on his motorcycle – a BMW R65 older than he was – only to spend three minutes with Chloe beneath Nurbanu Hanım's plane tree. Could he have had an accident? Or gotten frostbite while waiting for her late at night, in the heart of winter, when her mother delayed going to bed or tried to prevent Chloe from going to the mini-market for a magazine? Of course, he could have. But Benyamin didn't even think about that.

One evening after graduation, while he was lying in bed with Chloe, he said the thing that he'd been avoiding for months: "It's because I'm Jewish, isn't it? That's why your mother doesn't want to meet me." He spoke in Turkish, their common language.

"No," said Chloe.

He nuzzled his face in her hair, which always smelled of sweet printing ink due to her habit of falling asleep with her head on an open book. "Rums fear assimilation, just like Jews. It's understandable that your mother doesn't want you to marry outside your community. She's afraid you'll lose your identity, your history."

Chloe's eyes half closed. "It's because of numbers. My mother evaluates mathematically."

"I'm 180cm," said Benyamin, frustrated that Chloe was falling asleep. "And at least 17cm —"

Chloe's eyes flashed open. "Salary, not size, Benya!"

"But if she met me, then maybe . . ."

"I love you because you're a normal man. She doesn't get that. It's not personal."

Benyamin rolled onto his back. Staring at the ceiling's elaborate woodwork, he said, "Circumstances aren't in our favor. One day you'll leave me."

"Give me your hand," she said.

He did. She sat up and jabbed her nails into his skin. Her middle, ring, and pinky nails left red marks. Her index nail left a half moon of blood. "That wound will remain," she said, "reminding you of what you said. If we're together, I'll remind you myself."

•

Benyamin eventually did meet Madame Eva by accident — or at least that's what it was meant to look like — after he and Chloe had been dating for a full year. Eva returned to Tarabya unexpectedly on a Sunday morning in early October 2016, while Chloe was playing the Bösendorfer in preparation for a teaching interview. Benyamin was sitting beside Chloe, watching her pale hands dance over the yellowing keys: just from looking at them you could tell that she was a book and music person. Nobody who spent any time outdoors could have hands that white.

A warm breeze rushed into the yalı's piano room. Because no furniture blocked their path, the curtains billowed like sails. That, he realized, was what it meant to be wealthy: one had enough space to dedicate an entire room to a piano. In Benyamin's dim family flat in Kurtuluş, they pulled desks and sofas and tables as close as possible to the high windows with views of cement walls and satellite dishes. In Chloe's piano room, one had windows to waste: three facing the water, one side-window looking up toward the Black Sea, another looking down toward the Sea of Marmara. Benyamin had even spotted dolphins – a whole school of them – from that window. Perhaps they'd come to listen to Chloe.

A shadow obscured the sunlight flooding the room. Red fingernails tapped the piano's round shoulder. Benyamin's eyes travelled up the thick forearm, over the loose tricep, exposed shoulder and leathery neck to an expressionless face that he recognized from the photos in the living room – Madame Eva. She carried a folding chair, wooden and inlaid with mother-of-pearl.

Chloe stopped playing mid-piece. She never did that. Benyamin called her his pit bull because she couldn't let go of her music until she reached the proper end. "In summer," said Madame Eva, her voice as melodious and clear as the Bösendorfer's, "the Black Sea dolphins come all the way to Tarabya, but no further. They're afraid of the lower Bosporus."

"I've seen them," said Benyamin, standing.

Eva set up her chair by the window. "I've counted three just this year."

He approached her and extended his hand. "Benyamin Alhadeff. Pleased to –"

"I know." Eva dropped his hand as quickly as she took it. "Have you gone swimming here?"

"No."

"You should. The salt doesn't burn your eyes, as it does in the Aegean. But the currents can be dangerous. Sometimes up to four knots." Eva crossed one bare ankle over the other. Benyamin thought he could see sand on her tennis shoes. Chloe, who, just minutes ago, had been inhaling hypnotically at the music rests and exhaling just after the onsets, now seemed to be holding her breath. Eva opened her arms. "Come, *yavri*." Chloe was twenty-four, but her mother still used the Turkish pet name yavri, baby.

Chloe crossed the room and sat on her mother's lap. Eva sang the slow, tender beginning of a Rum folk song about a vest sewn with bitterness and trouble. She widened her eyes and then, with a strength that Benyamin did not expect from her chubby legs, bounced her daughter to the playful refrain about scolding the vest's wearer — either a child or a lover — and afterward repenting. Chloe laughed like a toddler. Benyamin hadn't suspected that she would be just as tender with her mother as she was with him.

Eva planted her lips on her daughter's head and inhaled. Benyamin wondered what Chloe's hair smelled like to her. Did she identify the printing ink? Or only the lavender shampoo with which she herself stocked Chloe's shower?

"I need to get your lunch ready for tomorrow, yavri. And pick out your dress for tonight."

"Tonight?" said Chloe.

"I didn't tell you?" said Eva, switching from Turkish to Greek.

Having spent hundreds of hours playing ball with his Rum friends, as well as endless afternoons sitting at their cramped kitchen tables beneath Blessed Mother icons, ever-burning oil lamps, photographs of dead forebears, and bunches of dried flowers tied to gas pipes, Benyamin understood the language even though he didn't speak it.

Eva continued: "The Athenian banker is taking you out." She set Chloe on her feet and proceeded to the door without inviting Benyamin to tea, without saying that she was pleased to meet him, without even looking him in the eye.

Staring at the empty folding chair, he whispered to Chloe, "Are you going?"

She ran her fingertips over her name, which had been engraved into the gold-painted music stand. "It's just to placate mama. Nothing more."

*

The following February, after an intense altercation with her mother over her "superficiality" (that is, her attachment to Benyamin), Chloe called and asked him to meet her on the quay. He immediately turned off his laptop, hopped on his motorcycle, and sped to their favorite seaside bench in Tarabya; after all, it was a chilly, overcast day, and he didn't want Chloe catching cold. As soon as he arrived, he tried to calm her, but she didn't want comforting. They went for a walk along the Bosporus instead. When Chloe tired, they perched themselves on the edge of the quay. Across the strait were some of the last rolling green hills of the Asian side. In ten years, they, too, would probably be built up and covered with concrete.

"The Bösendorfer was made for a wealthy Jewish family in Budapest," Chloe said.

Benyamin felt a sharp pain in his throat, as if he'd swallowed a fishhook. Was the announcement her way of forcing him to end things? Did she want him to reject the unacceptable and thereby spare her further confrontation with Madame Eva?

"So the Bösendorfer is Holocaust spoils?"

"Absolutely not. My grandmother's family bought it for her in 1931, when she was a baby. I just wanted you to know its history . . . *my* history. The Bösendorfer is a part of me."

Benyamin exhaled. The piano had nothing to do with the Shoah. Furthermore, Chloe wasn't trying to cast him off. "That's a relief, because I wouldn't have been able to . . ."

"What?"

"I'm glad it was never mixed up in anything." A passing ship blew its low horn. The seagulls screeched in reply. Chloe said nothing. Realizing it would be best to steer the conversation elsewhere, Benyamin said, "Wasn't it presumptuous of your grandmother's family to buy her a piano when she was just a baby? What if she didn't want to play?"

Chloe stared at him as if he were speaking Chinese. "All girls learned piano."

"My grandmothers didn't." He realized what he'd said as soon as it was out of his mouth. His maternal grandmother had been a seamstress. His paternal grandmother had given birth to her first child at the age of seventeen. Piano playing was a luxury.

"All girls from *houses*," Chloe said.

"And my grandmothers were from stables?"

Chloe flinched. It felt, for a second, as if a tanker ship with a broken rudder or a drunken captain had crashed straight into a bicentenarian yalı, as too often happened on the Bosporus. "I didn't mean *that*," she said.

He put his finger to her lips. "I know you didn't."

"My parents will have left by now. Let's go." She stood, brushed dried seaweed and dust from her trousers and coat, and led him back toward the yalı. A stray dog — half Kangal and half shepherd — struggled to its feet and followed them. That always happened with Chloe. Even the strays wanted to claim her. At the mansion's gate she caressed the dog's ears, called him *canım*, Turkish for "my soul," and passed inside the yard without looking back.

They went straight to the piano room. She retook her seat at the Bösendorfer and began playing a slow and graceful piece that Benyamin had never heard before. It seemed to him, even before she revealed the name of the piece, that the music expressed not only her desire, but also her power to limit and conceal. He stood in his usual place, behind the Bösendorfer's tail, legs spread, arms folded across his chest, declaring with his stance that he was determined to wait her out. "Title?" he asked.

Chloe played all the way to the end, which finished with a left-hand solo, just as it had begun. Without raising her eyes from the keys, she said, "*Secret Engagements*."

•

In April 2017, Benyamin landed a job at *Neşama News*, Istanbul's Jewish newspaper. The extra money — combined with what he already earned from pizza delivery, as well as Chloe's salary as a piano teacher in an upscale conservatory — made it possible for them to think about living together. He tried to show her a few internet rental advertisements as they sat on the piano bench one Sunday. She looked at the photos on his phone while playing the introduction to one of her favorite pieces. Benyamin had the impression that she was both drawing him near and simultaneously prolonging the pauses, turning them into voids through which he might accidentally slip. Her left hand rose to join the right. Her pupils dilated. The piece's tone changed from inquisitive to tense. Her hands began running, chasing each other. Her breath shortened. The tiny, chicken-like bones beneath her transparent skin and blue veins rose and fell as if they, too, were part of the instrument. The pads of her fingers slipped along the keys from top to bottom, sputtered between them, played deeply.

He had read that an American anesthesiologist and a British physicist had discovered the location of the soul: the microtubules of our brain cells. The ancient Egyptians, on the other hand, had thought the soul could be found in the heart, whereas Leonardo da Vinci believed the soul resided in the center of the head. Da Vinci had even dissected a corpse to prove his theory. Watching Chloe play, Benyamin believed that he grasped what had escaped da Vinci, the Egyptians, and modern scientists alike: the soul couldn't be found in the mind, nor in the heart, nor in some invisible aura or microtubules, but in the hands.

At the most intense moment of the chase, Chloe raised her wrists, bringing the piece to a seemingly premature finish. Her eyes – owlish green with a brown limbal ring – were always more beautiful when she sat at the piano. She said, "And the Bösendorfer?"

"We'll take her with us."

The Bosporus turned a muddy pond color beneath the clouds riding in on the back of the Etesians. The winds also carried pine pollen, which was the cause of the annoying surging in Benyamin's nose. Chloe reached into her pocket, took a tissue for herself, and handed the packet to him. They said in unison, "Three, two, one." Then they blew as hard and as noisily as they could.

"Winner!" said Benyamin, holding up his hands in victory.

"I give in," said Chloe.

"I was obviously louder. Way more snot."

"I mean I'll move out of the house."

It was the best thing he'd ever heard. Better, even, than I love you. It meant that Chloe's mother's efforts to arrange a match with a wealthy Athenian, or the son of a Rum council president, or the nephew of an archbishop were to come to an end. It meant that Chloe had finally decided not just to love him, but to claim him.

Benyamin picked up her hand and held it to his nose: the sandalwood oil that she wore had merged with the Bösendorfer's spruce. Benyamin recalled the Orthodox rabbi who had arrived from Toronto a decade before. Istanbul's liberal Jewish community – Benyamin included – had trouble digesting the rabbi's hands-at-sides bow to women. But every time Benyamin touched Chloe's hands, his understanding of the rabbi grew: handshaking could be an almost amatory act.

Chloe tried to pull her hand away. "We just blew our noses."

"I'd dry my face with a towel you'd used on dirty feet," said Benyamin. He put her fingers into his mouth one by one, sucking from base to knuckle to fingernail. She shivered. He lifted her off the piano bench and set her down beside one of the massive hexagonal legs, on the Ushak carpet, which was surely worth more than he would make in five years as a newspaper columnist.

•

Standing outside the yalı on moving day, Benyamin took a deep breath: the Bosporus smelled more sharply than usual, probably because of the *Emiliania huxleyi*. He'd read that the plankton was a coccolithopore: a seed that bore rock. Apparently, the mosaic cages of microscopic calcium carbonate plates enclosing the single-celled organism were not only responsible for the Bosporus's unusual color, but, as the plankton lived and died in millions, the same plates would settle on the strait's floor and form rocks above the shipwrecks, rubbish, and bits of yalı mansions destroyed by renegade cargo vessels.

The crane's hoist line tightened and began to reel in, pulling the piano up. Benyamin would have liked to be with Chloe, comforting her while she watched Old Lady Bösendorfer dancing on *corde lisse*. But

Chloe would be down soon enough. He'd take her into his arms. The piano would be placed safely in the truck, and they would start their life together.

The yellow straps rose above the balcony railing, followed by the piano's tail, covered in padded blankets. The crane hoisted higher and higher, first to clear the railings, then the gutters. The main hoist rotated again, ever so slowly, flying the Bösendorfer between Chloe's mansion and the neighbor's to reduce damages in case of accident. Finally, the telescope retracted. The piano had made half its exodus.

The movers, each carrying a swaddled piano leg, descended the mansion's front steps. Chloe pushed past them to Benyamin. She wrapped her arms around his neck, planted her wet cheek against his. He kissed her tears. They were saltier than the Bosporus. If he and Chloe were to have a snot-blowing competition now, she would win.

"The hardest part is done," he said.

"It's not that." She pushed out her lips. Her expression was childish, imploring. He knew that look. She was asking for a solution. Benyamin pulled away. Chloe turned toward the mansion. Sandwiched between the sheer curtains and the window above the main door stood Madame Eva. Perhaps she was counting dolphins. Or deciding where to throw her poison.

"You can visit her whenever you want," said Benyamin.

Chloe covered her eyes with her hands. "She won't let me."

He again looked up at the window. Now Madame Eva was staring straight at him. He thought he could make out a sneer, an expression that said, *I win*.

"She threatened you," he said.

Chloe remained silent. He could have solved any problem but this one. Why was she telling him now? Couldn't she have waited until they had moved the piano into the new flat? If she was telling him *now*, then … he embraced Chloe as tightly as he could without hurting her.

She said, her voice muffled in his chest, "Every romance has an expiration date."

"Who would dare put an expiration date on love?" he said.

Chloe didn't reply. This had to be the reason her father was always "working." Eva's maternal devotion left no place for him. No place for anyone.

"Stop!" Benyamin yelled to the crane operator. He jogged to the hoist, waving both hands overhead like malfunctioning windshield wipers.

The machine paused. The operator poked his head out of the window. "What happened?"

"Stop," he said.

"But it's going well."

"I need a minute."

Benyamin sat on the slate stones surrounding Nurbanu Hanım's plane tree. He'd faced Chloe's hesitation before. The first time they'd been intimate: it had taken all night because she had been so afraid of the pain. He didn't want to force her. They had held each other, cried together, grasped at each other, slipped away, returned, until finally, exhausted, he decided to spare them both the frustration of defeat. Benyamin remembered his father's words. "If it's really love, you shouldn't be asking. You should be *announcing*." He saw the calcium carbonate cages of the *Emiliania huxleyi* falling to the Bosporus floor, the anchovies devouring as many as they could.

Chloe sat beside him. He sensed that she was looking into his eyes, but he avoided her gaze. She reached for his hand. He pulled it away, stood, and called out, "Put it back!"

"Excuse me?" returned the crane operator.

"I'll pay what we agreed. Have them set it up exactly as it was."

"She changed her mind?"

Benyamin held his right hand to the sunlight peeking through the plane tree's leaves. The pink half-moon scar was still there, a year after she'd carved it into his hand. In his head, he heard his father say *haberes buenos*. Out loud, Benyamin said to the crane operator, "No. *I* changed mine."

The Cactus

MOHAMMED AL NAAS
Translated from the Arabic by Rana Asfour

"I've killed two already. Don't let this be our third," she told him. Her desolation, he noted, lent her eyes even greater beauty. She added: "I want you to take good care of this one. Do it for me."

"For you, anything," he answered.

He had wanted to say something more profound, but staring at her lips arrested the words escaping from his own.

•

He had had every intention of emailing her, despite his belief in the inadequacy and triviality of the medium. But she occupied a time and space in which he longed to belong, with her. If he were being honest, he'd say that he had never liked being a writer; that, in fact, he felt like an impostor each time he wrote anything. Generally speaking, he'd always thought of himself as insignificant and foolish.

He started to clear the table. Everything in his room reminded him of her: his clothes, his books, his notes, his toothbrush, his coffee cup, his cologne, his leather jacket and that little cactus occupying pride of place in the middle of the well-worn granite table. He wanted to make space for his computer so that he might sit down and try, once more, to write to her. He unconsciously rubbed his thumb against his fingers, recalling the previous day's pain when he'd attempted the same. He had been struggling to find the words to write to her when, in frustration, he had gotten up to clear the potted plant off the table. When it slipped from his fingers, he reflexively grabbed the prickly thing, and its spines, each no longer than a grain of rice, sank into his flesh.

•

"I should lock you up now and throw away the key," she said. She'd been sitting on his thigh, her gaze playing havoc with his heartstrings.

"I'll find a way to escape," he'd replied, with his usual foolishness. He loved to provoke her just so he could observe with fascination the unraveling of her reaction.

"I would do it. I would lock you up right here. I would tell my family that I kidnapped you, and that if anyone wanted you free they would first have to marry us," she said.

"But how would I eat? How would I smoke? How would I drink coffee? On what would I survive?" he asked.

"You would want for nothing as long as I give you this," she said, reaching for his hand and placing it between her thighs.

●

Again he stared at the cactus, and then at the window. *Appear. Please appear*, he entreated what lay beyond the closed shutters. He made to open them until he remembered he'd promised himself to keep them bolted at all times, even though it meant denying himself a repeat of the scene that had arrested him the first day he'd arrived in the Old City. She'd materialized like an apparition, silhouetted against her kitchen window which looked on to his room. Since then, he'd taken to guessing what she was cooking as fragrant scents seeped through the perforations of his window's wooden shutters and wafted towards him. He imagined the heat rising in her kitchen to coax out the sweat beads glistening on her forehead. He envisioned the moist droplets running down her face trapping, in their descent, the aromas of cooked fish, tomatoes, pigweed, and onions before sliding down her neck and ultimately pooling in a mass between her breasts. He wished he could ask her how she bore living amidst all the hardships within the alleys of the Old City. He passed his hand over the wooden shutters as if willing them to magically open of their own accord, his eyes pleading for one more sighting. For a brief moment, his gaze shifted to the bathtub placed outside on his balcony, and the combined scents of the yellow flowers bathing inside it alongside pungent mint leaves served to further inflame his lust.

*

Perhaps her name is Céline, he mused, likening her to his beloved from whom distance, war, and the scrum of life separated him. He surveyed the flowers, trees, bushes, and shrubs in this city, nicknamed the "City of Jasmine" and marvelled at the constant intermingled scent of jasmine and strewn garbage. There'd been a time when he hadn't had to make such promises to himself, a time when he could have opened the window to anything and anyone, to the sight of an entire garden of blue, yellow, red, purple, and orange flowers in which insects and birds sang along to the rhythm of the sea that adjoined the villa of the French journalist now buried in its grounds.

*

"You know I have to leave," he told her while stroking her hair.

"Yes I know," she replied, desperately wishing it were otherwise.

"This is my chance; I'm going to write down everything. Absolutely everything," he said.

"Yes. You will write, and I will love it all," she replied. He knew that if he were to taste her tears he'd fall into a drunken stupor.

"You know I will never give up on us," he said instead. "It's only for a few months. We can do it. Everything will be all right," he added, confident in his sentiments.

"I fear otherwise," she said. "But I understand your need to travel and to experience the world. You've always cherished that idea," she added, trying to save him the embarrassment of further deceit.

"Yes. I've always cherished the idea," he repeated. He kissed her then, slipping his hand under her skirt.

*

He snapped back from his reveries and moved away from the shuttered window. He could feel the cactus watching him, and he, in turn, gazed back at it. Gripped by a sudden impulse to leave he grabbed his leather jacket and headed out. Nothing around him resembled his country. Everything was so different: the cold, the air, the smells, the songs, the color of the sky, and people's clothes, conversations, and shenanigans. Even the city's gateway to the sea was in huge contrast with Tripoli's Bab al-Bahr.

It amazed him when his friend Oren, a poet he'd met at the French journalist's house, detailed the similarities between the two countries, and waxed lyrical about the effervescence of his city and its stories. He failed to see the likeness that would inspire his friend's poetry each morning on the subject.

He realized that he had reached a street commemorating the man who had begat freedom a home in Tunis. He noted that the cold hadn't impeded the birds from confiding their secrets to the trees strung along both sides of the street. As he made his way through the corridor of people accompanied by the trilling symphony of African reed warblers, it occurred to him that if Céline, who hated all birds, had been with him at that moment, she would certainly have collapsed from the intensity of birdsong.

Every day since arriving in the City of Jasmine, he would walk for an hour in the villa's garden. The dusty paths were bursting with foliage, and he couldn't help noticing their lushness compared to his puny, rigid, and prickly cactus at home. And as he maneuvered his way through the masses of bodies in the street of that beloved man, his Bedouin passions awakened to the women around him, his ardor inflamed by the myriad colors of their hair: blue, yellow, red, purple, and orange, a blooming garden with no danger of a single thorn in sight to puncture his heart.

•

"I will write to you," he said, as he made his farewells.

"That's good," she replied, her eyes never letting go of his.

"Every day," he added for good measure. "About everything. It will seem as if we're barely apart. As you read my words, it'll be as if my mouth were close enough for your fingers to trace the lips that speak words created just for you."

"Stay a while," she pleaded, desperate now that he was finally getting ready to leave. "I want to hang on to your scent, your kisses, and your

warm hands a bit longer. Won't you stay?" Forever was what she wanted to add, but didn't.

"I'll stay another hour," he offered as he encircled her waist.

"I wish I could conceal you from the world, hidden here within my embrace," she said, squeezing him tightly to her as though coercing his body to fuse with hers.

His hands reached under her shirt to squeeze her breasts as he kissed her neck, ears, and shoulders. He slid his hands downward, slipping them under her skirt where they got busy relieving her of her underpants. "If I am to take the cactus with me like you want me to," he said, "these will have to be part of the bargain too."

"You can't do that," she said.

"Then it'll just have to be something else in return for my troubles," he said pointedly.

●

When he'd finally left, he'd taken the cactus with him, but not before he'd kissed his love one final time, her eyes shining like two precious pearls he wished he could steal for safekeeping. Eventually, he'd stopped trying to count the number of times the hairline spikes had made a meal of his fingers. When he was ready to leave, he'd packed the plant in his suitcase, but not before another batch of spines had had a go at his flesh. On the plane, all he could think about was the cactus and whether or not it would survive the ten-hour flight delay. As he looked down at the pale, dusty palms, olive trees and cypresses, he had prayed his plant would have enough oxygen to last it the journey. *I'll have to carry it back with me,* he'd thought to himself, imagining its size six months down the line and the amused looks he was certain to receive from his fellow passengers as he boarded the plane. He quickly dismissed this last image, knowing he'd never be allowed to bring the plant aboard anyway.

●

After a full day's delay, feeling thoroughly spent, he'd arrived in the City of Jasmine in the early hours of the morning, and had finally been able to unpack the cactus from his suitcase before crashing into bed until midday. He wasn't sure whether the sounds of rumbling waves were coming from somewhere close by, or if they were part of his dream in which he dove into the water over and over again to scoop up his love's pearly eyes, only to come up for air to myriad cactus spines impaling the tender flesh under his fingernails instead.

Three months later, he still hadn't written a single word. Not about her, for her, or even to her. Each day he woke up to the same morning routine, which started with a breakfast of eggs, coffee, butter, strawberry jam, and a croissant. Most days were spent in the company of Oren, whose habit of bellowing his verses out at the sea had both men falling to the ground in rapturous laughter. Other days he'd spend in solitary walks around the garden, stopping for a rest at his favorite bench beside a nearby pond. It never failed to amuse him how his arrival always startled the frogs, who leapt into the water and upset the serenity of the bright-colored lilies floating gracefully on the surface. Were his love here, he would have reached down and plucked one out of the water in offering. As if privy to his intent to de-home them, the lilies appeared to keep their distance, drifting – it seemed – as far away as they could from where he stood watching them. He named them all Céline.

As he watched the frogs return to the surface, the scene reminded him of a childhood resplendent with stories of frogs, ghosts, and flowers as well as thorns, death, and escape. He supposed that a novel about his childhood might just be the thing he needed to work on. He recalled how Céline had relished his stories, her eyes melting into his as he regaled her, her attraction turning to devotion by the time he came to the end. Buoyed by the memory, he resolved to follow through with this idea, unaware of its folly.

He returned to his room to find the cactus right where he'd left her. As he watered the plant he conceded to himself that its care was turning out to be a burdensome, loveless obligation akin to that of caring for an irksome child. Nevertheless, he carried out his duty, all the while resenting that all the ungrateful plant administered in return was pain.

He picked up a guidebook for writers that he had taken to reading each night before going to sleep, knowing full well that in a few hours he would wake up to another day that would siphon away a little more of his desire to write as he negotiated all the excuses and distractions that kept him from sending her a single word.

The following evening, when the full moon was already high up in the sky and the tide had gone way out, the two friends met at their usual spot at the top of a slight slope overlooking the sea. When each had picked a comfortable rocky surface to sit on, it struck him how the cacti dotted around them bore no resemblance to the one waiting for him at home. It wasn't long before the two of them were deep in conversation about the war, the sea, God, and all living beings.

"Say, Oren, do you know the names of these plants?"

"Are you asking me from a scientific or aesthetic point of view?" Oren asked glibly, which only reminded him that Oren had trained as a doctor long before turning to poetry.

"For a scientific answer you'll need an encyclopedia. However, as any poet worth his salt will tell you, one is free to name things as one pleases." Oren's answer only served to replace his friend's previous look of confusion with one of frustration.

"For example?"

"Well, take the cactus over there. Who's to tell me I can't call it the *orange-hued cactus*, when clearly it is orange? Or the blue-colored one right next to it. Why can't I name it *the cactus that lives beside the orange-hued cactus*?"

They both went silent after that.

"I believe plants have feelings," he said, startling them both out of their lull. "That's why I can't stand vegetarians who cry to anyone who'll listen about how animals have feelings, but then dismiss the notion that plants, as living beings, could have feelings, too."

"Not all vegetarians are like that, my friend," answered Oren. He sensed, probably for the first time, that Oren had more to say but was being uncharacteristically hesitant. "In the West, animals are subject to terrible conditions," Oren continued, "cramped pens, growth-promoting hormones, and filthy quarters." "But who's to say that plants, too, do not loathe being confined in pots, walled gardens, and cramped beds, harvested according to man's whims?"

"Science hasn't yet confirmed whether plants have feelings or not. As for animals, any human with eyes can see the suffering they're being put through."

When he'd packed his bags to move to the Old City, he'd decided that the cactus would travel on his lap in the taxi. When he'd gotten into the car, the driver greeted him while throwing several curious glances at the plant.

"*Hindis* are tasty plants," said the driver in a bid to engage with him while misidentifying the cactus as an Indian costus.

"True, but this is a different type of cactus," he replied, trying to balance the plant on his lap while avoiding contact with its barbs.

The journey was long and difficult. The taxi driver appeared frustrated by his passenger, who seemed reluctant to engage in conversation, prickly or otherwise, and while away the monotonous journey between the two cities. He finally gave up and switched on the radio to keep company with his thoughts.

When the taxi dropped him off at the station closest to the Old City, he discovered that he'd have to walk the remaining distance to the guest house. And so it was that he navigated the last kilometer dragging a heavy suitcase in one hand and carrying a potted plant in the other, making his way through the narrow alleys and markets. By the time he arrived, cranky and sweating, he felt completely spent, his thoughts flashing back to their last time together.

•

"Keeping this cactus alive proves you're ready to care for our future child," Céline said.

"Based on our track record it means our first two will die," he joked. Then, more soberly, he remarked: "I seriously don't know where you get these crazy notions — of signs and symbols — from."

166

"From here," she said, tapping her index finger on her forehead. "Most likely from back here," he said, slipping a finger to reach back there where he —

Just then, the pot slipped from his grasp, smashing to pieces on the street. The cactus lay sprawled on the dirt, its roots naked, exposed, unearthed from their sanctuary beneath the soil. The dirt seemed to come to life as a light breeze arrived, scattering it every which way, while whatever remained was trampled underfoot by passing pedestrians. As he surveyed the scene, he registered his incompetence, his worthlessness at keeping anything alive, let alone the child that Céline desired. When he glanced back at the cactus he could feel her pleading with him to rescue her. A sudden urge to abandon her exactly where she was overwhelmed him, but it disappeared just as quickly and he sprang into action. He collected as much of the soil as remained and stuffed the roots back into it. Fairly satisfied, he continued on his way to his new abode.

•

"It's settled. You are taking her with you," she demanded.

"Aside from everything, why are you so insistent that I do?"

"She's my informant. Anything you do, she'll let me know."

"But plants can't speak," he said. The hypocrisy of his words struck him. Didn't this contradict his theory about plants as sentient beings?

"She may not be able to speak our language, but she can still prick you whenever she knows you've strayed," she answered. She turned to the plant then, and, gripping the pot in both hands, she leaned in to address it: "Promise me you'll plant your spikes into him when he thinks of cheating on me."

"I promise," he replied playfully putting on a voice he thought the plant might make. They both laughed then, although the incident had left him with an unsettled feeling.

•

That evening, just before sunset, he took a seat at a café he happened to pass by on his way home. It had been three hours since he'd ordered his first coffee, and both the frequency with which customers entered the café and the number of people in the street were visibly dwindling. Having lost count of the number of coffees he'd consumed and the chain of cigarettes he'd smoked, he looked around to find that except for two other tables – one occupied by a man and two women eating their dinner and another taken by three Libyan youths he could hear conversing about the war – the café was empty. The cat roaming around the place entreating its patrons for food certainly didn't count; neither did the overweight flower vendor trying to forcefully sell off what remained of her roses to unwilling customers. It wasn't until he shifted in place that he noticed a woman sitting alone at a table eating an ice cream, whom he'd missed seeing earlier. A powerful longing to get up, converse with her, and to watch her as she ate, washed over him. The emotion dislodged a memory of a long-ago conversation with Céline.

●

"I dreamed that I was alone when I gave birth to a baby girl," she said. "I suppose you had traveled, as you always do. She felt like something alien, foreign to me, so that I found it very hard to bond with her, even to look at her. I couldn't even tell you the color of her eyes, her hair, her skin. I felt neither tenderness nor love towards her. Breastfeeding her felt like a duty rather than an act of motherly devotion."

"Why?" he asked.

"I don't understand it myself," she answered. "Maybe . . . if only . . . I'd allowed myself to look into her eyes, I'd have found some answer."

●

He spent the rest of the evening alone at his table, imbibing what energy he could from the constantly dwindling flow of passersby. He scrutinized faces, lingering longer on the women. The absence of birdsong aroused an intense desire for the voice of that other woman, who he surmised to be in her thirties, the beauty he stole glimpses of in the window across the alley, the wife of an absent husband, and the mother of the little girl she sang to.

His lucid thoughts were cut short by the shouts of the flower vendor, who was now making him the target of her aggressive designs. *Go on!* she shouted, pushing a rose towards him. *Just take it.* He thanked her and declined. He thought of his cactus, and the promise he'd made to covet no other but her. But the woman was relentless, and tried several times to place the flower behind his ear, telling him how handsome it made him look. *Dammit it, woman, I said no!* he said, his rebuke more aggressive than it should have been. *You're unworthy!* the woman spat before gathering her flowers and moving away from the table.

The encounter put him on edge and rattled his nerves. Drained and exhausted, he was barely able to carry himself home, where he was greeted with a familiar melody as soon as he'd stepped into the room and closed the door behind him. Despite not opening his own shutters, he knew that her kitchen window was open, as the verses of her song drifted towards him loud and clear: "*The resentful begrudge me my love . . . they asked me, what it is that I saw in her? To refute my detractors I told them . . . Take my eyes and look through them. . .*"

He moved towards the table and took a seat opposite the cactus, which appeared to him to be transfixed by the melodious voice as much as he was. They sat and listened to the woman singing her heart out as she washed the dishes. It seemed that they would spend all night this way, until the calling of *Mama, Mama* interrupted the woman's flow. *What is it?* she asked her little girl. *I'm hungry,* came the reply. *Alright, I'll fix you something to eat,* she replied.

He could detect a palpable change in her tone, one that had gone from seductive melody to another laced with frustration and resignation. He felt a twinge in his chest, so he got up from his chair and moved to the window, hoping to catch a glimpse of her face through the openings of the wooden louvered shutters. A while later, the clatter of pots and pans could be heard as she resumed her place at her kitchen window. He detected the faintest sound of a tune that he couldn't make out this time. From this viewpoint, he watched her like a hawk as her silhouette moved about the kitchen, amazed how much it resembled that of the one he loved.

Overcome with exhaustion, he finally retired to his bedroom, all notions of writing long gone from his mind. As he set eyes on his cactus for the last time that day, he could feel her thistles piercing holes in his heart, and as he fought the urge to close his eyes and succumb to sleep, he was reminded of a conversation he'd once had with Oren not too long before.

"All women will come to resemble the one you love, but only if you truly love her," Oren had said.

"But no two women are ever the same," he'd replied.

"Try it. Imagine a woman. What does she look like?"

"Exactly like the woman I love. But this proves nothing. There are more than a thousand species of cacti, and any similarities they share does not mean that they are one and the same."

Before he finally drifted off to sleep that night, he resolved that the first thing he was going to do the following morning was to relegate the cactus to the dumpster.

Counter Strike

MK HARB

SUNDAYS IN BEIRUT ARE EMPTY WITH SOMETHING MORE THAN quietness. This Sunday was no different. My grandmother, armed with flour and olive oil, kneaded the *ajeen* (dough) on the balcony table until it bent to her will. She flattened the center with her elbow and said: half of the city is at the beach and the other half are back in their villages, and you have the luck of being with me. Shuf, true Beirutis do not leave their home, even on Sunday. You never know who will squat in your house! My mother, sat on the couch in her green prayer gown, moved her neck left and right to end her *salat* and said: stop feeding Malek's head with nonsense. We stay here on Sundays because we enjoy the calm of the city. Not out of fear of squatters!

"Uff, Nadine. You have the audacity to say this when your trip to Syria is next week. They occupied half the homes in Ras Beirut, including yours on Makdisi Street and Hariri's blood is still fresh. Allah Yerhamo, steheh!" my grandma responded.

"Khalas, Mama. We go to Syria every year. Zahi's sister has been there for two decades, but each summer you make a fuss out of it. It's not like Hend assassinated Hariri!" my mother replied. "Malek, go inside and call Ghaith. Ask him what they need us to bring down to Damascus," she commanded –

I went to my teta's room to get the *handy*, the phone I spent much of my life on. Twice a week I would call my friend, Maya, and we would imagine we were celebrities living in Beirut. We acted out the ego, the confidence and the drama, but we did not know what our profession was. One time she called and asked: did you send me those beautiful red flowers? The concierge just delivered them. Even though I was half asleep, I joined her act and said: No, I was sent some too. Do you think it's an admirer?

I called Ogero and requested an international line to Damascus. After a few rings I heard an excited Ghaith say: Maloukkkk, shlonak habibi? – "Meshta'lak. I can't wait to see you. Mom is asking what you want us to bring down from Beirut," I replied. "Yes, I have the list here. Two packets of Tegretol 200 MG, Sara's seizures are worse. A few Javel bleach, a couple of Pepsi and KitKat boxes, an Eastpak bag for Luna, soon in grade 10 at the German school and whatever new DVDs are available at NabilNet," he said. "Tekram, is that all?" I asked. "Of course not. Don't forget the McDonalds and KFC on the way. Get as many burgers as you can. We can sell them to the neighborhood boys for fifty lira per burger. And a few twister sandwiches to bribe the customs officers," he said as he laughed. His chuckles now carried a pubescent tone, years ahead of mine. "Malouk this trip will be your favorite one. I made so many new friends in El Mazzeh and I told them all about you. Ramez, Moaz, and Adam. We are hooked on this new game called *Counter Strike*. You get to fight like in the American war movies," he said.

"Eh it's popular in Beirut too, boys play it at NabilNet. Yala habibi I will see you in a week. My mom will come in and yell about the phone bill if we talk more," I replied. When he hung up, a trepidation creeped up on me. Ghaith was my favorite cousin, the one who drove me around Qasyoun Mountain, buying me *sobar* (prickly pears) and shawarma from Abu El Meesh in Bab Touma. Now I had to share him and carry guns!

◆

The next day, I woke up determined to fight. Not just for Ghaith's attention, but the militias in *Counter Strike*. I gulped my Nescafé, ate the *manakeesh,* wore a military cap and marched over to NabilNet. Nabil, herculean built, with a face that refused to express any emotion, ate a kunefe sandwich behind his desk. He spoke with a confidence that asserted his godliness in Lebanon. Teenagers and old men alike scurried from across the country for his bootleg DVDs. Some movies like *Shakespeare in Love* had the best quality available, others were recorded in a cinema in Dearborn, Michigan, with theatergoers walking across the screen while we watched. Once, during *Vanilla Sky*, I heard a movie goer eat popcorn, but I did not mind it, it was like being in the US.

"Ahlen Malouk. How was the *Princess Diaries*?" Nabil asked. "Oh, my mom and I loved it," I replied. "I'm glad to hear. So, what are you in for this time?" Nabil said. "A two-hour internet card for *Counter Strike*," I said, pulling out a ten thousand–lira bill. "It's all the rage now. Making me more money than these DVDs. Are you sure you want to play with these jungleboyz?" he asked, nodding his nose to the middle of the café. It was Ramy, Omar and Jad, with their hairy legs, sitting in unison. Ramy was the worst of the jungleboyz, often squirting juice out of his nose to impress the girls of the neighborhood. Little did he know the girls called him *Makhta*, a snot. Omar, wearing his New York Yankees hat, the one he told me a million times his uncle brought back with him from Daytona Beach. And Jad, fourteen with the muscular frame of a body builder and the moustache of a bodega owner.

My recharge card was for computer 15 in a dimly lit corner that smelled like cum and sweat. The keyboards were sticky, dirtied with dust and cigarette buds. I logged in, chose "VerdunBoy23" as my username and found myself in an abandoned beige building in Havana. My fighter was already injured, he huffed and puffed in the manner of an asthmatic child. I clicked the red cross icon and brought him back to full health. Hearing the footsteps of other fighters, I ran across the stairs and ducked behind a yellow Mercedes from the eighties.

"Who the fuck is VerdunBoy23?" yelled Ramy. "No clue, but let's take him out," Omar replied as he switched his hat around. Weary of my imminent death, I ran to the basilica across the road, my legs shaking. I hid behind the altar and moved my focus left and right to catch any intruder. Ten minutes later I dashed out of the basilica only to hear a loud sniper shot and see my fighter collapse. "Khod! You think you can face the boys of NabilNet," Jad yelled as he pounded his

hand on the desk. "Bas wle, I will make you pay for that," Nabil repri-
manded him from across his office. I joined the yelling and said: Why
did you kill me Jad? I stepped out of the dark room and continued to
say: It was me. I am trying to learn the game and you guys just wasted
a two-hour recharge card. "Malouk?" Jad said with a look of surprise.
"Why didn't you tell us it was you?" – "Eh Malek, why didn't you tell
us it was you? This is a game for men. You should join GTA and play
as a stripper instead," Ramy snickered while Omar laughed and blew
air into his fist. Jad smacked Ramy's head so hard his eyes jumped out
of his face. "Kess emak, shut up Ramy! Malek, come sit next to me, I'll
show you how to play," Jad said.

I watched Jad play for an hour, his arms out and his eyes sunken.
The jungleboyz left the game, assuming the role of cheerleaders,
drumming on the table and chanting: Jad with the goodkill. He was
merciless, killing all sorts of fighters, one in Siberia, shooting him in
the chest while he was camouflaged behind a tree and another in a
post-nuclear Paris, standing on top of the Eiffel Tower, watching the
city set ablaze, killing six men in a row. When he finished, ranking
number four in Beirut, he unclenched his jaw and stretched his arms.
His face was solemn like a statue, but a minute later, he exited his
trance and said: ya hek ya bala. The jungleboyz jumped and Jad stood
up, his large dick shaking between his baggy shorts.

That evening, I stayed longer at NabilNet, my parents were in the
mountains and the jungleboyz scored more recharge cards through
Omar's Eid money. I watched their techniques, Omar skilled at duck-
ing, Jad with a falcon's eye and Ramy a patient observer, willing to wait
out any opponent. At eight p.m., a tall boy flaunting a medallion of
the Imam Ali entered the café. He asked for a one-hour recharge card
and took the computer across from Jad. He looked at us and said: Shu
shabeb? Anyone up for a fight?

"Umm, sure, you can join our tour. But be warned, I don't show
mercy to strangers," Jad said.

"I don't either," Zaher replied.

Ramy inched closer to Omar and whispered: That's the Shiite boy, Zaher, who moved here. His dad opened that bakery Pizza Hiba. They say they are Hezbollah spies. Ramy and Omar stayed out of the game, leaving Zaher and Jad to duel it out. The setting of this tour was vague, the fighters perched on the roof of an industrial building during a thunder storm. They shot at each other for thirty minutes, missing by a slight mark. Near the end of the game, Jad managed to shoot Zaher in the leg. Injured, Zaher ducked behind a collapsed satellite dish, clicking the red cross icon at a frenetic pace. Jad got closer and said: this will be a good kill. Omar and Ramy, noticing Nabil's absence, stood up, drummed across the desk and sang: good kill, good kill, good kill, Jad with the good kill. Jad stood tall, wiped the sweat off his face, looked at Zaher and said: coming here was a mistake. A minute later, a loud gunshot was heard and Jad, in disbelief fell. Zaher used a hand gun and surprised Jad with a sudden death. The game ended and Zaher was crowned king of NabilNet for the day.

The jungleboyz went quiet, packed their bags and shut off their computers. Zaher broke the silence and said: good game men. Anyone up for some shisha to celebrate?

"Nfokho," Ramy yelled. "Come on boys, let's have some ice cream away from this twat," he continued to say. Zaher fiddled with his necklace, looked at me and said: are they always jerks?

"Ramy more so than others," I replied. His sorrow-filled eyes saddened me, but in that very moment I knew that to be a great fighter I had to learn from him, not Jad. "Listen, I have a proposition for you," I said. "I want to train in combat and you have what it takes. I have a tournament coming up. How about you teach me?" – "What's in it for me?" Zaher asked. "I will pay for your recharge cards for a week," I replied. "Add chips and two cans of Pepsi and we have a deal," he said. "Manak hayen, yes, we have a deal," I said. His face wore an impish smile and he replied: see you tomorrow.

•

At five p.m., I was at NabilNet. I bought two internet recharge cards, two bags of Fantasia chips and two cans of Pepsi. I took the corner computers again, away from the jungleboyz and waited for Zaher's arrival. Ten minutes later, he walked in, ginger curls dangling from his head, delicious pecs imprinted on his shirt and long black lashes that caressed the air around him. He sat with his legs wide open and said: did you log in yet?

No, I haven't.

Well before you do, you need to change your username.

What's wrong with VerdunBoy23?

It sounds like a girl's username. And we are men here! Pick a name that will strike fear in the heart of your enemies. Like Jaafar!

I went quiet for a few minutes and workshopped names in my head until I found it: Abdulrahman's Sword. Inspired by my uncle Abed, a brutish man who after a few glasses of cognac spoke with a voice so loud it woke our neighbors. Zaher winked and said: now we're talking. We logged in to our computers and got transported to a dusty Fallujah in the midst of a busy spice bazaar. Zaher stood behind one of the vendors and I stood at the entrance of a residential building. The floor was cracked, riddled with damaged rubber tree plants, a broken office chair and a collapsed frame of *The Righteous Names of God*. A woman wearing a green hijab hid her son behind her back. "Hey are you okay?" I asked. She did not respond and just breathed. Zaher squeezed my hand and said: focus and follow me. We ran towards an empty square surrounded by four palm trees, ash brown in color. "Don't move," he yelled. I heard gun shots and saw a man falling from behind one of the palms. Zaher elbowed me and said: stay behind me, I will protect you until you are strong enough to fight.

For a week, Zaher and I camped around computers fifteen and sixteen, inhaling and exhaling together, sharing Unica bars and Fantasia chips until at one point we found our hands inside the same salt and vinegar bag. Zaher laughed, took a few of the chips out and handed them to me. The jungleboyz ignored us except Jad who assailed me with his eyes, angry at my betrayal. Though I did not care. Zaher was all I needed. He taught me the thrill of the fight. One evening, he played for four hours straight, the boys pouring in from across Hamra and Verdun to witness his marvel. Nabil, never one to miss an opportunity, charged each one of them a watching fee of five thousand liras. I sat next to him, opening his fourth Pepsi can as he shot every fighter he came across. His rage was endless. He entered the fifth hour, it was getting dark, the boys tired from standing, left one after another, gifting NabilNet to Zaher and me. Catching a breath, he looked at me and said: feed me some chips. I reached for the cheese-flavored Fantasia and put some over his tongue and bits of my right finger entered his mouth. I repeated this act, until Zaher, satiated, said: khalas, thanks habibi. We neared the end of the game, he was overcome with excitement, his body hotter than the modem next to us. His right leg shook with an intensity that caused our chairs to move as if we were in an earthquake. I closed my eyes and took in this euphoria, shaking along with him. A voice then woke me up from my trance, it was Zaher yelling: ЕНННННН. His elated tone carried a feminine inflection within it. He ended the fight and moved his index finger across the screen, counting the nationwide rankings: Zaher number two. He stood up, championed his arms in the air and looked around the café only to realize it was just us and Nabil, having his falafel sandwich. I opened a Unica bar for him and said: who cares about these assholes?

He walked over to the door and yelled to the air: exactly, who cares about these assholes! He then looked at me and said: I'm glad my best bro was here with me. Hearing him say that, my heart jumped out of my chest. To celebrate, we walked over to Mahmaset Rabea, one of the few stores that imported green apple Airheads from the US. We sat in the parking lot of my building, under a Jacaranda tree, the leaves of which filtered out the light from the streetlamps, revealing red veins swimming inside Zaher's green eyes. He ate the last of the Airheads, licking his tongue and making a loud bang sound. He fist-bumped me and said: it's time to find a service (taxi) home. "It's not safe at this hour," I said. "Oh please, I used to take taxis from Bent Jbeil to Beirut at the age of ten. See these guns, they're all I need," he said while he kissed his right bicep. I wished I could kiss them too.

Knocking my house door, teta greeted me with her inquisitive eyes, covered in a fume of double apple shisha. "Sorry I'm late. I didn't realize the time," I said. "I won't tell your mom if you won't tell her I'm feeding the snake," she said, a term she loved to use when she smoked shisha. "No humidity tonight, thank god," I said. "We are lucky to have this balcony. My mother, allah yerhama, was always in heat in Beirut. She came from the north and prayed that God shelters her from the humidity. And since that prayer, the breeze never left this house," she said while smoking her shisha. "Listen, I'm happy you're enjoying the summer with new friends, but I don't want you to hang out with this Zaher kid so much. Jad's mother told me about him," she continued to say. "Why? He's sweet and polite. And he's teaching me some games," I replied.

"I'm sure he is. But you know ever since Rafiq Al Hariri was assassinated, the situation is tense. And I heard from Latifa who heard from Abu Mahmud that Hezbollah is funding his father to open a bakery in our neighborhood. They are spies. Be careful," she said while changing the coal over her shisha. A bit of the ash fell to the ground, she ignored it and said: I'll clean it later.

"You're watching too many movies, teta," I replied. "Malek, you did not live through the war. Think about it. Now it's time for bed, go inside and close the balcony door behind you," she commanded. Sitting in bed, watching the ceiling fan spin out of control, the flowers carved on it dancing like dervishes, I replayed feeding Zaher chips in my head. I left my grandmother's words on the balcony, what did she know!

•

It's three days till Damascus, I was happy to see Ghaith, but sad to leave Zaher. My parents went to the mountains to clean and lock our house and my grandma went to her sister's home in Zareef. Heading down to the taxi she yelled: Why can't Sumayyah come here? That part of Beirut smells like *Baharat* (seven spices)! At five p.m. I was at NabilNet waiting for Zaher. He came in fifteen minutes later, this time his smell proceeded him. It was a strange fragrance, as if one drowsed a field of lilies with gasoline. "Nice perfume," I said. "Man, this is all the rage. Fahrenheit by this brand called Dior. I know this woman Zainab who sells unbought testers from the airport duty free. Only fifty thousand liras!" he said, happy I noticed his scent. "I'll buy you one next time I go to her shop," he continued to say. This time I could not hide my explosive smile as I said: hey listen, my parents are out of town till ten p.m. You want to come over? We can take a break from *Counter* and watch the Comedy Channel. Why not? Do you have a shisha at home? Eh, my grandma smokes, but I don't know how to make it. Bro, I'm the *argileh* king, I'll make it.

Entering the house, Zaher took his shoes off, put them aside and went into the kitchen. He maneuvered his way around it with ease, as if he had been here many times before. I watched his feet dance around our blue and white terrazzo tiles and his long arms reach for the cupboards, conjuring an afternoon snack of Lays chips, *janarek* (sour green plums) and Pepsi. "You can call me Argaljeh," he said. "I love calling you Zaher," I said with a muffled tone. When he finished his shisha operation, he smiled and said: let's smoke it on the balcony, it's nicer with the breeze. I loved that he indulged himself in the manner of an Ottoman prince.

Sitting on the balcony, I was faced with my grandfather's sepia portrait, with his almond-shaped eyes and his olive-colored suit. He had a black line painted over his head, a sign that someone was martyred. Though he was no martyr, in fact he was an infamous womanizer, who died in the arms of a prostitute who lived near the port of Beirut. Her name was Warde and she wore silk whenever she saw him. My grandfather spent three nights a week at Warde's house, returning home, with a smile cast in iron, and smelling of rose water. My grandmother could not handle that he died in the arms of his mistress so she lied and added the black line.

•

Zaher, sitting under my grandfather, smoked his shisha, pursed his lips together and blew large circles of smoke. At one point, he put his finger in the middle of a circle, bringing it back and forth, until the smoke dissipated. Watching him, the tingling sensation in my groin returned.

My ears turned red and I felt as hot as Zaher's computer during a game. "Come sit next to me and try it," Zaher said. I jumped across to the couch with an attempt to hide my erection. "Ntebeh, you might break your grandma's shisha," he said while laughing. I sat quietly next to him for a few minutes, the pipe and its burly sounds between our legs. I broke the silence and said: I'm glad we became friends. "We're not friends. We're brothers," he said, pressing his hairy arms around my back. I saw an erection coming out of his shorts and it was the sign I needed to know he's comfortable. I reclined my head on his chest while he played with my hair and smoked his shisha, sending a double apple cloud out to the streets.

We stayed like that for ten minutes, in solitude like a Beirut Sunday, until Zaher, noticing my mother's orange Nokia phone, said: damn is that a Nokia 5200?!

Eh, it's my mom's. She leaves it here when she goes to the mountains, in case I need to reach her. There's no landline there.

Can I see it?

Sure, we can play Snake if you want.

Zaher reached for the phone, his face a hall of excited impressions. I helped him slide it up and we opened the game. He played a round of Snake, called my house phone as I answered and said: hello you've reached KFC Rouche and laughed.

I watched him play, mesmerized, but I wanted to get his attention again. "You can also send pictures to others via Bluetooth, my mom does that all the time," I said. "Here, let me show you," I continued to say.

I opened the Bluetooth gallery and when I clicked on the latest photo, my heart dropped to my knees. It was a meme of Hassan Nasrallah, Hezbollah's spiritual and political leader, superimposed on Haifa Wehbe's album cover, *Bady Eeesh*. Haifa, wearing pink silk, posing in a bout of ennui, with her right index finger in her mouth. Except this time, it was not the face of a seductress, it was the face of Hassan Nasrallah floating over her body.

Never mind, I said, I don't think it's working.

What's wrong?

Nothing, ensa.

"Shu fee," he exclaimed as he stole the phone and opened the gallery. It took him a minute to take it in and then he looked at me and smacked my chin with the phone, closing the slider. He stood up and said: you are just like those assholes at NabilNet.

It's not me! It's my mother's phone, Zaher come on!

Fuck you. You were just using me to learn *Counter* and fit in with the rest of them.

He rushed to the door to put on his shoes.

"Zaher please I'm sorry," I yelled.

He stood at the door and said: if you ever come near me again, I will break your legs. He slammed the door causing my neighbor Nada to open hers and yell: Shu fee!

I went back to the balcony, still smelling of double apple, cursing my luck. A bird came out of my grandma's clock announcing it was ten p.m. My parents were almost home! I cleaned the shisha to the bone, took out the garbage and rubbed a few of the naphthalene balls on the couch.

When my mother arrived with a dusty and drab look, she said: yih yih, I need a shower and rushed to the bathroom. I was relieved she did not have time to take notice of the house and I went to bed, with an anger festering towards her and her memes.

The next day, I camped out at NabilNet for hours. Sequestered in my dark room, I watched the door from the corners of computer fifteen and awaited his arrival with a bag of Airheads and Pepsi. An hour passed and so did the jungleboyz, who drenched the floor with their wet bathing suits, returning from their swim at the military beach. "Ya kleb! Go outside now. You think you can just come and play with your wet clothes like monkeys! La barra." Nabil yelled. At eight p.m., during the call for prayer, I accepted my defeat and walked home. The *athan* sounded more melancholic today, slow and elongated pronunciations, like the prayer recital for the deceased. Entering the house, my grandma greeted me with a plate of *lahm b ajeen*. "Have some good food before you go to all that fat and lard in Syria," she said. I had four of them, oily and crispy, with the taste of the minced meat waltzing inside my mouth. My grandma did not bother asking what happened, though reading my facial expressions, she assumed Zaher and I were no more and it made her happy.

●

During my last days in Beirut, I avoided walking by Pizza Hiba, taking the longer route to Hamra up the Koraytem hill. Zaher stopped coming to NabilNet, which made the jungleboyz happy, Ramy saying: back to southern Beirut where he belongs. If only they understood his beauty and the way he embraced me.

That summer in Damascus, Zaher's words stayed with me: Shift left. Duck. Walk slower. Shoot from the right side of the eye. Don't hide behind cars. His training led me to the top five fighters list in Damascus, my cousin, starstruck, showed me off in front of his friends. "I told you he was Kafou," he said. Soon after, I forgot about Zaher. A few months later, playing at NabilNet, the jungleboyz, now my cheerleaders, applauded and drummed for me: Malek with the good kill. Jad stood next to me, proud that I was back in their terrain, and watched as I neared the end of the game. I saw the last remaining fighter, hiding behind a car, his gun peeping. "Amateur," I shouted. As I pointed at him from across a town square, he ambushed me, shooting from beneath the car. I fell, the jungleboyz yelling: nooooooo. Jad comforted me and said: it happens to the best of us. I looked across the screen, curious to see who he was, and the name said: Zaher.

Raise Your Head High

LEILA ABOULELA

TANTE WALAA WAS MY SISTER'S MOTHER-IN-LAW. IN A ROUND-about way she was family and I could not wriggle away from her. She was a widow with two sons; the eldest, Amer, was married to my sister Dunia and the younger, Shadi, was still in school, struggling with his coursework. I was asked to tutor him in physics but I said no. It wasn't only because Tante Walaa had no intention to pay me. It was because I knew Shadi was a weak student and, to be honest, I couldn't be bothered. When I said I was too busy to give private lessons Dunia looked at me with silent reproach and Amer asked, more annoyed than curious, "Busy with what?" I just ignored him. Tante Walaa, on the other hand, kept pretending that sometime soon I was going to get round to helping Shadi with his GCSE physics. She would call me and seeing her name on the screen, I wouldn't pick up. She left messages using my nickname and saying that she missed me. "You're a naughty girl, dodging me," she'd say. "But I know that you love us and want the best for Shadi."

One day I found myself alone in her flat. By alone, I meant in her company without Dunia or Amer. It was like I needed them to justify my connection to her or act as go-betweens. Tante Walaa lived in a flat above them and I had been there before, joining in family meals where the table was overladen with food that was varied but not especially tasty. On that afternoon it was winter, the sky threatening rain and in the streets men covered their mouths with woolen scarves which made their eyes look even more sullen.

It happened like this. First, I was visiting Dunia and she said we should go out to eat. I would rather have stayed in the warmth but she insisted. "I can't imprison myself at home waiting for the repairman, I need to live my life." Telephone in hand, she'd been threatening and pleading with the shop where she had bought her dishwasher. Two nights earlier, it flooded the floor with dirty water. Since then an electrician was meant to visit but so far he hadn't shown up and Dunia was becoming frustrated, afraid to use the dishwasher and make another mess.

As we stepped out into the landing, she said, "I need to nip upstairs to Tante Walaa and leave her my key in case he finally does show up. Then I will tell the doorman to send him up to her." I could have waited while Dunia ran upstairs with the key or I could have gone down to the street without her. But she said, "Come with me to say a quick hello to Tante Walaa." I groaned out loud but she pulled my arm. I figured it would be rude to refuse to go up. It would look as if I hated her mother-in-law. "We'll be quick," she reassured me. "We won't even have to go in."

My sister bounded up ahead of me. The staircase was dark and smelled of garbage. Dunia was flexible and strong. At least in comparison to me. I had a handicap that was slight enough to go almost unnoticed; it was a secret that only doctors, Dunia and our late parents knew about. I kept it close to myself and didn't talk about it. I was holding down a job that many would consider good. What else did people want from me? Tante Walaa opened the door of her flat and was happy to see me. "Come in, Nada. You must come in," she repeated while Dunia made up excuses and held out the key of her flat explaining about the repairman on his way to fix the dishwasher.

Suddenly we heard him below us, dropping his toolbox on the floor and ringing the bell. Dunia dashed downstairs, calling out to him that she was on her way. "Come in," Tante Walaa was beaming at me. "You can't stand in the doorway like that."

Her flat was the exact layout as Amer and Dunia's except that everything in theirs was brand new and hers was like stepping into the past. There was a complicated reason why she hadn't swapped flats with Amer and Dunia so as to climb fewer stairs. I had heard it once and it made perfect sense at the time but now I couldn't remember. There was no elevator in the building and she struggled with or without shopping. I stepped into her sitting room. It was full of formal, heavy furniture, oversize sofas that only guests sat on and an elaborate, large dining table. In summary, ugly.

The dining table was laden with plastic bags, disjointed objects and what looked like bric-a-brac. "I'm selling all this for charity," she explained. "I'm helping a widowed mother. Here have a look!"

She seated me at the dining table and began to show me the things. "That's nice," I said fingering a prayer set with embroidery around the edges.

"It's for you," she said, bundling the set into a plastic bag and shoving it towards me. She named a high price. I started to tell her that I already had one but she cut me off.

"For charity," she said, her nose shining. "We have to help those less fortunate than us. Don't we? I feel so sorry for this lady. She has a son who needs private tutors on top of the school fees. So expensive. Look at this. What do you think?" She held out a brass candleholder.

"I never light candles," I said.

"But you're helping someone and getting something pretty too." She placed it on top of the prayer set. "And here's a lovely pair of pajamas." They weren't lovely. They were in a ghastly shade of green. "Try them on. Go on. I am quite alone. There is no one here. Or go change in the bathroom if you like."

"No need." I mumbled.

She was already walking away towards the kitchen. I knew she was going to bring me a drink or sweets. I should have stopped her and insisted that I needed to go down to Dunia. To be with her while the repairman dealt with the dishwasher.

Tante Walaa came out of the kitchen with a can of Miranda and a glass on a tray. "I'm glad the pajamas are your size," she said as if the matter was settled.

"Look," I protested. "I don't want the pajamas or anything."

"Why not? It's not as if you can't afford them." There was a sting in her voice.

"Where did you get all these things from?" I asked her.

"They're brand new," she said as if taking offense. "Don't think they're second hand or anything like that! Would I be cheating you?" Her voice rose, "That poor widow has an older son but he's married now. His flat is full of brand new things. And that's not easy, that's a strain so she doesn't like to impose on him and ask for money. He does help her from time to time, but his focus is on his new wife now. It's natural I suppose. Can't blame him."

I nodded. A widow with two sons, the older newly married and the younger in school. What a coincidence! But surely she wouldn't be so blatant. Or would she?

"Look, this is really special." With pride, she lifted up a box. There was a saucepan inside it. "It's no ordinary saucepan. You plug it into the wall and it cooks everything extremely slowly. Perfect for you. While you're at work, it does all the cooking." She named a price.

"Impossible." I stood up and started heading towards the door.

She grabbed my shoulder and her voice rose. "Don't turn me down. For the soul of your mother. For her dear soul. You will not turn me down." Her grip on my shoulder tightened, like it wasn't friendly anymore. She almost pushed me so that I was sitting down at the dining table again. "Nada, be reasonable now. Consider the money you are spending as a mercy towards your mother."

It upset me that she mentioned my mother. I remembered the first time she collapsed, and I took her to hospital. They wouldn't even examine her until we paid straight up. The way they treated us — it was as if we weren't human. I was only in my second year at university and my bankcard didn't have enough on it.

Tante Walaa was going on and on about the slow cooker. We started to haggle over the price. Back and forth. I pushed. I went through the motions but she was tough and it wasn't as if I were in a shop. I felt restricted. At the end of the day she was family so there were certain lines I couldn't cross. She went on praising the cooker. "When you come home, there'll be a freshly cooked warm meal waiting for you. I know you work hard. This is exactly what you need."

I explained in detail why I wouldn't use it. It was as if I hadn't spoken. She dashed into the kitchen again determined to bring me all the other accessories that came with the cooker. I walked over to the window. High identical buildings, painted grey with pollution, crammed with people and their junk. The washing lines were heavy with winter clothes, puffy dressing gowns and men's pajamas. Dirt stuck to everything, even to the leaves of the trees. Down in the street, a little girl with uncombed hair was rummaging through the trash. She wore a jumper, but no socks, her dirty feet in plastic slippers. Cold, poor and unschooled. Yet she could hurt me if she needed to and, given half a chance, steal my handbag. She would tell lies and use filthy swear words.

When I turned away from the window, the vision in my left eye was blurred. I could see properly only to one side so I tipped my head and scrunched up my nose. In the gilded mirror above the settee, my face looked pale and stretched. Tante Walaa looked solid and happy. "These things could be for your trousseau, Nada. Yes, why not? Soon you too will find a bridegroom. Nowadays young men want a strong earner like you. It's hard times not like in the old days. Believe me, they will overlook other things." My legs felt heavy and my feet too small as if I were a boxing stand. When punched I would sway but never ever fall over. I started to answer her but something in the way she said that last bit about overlooking faults made me stop.

It went on and on. She was sure I needed a garish painting, a set of mugs, a handbag and a linen set. I suddenly had this strange detached feeling that I was waiting for her to reach a level of satisfaction, only then would she let me get out of here. I wanted her satiated but her appetite was strong. When the cash in my handbag wasn't enough, she made me sign receipts that added up to a whole month's salary. I felt a sweeping down pressure inside my stomach. She looked triumphant and I felt sick.

The walk down the dark staircase to Dunia's flat was even more blurred. Amer was now with her. I stood in front of them in the living room, the splashing sound of the now functioning dishwasher in the background. They were not a romantic couple; I could never pick up a sexual charge between them or a thick longing. Not like it had been with Dunia's ex-boyfriend, Emad. They had been passionately in love but Dunia wanted everything perfect. When she caught him out once – no, not with another woman – but walking into a psychiatrist's office, she dumped him. Then picked Amer up. He was flattered and grateful at the beginning but over time, and especially after our father's death, Amer was hardening. I had never heard him and Dunia talk about anything except their flat and its contents, about shopping deals and prices. They were life partners and not lovers; they were colleagues not mates. You'd think they were in the same business together, the project of setting up, stocking and maintaining a new flat.

They exclaimed over my purchases but did not seem to need much explanation; it was as if they already understood. I complained about my migraine. Dunia gave me Valium and I headed straight for their guest room. I had stayed over with them many times and the room was familiar. I lay down on the bed and dozed. I know it sounds over the top and most likely it was a scene from a film I've watched, but I dreamt that I was toiling away in the building of a pyramid. Around me the other slaves were being whipped and shouted at. When one of them collapsed to the ground, the rock he had been carrying rolled towards me, to crush me and no one could stop it because everyone else was struggling with their lot.

Dunia and Amer were talking about me. Perhaps they did not feel the need to whisper. Amer said, "Serves her right for refusing to tutor Shadi. It's not as if she doesn't know how much private lessons will cost!" I sat up in order to listen but only Amer's words were clear. Dunia's tone of voice sounded like she was defending me. He replied, "She's sorted with that computer job of hers. No one hit her on her hand." He meant I wasn't forced into buying anything. He said, "Your beloved sister earns more than me," as if it was all my fault. Dunia's whine made me frightened. I guessed that she had aggravated him by criticizing his mother.

The medicine made me doze until I felt her cool hand on my forehead, her voice gentle with concern. After our mother passed away, Dunia started mothering me. I looked up to her and always asked her advice. Today she was wearing her checkered coat, the one we bought together at the sales. "I have to go to my shift now, Nada. Don't get up till you're well enough to drive. Promise me. Wait till I come back and we can eat together. Or you can even spend the night. Yes, that would be best."

I woke up to his voice. It sounded reproachful and mocking. Amer was sitting close to me on the side of the bed. He tugged my ear in a playful way but it was painful and his voice was mean. "Why did you buy too many things? Throwing money around like a millionaire, then you have the nerve to complain! Speak. Speak up." His finger was now below my chin, jerking my jaw upwards. "Look at me! Speak. Don't you have a tongue?" I ground my teeth together. If I let them go slack, my teeth would rattle. I moved my head away and tried to sit up. He pushed me down. He smelled of cigarettes and his leather jacket. I started to kick and shout. But women shouted up and down this building all the time, no one paid any attention.

The more I fought him, the stronger he became. "You have the nerve to blame my mother! How dare you. She's better than you. A hundred times over. Say it! Say, she's better than me." His other hand was now inside in my hair, the fingers pressed into my skull. He tilted my head back as if I were at the dentist and my mouth forced open ready for the cold pain. "Don't. Please don't."

He yanked at my hair, "You have to repeat it. You have to say it in a loud voice."

"She is better than me," I whispered.

"A hundred times over. Say it."

"A hundred times over."

He smiled. "Good. You should go out of your way to please her. That's how it should be."

"Let me go." With all my energy, I pushed him away. "Get away from me."

He stood up but his hand still jabbed at my forehead tipping it back. "What's all the fuss about? Do you think I'm going to rape you? In your dreams. I'm not even attracted to you. No man would be." He looked down at my thigh as if he could see through my jeans. "Dunia said it's the ugliest piece of skin she'd ever seen in her life. It gave her nightmares." I gasped at the shock. She had told him; she had actually told him.

I was already in the car, cold fingers round the steering wheel, when he came down carrying my things. He tossed them in the back seat as if this was a normal day and he was helping me with my shopping. My heart sank when he said he needed to go back upstairs and get the rest of the things, they were that many! I should have opened the boot for him and tidied things up. But I felt safe in the driver's seat, belt locked and the engine running. When I drove off, the back seat was littered and piled with stuff I neither needed nor liked.

The migraine made the drive home feel weird, the city uglier than ever. Not the City Victorious but the City Oppressor. I drove through damp muddy streets, other cars pressed against me, their drivers hating me. A few drops of rain fell on the windshield, wiping it left streaks of dirt. I passed the City of the Dead, those houses that looked like houses but were empty if you passed through the tall metal gates. No buildings, no pyramids, just wrapped dead bodies under the ground, without earth surrounding them, scattered in a room to become sacks of bones.

The medicine made me slow, and all the things around closer than they usually were. Stopping at the traffic light, I heard pounding. Someone was trying to smash the back window. I started to shout and even beeped my horn to scare them off. Instead, one of them used a stick and the glass shattered. A hand reached inside and grabbed at the plastic bags piled on the seat. Another pair of thin arms covered in dirty and faded flowery material were hauling what they could, lifting out then reaching in again. The light changed, I pressed the accelerator and heard her scream. "You broke it, you bitch." Later in every nightmare I would hear the bone crack.

This was what the city's billboards were saying, the meanings hidden behind conventional words. This was the graffiti on the walls. The hieroglyphs on stone. This was the city's survival tactics, its street wisdom and rules. More visceral than poetry, deeper than propaganda. What I read, what I heard, what was taught, what was known. *Lie when you are in a tight spot / It is normal to hate the weak. It is their fault that they are weak. The weak need protection. They will pay for it with money and labor or obedience and loyalty, they will pay for it with their honor. Complexity is superior to simplicity / Underestimating or overestimating are serious mistakes / Every single encounter is a power struggle / Underline your accomplishments. Boast of your success. Otherwise someone else will take all the credit.*

•

Dunia and I had always been close. I was furious that she had shared my secret. Years ago, our parents had told us not to speak of it. They did not want me to be pitied or looked at with disgust. A fourth-degree burn caused by a childhood accident. When it healed it looked like a large flat navel on my inner thigh. I got used to it; I stopped thinking about it. At the beach I wore leggings under my swimsuit, and everyone thought I was being modest. I could have had plastic surgery, but my parents said no need, too much expense, thank God it's not her face. Would she find a husband? Sure, "all women are alike in the dark."

Amer denied that he had even entered the guest room let alone touched me. *Lie when you are in a tight spot.* He claimed that I was accusing him of rape (I never did) due to my "sick imagination" and "state of deprivation as an unmarried woman." In a flash, he became the injured party and I, the jealous younger sister, the warped homewrecker. When I reached out to Dunia she snubbed me; when I phoned, she didn't pick up.

I took my car to the dealer to get the smashed window fixed. The mechanic I spoke to said he was too busy to get the work done within an hour, it would have to wait. Until when? He just shrugged his shoulders. He looked at me with complete disinterest as if he was too world-weary and important to deal with my request. A 20-pound note would get him moving and he would take it in broad daylight even though the office of his superior with its glass windows was just behind him. After what happened with Tante Walaa, I was in no position to part with more money. So, there I was in the garage arguing and pleading, when a man walked out of the office and called my name. I didn't recognize him at first — glasses instead of contact lenses, hair slightly longer. He turned out to be Emad, Dunia's ex, the one she had dumped after finding out that he was getting psychiatric treatment. Emad said he was working for his father now. I hadn't known that the garage belonged to his father. He turned to the mechanic who was already standing straighter. "What's the car needing?" The mechanic replied that fixing the window was simple and he could get it done within an hour. *Every encounter is a power struggle.*

"Why don't you come and wait inside," Emad said.

Normally I would have said no thanks, hopped into a taxi and killed the time at Dunia's. My only other option now was to wander around and find a coffee shop with good Wi-Fi. It was cold and miserable, so I accepted Emad's invitation. Besides, seeing me on friendly terms with the owner's son, the mechanic was bound to get my window fixed in the shortest possible time.

Emad's office was protected from the draft and he ordered me a hot drink. We exchanged small talk but didn't mention Dunia. He expressed his condolences for the death of our mother. We shared memories of her. I sipped my drink and started to relax. A woman walked in. She was visibly pregnant. What startled me was how uninhibited she was. "Come with me to the demonstration," she said to Emad. I remembered the video that was doing the rounds on social media. *Meet in the square on Tuesday, enough is enough with this government, let's make a change.*

Her name was Sally. I immediately sent a text to Dunia. "You won't believe who I'm with now? Emad's wife." *Underline your accomplishments. Boast of your success.* Dunia was bound to be interested in her ex. And we could slip back to how we were, our stupid quarrel forgotten.

Sally was different than Dunia — especially in looks, hair all naturally frizzy and wearing dungarees. But there is no need to describe her because the whole world got to know her. She was the one in the news photo that spread from Washington to Kuala Lumpur. The pregnant woman standing up to the snarling soldier, her belly between them, her unborn baby inches away from his gun. Sally the icon of the revolution, the face of the Arab Spring. That taut bulging stomach thrust out against the brutality. Innocence and hope leading the rebellion, coming smack up against the vicious army. But that came later. As did all the praise — *Our Revolution is a Mother. We're sacrificing for our unborn children. Fearless Sally*... And then the condemnation and envy — *But how could she expose her unborn child to the teargas ... How could she be so careless ... What kind of mother-to-be is that ... For God's sake the battleground is no place for a six-month-old fetus.* To be honest, Emad said this last sentence to her too but in gentle tones, more timid than assertive, nothing like the venom poured on her on social media. But the photo and all that it brought was still in the future. On that afternoon when my car window was getting fixed, she was still a stranger to me. I witnessed the exchange between her and Emad. Sally, insistent that he shut down the garage for the day and let his employees go to the protest.

I kept glancing at my phone waiting for Dunia to answer my text. Instead of feeling awkward, I was captivated by the discussion between Emad and Sally. "I have my father to think of," he said. "I am not my own man."

"Yes, you are. I'm sure of it," she said, with the kind of confidence that was contagious.

I got to know them well after that, indeed it was with Sally that I went to my very first protest. She was a natural leader; there was a charisma about her and an ancient fearlessness which that famous photo later captured. "My new friends," I sent a selfie of the three of us to the silent Dunia but instead of the grudging but affectionate reply I expected, she wrote, "I can't believe you can be so inconsiderate."

I phoned and she did not reply. I rang the bell of her flat and she didn't open though I knew she was inside. Surely, she would soften. Surely, she would be missing me by now. *Overestimating is a serious error.*

No longer seeing her or going over to her place, I suddenly had plenty of time on my hands and a lot of bewilderment. Emad and Sally took me in or at least partially filled the gap. Sally wanted another listener, another follower. Emad was happy to make her happy. I had never been greatly interested in activism. My knowledge of local and international politics was shaky. But now when Sally spoke about power and injustice, I understood.

Things got to the point with Dunia where I was desperate enough to appeal to Tante Walaa. I dragged myself up the stairs. Shadi opened the door for me. I hadn't seen him for quite some time. He had shot up and now had a new wisp of a moustache. Behind him the dining table was empty. He looked at me as if he didn't know who I was. It occurred to me that everything was his fault. Or rather my fault for refusing to tutor him. One "no" had let lose all this animosity and lost me my sister. *Underestimating is a serious mistake.*

"How's the physics going, Shadi?" I couldn't help myself.

Tante Walaa's appearance saved him the trouble of answering. She didn't invite me to sit. "How dare you!" she shouted. "After all we've done for you."

What had they done for me? I couldn't remember any favors.

"Dunia took care of you after your parents died. She put up with your defect. And in return you want to wreck her home! Your heart is black. Do you think I would welcome you after what you said about my son! He was decisive. He said, 'Dunia, it's either me or your sister, choose.' And here you are playing dumb. A speciality with you. So, let me tell it to you straight. Don't you dare step into my home again. This whole building is forbidden to you."

I left but not before abusing both her sons. The elder for being a bully and the younger for being a lazy student. "I hope to God he fails physics," I said but as I spoke, I realized that it was easy to turn on those who were younger. *It is normal to hate the weak. It is their fault that they are weak.* My new friends had made me aware that this was cowardly. I took a deep breath and faced the one who was older than me, the one who had more power. "You're a liar," I said to Tante Walaa. "Pretending to sell all this junk for charity when you were keeping all the money for yourself."

Months passed when I neither met Dunia nor spoke to her on the phone.

I missed her so much that I sometimes wanted to apologize to her and Amer, even though I was the one wronged. They were the only family I had. When I heard Sally talking about how in police cells and secret prisons people were confessing to crimes they hadn't committed, I understood. I could imagine that you only had to squeeze someone hard enough and repeat the lie over and over again. Then they would name names and – without the need to invent for it would be spelt out for them – they would tell their interrogators everything they wanted to hear.

The city erupted. Individually, collectively, in clusters and in groups people took to the streets and protested. For years, some people had been demonstrating against the government, but no one took them seriously. My parents thought of them as troublemakers. That January and February it was different. The protests built up momentum, people at work were leaving early, or weren't showing up at all. One afternoon I was the only one under thirty still at my desk. As always, the work absorbed me but I felt left out. The protests were where it was all happening, the square was the place to be.

When the government shut down the internet, Sally called and asked for my help. "You are a computer whiz," she said. "Come over and help." I didn't hesitate. It was a challenge after all and as I drove away from the office, I had all sorts of ideas on how to bypass the regular access and get round the shutdown. Within the hour I was with a group of computer engineers and programmers like myself. Try this and that; be creative, go on and don't give up. For several hours, I was so absorbed that I almost forgot why we were doing this. Maybe for the others getting back the internet was a means to an end but for me it became the ultimate achievement. Eventually we pulled it off. We managed to find a way to circumvent the shutoff by going back to old-fashioned dial-up. The breakthrough was pure joy. I almost cried. After that there was no going back. The revolution was not an abstract concept, I was in the thick of it, a hacker, someone who had taken part!

We marched to the square and though, at first, I felt self-conscious, the mood took a hold of me. Here was a place where I could never be lonely, where I didn't feel helpless and I didn't feel handicapped. Demanding change, urging each other to be proud. "Raise your head up high," we chanted. "You are more honorable than the one who trampled you." The sit-in started; the tents set up. Portable toilets, vendors selling snacks, rotas for meals and for standing guard. Such good will, such purity of intention. Street art. A concert, talks, Friday prayers, Coptic Mass, bride and groom in all their wedding finery, sandwiches and tea. In the square at night, around a small fire in a brazier, I started to believe in a change that would put everything to rights.

Photos, even that famous one of Sally, don't tell the whole story. What we heard, what we felt in the streets. The acrid constant fear, the heat, the beat of a drum, the hubbub of voices, a high pitch of a woman calling out, the low rustle of wind through the trees, the sudden loud din and tinny echo of a microphone getting started. Sweaty palms and hoarse throats. The exhilaration of being all together, anger coalesced, a cry against injustice and fear, and later collective grief.

When we sang the national anthem tears ran down my face. Love was the flag swaying, love for this homeland with all its shame and damning faults, this city with its new alien ugliness, the desert and river that pulsed the span of our lives.

Voice messages to Dunia ... *I might die any day here and you are my flesh and blood ... How can you be so hard-hearted ... When I see Emad with Sally I know that you married the wrong man . . . Get out of this marriage, Dunia, you deserve better . . .* Her reply eventually came, her voice . . . *Can't you see that you are making things worse? Putting me in an impossible situation . . .*

Day after day, I carried cartons of water to the protestors in the square, I carried medical supplies and blankets. At times people referred to me as "Sally's friend" and I glowed. When I got tired, which often happened sooner than I wanted, I would sit down and upload material on social media. I would write to Dunia and say to her, "Here is where you need to be." Around me others were carrying Molotov cocktails in Pepsi crates. They crouched behind metal barriers they had ripped up from the petrol station.

One night I saw her, Dunia. It must be her; it must be. I shoved my laptop in my bag and stood up. Suddenly it was as if everyone was shouting orders. The dreaded sound was either rubber bullets or stones beating against the lampposts and the tents. Through the gas and smoke, I could still see Dunia's checkered coat. I hobbled up to her, the tears streaming down my face. I wanted a hug. My sister was here because she understood. Everything would be alright between us like it was before. Dunia turned to face me. "Run," she screamed. The security forces were firing birdshot. I looked behind me and we started to run from the truncheons and the thugs.

Here, Freedom

DANIAL HAGHIGHI

Translated from Persian by Salar Abdoh

WE WERE SITTING ON THE BALCONY WATCHING VIDEOS OF THE demonstrations in Tehran on our cellphones.

I told her, "This is the big one. This time they can't just roll things up like all the times before."

She was resting her head on my chest, watching the screen. "Is it really possible? Talk to me, Asghar. Tell me we'll be free. We could go to concerts from now on. Go to the beach — and I could wear a bikini! Tell me it's not all a dream."

"It's not a dream, my love. It's real. We've turned into a nation of lions."

"But the other afternoon when you were away, it got pretty rough around here. They hurt a lot of people."

"I know. But it's different this time. Don't look at this nowhere town we live in. In the big cities, and not just in Tehran, no one's backing down."

She did not skip a beat: "Then I'm not wearing a hijab either, from now on. I'm going to the salon to bleach my hair. Afterwards, I'm going to the city."

"City? What city?"

"You just called this a 'nowhere town.' And I agree. I want to go where the action is. Tehran, Mashhad, Tabriz, Esfahan . . . wherever."

"What about me?"

"You can get yourself a new wife, darling."

"I don't want a new wife."

"But ours was an arranged marriage."

"Of course it was. Every marriage is arranged in this town. And what's wrong with that?"

"Everything's wrong with it. My youth was wasted on us, my dear. I like you, but I don't love you. This town has slim pickings, and you and I got paired. Now I want out." She pulled herself upright, put the cellphone away, and stared into my eyes. "If women are going to get their freedom, why should I spend the rest of my life with you? I don't even like a man with blue eyes."

"You don't like my blue eyes?"

"I don't trust them."

"Then you're going to find someone with brown eyes?"

"What I mean is, I'm not staying in this backwater anymore."

"Fine. We'll go to Rasht. Maybe even Shiraz. But, let's admit, Tehran's a bit expensive."

She rolled her eyes. "If this government goes, you'll have an army of women who'll love your light hair and blue eyes. Come, let's agree to get a divorce. Don't waste yourself on me, dearest."

"You're being serious? If this regime falls, you want a divorce?"

"Yes."

"Not on my life."

"I am being honest with you, Asghar. How can you say you love me if you don't appreciate my honesty?"

"I actually never said I loved you."

"See? If you don't love me, so much the more reason we should go our separate ways."

"Are you insane? I'm out there every day, working myself stiff for a piece of bread and a roof over our heads, and you're talking about divorce?"

"Asghar, whether you like it or not, I want a divorce."

"But why?"

"Why? Because this life we live is empty. Empty! You think anyone will ever again want to watch a film with a woman wearing hijab once we're free? Our lives are a lie, my precious. A woman in her own kitchen wearing hijab because she in a movie or a TV series. Do I wear a hijab in my kitchen?"

I shook my head.

"Exactly. It's all a big lie. Admit it. And now the big lie is ending. Get used to it."

She got up and left without another word. Went to her mother's house, like all the other times we'd had a falling-out. Two days later, when she returned, I'd been thinking.

I said, "I'll give you back your dowry. Go do whatever the hell you want with it."

"And what do you want?" she asked.

"A Peugeot. I've always wanted to drive a Peugeot. Without both of us to support, I can buy myself one of those beauties and move to Tehran and take my blue eyes with me."

"So all that talk of 'you are my one and only' was just for show?"

"I swear, the thought of freedom got me truly thinking."

"You're not man enough yet for freedom. I was testing you to see what you'd do. You want a damn Peugeot out of all this. That's all you care about."

"But —"

"No *but*. Let's watch some 'Woman, Life, Freedom' videos tonight. What do you say?"

". . . I say whatever you say, my one and only."

The Agency

NATASHA TYNES

NOOR TOOK METICULOUS NOTES ON HER LAPTOP WHILE HER client Fadi described his ideal candidate. He was a first-generation Jordanian American with a 1950s mindset. He wanted his future wife to be educated but didn't want her to work outside the house. Typical, thought Noor. He also wanted her to be between 20 and 25 years old, and he was unwilling to budge. Twenty-five was the absolute maximum he would accept. He preferred a blonde but was willing to compromise for a brunette.

Noor typed away in her office on the third floor of a high-rise building in Amman while her client talked and smoked what looked like a Cuban cigar. He leaned back on a black leather recliner chair and occasionally looked outside her office window as if lost in thought. Noor continued to take detailed notes on his future wife's (or *el arous* as he called her) height, weight, family status, complexion, and what she had dubbed a "virginity level." It was a scale she had created after five years in the business. It was her trademark. Some of her friends had even encouraged her to patent it.

Of course, every one of the candidates should be virgins. There was no question about that, but what really mattered was the level of virginity. There were those whom Noor categorized as "Pure Virgins," who had lived with their parents all their life, had gone to an all-girls school, and had had almost zero interaction with the opposite sex, with the exception of their fathers and brothers. They had never held a man's hand or were ever found alone behind closed doors with someone from the opposite sex. Then there were those who had experimented with men. A kiss here, a kiss there, and maybe a slight touching of body parts. Noor referred to them as "Quasi Virgins." Finally, there were those who had kissed, touched, and more, who experimented with various sexual acts but refrained from the final act of submission. Anything but the intercourse. On Noor's scale, those were called "Technical Virgins."

Noor never dealt with those who were in fact non-virgins. Those were the rare minority, the pariahs on whom Noor didn't want to take a chance. Dealing with them might have cost her the whole business, so she always rejected their cases. Just the other day, she read on CNN.com about an Iraqi man in Chicago who ran over his daughter because she had become too westernized. The last thing Noor wanted was for her clients to run over their wives because she had made the wrong choice.

She never shared her notes with her clients or asked them their preference regarding the virginity level. She knew better. Years of experience in the business had taught her to determine the level of virginity that her clients were seeking without asking them directly or even requiring them to fill out an application form. She quickly figured out that her client Fadi was looking for a Pure Virgin. A blonde, Pure Virgin. That was obviously hard to find since blondes were rare in Amman and were mostly either Quasi Virgins or Technical Virgins. However, Noor was willing to take on the challenge. She even considered charging him a "rush fee" since his requirements were tough and he was pressed for time.

Fadi had a list of unusual requests. In addition to his "Pure Virgin" he wanted the bride to speak two languages besides Arabic. English, of course, since she would live in America, and French. "It just sounds so feminine, and I'd love for my wife to speak it," the client told Noor, who just nodded, smiled, and kept typing.

"I also want her to have a degree in something related to science, maybe pharmaceutical sciences. It's just so perfect for a woman," he said while puffing his cigar. "As I told you, I really don't want her to work outside the house, but I want her to be educated so that she can pass her education on to my children."

"I understand," said Noor in a perfect American accent, which she had picked up during her graduate years at George Washington University. There was no need to embarrass her American-born client by testing his broken Arabic.

"Do you need anything else from me?" asked Fadi, preparing to leave.

"No, that's it for now. What's your deadline?" asked Noor.

"I'm leaving in three weeks, but I travel to Jordan often, so hopefully, we can work something out."

"Okay, let's try to find someone in three weeks," Noor stood up and shook Fadi's hand. She handed him her business card that said: Noor Tadros, CEO, Marriage Liaisons Inc. "We'll start working on your case immediately, and you should hear back from us by the end of the day tomorrow," she said smiling.

"Really, that fast?" he said, cocking his head.

"Yes. We're efficient. We'll present you with five options. This should give you enough time to meet them and decide who's the most suitable."

He ran his fingers through his black hair. "Great. Thank you very much, Noor. How do I pay?"

"Just stop by the receptionist's office on your way out and make your down payment," she said, pointing to the room next to her office. "We take credit or cash. No checks, please. You pay the rest when you sign the marriage certificate. Have a good day, Mr. Fadi."

"You too, Noor," he said, extending his hand again. "Burberry, correct?"

"Excuse me?" she asked, shaking her head.

"Your perfume?"

"Yes, that's right."

"I've always liked it."

"Then I'll make sure to find you a wife who wears Burberry," she said, smiling as she let go of his hand.

Noor went back to her desk and opened a new Excel sheet. She saved it as "Fadi Ibrahim – Pure Virgin" and typed down his preferences. She looked at her database and spent two hours trying to find the best ten matches for him. She had a total of 540 names saved in her system, but she focused her attention on the Pure Virgins category, where there were 196. The manual search was tedious, and Noor was looking forward to the fall when the software company she had hired was supposed to finish the digital search program she had hired them to create. She was making enough money and had enough clients that it was a good time to use a more advanced system instead of the old-fashioned Excel sheet.

After she finished, she emailed the document to her assistant Lobna and then walked to her office.

"I just sent you ten options. Take a look and give me five."

"Why only five?" asked Lobna.

"He's picky."

"I don't blame him. He's gorgeous," said Lobna.

"Seriously?" Noor said, raising her eyebrows.

He was tall with salt and pepper hair, light green eyes, and an olive complexion. She wondered if he had been married before and if he was trying the traditional route after failing the first time. She had a lot of those clients. Always looking for a second chance. A redemption. To correct their previous failed marital decisions by finding a homeland bride. Many of them picked the first one to legalize their status, get their Green Card, and maybe, just maybe, give this marriage to an American a chance. The majority failed and came running to her to find the one, the traditional one, the good one, the one the West had not tarnished.

"Did you even look at him? He looks like Jon Hamm."

"Who?"

"You know, Jon Hamm, the American actor from *Mad Men*."

Noor raised her eyebrows. "Oh, please! Can you get to work now?"

Beautiful eyes, seductive. Too bad he is so backward, traditional, controlling. Misery is what awaits his future wife.

"Okay. Shall I ask Afaf to make some calls as a backup?"

"Let's see if he likes our choices first, then move to Afaf. He's leaving in three weeks, so I want you to make this your top priority. Understood?"

"That's really fast," she said, a look of concern on her face. "Will we be able to find him a wife in three weeks?"

"Yeah, it's doable. My cousin found his wife in a week before he headed back to Chicago. This Fadi guy comes here often, so we can ask for more time, but I want to impress him by finding him a wife soon. Anyway, I have to head home early today to pack for tomorrow's trip."

"Yeah, right. Good luck. Who are you meeting with there?"

"Some rich Arab American who was too lazy to come here and offered to pay all my expenses to meet him in Washington."

"That's pretty generous."

Noor shrugged. "I guess. I really miss DC. I haven't been there since grad school."

●

Noor's direct flight from Amman to DC was uneventful. On the plane, she mostly read and watched movies. She had expected some scrutiny at Dulles Airport, but the border patrol agent let her go with no questions asked. She wondered if the cross that she had around her neck had eased her entry to what she perceived as a Christian land.

The DC meeting was more than what Noor could have asked for. Not only did her client sign the contract, but he also offered to be her business partner if she ever decided to open a branch in the US.

"All we need is some extra funding, and we'll make it happen," said Rami, a middle-aged divorced man with a grey goatee and black hair. His first marriage to an American lady had collapsed after 15 years, and now he was going the traditional route. "Heck, we can open more than one branch. We can choose the best three locations where Arabs live. Let me see: Detroit, Anaheim, and maybe someplace in New Jersey. What do you think?"

"Great idea, but not sure I can get enough cash flow to start this."

He ran his fingers through his goatee. "I can put in some funds, but you really only need one more investor. Just keep looking for someone."

After the meeting, Noor took the Red Line to meet her good friend Amir downtown. As she settled in her seat on the train, she noticed the familiar maroon carpet, although a bit more run down, with more stains and a more pungent moldy smell than five years ago.

There was something else.

What's with the yelling kids on the metro? When did having children become so trendy in the US? Kids, kids everywhere.

Noor started thinking of the marathon, the procreation marathon that women had to be part of to fit in. She was taught that that particular race usually ended when women reached menopause. In some cases, the end of that marathon can signal the end of life, especially as the word menopause in Arabic, *Sin Al Ya's,* translated into "the age of despair." While on the train, she realized that the age of despair is not totally Eastern but universal. She looked at a woman across from her on the train. She was seated next to a child eating Cheerios from a blue plastic container. The woman was reading him a book as he listened intently. The book had the title *Ten Little Fingers.* The woman had black circles under her eyes, as if she hadn't slept in years.

Women, all women, Eastern or Western, were running their own marathons. They all wanted to reach their life goal, to get to the age of despair armed with a kid or two to prove they had made the journey with dignity. At 33, Noor realized that she had maybe seven years or so before she would reach the age of despair. Was she ready to face it with no children by her side, no husband to go home to? Was she that empowered that the idea of perpetual loneliness didn't bother her?

She sighed. She looked again at the woman on the train with the Cheerio-eating child and thought that someday she might want to read to her own child. When? How? She didn't know. All she knew was that time was running fast.

When Noor reached her metro stop, she bumped into a stroller on her way out, but hurried away.

Her friend Amir had picked the meeting place: Kostas Books in Dupont Circle.

"So, are you still running this marriage agency thing?" he asked as soon as they got seated on the patio sniffing the air of that unusually crisp summer day.

"Yes, of course. I'd have told you if I changed jobs. Can we order food before you start harassing me?" said Noor, flipping the menu.

"Come on, don't be sensitive. I really find what you do fascinating. Are you still doing that scale thing? The virginity scale thing?" He smiled, showing the dimples on his cheek.

She rolled her eyes. "It's the secret of our success."

"So let's see. You're, hmm . . . technical? You haven't moved up the scale yet, have you? Or you would have told me, right?"

"Shut up. People can hear us, you know."

"Do you think anyone here cares? It's only in the Middle East where people care about this shit," he said, his skinny left leg bouncing up and down.

"I wish you could stop being so bitter about where you come from. People make choices, you know?" she said.

He snickered. "Choices? Do you think it was your choice to remain quote-unquote technical?"

"It's really none of your damn business."

"Wasn't this why Mark left you? Because you insisted on wanting to bleed on your wedding night like all the good girls in Amman?"

She raised her eyebrows. "Really, you think that's what happened? Mark didn't leave me because I didn't sleep with him. I dumped him because he was a loser. He dropped out of college to be a full-time musician?" said Noor shaking her head. "What's up your ass today, anyway?"

A 20-something waiter approached their table. They both asked for the house red.

"What's wrong, habibi? What happened to you since I last saw you?" she asked.

Amir went silent and focused his attention on the street. It was the end of the workday in DC, and people were heading home. The younger ones stopped by bars and restaurants to wind down, while the rest commuted back to the suburbs to pick up their kids from summer camps, make dinner, and fall asleep watching reality TV.

"It's my dad. He has cancer."

Noor thought of Amir's father, the owner of various food factories in Jordan. Larger than life, patriarch to seven children. Would cancer really get him?

"Oh no. I'm so sorry," she said.

"It's testicular cancer, so there's hope."

"I hear King Hussein Cancer Center is doing amazing work. Cancer research has progressed."

"I know. Doctors think he'll make a full recovery. But that's not all of it," he said, sipping the wine the waiter had just brought. "He keeps telling me about dying and stuff and wants to see me married before he dies."

Noor sighed. "He doesn't know, does he?"

Amir leaned back in his chair. "Of course not!"

"That's tough," she said, twirling her wine, staring at the glass. "What are you gonna do?"

He let out a big sigh. "My work permit was canceled after I was laid off, and I don't have a choice but to go back."

"To Amman?" she said, raising her eyebrows.

"Where else? You know this means I have to get married."

"Geez! Maybe you should tell your dad?"

"Are you crazy? What do you want me to tell him? That I screw men? Now, that would kill him."

Noor thought about Amir's previous boyfriend, Alfonso, the love of his life. Tall, dark, and gorgeous. They met at the gym and became inseparable. She thought about how happy Amir had been when he was around him, which made her envious. She wanted a love like that. Alfonso eventually went back to São Paolo after his visa had expired.

"So what now?"

He shrugged. "Nothing. I don't have a choice."

She held his hand. "I'm so sorry."

"It's okay. Now you need to find me a wife. How much do you charge?"

"For you, I'll do it pro bono," said Noor, smiling.

"Make sure to get me a Pure Virgin."

"Of course. I know better." she chuckled.

"I have a better idea. Why don't you and I get married? This way, we will pursue our love lives while making society happy. What do you think? Win-win?"

"Funny! Now Let's order some crab cakes."

•

Noor's flight back to Amman felt longer than usual. She passed the time by catching up on 33 recommendations that needed classification. Most of the recommendations were unsolicited. People called her office nonstop to drop in the names of their sisters, daughters, cousins, and nieces who were about to miss the infamous marriage train and needed urgent help before they hit 30, that dreadful age when women's body parts start falling apart, and their eggs begin to shrink and rot.

Noor's main task was to look at the recommendations usually entered by her receptionist, Afaf, who took the calls. Noor was the brainpower of the agency, the one who did the most crucial part of the process: the classification. Afterward, she would pass her recommendations to Lobna, who would set up appointments and handle the logistics. It was a smooth workflow that Noor came up with as soon as she started her own business. The seed funding for her agency came from her father, who gave her financial support as soon as she got her MBA, and right after, she pitched her idea to him. "It's a good business model," her dad agreed. "First of its kind. Highly needed in this town." Matchmaking had always been done by word of mouth in Amman. A professional agency with a nine-to-five staff had never existed in the city. It was a novelty, a shrewd business idea that her dad was all over.

"Glad to see all the money I spent on your MBA didn't go to waste," he said as he handed over the first big check.

Going through the recommendations and classifying them took her six hours. There were 20 Pures, 5 Quasis, and 8 Technicals. The Technicals are gaining momentum, thought Noor as she drifted to sleep. *Good for them.*

When Noor returned to the office the next day, Lobna was doing her usual annoying giggle on the phone. *It's that Ahmad guy again!* Ahmad would be the least of Noor's problems that day. As soon as Noor got settled in her office, Lobna was quick to tell her about "the problem," which involved their client Fadi. He was unhappy with choice number three, who admitted to him on their fourth date that she had had a boyfriend in college. Fadi had appeared in the office, yelled at Lobna, and demanded a refund.

When Noor heard the news, she wanted to chop Lobna's head off along with her boyfriend's testicles. She wanted to rip both of their body parts and feed them to all the tail-less, stray cats in Amman.

"How did that happen? I gave you 10 choices to pick from. What went wrong?"

"Well, one of them turned out to be a Quasi. We had her in the system as a Pure. It wasn't my fault!"

"Are you sure this is what happened? I've never made any classification mistake before. Are you sure you didn't give him the wrong candidate by mistake?"

"I'm sure. I used the list you gave me," said Lobna looking annoyed.

"I don't even know how you can focus on anything when you're always on the phone with that Ahmad guy." She sighed. "Let me handle this disaster. And by the way, I don't want you to make personal calls during work hours. Understood? You call your boyfriend or whoever after hours."

"But what if there was an emergency?"

"We'll handle it then."

"Fine," said Lobna, marching back to her office.

When Noor called Fadi, he asked to see her immediately. He told her he wanted to meet her at a coffee shop in West Amman to go over things. Noor grabbed her notes and agreed to meet him in an hour. When she saw him, he was wearing a black suit with a black tie. *Who the hell is he mourning? His sense of humor?* He was sipping a cappuccino and reading the *Jordan Times*.

When he saw Noor, he smiled, stood up, and shook her hand. She tried to apologize for the mistake, but he had a different reaction than she had expected. He put his left hand on hers and said: "It's okay. Don't worry about it." Noor immediately pulled her hand away. "We'll refund you the down payment. We'll even offer you a 10 percent discount if you decide to use our services again."

Fadi continued to smile and nod his head. "I'm not here for business, Noor. I'm here for you. I want to get to know you better."

Noor's immediate thought was to pack her stuff, say her goodbyes, and then pour the cappuccino in his lap, right on his manhood. Instead, she reminded herself how important her business was to her sanity. "Excuse me? I don't think so. I'm definitely not your type."

"I know, but I think you and I will have a great future together."

"I need to go now. Have a nice day."

"I see a great life for us. I know you're a career woman. I've already thought about this. I can help you start the same business in the US. Even when our children are born, I won't mind you working from home. You'll be able to telecommute. Everyone does that over there."

"Mr. Fadi, I don't think I'm your type. I need to get back to the office now. Please make sure to get in touch with Lobna to get your down payment back."

"Noor, think about it. I'll make you happy," he pleaded. "You know I like blondes, but I will give that up for you. I think your long dark hair is very attractive. I'm willing to compromise on many levels to make you happy."

She sighed. "Okay. There is no better way to say this, but here you go. I've had a boyfriend or two. I'm not who you think I am."

"Oh, I see," he said. "Let me think about it."

"There is no need to think about anything. I don't see a future for us. Now I really need to go."

Noor grabbed her purse and headed back to her car.

Is this who I'm going to end up with after thirty? A controlling man who wants to lock up his wife?

Did I fast all these years to break my fast with an onion, just like the Arabic saying?

After their coffee shop meeting, Noor thought Fadi was gone from her life for good. She thought admitting her past experiences to someone looking for the Virgin Mary was the best deterrent she could ever think of. She was mistaken. Fadi called Noor the next day and kept calling twice a week. She picked up occasionally and asked him politely to stop calling her, but that didn't work. Flowers were delivered to her office every day at 9:00 a.m. for 10 days straight until she finally told him that she didn't want to hear from him ever again, that she had put all of his flowers in the dumpster, and that her neighborhood stray cats were probably eating them by now. It was the first time she was ever rude to any of her clients, but she had had enough.

"You're funny. That's another reason I like you," Fadi said over the phone.

"I also deleted your contact info from my phone and used your cards as coasters for my afternoon teas," said Noor, then hung up and rushed to meet her friend Maysoon for lunch at Romero's. Maysoon had called earlier, and Noor sensed a looming disaster when she heard her voice.

•

"Screw you, Noor," said Maysoon as soon as she saw her.

"Good evening to you too. What's the matter?"

"Screw you and your damn business," she said while the waiter walked them to their usual table.

"What's the matter?"

"I'll tell you what's the matter. I received a call from your office. Apparently, I've been recommended to a client, and he wanted to see me."

"What? Impossible. You're not on the list."

"I am. Your assistant called me to tell me the good news."

"That damn Lobna! I don't know where she got your name from. I screen all the names before we put them in the system. Don't worry about this; it's a mistake. I'll remove your name. She should know who to exclude from the list."

"So, what do I qualify under? Technical Virgin? Is that where I am now?"

"Come on, Maysoon. Don't worry about it. You shouldn't be on the list at all. We all know this is not how you want to get married. My business serves a specific clientele, the nouveau riche. You know it was a mistake."

"Let me tell you something. I'm no longer a Technical Virgin if that's what you have me under. I would qualify as a pariah. Isn't that what you call us?"

"What?" she said as her heart skipped a beat. "Yes."

"When?"

"A few weeks ago."

"Who with?"

"None of your business."

"Come on, Maysoon. I need to know."

"Why, so that you can reclassify me in your lovely database? Oh, no, I forgot, pariahs don't even make it to your precious list."

"Cut it out, Maysoon. I told you it was a mistake. I'll take care of it."

Noor drove back to her office in a daze. While dodging Korean-made cars and cursing drivers, Noor thought of her friend.

Maysoon, of all people? How, when, and why? And how could she? How is she going to live with that, and who is going to marry her now? How did it feel the first time?

Noor couldn't stop thinking about the moment when Maysoon finally gave in. Does she have any regret? How could Maysoon do it, and she couldn't? Do you stop caring, as you get older?

Noor thought of Mark and how she had been so close to going ahead with it. She even bought her first lingerie that night. They had it all planned. They met at his studio in DC's Adams Morgan quarter.

He had the place lit with candles and scented with burning incense. It was clear to Noor that Mark, who was not the romantic type, was putting extra effort into making it special. Noor had dated Mark because she was lonely, and he was available and interested. He was witty and well-read. She admired his love of historical mystery novels and French movies. She knew he would be just a fling, but what the hell? She was in DC, and she could do whatever she wanted. She called him one day and told him she was ready.

"Are you sure?" he asked. "You know women never forget their first time."

"I'm very sure."

That night Mark was trying hard to make it memorable, his moves were slow and cautious, as if he was doing it for the first time, but Noor couldn't tolerate the initial pain and stopped him. It was not the physical pain but the mental pain that was agonizing her. "I really can't do this. There's too much at stake here."

As she neared her office, Noor kept thinking of the best way to punish Lobna. She was going to cost her both her business and her friends. *Yela'an abouha* (May God curse her father.)

When she got back to the office, Lobna was on the phone. *Bitch!*

"Your mom called," yelled Lobna from her office.

"I'll call her, but first, we need to talk. Can you get off the phone and come to my office immediately?"

When Lobna came to Noor's office, she expected her to be afraid, even shaking, at the possibility of losing her livelihood. Instead, Lobna had a look of defiance that Noor had never seen before. It seemed as if having this Ahmad guy in her life gave her enough self-confidence that enabled her to move mountains if she wished. Noor felt jealousy at that moment as she stumbled with words when she saw Lobna in her new state. The last thing she expected was a confident assistant instead of the submissive, meek 21-year-old she had hired right out of college.

Lobna was from East Amman, a neighborhood for the less fortunate. She had a mediocre education, but she was in love, employed, and had her life mapped out for her. A husband, kids, a decent job, and a supportive family. How had this Lobna figured it out, and she hadn't?

"You called my friend Maysoon. How the hell did she make it to the list? Didn't I teach you to carefully scrutinize all the recommendations we get from West Amman and remove those who don't qualify?" said Noor while seated in her leather chair, her elbows on the desk.

"Her aunt recommended her."

"So what?"

"Her aunt kept nagging and said she would pay us double if we added her, so I did. I thought I was doing you a favor."

"What? A favor? I didn't hire you to make executive decisions. You just do what I say. You've been making a lot of mistakes lately, and that's because you spend most of your time with this Ahmad guy. I'm giving you a warning. One more mistake, and you're out."

"A warning! That's not fair. I work overtime and never get paid. I don't get any raises or bonuses, and you're firing me?"

"Your performance is slipping. This all started after you started going out with Ahmad."

"Can you leave Ahmad out of this? You're just jealous."

"How dare you say that?" she said, banging on her desk.

"Of course you are. I have a man in my life. You don't have anyone. All you have is your business and your chi chi girlfriends and gay men."

"That's it, Lobna. You have until the end of the day to pack your stuff and leave. I've had it with your shit."

Lobna left Noor's office, slamming the door behind her.

Noor leaned back in her leather chair. Her hands were shaking, and she was feeling nauseous. She put her hands on her face and rubbed her eyes. *I should have fired her ass a long time ago.* She opened her eyes to see a yellow Post-It Note on her desk: "Call your mom. She says it's urgent." Noor dialed her parents' home number. "What is it, Mom?" she said as soon as her mom picked up. No hellos or how are yous.

"Amir called."

"Really? He must be in town."

"He says he doesn't have a cell phone."

"I'll call his parents' house." Noor could hear the sound of the TV in their family room blasting what sounded like an Egyptian drama.

"There's something else," her mom said.

She sighed. "What? I'm in a hurry."

"Someone called Fadi asked to see your dad."

"What? That guy is unbelievable. He never stops."

"He seems like a nice guy."

"Mama, don't start this now. He's not my type," she said, her voice increasing in volume.

"Type? Come on, Noor. You're 33. You shouldn't think of types at your age. Do you ever want to have kids? It's not like you have much time left."

Noor bit her lip. "Here we go again with kids. I don't wanna hear this."

"Noor, listen to me."

"I know what you're going to say, that after 30, women are left with either a divorcé or a widower."

"Glad you still remember." Her mom chuckled.

"You know what? I'd rather be with a divorced man or a widower than be with this Fadi guy," Noor shouted.

"You're making a big mistake, Noor. You'll regret this for the rest of your life. I'm your mother. I know these things. Do you want to end up a lonely spinster like your aunt Rula?"

"Bye, Mom."

"Wait! Did you see today's newspaper?"

"No! Why?"

"Look at the business section."

"I don't have time for this; what is it?"

"There's an article about Fadi. He's in Jordan to start a local office for Google. He's rich and smart. He is even good-looking. Can't you see that? If you really want to start a business in the US, then he'll be able to help you."

"Bye."

Noor hung up, leaned back on her chair, and put her feet on her desk. She grabbed a pack of Marlboro Lights from her purse and lit a cigarette. She was not a smoker but always kept a pack in case of an emergency. No one was allowed to smoke at her office (except for wealthy clients). She hated the smell of smoke on her expensive leather furniture, but she was the boss and could do whatever she wanted.

Damn it! She sprung off her chair and approached the mirror with the golden frame on the wall across from her desk. There it was. Yet another grey hair. It's because of that sharmouta *Lobna.*

Noor returned to her chair and looked outside her office window. Construction workers were putting the last touches on a new state-of-the-art highrise, across the street.

Skyscrapers were becoming trendy – Amman had high ambitions. The city's new slogan splashed across the streets' billboards: "The Sky is Not the Limit."

Noor kept puffing away as she gathered her thoughts. She thought of Maysoon and how she had betrayed her. She never thought she would do this without discussing it with her first. How did Maysoon find the courage? She had no fear of retribution, which puzzled her. Noor considered her prospects and whether she was doomed to a life of virginity. She thought of Amir and his offer. Would marrying him liberate her? Would she be able to have affairs with whomever she desired while married to her gay best friend? Would she be as free and as happy as he suggested? Would they even have kids?

She let out a big sigh, put her feet down, and moved to the end of her office to where the trash can was. She rummaged through the receipts and tissue papers and found the card that came along with the flowers that Fadi had sent her this morning. She went back to her desk and let out a sigh. She dialed his number.

After all, she was still a virgin.

PART THREE

The Roots of Heaven

"I remember madness leaning for the first time
   on the mind's pillow.
   I was talking to my body then and my body was
   an idea I wrote in red."

      ADONIS
      Selected Poems

The Long Walk of
the Martyr

SALAR ABDOH

SEYED HASAN HELD HIS BREATH AND TOOK A SHOT THAT RE-
verberated through all of Nineveh province. No one had taught him
by-the-book counter-sniping; rather, he just sort of picked it up
through trial and error. Those two years in the ditches of northern
Iraq, while I tried to take notes for my damn book, Seyed Hasan, who
barely reached my shoulders, would crawl into the spaces no one else
had the stomach for and do what needed to be done. The shot that
would finally bring down the Chechen "Ghost" would be the talk of the
Hashd forces long after our war was over and we had buried our dead
and returned to Tehran.

I did what anyone does back home. I drank. Hesitantly at first,
and ashamed. Then the floodgates opened. Soon every *arak* dealer
between Imam Khomeini Boulevard and Motahari had my number.
Whenever I went online, there would be a fresh funeral for another
martyr back there in Iraq. People we'd known. I'd believed the war was
over. So why the dying this late?

The war was never completely over.

I drank more.

Until one day Seyed Hasan showed up at my door.

"Arash, you smell like blasphemy."

"I feel like it."

He had never been to my place. In general, back in Tehran I tried
to keep my distance from the vets of Iraq and Syria. Most of them

221

came from working-class families, and God was their thing. God was my thing too, lately. But only because I'd been having intimations of mortality, and not having God around seemed like a losing proposition.

I said, "I don't know how to live with peace, Seyed *jaan*."

He began weeping right there at the window, which overlooked the synagogue across the street.

It was a Saturday, and it was the month of Ramadan. In the courtyard of the synagogue a fellow wearing a *tallit* was on his cellphone. I suspected he shouldn't be on his cellphone on a Saturday, and in the synagogue at that. This was about as much as I knew about the guy's religion and still I took it personally, with almost a mind to go over to tell him to get off the phone. Then the absurdity of it all hit me – the weeping Seyed Hasan and his legendary kill back in Iraq, my alcohol breath, and that man and his phone in the synagogue during the month of fasting in Tehran.

We were womenless men. We suffered for it. We had no money and the war had been a way out of our gloom. Now what?

❉

That night, Seyed Hasan rode on the back of my bike to Khayyam, near the Grand Bazaar. The area is a desert at night. A lone garbage truck might pass. Otherwise it's just the city's street sweepers in their yellow outfits and brooms, and the echo of their rhythmic brushing on tired asphalt.

Another old comrade, Kazem, had become one such sweeper. He said the labor was a ritual that he would never give up, and that it was for the good of the Earth. Before all this, he'd owned a hole-in-the-wall cubicle in the outer reaches of the brassworkers' quarter in the Bazaar, where he dealt in watches and second hand shoes. When the war came to Syria, he sold everything to go protect the holy places. In Samarra he fed us, the Iranian contingent, until his money ran out, believing all the while that martyrdom was near and he wouldn't have to return to Tehran and face the wasteland of no war and no cubicle in the Bazaar.

No such luck.

"Brother Arash, they don't make posters for the living," Kazem was saying. He tousled Seyed Hasan's hair. They'd been inseparable in Iraq, and both had nearly caught it in Syria. Yet here they were, alive and therefore unlucky. "Did you ever finish that book about the war?" he asked.

"Working on it."

"He drinks," Seyed Hasan said, ratting on me. "Alcohol."

"Is this true?"

"I've been having a bad season for the last few months. I apologize."

The three of us looked up simultaneously across the street at the enormous poster of our late commander. His posters had been on display everywhere since winter, when he had been assassinated back in Baghdad. In this poster he looked positively angelic, his determined, angular face burdened with something from the next world, the khaki of his uniform slightly faded as if he was still on a long desert march.

That night I spent with Kazem and Seyed Hasan in the broken place they rented below the Shush district. The place had missing windows, and any Shush junkie could have stepped in to help themselves to nothing. But the half-dozen men who lived there, all of them vets of Syria/Iraq, were not nothing. They'd teach you a lesson if you crossed them. They, too, hadn't had the luck of martyrdom, and they weren't celebrated back home for having protected or defended anything. The world had passed them by. I was one of them, except I still believed some book might come out of my troubles. No such luck yet. I had a side job teaching conversational Iraqi Arabic, and that was about it. There was also a club where they'd needed a sharpshooting coach for the rich bastards who lived uptown and didn't know how to spend their money fast enough. But there were only air guns, the ammo just BB pellets, and the first time I stuck the barrel of the gun in my mouth to chase boredom away the owner politely said that I was fired — *you're not setting the proper example*.

I couldn't argue with that.

Before sunrise, Seyed Hasan woke me up. He had some dates and flatbread and tea for us for our *sahari*.

"I don't fast, brother," I told him. "The month of Ramadan and me, we're not intimates."

He eyeballed me. In the tired quiet of Shush, three other veterans were up finishing their brief morning prayers. Kazem slept. He'd sleep right through the day and eat after sunset, before going back to sweep on Khayyam and the wide cobblestone walkway of the Grand Bazaar.

"Is this why we fought? Look at us."

What could I tell him? A fellow can have a thousand and one reasons for going off to die. If he's not lucky enough to get his wish, he's not lucky. Nothing to be done about that.

"Arash, tell me please, is this why we fought? I don't have a job. I don't have a wife. I don't have a future. Our *Sardar* is dead and they have his posters everywhere. I don't even have a poster."

"You want a poster of you? I'll make you a fucking poster. What do you want me to say?"

"Why did the Americans have to assassinate him?"

"Because he was good at what he did. The best field commander there ever was. He kicked their asses and they were jealous of him."

"We really were the best, Arash. Weren't we?"

"We were pretty damn good. You, my friend, were *great*."

"Now I live in a half-abandoned building in Shush and push a cart in the Bazaar all day. Do you know how much I make every day?"

"How much, my brother?"

He burst into tears again. The other vets, breaking bread now, turned for a moment to look at us. Then they turned back to chewing in silence.

•

Abu Amin was apparently coming from Baghdad. This was the gist of our misery. We loved Abu Amin. An Iraqi, he'd been specifically in charge of intelligence for us Iranians operating in northern Iraq and the Syrian border. Mostly he humored us, and tried to make sure we didn't get ourselves killed. In this effort, his aims and ours were somewhat at odds. But we loved him anyway. During the war he had had the flair of a man engaged in important things. Now he was reduced to coming to Tehran to have his poorly functioning heart operated on. He had written to me and some other guys that he wanted to see us, and that he'd be a guest at Majid Safi's house.

It was this guy, Majid Safi, that was the real issue. Safi had inherited a cloth business from his *baba* in one of the prime locations at the smaller Bazaar of Tajrish, in the north end of the city. I'd been there a few times after we all came back, and Safi, imagining I was going to make him the hero of whatever I had been prepaid to write, had invited me up there and fed me kebab and rice. You could say that Kazem, our street-sweeping brother, and Safi were martyrdom's truth and lie. Whereas Kazem had sold the shirt off his back to go to Iraq and Syria to die, Safi had simply closed up shop for six months to go and *pretend* he wanted to die. He got a hero's welcome on his return, while Seyed Hasan and Kazem got a place you wouldn't want to take for free in Shush. In the spice-sellers' quarter of Tajrish, I'd overheard a woman consider the mound of turmeric in front of her and opine to the merchant that Majid Safi was one of the most desirable bachelors around.

The fact that Abu Amin had come from Baghdad to stay with Safi was a punch in the gut. But where else was he going to stay? In Shush? Or in my dilapidated one-bedroom across from the synagogue?

Seyed Hasan said, "I could kill Safi, you know."

"You mean you have that kind of sentiment toward him in general, or that you want to really kill, as in *kill*, him?"

"The second, brother Arash."

"Because he has money?"

"Because he came to defend the holy places for all the wrong reasons."

"You could say the same about me."

"How so?"

"I had a contract to write about you guys."

Seyed Hasan considered this.

"I can't accept that. A man does not risk getting it from a DShK round for the sake of some words. I don't care how much they paid you. Besides, you are just as much of a wreck now as I am. Safi, he's not a wreck. He's the number-one cloth merchant of Tajrish, and now he is going to be entertaining Abu Amin while we eat dirt."

"Why not go visit him?" I suggested.

Seyed Hasan frowned. "To do what?"

"We could start by telling him we've come to visit Abu Amin. Our old Arab officer-in-charge belongs to all of us."

Tajrish was packed at 9 p.m. on a Ramadan night. This was where I'd actually grown up, on Darband Road, where the mountains begin and you can hike a few days right across that harsh terrain all the way to the Caspian Sea. It had been a childhood of snowstorms and snow days off from school. Eating warm, sweet beets in Tajrish Bazaar at nights, and running around to get lost in its maze of shops and the bottoms of women's long black *chadors*. Now I hardly ever ventured so far north in the city. This much vibrancy can unsettle a man who has been tasked to write about martyrs.

The last time I was here, they'd put up a minaret-sized poster of one of our dead behind the Bazaar, at the mosque of Imamzadeh Saleh. A boy, really, this martyr. He'd been with us during the siege of Mosul, but then disappeared, and next we knew he was in Syria and his head had been severed. The cut-off head made news, and I thought: *I don't care who wants to be a martyr, I'm not writing about the cut-off head of a brother. I have red lines I won't cross.*

Seyed Hasan and I pushed past the crowds at the Bazaar's vegetable market until the crush of bodies got thinner, and we were at last standing in front of Safi's cloth shop.

He was busy. A blown-up photograph of him, which I had taken, in uniform up by Tel Afar just before we liberated the city. He's looking into the camera and probably thinking about the day he'll have a life-sized copy of the picture put in his store.

Seyed Hasan said, "I don't have the stomach for it."

"Don't be a child. We'll just wait a bit."

Women, and a few men, were lined up behind Safi's counter, running their hands on various fabrics and asking him questions. He looked elated. Ramadan became him. I could not deny that he was handsome: His broad shoulders turning with ease every which way to deal with customers, his honeyed voice giving discounts even before being asked. He looked well-fed and darkly handsome with those thick eyelashes.

"I want his life," Seyed Hasan murmured.

"No, you don't."

Seyed Hasan did not want anybody's life; he wanted death. But on terms that would bring him immortality. I thought of that boy with the severed head whose poster I'd last seen at the Imamzadeh Saleh mosque next door.

"I'll be back," I told Seyed Hasan.

"Don't leave me, Arash. Don't leave me here to watch Majid Safi."

"Think of it as therapy."

"As *what*?"

"Think of it as facing your worst nightmares so that you can overcome them."

"Safi is not my nightmare. He's just someone I want to kill."

"We're not at war anymore."

"I should have killed him in Iraq. Accidentally."

This was going nowhere. I left him to his protestations and soon was standing in the wide-open space outside of Imamzadeh Saleh, with a thousand worshippers meaning to go inside. The poster of the martyr was no longer there, and I hadn't expected it to be. It was something of a carnival here. Families drinking sherbet and tea. Spreads of food laid out everywhere. Under the wall where the martyr's poster had been, three boys did Persian street rap for money.

The idea came as a gift. I saw him. Right above the heads of those Persian rappers with their baseball caps, loose jeans and T-shirts bearing the faces of their beloved American rap martyrs. Seyed Hasan was going to be up there on that wall. His mug, that of the freshest among those killed in a war we had imagined we'd won.

Nothing had ended. And we'd won nothing.

That night, after Safi closed up shop, he entertained us. He lied, saying that Abu Amin had not arrived from Baghdad yet. Instead he took us with him to a plush hotel with a swimming pool that he and his friends rented in the nearby Niavaran district during Ramadan. Their pretend fasting consisted of being served by the hotel staff, horse-playing in the water with each other and gorging themselves on tray after tray of food brought to them until dawn broke. After which they went home and slept off the daylight hours and the fast, only to wake up at sundown to open up their shops and imagine their version of Ramadan was going impeccably.

After an hour of watching them at the swimming pool, I sent the outraged Seyed Hasan home. Safi could not have been kinder. He would not take no for an answer, and had the hotel wrap several plates of rice and meat and chicken and sweets to be sent along in a cab that he ordered for Seyed Hasan.

"You're not coming?"

"I still have some business with Safi here."

Seyed Hasan gestured at the half-dozen young men laughing, splashing in the water, and swimming to the edges of the pool to stuff themselves on the rich trays of grapes and lamb stew and pastries. In the one hour that we had been there, not one of Safi's friends, all of them sons of rich Bazaar merchants, had so much as acknowledged our presence. We were invisible. Peace – the absence of war – had made us that way.

"What possible business can you have here? Look at them. These guys make a mockery of Ramadan. They eat all night and sleep all day and call that fasting."

I thought he was going to burst into tears again.

"Go home, Seyed *jaan*."

"Home? That no-place in Shush?"

"We were in worse places in Iraq."

"That was war."

"So is this."

Three months later Seyed Hasan's posters would be up around the city – the Iranian martyr and sniping legend who brought down the Chechen ace in northern Iraq.

Not every martyrdom is a negotiation, but this one was. That morning, when Safi and I left the swimming pool after he had said his goodbyes to his bloated friends, I told him, "You are a piece of shit!"

"This means you won't make me the hero of your book?"

"Actually, it means that I will."

"How much do you want for it?"

We stood in his shop at seven in the morning. He had come to pick up some expensive fabric to take home. I knew what he was up to. He was taking gifts from his store for Abu Amin.

"I want something else."

"Name it."

"Take me to Abu Amin." When he tried to deny that Abu Amin was staying at his place, I slapped him. "Do you want to be the hero of my book or not?"

Rubbing his reddened face in shock, he said yes and reluctantly took me to the great man.

It took some convincing. Abu Amin was certainly not exactly the Abu Amin we'd known back in Iraq. But I finally managed to talk him into signing Seyed Hasan back on the books in Baghdad.

It was a jolt to see the old intelligence officer. During the dog days of the war, the convoys that escorted him never sported fewer than half a dozen pick-ups with men armed to the teeth. That was just a year ago. Now he lay flat on a couch with a *keffiyeh* wrapped around his head, his eyes tired and dulled.

"Why do you want to send your friend back to Baghdad?"

"Tehran is not for him, *ya* Abu Amin."

"Don't give me stupid reasons. Tell me why."

"He needs to try his chance one more time at martyrdom."

"The war is over."

"You and I know, Abu Amin, this is not the case. There are plenty of pockets of trouble you could send him to."

"To die?"

I nodded.

I saw Safi hovering just outside the living room, curious and nervous. This was about all of us. Seyed Hasan's wish to become a poster, Safi's to become the hero of my book about the war, mine to write the bloody thing, and Abu Amin's to have the best care he was going to get in Tehran for his open-heart surgery.

"Consider it done," he said.

When I tried to relay to him that Safi was going to take on any extra expense for the care he was receiving in Tehran, he put his hand up to hush me.

"I don't want to hear about compensation. I would have done this for your friend, for Seyed Hasan, for free. I will make arrangements for him to join one of the units in Syria."

"Dangerous?"

"Deadly."

"Then God be praised!"

Four months later, when the good news came about Seyed Hasan, I had already given up trying to write the book several weeks earlier. My heart wasn't in it. I was sure the government publisher would take me to court for it. But by then I would find more work teaching rich folks how to shoot stupid air guns so I could pay back the unearned money the regime had given me to start the project.

Abu Amin himself would only live another couple of months past Seyed Hasan. Long enough to vouch that Seyed had died a martyr's death. I never visited Imamzadeh Saleh again to see if they had put up Seyed Hasan's poster in that location. But I knew the posters were up in other spots in the city, since I'd been contacted about supplying a few photos of the martyr from our time in combat. I sent the pictures that I thought were suitable; then, finally, one day I ran into a poster of Seyed Hasan down by the Grand Bazaar where Kazem continued to sweep the ground at nights. It wasn't too far from where the poster of our late commander had been, maybe seven buildings down on Khayyam. And there he was, Seyed Hasan, my dear friend and the nemesis of all the enemy snipers of the war. I had touched up the picture and purposefully faded his uniform so that the same hint of nostalgia that had suffused the commander's poster would also accompany Seyed Hasan's.

It was a busy day on Khayyam and the Grand Bazaar. A Wednesday. No one was paying Seyed Hasan and his poster any attention. Men fought over parking spaces. A little boy spilled his carrot juice and cried. A mother bought an electric fan.

When I went to give the good news about our Seyed's poster to Kazem and the boys at that old Shush dump, I saw that their place was in the process of being razed to make way for a new apartment building.

I could have called Kazem and tried to find him. But I didn't bother.

Then, on a Saturday, as I was watching the same man in the synagogue across from my apartment use his cellphone and thinking I'd go down there to talk to him about what I assumed was a religious infraction, I saw a familiar face. It was Safi, lurking outside the walls of the synagogue. I had promised him I'd call to set up an appointment for an interview about his past, his present, and his exploits in Iraq. But I had not given him another thought until now.

He looked up and our eyes met – me standing by my third-floor window, and him by the wall of the synagogue, where someone had spray-painted something having to do with *death to the king*.

What king? This country hadn't had a king in over forty years. Maybe "King" was someone's nickname in the neighborhood, though I doubted it.

I retreated from my window, and Safi never rang my bell. And if he did, I didn't hear it. The bell hadn't worked since before the war.

The Burden of Inheritance

MAI AL-NAKIB

MERAKI-MOU, TAKE BETTER CARE OF YOUR SWAN'S NECK. I thought it was the delirium of dying. I had never seen a living swan in my life. With more energy than he had mustered in weeks, he jerked his head right off the pillow. I leaned over to reposition it, and he pressed his face against my neck, his eyes jelly-cold. He repeated what he said, then slumped back down. His final words a command to take better care of my neck.

That was ten years ago.

I would rather he had instructed me on what to do with his fucking work. His paintings climb the walls of my apartment, sullen stacks of oversized canvases closing in. I can slap cream on my neck, but what do I do with his avalanche of paintings?

I am tempted to dump them into the sea.

•

Overnight, Theo was in pain; inside a couple of months, he was dead. By then the girls were in their late twenties, tracing the path of their lives. The funeral arranged itself, like a library. I don't remember who came or what people said. I only remember focusing on not crying, because sorrow, like dreaming, is private.

The day after Theo was packed tight in the ground, the calls began. His agent, then a few gallery owners. They were sorry, they said, so sorry he was gone, and then they asked where I wanted his paintings sent. I didn't get it. The paintings were the paintings, with or without Theo, and, to the extent that I understood anything about the art world, death could only add value. They agreed, but the calls kept coming. Later I would learn that his paintings had stopped selling, that he had kept it secret from me.

They arrived from all corners of the earth. Every doorbell announced another one. I wept and moaned as I signed countless DHL slips handed to me by embarrassed deliverymen. By week's end, the paintings had piled up to the ceiling. I stared in bewilderment at the tower in the foyer. His studio contained at least four additional stacks. His office at the Athens School of Fine Arts, more still. I anticipated other paintings would arrive over the next month as news of his death spread.

The only solution was to put them in storage. My tears dried up, and I spent the next few weeks lugging canvases from the apartment to a large, rented storage space on the outskirts of Athens. Once the apartment was cleared, I moved on to his studio, back and forth. Then from the studio to his office, with its wall of steel cabinets full of endless sketches in labeled folders and hundreds of notebooks arranged by spine heights on shelves. I must have entered and exited that storage space 1,000 times. Lit by a dim bulb dangling from the high cement ceiling, thin shadows fringed my memories as I worked. Scuttling in and out of that place was a version of grief. Remembering all the things, then forcing myself to forget. I terminated the lease on his studio and handed his office key to a shiny young artist singing his condolences as he sped past me.

◆

A few months later, I packed a suitcase and persuaded my girls to come with me to Iceland in the vortex of winter. An outside that I imagined would be an extension of my inside. They agreed to come because I was paying and because they were, they explained, not happy with the way I was handling their father's death. *Their father.* Their father had spent hours each day painting, and when he wasn't painting, he was walking. It was a religion with him. Up and down the hills of Lycabettus, Parnitha, Pentelikon, and when wild brush and trees were scorched by arsonists, he found other hills to climb. He was working, he said, painting as he walked. I never did any of that because our two daughters were on me. They tucked themselves into warm corners of their shared bedroom, mostly raising themselves. They owe me nothing. They owe him even less.

In Reykjavík, I walked out onto a frozen pond for the first time. I could feel the water sludge under my feet, despite the thick layer of ice between my soles and the flow. That dark gray liquid was death. It's where Theo was. I was shuffling on ice, but I couldn't make out any difference between Theo under it and me on top. It all seemed part of the same gray mush. But even as I was having that thought, I knew it was more Theo's than my own. Under and over were opposites, not at all the same. Theo was embedded forever beneath the mercurial light and dark of an Icelandic winter morning. I was still in the thick of things, like the swans gliding across the slice of pond where the water was kept artificially warm for them in winter.

Every year since, always in winter, I pack my bag and head to unfamiliar places to get myself lost. Peru, Nepal, Morocco, Zanzibar. Sometimes with the girls, more often alone. A month each year. That's something Theo and I never did together. We were always working. Art is work. The fantasy of art as celestial inspiration and flapping around a studio – that isn't it. There was no room for family travel, no time to pause.

I still paint his designs on my ceramics, organic shapes suggestive of primeval life, of scrawls on cave walls. There's no getting away from him, everywhere I turn. Even after ten years, his lines still mark my clay.

•

When we were together, it was like being burned alive. Right away he called me *Meraki* – creativity and soul. A month after we met at art school, he asked me to go with him to Koufonisia. In those days, a deserted island was a deserted island. We spent two weeks naked under the sun. *You belong to me, Merkai-mou.* I remember holding his hands up to the sun, thinking how transparent skin was, like porcelain. As the sun set, bats replaced gulls, and he would build us a fire on the beach.

Tree shadows slunk across sand like sharp bones. It was a prelude to the life we were going to share.

•

Nikos Dimou says, *Man longs for immortality. Whereas the only thing he knows for certain about the future is that eventually he'll die.* So what do we do? Dimou says that the artist fills the gap between desire and lack of fulfillment with forms. Theo was obsessed with death. A long series of his paintings are of aging skin. Putty-colored crevasses over massive canvases like networks or constellations. Stand far enough away and you might make out a hand or neck or breast; step forward again and the less troubling patterns and trails reassert themselves.

When Theo was a boy, he had a nanny he adored. He spent more time with her than with his own mother. Evangelina seemed old to him when he was little, and of all his nightmares, her death was the most terrifying. She was only forty then, but compared with his young and exquisite mother, Evangelina seemed ancient. Theo used to pray each night for his beloved nanny not to die in her sleep. He invented covert strategies to keep her alive. One of those strategies involved making drawings of women who looked even older than Evangelina. Women with crinkled skin sagging off their skulls and joints. He was seven, maybe eight, when his peculiar obsession with wrinkled skin started. Small squares of paper scratched over with ballpoint blue. Nobody could tell what they were. I still have them. They were filed in one of the cabinets in his office. He filled his life with forms to stave off mortality. And Evangelina? She lived past a hundred. He died before she did. His mother died before her, too.

There's another way Theo filled the gap between desire and the impossibility of satisfaction. We were young. It happened then, and it happened long after we were young, always with women younger than himself and me. We were not moralistic. He was free, I was free. We must have been jealous, but we would never have admitted it. It became more difficult as I got older. Forty may be the new thirty, fifty the new forty, but that's not how it was when I was forty and fifty. His line of willing women never shortened, but I didn't have the equivalent in men. Men are mean that way. All they see is the neck sagging or about to sag. Even almost-dead men, apparently.

∗

I can no longer afford to pay for the storage unit. When I first rented it — almost as large as our apartment — it was supposed to be a temporary reprieve so that I could figure out what to do. That storage unit cost more than half my monthly income. For ten years I've been storing Theo so that I don't have to deal with the burden of his inheritance. But I no longer have a choice. I've hardly saved a penny. Art pays only the few. I suddenly understand what my girls have been squawking about, why they have become so critical of my annual trips.

I've spent the last week moving all his work out of storage and into my apartment, reversing the actions of ten years ago under the flickering light of that swaying bulb. A carpenter has spent the last month at my place building vertical shelves for Theo's canvases across every available wall and corner, shelves that cover up even the largest windows, leaving me only a sliver of access to the balcony and almost no natural light. I've gotten rid of many of my own things to accommodate his work. That wasn't hard. There is pleasure in ruthlessly clearing out what starts off important and, over years, transforms into clutter: clothes that no longer fit, accumulated kitsch, my daughters' toys, books I've never read or won't reread, chipped china, dented utensils, forgotten mementos, cassettes and video tapes, reams of paper I couldn't bring myself to sift through, pillars of faded pink folders. My heart hardened, and I tossed it all away. I felt light until the carpenter arrived. Vertical storage shelves, floor to ceiling. Sawing and pounding and sawdust in every crevice. I escaped to my studio while the man reshaped my walls.

Theo is now the membrane of my apartment. *My apartment.* It's the apartment I chose for us in Kolonaki forty years ago. He paid for it with paintings commissioned by Swiss banks, but it was the space I chose. The tall windows let in rose-gold Athenian light. The wraparound balcony was where I went to breathe, away from him and the girls. I was the one who had selected the furniture from a hidden gallery off Monastiraki, mid-century pieces out of sync with the eighties. Theo didn't waste a second making decisions that, ultimately, he would insist, mattered not at all. In the end it was my saggy neck that mattered. My droopy, unswanlike neck. Not the loft, not the light, and most certainly not the lounge chair and ottoman buried under rolls of artwork that do not slide conveniently into vertical shelves.

◆

No museum or art school or library will have it. He's not that kind of famous. People forget. He garnered some attention, but it's been a decade since he died. In the last five years, I've organized three exhibitions of his work at galleries here in Greece. Not my work. *His.* I managed to sell a few pieces, but attention spans are short and seem to be getting shorter. He's no Kessanlis or Caniaris. In a few years, who will remember? A lifetime of energy expended, a mountain of production, and none of it wins him immortality. After I'm dead, after his daughters die, he will be forgotten.

You are a woman from another time. My daughters say that to me. They may be right. It is terrible to love a man more than he loves you. Then, for the rest of your life, to continue to love him that way. Even after he's dead, to go on as if nothing much has changed because, if I'm honest, not much has.

But they may be wrong. I didn't chase after fame. I did what I pleased. I wanted to work with my hands, to inhabit landscapes and weather through color and clay, to ground myself. If people liked what I was doing, well and good. If they didn't, that was okay, too. Attention, like money, is a kind of filth I wanted nothing to do with.

Theo did.

◆

I don't normally look like this, frizzy hair, unmade face. It's been a crazy month.

In my studio, I keep an envelope of photos along with brochures from my past exhibitions. They are warped, damaged by a flood in our basement six years ago. The basement is shared by all the owners of apartments in my building. Each of us gets a taped-off square of space where we can heap boxes as high as we can manage to balance them. The flood was unexpected. Not rain, but busted pipes, a vile mix of rusty water and sewage. It hadn't been prudent to store our lifetime of photographs down there, but I couldn't bear to keep them in the apartment with me. I had stashed them in shoeboxes after Theo died. I deserved to lose them. The few that survive intact happened to be in a zippered plastic sleeve. Someone had taken some shots of Theo and me in Paris, side by side on the curb outside the gallery where we were setting up his exhibition. It's late. I'm smoking a cigarette. The images are blurry, but in one of them, we're grinning widely at each other, our feet pointing in the same direction. What I wouldn't give to remember what we found so amusing.

Tucked between those photos in the plastic sleeve were a few of my early brochures that used my favorite headshot. Look at me! Twenty-seven years old. It shocks me to see my young face. I'm a stranger to myself. The truth is, I don't feel different. No, that's not true. I do feel different. Everything is different. He's dead, and I carry the weight of his legacy. That kind of responsibility ages a person. I had sharp cheekbones and wore my black hair long, with blunt bangs. My dark eyes spell trouble in that photograph, the kind of trouble some men found irresistible. Theo was right: my neck is as long and slim as a swan's. It felt like the whole world was mine. But the world proceeds without paying attention to anyone. I find this planetary in-difference soothing.

I take reasonably good care of myself now. I didn't when we were together. Too much to do and still young enough to take elasticity for granted. I'm no fresh cygnet, and I don't look anything like I did in that headshot, but I don't normally look as bad as I do today, roots show-ing, face exposed. My poor, ravaged face – unavoidable extension of my neck.

•

He's gone, and I hold his *forever* in my hands. In the process of dis-posing of so much to make room for the shelves to store his canvases,

I daydreamed about adding those canvases to the growing mound of junk. He saved every sketch, every scrap and note. All of it archived. The pink folders I threw away didn't belong to him. They were mine: notes for my projects and exhibitions, folders full of my children's drawings, report cards, invitations to summer plays they staged on the balcony when they were small. I am a demon. I shoved it all into black trashbags and dropped them into the dumpster two neighborhoods down from mine. I didn't want to be tempted to retrieve anything in the middle of the night. But his notes, his sketches, his scraps – I saved all of it.

One especially aggravating morning, I crumpled a sketch he had done of me into a tight ball. I held it in my palm for an hour, trying to convince myself to throw it out exactly the way I had been throwing out everything else over the last month. I couldn't do it. The sweat of my palm made the thick paper feel like leather. I unclenched my fist and smoothed out the sketch on the marble table, placed it back in the folder he had labeled *MERAKI*. How could I throw it away? It had my name on it. In that moment, it felt as if he had just died, and like we had just met. *Meraki-mou, your neck. Meraki-mou, you belong to me.* Time has me tangled up. The future has been stored for ten years. Now it's here, and I think I've made a colossal mistake.

•

I put this burden on myself. Everything moves fast and I remain slow as clay. Where do I offload it?

Into the sea.

I don't care about much anymore, and I've become incapable of pretending I do, which makes me a less social being. It's the privilege of age. To care less, to pretend less, to be only as genial as it suits me to be. The company of my old friends, I find grating. The company of strangers, intolerable. The world is spiraling out of control. The plastic bothers me more than anything. I don't eat fish anymore. I read somewhere that by 2050 there will be more plastic than fish in the sea. I won't be around, but it's coming.

The vertical shelves are installed and filled. He has been contained, but at a price too high. My daughters refuse to step foot in the apartment, tell me I've lost my grip. I glance around my darkened space. The smell of raw wood inflames my lungs, keeps me from sleep. *Only the "now" has the value of "forever."* Theo never read Dimou. He should have. Those were Theo's wrinkles, not Evangelina's, not mine.

Canvas is not plastic. It is not of this century. I could sink him into dark water now, my footsteps crunching forever the ice between him and me.

Eleazar

KARIM KATTAN

DAWN IS TRULY STRANGE, ISN'T IT? SUCH A POWERFULLY weird moment. Even amid grief, one feels hopeful at dawn, doesn't one? It's like a take-off. Mariam was happy to tell her guests whatever they wished to know. She wasn't one for hiding. She never really understood the urge to do so. And now, anyway, what did she have to lose, she wondered, looking outside the kitchen window at the patio, shaded by the fig tree. Well, yes – there was the small matter of how their parents had died. Mariam realized this. It was eerie – upsetting, even – how similar it was. The brutish manner; one felt it was the work of someone who had no idea what they were doing. Surprising, this similarity. She'd be lying if she pretended otherwise; and she'd be lying if she didn't say outright that she felt like she'd been punched in the gut when the police called her.

But these things – they happen, often. She'd heard somewhere, or perhaps read in the paper, that it was the leading cause of death in this region. Well, after getting shot in the head by a soldier, that is. But that's another matter. Somehow, that felt habitual, less sinister.

Is the chair comfortable? Mariam is sorry, she didn't expect them so early in the morning. Would they like some sage? She brews a pot every morning. You know, that's why her parents called her Mariam, because all her mother wanted to drink when she was pregnant was sage, *maramiye*. Isn't that funny. She's always felt very, she paused, fumbling for the word, connected to this herb. She misses her parents very much, especially now. Now she's all alone. She'd never been so alone.

When Zar and Marta were still here – sure, there was a lot of noise, and Marta could fly off the handle at any moment, but at least it was – well, family, right? And in the evening, she'd pour sage in these little rusty cups and Zar would drink it silently and Marta would be too busy doing this and that and her tea would go cold and then Mariam would have to brew a new pot but Marta would end up never drinking it because she could never really just sit down and drink sage; that's what she was like.

The sage is from the garden. Yes, of course, Mariam said, she can answer any question. She does not have anything to hide. She knows that everyone around town thought Zar was dumb. He was slow, he stuttered sometimes; and when he was excited (how odd, only then), he lisped a bit. He smiled easily, and only rarely showed anger. A sweet kid, a sweet sweet kid. He didn't yell when someone cut in line in front of him at the baker. He waited patiently when person after person, at the pharmacy, squeezed past him, shoved him aside, even though he had been there for more than fifteen minutes. People felt this was an unforgivable sign of weakness. Mariam, however, disagreed. Zar was meek, perhaps. Yes, that's the word, and isn't that a good quality, she asked. He drifts away sometimes, just like that.

Marta, on the other hand, didn't think that Zar *drifted*. Marta thought that Zar was a good-for-nothing. She never said so, but she made it abundantly clear. (Mariam thought that Marta didn't show it on purpose; she just loudly embodied everything Zar was not.) She would swoop in at the supermarket, as Zar waited, and she would cut the line, yelling and screaming, and drag Zar along with her. *She's* – well, you know – she always knew what she wanted and what she thought was best for everyone and *he's* ... well – Mariam gestured with her hand, as if swatting flies away. He's Zar, you know. Now, it's not that they hated each other. They simply ... well, I'd say they didn't get along, yes. Something like that. Mariam pursed her lips regretfully.

Mariam had learned, early and fast, that to survive one needed to blur the borders of one's knowledge. Pretend you don't know; pretend you weren't exactly there and didn't have an opinion to begin with. She had learned this, as a child, when both her parents – and often Marta with them – would erupt like volcanoes and Zar was off somewhere in the woods. (To get to the woods, from here, was quite the walk. That he did it every day was a testament to Zar's flashes of stubbornness.) For Mariam, it was easiest to stay still and never get involved. When she did intervene, it was in the most innocent of ways; with a voice like a massage to the temples, like a hush to the soul, a refreshing pedicure contained in a couple of syllables.

Mariam had consciously developed this voice. She had shaped it, through trial and error. Her natural voice was actually a monotone, much like Zar's (but Zar's monotone was disconcerting, it's true, like a voice not quite human). She'd learned to modulate it into a reassuring shape.

Mariam thought of herself as a survivor. Zar and Marta, on the other hand, for all their differences, were not. And then there was the business of – you know. Of when Marta flew off the handle, that time, when it was really bad. Yes, that was something. Mariam supposed Zar knew it wasn't Marta's fault; that's just the way she is, he said, she said, everyone said so. As if her very being was a howl. But he also never forgave her.

As for Zar, well, he was fanciful, you know. He saw things. Their parents, they were very nice, yes, they did the best they could, like all parents do, she said thoughtfully. All any parent can do is the best they can. Did you ever stop and think about how bad the world is, that humans must be parents? What if, for instance, we had another species, much better than ours, much more evolved, who could serve as the caregivers and guardians of children of humans until they came of age? You know? Everyone would be better adjusted, wouldn't they? Mariam often thought of that; this was the fundamental flaw in society, that we had to rear our own.

She was sorry for the strong smell. Muskroot. It's a smell she enjoys, she sprays some in every corner of the house each morning. It vivifies the air. Cleanses. That word, she relishes it: to cleanse. Yes. She enjoys the smell of muskroot but she knows people who don't like it.

She usually sprays it early in the day, as the smell will have evaporated by the time she greets her first guests. She didn't expect them to arrive this early.

And yes, well – now, there's no one at home to drink the sage with her. But she has all her neighbors. Mariam enjoys a quiet life in her garden, but it's nice to have habits shared with others. It created a sense of community, you know? And this town, this house of affliction (or was it figs? She never could remember where the name of the city came from), this valley of vice where they lived, where neither the bald-headed, smug consuls nor their servile assistants; neither the generals nor their minions dared step foot except to buy a woman or a cheap part for their cars, it could reveal itself to be quite welcoming sometimes. The neighbors took care of her. Not that she needed it, mind you, but it was nice nonetheless to be cared *for*, you know?

Anyway, what she thinks, most of all, was that it was extremely unfortunate that Zar was a man and Marta a woman. If it had been the other way around, Mariam feels, things would have gone differently. And she thinks they both knew it. They knew somehow, they had been switched right before birth, some sort of cosmic flaw, a bug if you will, had occurred. And sometimes, when Mariam thinks about it, she figures that this fieriness, this electricity, that Marta radiated was the resentment she felt that Zar somehow had taken her place. A usurper. This was the root of her violence.

Well, you know, Mariam feels like she has to insist on that, the guests would not understand otherwise. *Violence*, she said, again. You know where we live. It's all around us. It's in the air we breathe, it's in our muscles. So, yes, naturally, our parents were, and Marta too and so was Zar sometimes and – well, she herself, Mariam, she was not beyond it, she did yell occasionally, why, in fact once she yelled at Marta so loudly you should have seen the look of surprise in her eyes, that shifted into fear, then outrage, yes, outrage that Mariam would yell at her; Marta she was like that, but she didn't mean any wrong, she didn't know (Marta, didn't) what she wanted; you know she just did everything forcefully barely knowing what she was doing, and her whole life had been like a Band-Aid to her childhood. Yes, that's right a Band-Aid to a childhood being born not a boy, and bowing her head when she walked by soldiers, and swallowing day in day out the intoxicating mix of shame, violence, fear, in front of these soldiers and –

My, she's been blabbering for a while now. When she starts talking, it's true, she doesn't stop. Not only that but the more she talks, the less she feels like she makes sense; and then the next day, she feels very stupid, and so inarticulate. You know, she often thought about how pitch black the night was in these parts. Sure, the city folk had built all these roads leading into town, and had lined them with these great lamps. It was all very modern. So modern that it felt like it belonged to another country. (The highways! So clean, so infinite, a promise of eternity. Who has highways like that?) Anyway, the boys of the town had already started stealing the electric cables from the lamps, and sometimes climbed up to unscrew the bulbs and sell them on the market. And sure, the checkpoint at the entrance of the town beamed a searchlight which intruded on them all the time. Yet, the night remained *pitch black.* How this was possible, she could not say. Some sort of strange magic that protected, at night, the boys from the soldiers.

Mariam would like to insist on the fact that what the soldiers do is not arrest boys but abduct them. She hopes the guests don't mind her being so emphatic about this, it's important. It's important also to understand she and Zar and Marta had grown up with the fear of being abducted by soldiers with high-tech weapons that shoot lasers in the night sky and taken somewhere where the searchlights and the floodlights never stop burning their eyes, drilling their souls. Anyway, she was saying how eerie it was, that all the night lights seemed self-contained: the soldiers' searchlight could not dig into the solidity of night. The dark was of another essence than the light. And so, she'd taken the habit of spraying muskroot to greet the daylight and thank the night for its small graces.

There's a nice breeze this morning. Mariam is available until ten, then she has some other guests who are supposed to come. Imm Nabil, her neighbor. This one, she comes daily. It's awfully nice of her.

Any other village or city here and she would have been shunned, she knows, for her work and the matter of her parents, and the matter of her brother and sister. Really just a run of bad luck; but other villages would have thought Mariam deserved it, that somehow it was all her fault. But not here. Here, there was a sort of safety. Anyway, Imm Nabil wouldn't be here before ten. Mariam thinks the guests will really enjoy the shade of the fig tree, let's sit outside for a bit.

A funny thing about Zar and Marta is that they both had a very peculiar relationship with this tree. Zar talked to it, in whispers, when he thought no one was watching (often, it was in the dead of night or just before daybreak). But Mariam saw everything. She spent her life seeing and attending to others, so yes, she heard Zar, that hulky, massive man, with his big biceps, his enormous, muscular back, his curly hair (some of it white; can you believe that the man she's talking about is in his early forties? It feels like she's talking about a teenager); that man, on all fours, whispering things in his sing-song voice, his slight lisp, to the fig tree. As for Marta, she hated the tree. She refused to eat its figs. When she was angry, she even threatened to have it felled. *Felled*!

Mariam had hoped, always, that both Marta and Zar could heal. Their wounds were so deep, so unfathomable; she thought that they themselves couldn't understand them. Probably had no idea that they even had these wounds. They thought they were two warring continents but in fact they were just two gaping wounds unable to see or understand each other. Mariam knew they were both slightly crooked inside, and this crookedness gave them so much pain. You know, sometimes things are impossible to heal. How can one live without any hope like that?

The three of them, always on edge, always about to erupt. Well, Marta mostly. Zar was absent, and Mariam tried to smooth things over. In her good days, Marta was lovely – though self-involved. But on her bad days, she was so utterly terrifying – Mariam doesn't even have words to describe it. And then, one day later, she'd be back to normal. As if nothing had happened. Mariam really believed that Marta forgot. She could say all this now, but back then. Well, Mariam had become sort of like those machines that can predict earthquakes, you know? She picked up on the slightest variation in Marta's tone, any, microscopic edge; and she knew when it was time to hide.

There's still some time before Imm Nabil comes. It's getting a bit warmer, but it's still delightfully cool under the fig tree. Ah, Zar had a peculiar relationship to time. He floated in it. Mariam thought it was easier when their parents were alive. Much easier, yes, because they seemed to organize their time, Zar's time, especially; and they catalyzed Marta's energy. When they died, Zar didn't cry. He was a sensitive boy, he just didn't know how to show it. So, obviously, here, people thought he was a stone-faced, cold-hearted madman. But Mariam knew that was not the case.

Marta, on the other hand, was devastated. She had spent her life in an ongoing conflict with them, yet their deaths had made her completely unravel. Yes, somehow, Mariam guessed, both of them unraveled after that. When did the relationship between Marta and Zar become venomous? She mused a little while. It happened overnight. Human lives are such mysteries. Probably after their parents' death. Something went amiss; some secret equilibrium was disturbed for good.

But we live in such a venomous place, too, Mariam added. You know, we pretend it's not a problem, we make believe that we're fine with it and that we found ways to survive but really, seeing these soldiers, these rifles day in day out; this constant threat, it's bound to make you go a bit mad. In this little corner – forgive me, it's true – of an empire, really, how is one supposed to not be violent? You see the thing is, she's been thinking about violence for a long time. And it seemed to her, now, that violence seeps into every single aspect of one's life. Violence against the soldiers, but also against the house (some days she just wants to grab a pickaxe and hurl it at the stone walls), against the neighbors, the brother, the sister, against oneself. All of it is just one big web of violence, really, and one should be careful. Marta was like that, she had violence coiled up within her, ready to spring at any given moment. Even at its calmest, her voice carried the promise of storms. Zar, on the other hand, well, Mariam guessed his violence was a bit more insidious. Zar would target himself, his very soul, but no one else. His outbursts would shred at his spirit. He told her once – she remembers that distinctly – that he sometimes felt like a hand was clenching at his chest, at his lungs, and he couldn't breathe. She thinks that he said "sometimes" out of a sense of decency, but really, it was always.

It's not like Mariam was innocent or naïve, not at all. You can't survive here like that. No, but she knew where attention was wanted and where it wasn't. She knew – her job taught her that – when to close her eyes and why. And she never second guessed herself or her intuition about those things. She'd learned it, over long and difficult years. You see her sitting here, pouring sage in these old cups, looking rather peaceful though, granted, a bit flustered, and you think she's always been like this. But she has not. It required discipline to squelch every burst of anger inside and every time she wanted to let loose and bang her head on the walls. Perhaps she was luckier than both Zar and Marta. There was something the gods had made crooked there. She doesn't judge, it's not her place. Besides, it wasn't evil. It was a deep-seated inability to adapt.

She knew people tended to think of her as subservient. She wasn't. She simply knew how to bend when needed. Marta and Zar, they couldn't bend, they wouldn't even know how to try. That's why, eventually, they broke. Mariam was worried and upset often, too, of course; but she knew how to bide her time until the tides subsided. She knew how to wait for the calm to wash over.

Zar – she paused again. We shouldn't make much of it. He was moonstruck, he lived in some dark, nocturnal cloud cuckoo land; someone who'd spend his days whispering things to a fig tree wouldn't do that. Mariam thought that people read too much into Zar's attitudes. She knew him best, and knew there was nothing sinister about him. He was soft, a lamb really, not a viper. Of course, lambs could kill, yes, they could. But not Zar.

Once she had been watching him, as he sat under the fig tree, right here, where they are sitting, the moon shining on just one half of his face and she thought to herself, she had never seen him truer to himself. Did she mention she thought he was properly moonstruck? She thought about that often, these days. When he was born, a wandering priest had come into the house and said the child had moons in his eyes. Of course, no one should believe wandering priests, especially not in these parts (and if they wander, it means that someone is allowing them to. Priests who are in cahoots with soldiers? That doesn't sound too saintly to Mariam). But Zar did have them, she saw them often, these little dancing moons in his eyes. Sometimes they were beautiful, sometimes scary.

No, Zar would never do such a thing. Not her Zar. This she could tell the guests with absolutely certainty. Didn't they think, that she wanted her sister's murderer to be brought to justice? Yes, she did, though in this country, she was not sure what justice was worth. But what she knew, what she wanted to tell them, what she hoped she had shown them, what she truly believed, was that Eleazar didn't do it.

•

The sound of water. Gurgling, free flowing, streams far and near. He crouched in the tall grass and closed his eyes. A complex system of canals, small, lush gardens, and bridges extended all around him. Up here on this cliff, far removed both from the town and the city. This is where they came to get water when the soldiers cut off the supply. This was the only place they had, all three of them, had genuine fun well into adulthood, laughing, dancing in the water, spraying each other.

Eleazar didn't dislike his home, a town where the prostitutes, the thieves, the drug dealers, gathered and where their clients came to exploit them. It was no one's fault that they lived in such a terrible place. It was a place that laid bare how deeply flawed the world was. A den of iniquity, it was called. That was true. Except that everyone *else* (the johns and the rich in their nearby villas who sometimes sent a bit of money, a bit of food, a bit of goodwill) made it iniquitous. It had seemed evident, to Eleazar, that the skies would always be dust-yellow and that always, he would live in that half-town, the garbage of a nation that never came to be. Mariam sometimes talked about venom but he thought, rather, that it was dust. Just dust, and trash.

Marta and Mariam called him "Zar." Mariam said it with tenderness, Marta with something that sounded, sometimes, like scorn. They had called him Zar for so long that he felt he had lost his name. He was sitting cross-legged now, his back against a tree, and he whispered: "Eleazar." His name, resonating in the hills, felt like a little song, a bit of night music. Something mystical about it; a grand name really, the name of one who survives; one who dies and is born again; and again; and again; and again. One who testifies to miracles.

Most people, he felt, lived with a kind of will to exist, a will to do. They lived forcefully. There was a rage in them. He had a hard time understanding how it did not exhaust them. He was born in a country that does not exist, in a city that itself is unstable, always quivering and on the verge of vanishing; and he was born – he saw that now – maladapted for the fight this implied. It had drained him of all will to enact change in the world around him. He had learned – from Mariam, mostly – how to leave the world alone, so that the world left him alone. It was tricky; it did not always work. Becoming a shadow, sometimes, was a gamble. But it had been his life.

Eleazar had thought, often and long, about life and death and had come the conclusion that some people deserved to die. They deserved to be put out of their misery. It was a noble gift to give, and to receive. He wondered what Mariam would think of that. Mariam was well-adjusted, happy. Or, at least, she could be happy. She will be happy. Marta, on the other hand, was exactly like him. She was filled to the brim with misery. Any more and she would have started spilling misery, like a liquid, out of her mouth. No court in a just world would ever hold against him that he did to Marta the thing that he had hoped, his whole life, someone would be brave enough to do to him.

He had decided to do it a long time ago. After their parents died. Years ago, when she went crazy for a day and a half. She was screaming, threatening to slit his throat like a pig. Her skin sallow and her eyes dark. It was all he could do not to burst into tears at how pitiful she looked. And he had decided, then, that perhaps it was better for everyone, her included, to help her – well, get over life, really. That is all there is to it. He wondered why humans made such a big deal out of murder. What a very ugly word, too, that gave no justice to what he had done. There should be a new word for it, to differentiate this from that. The crime from the kindness.

The word for what he did was soft as a feather, and heavy like love. It was a bottle full of stars, a light kiss on someone's forehead when they're deeply asleep. It was the only act of real selflessness he had ever done in his life. It was an act so inexhaustibly kind, so beyond anything Eleazar ever thought himself capable of doing, that it made him dizzy.

Eleazar, mouth agape, looked at the trees that lined the banks of the little canals. It seemed to him that the quality of the air was different; it was charged differently, its texture made of atoms from another, better planet. And in the dead of night, the boughs were all aglow, pink and blue, as if a thousand magical fireflies had landed all along them and were dozing off.

From where he sat, he could also see the city lights dotting the horizon like some sort of magical painting. The city, so close to their town, yet a million miles away. And there, a million lives; some of them full of misery, others better adapted to this, all going about their evening activities.

What he learned today was that he loved Marta more fully, more beautifully, than he did Mariam. Because he had been able to give Marta what he could never give Mariam. A chunk of his life. He did not worry about Mariam, she would go on, drinking sage, cleaning the house, living modestly and comfortably off what was left of their parents' inheritance – and his, and Marta's – until they all became mere specks, memories of pain in old Mariam's mind. We forget. It is the deepest gift that the gods gave us; to forget. She will forget them; perhaps senility one day, in some decades, will finally free her from the memory of her crooked, pained, siblings, and she will then be free.

He wonders, for a second, what the funeral was like. Just half a second, not more. The whole village must have attended and Mariam must have looked very dignified in black, standing all alone, abandoned by everyone in her family, everyone dead or vanished, just like that. The widow of an undead country. She must have smelled of muskroot, which she wore like a protection. He didn't know if there was much of a body to bury but – he'd rather not think of that. It had been a hard task to accomplish, one he had forced himself, eyes wide shut, teeth clenched, to carry out until the end. Just like he had, a few years prior and – no, really, there was no use to think of that. Acts of selflessness. He deserved some peace of mind now. He owed it to himself.

He had a garden, pink and blue at night, to tend to. He had at least that. There was solace there. Marta, she had had nothing inside. Her soul (he knew! he knew it, and when she looked at him with eyes dark and full of the fury, he understood what she was asking him to do, and Mariam was too innocent to ever understand him and Marta), her soul was a desert, a very ugly, barren desert and perhaps in another world, some other universe, she would have been able to tend that desert, to make it a pretty little place, but she could not and all he did was help her. All he did was carry out what she had asked him to. It had been, he reflected, her last cruelty, to ask him to carry this weight for her.

The city, far away and below, glittered invitingly. And behind him, the town was in darkness (the residents had, recently, taken to stealing the street lamps; it felt like a joke, the ultimate snub to the city folk who arrogantly thought they'd bring them light). Somewhere there was Mariam, happily alone (though she did not know it yet; though she thought she missed him and Marta), going about her nightly chores before bed. There was Mariam, in quietude; there was serene Mariam. Soon he would vanish for good; and Mariam, once grief had subsided, would grow more peaceful.

The muscular hand, which had clenched at his lungs ever since he could remember, let go. He breathed in. The air was new. This was the most precious part of his soul, and here he was free.

Ride On, Shooting Star

MAY HADDAD

CARNA' KARAKI'S CERVA HAD JUST ENOUGH FUEL TO REACH THE
Narra Harbor. But as she struggled to maneuver her scooter through
the cosmic turbulence, she realized that, for the first time in her career
as a courier, she was running on empty. Securing her grappling hook
against the nearest comet, she landed on its surface as gently as she
could, then lay back and let gravity handle the rest. If she was lucky, she
could hitch a ride without refilling her tank.

*

Earlier, Carna' had gone missing and needed to be tracked down to
the resto-café at the other end of the universe. Though she was never
one for alcohol, Carna' could always drink her problems away here at
the Leafs of Lebanon. Except, that is, on the night that would've been
her thirtieth birthday back on Earth, where she just sat at the counter,
contemplatively staring down at the crystal glass in her hands as old
Fairuz songs played in the background.

Expecting the worst when her supervisor Achut arrived with the
return order stamped by the Courier-Master General herself, Carna'
was surprised to see him sit down quietly beside her instead and casually order tabbouleh and drinks. The man seemed to be minding
his own business, and for the first time, Carna' noticed that his carved
face had furrowed since she had first met him, giving him more distin-
guished features that had aged him beyond his years.

"You've finally joined me for a meal," Carna' mused out loud, hoping
to end the prolonged silence that seemed to dictate their conversations.

However, her manager chose not to reply, enjoying his salad silently, seemingly unconcerned with having to clock back in on time.

"You know…" Achut finally remarked, sipping at a shot of arak after the tabbouleh was picked to the last shred of parsley, "ever since you told me about this dish, I'd been meaning to try it when – if I ever made it back to Earth. But this might be my last chance … for a while … "

Carna' leaned in playfully. "Finally saved up enough for a vacation?"

"No," Achut dabbed his mouth with a napkin. "Not that I'm looking forward to leaving the UCS to become a shipping super." He then studied his watch, looking like he was fighting the urge to get up and go. "Moving on to more of the same isn't what I had in mind when I thought I'd finally get the chance to leave this job, but the husband and I are looking to adopt, and I can't afford to be doing this in my forties."

Carna' drunkenly rested her chin on her palm.

"Come on, being a courier's not that bad."

"You mean the low pay, long hours, and nonexistent benefits aren't that bad."

"Well, maybe a little."

"Like you, I signed up to be a courier because the final frontier was where I had to be, and money was an object. But, having done this for over a decade now, I wonder why I thought it would be any different than Earth."

"But, chasing me down's not so bad."

Achut opened his mouth to say something clever but seemed to reconsider before looking around the resto-café with a tinge of regret in his eyes and said:

"Yeah," he sighed. "Maybe it's not."

To think that Carna's fading nation could be found all the way across the known universe was as remarkable to her as her being here – here, instead of the monotony of life back in southern Lebanon after the last of the civil wars ended when she was a child. Though she found herself comforted by the familiarity of the establishment she was in, this served little to quell the profound wistfulness that had set in.

"I wish I could come here whenever I wanted."

"I'm sorry management felt the need to 'limit' your mobility after the last couple of 'detours.'"

"Come to think of it, this job was fine before that." Carna' buried her head in her hands and groaned. "You know — if you don't overthink the low pay, long hours, and nonexistent benefits. Being a courier meant there were places to be, people to meet, and all the adventure you could ever want out of life."

"Honestly, I've been meaning to ask for a while." Achut removed his spectacles and ran his hand over his face, rubbing his eyes. "But why haven't you left yet?"

Carna' was taken aback.

"What do you mean?" she asked, confused.

Achut turned away from her with a tinge of embarrassment.

"You seem miserable," he replied after a moment of silence.

Carna' frowned, but she understood why he'd asked. "I'm not sure. I'm having trouble figuring it out myself. Something doesn't feel right about leaving this life. I mean, what else would I do? Where else would I go?"

Achut sighed again. "It's going to be a pain. But . . . " He paused, looking like he wasn't sure if he wanted to propose something. "Before I vacate the position, I can sign off on an all-expenses-paid vacation that'll let you head back home. Of course, you'll have to spend most of it delivering packages to some of the most unsavory places on the planet, but it'll all be worth it with the low pay, long hours, and nonexistent benefits."

Carna' laughed. "Sounds lovely." Then she closed her eyes and tried to imagine what life would be like for her back on the farm. "Maybe . . . "

Now lost in her own thoughts (and five shots of arak), Carna' was on the verge of falling asleep when Achut suddenly snapped his fingers, bringing her back to the Leafs of Lebanon.

"I just remembered . . ." Achut seemed to speak sheepishly now. "There's one last assignment on your schedule before I can send you back. But . . . if you'd like, I can reassign it to —"

"No."

•

As Carna' made her way to one of the military stations off the moons of Resheph, she was surprised to find that her destination was not an outpost but one of the compounds that housed the families of those in service. These required less stringent background checks and pat-downs, but the sight of soldiers was all the same unsettling.

Parking her Cerva in one of the stations designated for guests, she entered the compound anxiously, only to be caught off guard by the immaculate presentation of it all. Carefully concreted paths led to scenic homes with trimmed lawns and identical vehicles designed only for transport in the facility.

The stroll to the home of Brigadier General Eleni Hiraya was, if nothing else, pleasant, though she found it too quiet for comfort. The Brigadier General waited for her outside her doorstep, cross-armed, in full uniform and shades. Standing there in silence, she cut an intimidating figure to Carna', who was nowhere near as tall, and though Carna' was muscular herself, she could not compare to the soldier's lifetime of dedicated weight work that had tightly toned every muscle in her body.

Carna' walked up to her with trepidation, but when the Brigadier General recognized the logo on Carna's bomber jacket, her expression lost some of its hard edge. Immediately reaching into her bridge coat, she pulled out what appeared to be a pouch and, nestling it in her hands, informed Carna' with a sincerity that seemed unusual for her:

"Please take care of this." She paused, then added with a chuckle. "It's for my parent. I hope you understand."

"Right." Carna' saluted respectfully before carefully taking the pouch and placing it in the pocket dimension inside her jacket. "This'll be there in no time."

Cautiously, the Brigadier General studied Carna' and seemed to like what she saw.

"If this is delivered intact and on time, we could use your services for the war effort."

Startled, Carna' did not react, but the Brigadier General seemed to pick up on the panic in her eyes.

"I'm not so sure I'll be able to commit to that with my current queue," Carna' eventually managed to say. "I hope I can —"

"Obviously, no one could ever turn this down. It's not exactly an option . . ." she cut her off, trying to respond as pragmatically as her stilted idiolect would allow. "Of course, you'll be well compensated for your time. More so than the UCS could ever provide on its own. Our partnership with them is well-established, and I'll reach out to them myself once all of this is settled."

"Of course." Carna' nodded, trying her best to hide what she was thinking. "I just need time to consider this . . ."

Memories of the war she had grown up with came flooding back, and the monotony of life in Southern Lebanon after it had ended suddenly wasn't so unappealing. Taking her leave as quickly as possible, she rushed straight to her Cerva, hoping she had enough fuel.

✦

No one knew what happened to the couriers who went AWOL. Carna' had never heard of anyone who had tried. The whispers passed along from those who had worked at the USC before her seemed just as unsure, if slightly more cautious, about the whole prospect.

Once the compounds were out of sight, Carna' slowed her vehicle down so she could check her map for somewhere that she would want to go, and that would be extremely difficult for the USC to track her down in. Having traversed far more of the known universe than most spacefarers, few locations piqued her interest. However, as she flicked through the location pins on the hologram, one image caught her eye with its intensity.

The globular cluster Araphel is said to be one of the most magnificent sites in the entire universe. With star interspersion ranging from one every 0.4 parsecs to 1,000 per cubic parsec, the cluster is immensely dense, offering a rare glimpse of brilliant intensity in an otherwise cold, barren universe. Gazing up at Araphel from the surface of a planet within its span would offer her a night sky to remember – one that Earth could no longer provide.

"Carna', is something wrong?" A text from Achut appeared on her visor, reminding her she no longer had the time to plan these excursions as she once did. "Incoming data says that your Cerva's stopped in the middle of nowhere, drifting away."

"Yes," Carna dictated a text back to him. "There's a minor mishap that'll be cleared, but it'll take time."

A brief eternity passed before Achut texted back.

"Understood" was all his message said before adding a moment later: "Be careful."

There was no doubt in her mind that she could hide out in the Araphel cluster before planning her next move, but how to get there was a matter that needed to be addressed immediately. The sideways path she mentally mapped would traverse a meteor shower that, if she could navigate, would make it costly for the UCS to chase after her.

Of course, there was risk involved. There was always risk in the life of a cosmic courier.

But, for the first time in a long while, that electrifying surge coursed through her, reinvigorating her dispirited pneuma as she leaned in and gripped the handlebars. Shifting gears towards her new destination, she activated her visor, perceptually slowing down her vision so that, when she hit the pedal, she could steer the Cerva as if she was riding her cobbled "scooter" back on Earth. With no time to spare, she opened the throttle, kicking everything into high gear as her tracker informed her that she was off course and quickly entering a red zone beyond which she should not venture.

"Carna'!" Achut's voice message coming in, his alarm and exasperation evident but forced. "Is the Cerva going haywire?!"

However, this stunt only encouraged her to go faster, and she found herself in the meteor shower, dodging fragments as she tried to make her way across. But, as she approached the end of it, a counter she'd never seen before began to tick down to an unspecified outcome.

This was when Achut's incoming call was activated automatically without her express permission.

"Carna' — we're unsure if you can hear us." She moved to end the call, but the screen before her did not respond to her input. "Your signal's too weak to track, and if you leave the known universe, it'll be impossible for us to intervene. Vitals and specs seemed fine when the last report came in, but I believe that something may have happened on your way there that could have damaged the vehicle." Flicking the switch to shut down all communication didn't work either, and she realized then that whatever control she thought she had over her scooter was a charitable pretense under which the UCS dealt with their couriers.

"If so, all I can do now is wish you good luck and hope you make the right choice . . . "

Despite fearing that the scooter would somehow immobilize her or, worse, self-destruct, she pressed on, knowing that this might be her only chance to make it out of this mess before she had to return to Earth and figure out how to get back here.

But it was no use.

As soon as she was out of the shower, the Cerva shut down, and Carna' was left stranded right before the bounds of the known universe with a signal sent out for rescue. The message on her visor explained that if she wanted to reactivate her vehicle, she would need to redirect it towards the drop-off point.

Though she was worn out in a way she had never been before, she knew that should the rescue crew bring her back in, she was as good as done, and the offer that her supervisor had made would remain on the table at the Leaves of Lebanon, along with her choices and future.

There was just no way around it.

A parcel needed to be delivered, and as a cosmic courier, she was the one to deliver it.

Whatever it took and whatever that meant anymore . . .

*

When Mx. Hiraya, the overseer of Narra Harbor, was notified that a lifeform was detected in one of the colony's comet collectors, xe rushed to the infirmary, hoping whoever was picked up by the drones was alive. But much to xeir dismay, xe found Carna' laid out, contorted beyond comfort, and prayed that her death was a painless one. Before xe could sign the cross, Carna' stirred and politely asked xer to quiet down and then, by habit, promptly turned over, revealing the "Cosmic Courier" logo on the back of her bomber jacket – before tumbling off the care bed. Having slept through solar storms as serenely as she had on her bunk back at the station, it would take a lot more than falling headfirst to wake her up, but now that Mx. Hiraya knew why she was here, she wanted answers.

After Carna's vitals were confirmed to be safe, xe ushered Carna' to xeir caregiver, GARISOL, who picked up Carna' as effortlessly as one would a child and carried her back to the farm.

*

It wasn't long before Carna' woke up to birds chirping. Though she knew where she was, when she stared out the window, she could've sworn she was back home on the hilly slopes of southern Lebanon. Evergreen hills stretched as far as the eyes could see. Pines, oaks, firs, beeches, cypresses, and junipers inhabited the landscape with turbines elongated high above them, patches of solar panels placed where they could not disturb them, and tidal fences constructed in the gentle streams that flowed amidst all of them. Bucolic in every sense, its vistas of sylvan charm harkened back to Mother Earth before humankind had traversed past its home planet into the boundless frontiers of space.

However, when she got out of bed, she almost didn't notice that for the first time since she had left to explore the universe, she could move around the same way she did on Earth.

But she couldn't. She didn't know how to anymore. And fatigue finally getting the best of her, she fell back onto the bed with a thud.

"Carna'!" Mx. Hiraya ran to the guest room, rushing over to inspect xeir guest.

Carna' gazed up at xeir statuesque face, only vaguely familiar to her, and noticed its graceful countenance even in a situation as concerning as this.

"How did you know my name?" Carna' asked, unusually at ease in xeir slender arms.

Losing no time, Mx. Hiraya responded with controlled urgency as xe inspected Carna's vitals: "To confirm your identity, we were given access to the tracer on the engine."

"That's where it is . . ." Carna' muttered in a daze. "If I could just . . . just . . ."

"Are you alright, Ms.?" Mx. Hiraya asked, worried that Carna' might not have had enough time to adjust to Narra Harbor's specifications, but Carna' replied without so much as a thought:

"Yes."

Having grown up in Earth's gravity, navigating outer space was as exhausting as it was thrilling. Each excursion out of the postal station left her enervated – so much so that it was only a matter of time before this would happen, but that was not what had startled her.

"What is it then?"

"This is just how I remember it . . ."

•

"Mx. Hiraya!" Carna' called out as she made her way down the stairs of the cabin. "Where are you?"

When she finally found the kitchen, GARISOL, preparing a spinach apple salad with honey balsamic vinaigrette, placed the ingredients on the counter to pull out a chair for its servee. Once Carna' sat down, GARISOL scanned her vitals before carrying on with its lovely salad. This act of kindness was made all the more amusing to Carna' as GARISOL seemed to be a repurposed War-Mech painted over in shamrock green and egg-shell white, its hulking figure meticulously arranging the apple slices standing in stark contrast to the picturesque kitchen they were in. Not that this sight was new to her. As a cosmic courier, she encountered more than her fair share of War-Mechs. But GARISOL, with its bulk and outdated tech and gadgets, was a model far older than any she had come across. There was something endearing about it, a gentleness in those old circuits known only to those who'd experienced war.

After carefully placing the salad on the dining table, GARISOL held out a knife before Carna', startling her until she realized she was being handed utensils.

"Carna'!" Mx. Hiraya called out from outside.

Carna' rose to meet xem, but GARISOL gently placed its rusted manus on her chest, softly guiding her back into her chair, and then pointed its index at the bowl. It then threw the towel over its angular shoulder blade and slowly trudged towards the front door.

Carna' chose to wait before digging in, but having not eaten since she set out here, that resolve did not last. By the time she had picked every last bit of spinach, GARISOL opened the door for Mx. Hiraya, and xe strode in with a smile that put her at ease.

"I'm told you've recovered fully." GARISOL pulled out a chair for Mx. Hiraya, who chose to stand. "Not that there was anything to recover from other than exhaustion. I must say hightailing a comet was an 'inventive,' if peculiar, way to make it to the harbor."

Mx. Hiraya finished off xeir comment with a self-satisfied smirk. Despite her desire to maintain professional cordiality, Carna' found herself smirking back.

"And, somehow, safer."

"Yes, and I'm sure that reducing battery expenses also plays a part."

"A part." Carna' affirmed, amused. "We couriers aren't exactly paid well."

Mx. Hiraya laughed, then sat down and untied xeir long black hair, letting xeir painstakingly brushed hair flow.

"How long before you have to head back?"

"This harbor is as remote as it gets for a courier in the known universe, so I've been given 'ample time,' considering I'm the first ever to journey out here."

"My, my. I guess you are. And you're so young, too. How on Earth were you talked into it?"

Carna' thought about it but couldn't come up with an answer. Mx. Hiraya carried on without missing a beat.

"And you must've bought yourself time with that extravagant joy-ride."

"I'm hoping to get back as soon as I can."

"Back to?"

"I'm not sure, to be honest." Carna's eyes went blank. "This might be my last delivery before I head back home."

"You don't seem to be happy about it."

"I won't know till I get back, I guess."

"You don't seem to enjoy your work much either." The vivacity in Mx. Hiraya's manner seemed to fade. "Not that I can blame you. I was in a similar position myself once upon a time."

"Were you a cosmic courier too?"

"Not exactly." Mx. Hiraya theatrically brought xeir palm to a heavy brow. "In some respects, it was far worse."

Carna' turned towards one of the windows and stared out into the evergreen hills with a disaffected gaze.

"Any advice on what I can do to get myself out of this rut?"

"That's a good question, and I think I might even be able to help."

Hearing this, Carna' lit up, but Mx. Hiraya seemed to be considering xeir next words carefully.

"Carna'," xe clasped xeir hands. "GARISOL and I were wondering if you'd be interested in helping out while you're here."

Farming was the last thing Carna' ever wanted to do. The agrarian life she led back on Earth was even more suffocating than working for the UCS. Still, she owed it to her host, who seemed keen on having her participate in it.

•

As Carna' put on her motorcycle helmet, a hover-tractor driven by GARISOL — now sporting what seemed to be an oversized, hand-woven straw hat — arrived to pick up Mx. Hiraya, who raised xeir baro't saya and hopped on. Taking the wheel, xe drove with exhilarated delight as GARISOL held onto its hat.

"Park over there, Carna'!" Mx. Hiraya called out.

Arriving first, xe positioned the tractor right in front of the entrance and then hopped off with an electrified zeal – unlike GARISOL, who, despite its lack of discernible facial features, seemed quite shaken from how long it awkwardly held on to the safety handle after the vehicle had stopped moving.

For some reason, Carna' expected a far more elaborate structure, but the aeroponic farm was modest, contained in a white translucent tent as far from the lodge as it would be sensible to traverse in regular intervals. By the time Carna' managed to find stable ground to park her Cerva safely, GARISOL was able to let go of the handle but chose to sit there silently, as if contemplating its choices in life.

"Are you alright?" Carna' asked, her helmet still on, but GARISOL did not reply, and she realized that she hadn't heard it say anything the entire time she was there. "We'll be inside if you need anything, GARISOL!"

Carna' left her helmet on the Cerva's handle, grateful that, for once, she didn't have to hide it in her scooter's seat before some punks spotted her until she realized that there was no fun in that.

•

Owing to the logistical difficulties of eking out an existence in such a remote location, Carna' expected to be introduced to an aeroponic farm unlike anything she had seen elsewhere. But it seemed just like the ones her family had back home. Worse yet, Mx. Hiraya inspected each crop in the aisle carefully, even though all the tech surrounding them gave Carna' the impression that there was no need to. "Is this it," she thought while trying to suppress the notion, but it only seemed to perplex her more. All the blood, sweat, and tears that went into taming the final frontier seemed to lead back to the same life she had abandoned back in southern Lebanon.

"It's not as intimidating as it seems," Mx. Hiraya commented without taking xeir eyes off the crops. "By the look on your face, I'm wondering if this is new to you."

"Maybe." Carna' shrugged. "Maybe not. I guess it is in a sense . . ."

"Oh!' Mx. Hiraya seemed intrigued. "I thought you were from one of the settlements."

Carna' suddenly couldn't hide her bewilderment. "Why?"

"Oh," Mx. Hiraya started grinning. "You give off the impression."

"No," Carna' audibly sucked in air through her teeth. "I wish I had lived in one of those settlements."

"You wish?" Mx. Hiraya raised an eyebrow. "Be careful what you wish for, dear."

For once, the cosmic courier thought a moment before responding.

"I guess life, where I'm from, is that solar dream without the punk ..."

"Oh, my lord. It can't be that bad. My guess, life there is . . ." Mx. Hiraya motioned xeir hands, trying to find the right word, but Carna' beat xem to it:

"Monotonous."

◆

Once they were outside again, Carna' kicked around as Mx. Hiraya got xeir things in order. Carna' assumed that it would be time to head back, but basket-in-hand, Mx. Hiraya walked away from the tractor, heading to what appeared to be a forest from a distance.

"Where are you going?" Carna' asked, exasperated. "Is there more to do?!"

Mx. Hiraya carried on cheerfully.

"Follow me."

Carna' got off her scooter and followed Mx. Hiraya, who led her through the forest and into a glade by a river where xe had placed a blanket and taken out food and drinks for what looked like a picnic. The spread was just as sumptuous as the dish she had back in the cabin, with the lentil bolognese and whole roasted cauliflower, in particular, enticing her appetite. However, having spent the last couple of years being worked to the bone, this all seemed too good to be true. Was their brief excursion back there in the aeroponic farm all the help that was needed from her?

"Are we really done with the work?" Carna' asked in a disconcerted tone that caught her off guard.

"Yes." Mx. Hiraya sat down and patted the ground. GARISOL walked past Carna' and sat down on the grass near xem. "GARISOL, and I thought you could use a change of pace."

"Is this it?" Carna' asked, sounding more dissatisfied than she would've liked.

"More or less." Mx. Hiraya laughed. "GARISOL and I could also use the company."

"Then why stay here at the harbor?"

"This is where I've always wanted to live. None of my friends and relatives seemed to share my desire to live here, but that wasn't going to stop me. Frankly, I've given them my time, as they have for me, and I decided to do this one selfish thing for myself for once. It wasn't easy to build this station, but nothing worth living forever is."

Carna' looked around as if she was flustered by the whole arrangement.

"You designed it?"

"Yes." Mx. Hiraya stood up to stretch xeir arms and legs. "Years of engineering finally put to good use."

"Why?" Carna' realized she sounded more baffled than she thought herself to be. "I mean, if you had the chance to design anything, why this?"

"Why not? Eventually, you reach a certain age where you can't take any of the hustle and bustle of life back there in the frontier and need to settle down somewhere safe and quiet."

"That's what I've been told," Carna' replied, sounding more disheartened than she realized.

"How bad could joining them here be," she thought, trying to talk herself into it. But, by the time she had her third biscuit, Carna' had already grown restless, staring off into the distance where she became transfixed with the path that led uphill to where a lone wind turbine had stood.

Without a word to Mx. Hiraya and GARISOL, she quietly stood up, brushed herself off, and walked towards it as if in a dream ...

*

The Narra Harbor was far larger than she could have ever imagined, but she did not know what this confirmation meant. Perhaps she was hoping for something different or even something she had grown familiar with over the years. From the peak, she could take in the expansive landscape in all its wonder, but to Carna', it was much of the same — just more of it.

All she wanted to do was take her Cerva up here to ride it off the cliff and see how far it would take off before she would need to hover. The thrill of the thought alone had her surging with renewed vitality. But that would disturb the carefully constructed serenity on which Mx. Hiraya was no doubt keen. There was a time and place for adventure, but it was not now and not here.

And, besides, she would have to go back eventually — as she always did.

•

When she returned to the farm, Mx. Hiraya and GARISOL greeted her in much the same way she would have expected her family member if she had ever returned to Earth.

"Where have you been?!" Mx. Hiraya asked, concerned. "Are you alright, my dear? You seem discouraged."

"Nothing happened," Carna' responded apathetically.

"We know." Mx. Hiraya brushed the hair out of her face, gazing at her with a tinge of worry. "That tracer installed in the Cerva allows us access to the chips installed in tracking your location and vitals at all times and warns us if you're in danger."

Carna' frowned. "I should head back."

"You really want it gone, don't you?" Mx. Hiraya put xeir hands on xeir hips, trying to size up the situation. "How are you liking the Harbor? It's a nice change of pace from the grind of spacefaring, isn't it?"

"It's wonderful," was all Carna' could reply, but Mx. Hiraya still looked concerned. Noticing xeir expression, Carna' silently walked away, making her way to the Cerva, where she discreetly pulled out the parcel from the pocket-dimension in her sac and placed it where

GARISOL and xe could see it. Without so much as a goodbye, she hit the pedal of her Cerva', speeding in the direction of the lone wind turbine up the slope where she would ride off the cliff and blast off into space.

•

There was no time to spare. While she flew within the confines of the Narra Harbor, a signal would not be sent back to the UCS HQ. But, as she exited the force-shield that encompassed it, she knew that the counter to shut down her scooter would start ticking and time was not on her side.

True, the distance between her and the boundaries of the known universe was shorter here at the edge of civilization, but that did not make anything easier. The UCS was on to her now, and there wasn't much Achut could say or even do to mitigate the fallout from this one.

Knowing that it was now or never, Carna' activated her visor and opened the throttle, reaching speeds that no sane courier would ever dare, just so she could buy enough time to hopefully make it into the unforgiving depths that no person in their right mind had ever traversed before.

And it was exhilarating.

Dodging debris and projectiles hurtling at her so fast that she barely could register their presence before having to avoid them left, right, up, or down, Carna' could feel life surging through her again. Every successful miss brought her atom-by-atom, scrap-by-scrap, closer to the freedom she had longed for when she was just that farm girl back on Earth. But the clock kept ticking. No matter what she dodged, no matter how fast or skillfully she maneuvered, the counter relentlessly ticked down. There would be no Achut this time to put his reputation on the line to intervene and talk some sense into her with messages, voice notes, or calls. Years of experience were finally being put to the test, and the weight of this strain would slowly but surely wear her out.

But she had to press on — she needed to. Except, that she didn't expect that she would drain so soon . . .

For the first time since hightailing that comet, she realized just how exhausted she was, and she could feel that numbness in her legs, that cramping in her hands that soon dulled their capabilities. Each dodge and maneuver was now less instinctive, less methodical, and that soon gave way to carelessness.

When her grip had finally locked on the handles in an uncomfortable clutch, she could do nothing but move left and right, up and down, unable to take her hands off the handlebars. Still, she hoped to outpace the timer at that speed now that her hands could no longer adjust.

But that would not make a difference. The Cerva's sensor glared red, suffocating Carna' in sight and sound, warning her of an asteroid that was coming straight at her.

Knowing what was coming, however, did not mean she could dodge it.

Carna's only hope now would be to relinquish control to the AI, but that would allow HQ to wrest over the Cerva from her and direct her back to the Narra Harbor – the last place she ever wanted to be, or perhaps, the penultimate one. Indifferent to a life that bound her to the Earth, she lay back and let gravity handle the rest. If she were lucky, she wouldn't feel a thing. Not that she felt much of anything as the asteroid hurtled toward her.

However, as she closed her eyes and accepted her fate, a hulking figure of shamrock green and egg-shell white soared before her visor – right before she passed out.

•

"Come now." Mx. Hiraya called xeir guest over with emphatic grace, taking her by the hand as she was preparing her Cerva to depart back to HQ and receive the brunt of Courier-Master General's unrestrained rage. "Our tea is waiting downstairs."

"Oh, I couldn't." Carna' sheepishly waved off the offer, needing as much time as she could save up to try and dismantle the tracer in her scooter. "I really have to head back now –"

But Mx. Hiraya wouldn't entertain the thought, and Carna' followed xem to the patio without protest. There, GARISOL was pouring green tea into yunomi against a backdrop of pastoral wonder. To think that it was only a short while ago that bulky frame had raced for her Cerva at the speed of light and smashed through an asteroid with a deteriorated manus. Having been all over, few things could wow Carna' in the known universe, but this old hunk of junk was somehow, someway, one of them.

Taking the chair facing the solar panel fields, Carna' sat there silently, taking it all in, wondering what her next move would be if there were one.

"Ms. Karaki," Mx. Hiraya turned to Carna' with a firm, but patient gaze, as GARISOL left their company. "I'm assuming that something was meant to be delivered to me."

"Oh, yes. I almost forgot." Carna' laughed nervously, unzipping her inner pocket-dimension and reaching inside to pull out a pouch that wasn't there. "Wait, but I left it back at —"

Mx. Hiraya nodded patiently.

"Yes, and here it is." Mx. Hiraya pulled the pouch out of her pocket and handed it to Carna'. "It would be ideal if the sensors picked up on the fact that you're handing it to me by hand, as opposed to leaving it near the woods. Don't you agree?"

Shamefacedly, Carna' nodded and promptly followed Mx. Hiraya's instructions. In spite of the terse turn their conversation had taken, no irritation or grievance could be discerned from xeir face, and Carna' found herself cheering up when xe lovingly cradled the sack in xeir hands with a smile that could melt Ganymede and untied it with bated breath.

"Oh, this is just what I've wanted!" Mx, Hiraya exclaimed, hands clasping xeir cheeks.

"My family would love this too." Carna' mused. "We used to plant these olive tree seeds back home."

Mx. Hiraya smiled coyly.

"You mean back on Earth?"

Startled, Carna' stood up straight in her seat.

"How did you know," she muttered under her breath.

Mx. Hiraya shook xeir head, trying xeir best not to chuckle.

"That look on your face back in that room. Let's say it's not one I'm unfamiliar with. Is that why you left?"

"No." Carna' struggled to find the words. "There was this yearning in me to blast off into space and live – for once."

"Ah," Hiraya smiled. "You're a sensation seeker."

Carna' nodded, though she had never thought of it that way. Hearing Mx. Hiraya say it, however, made it sound true.

"You're right. I am a sensation seeker, but I don't know if I could continue living a courier's life under the USC. This all makes me wonder if I should ..."

Carna' suddenly went quiet. The mere thought would've been unthinkable only a couple of years ago.

"In a way, I was once an explorer – one of the first, actually," Mx. Hiraya remarked, then, with an amused grin, glanced over at xeir guest. Carna' though taken back, tried not to show it. "That's all right. I know. I never seemed the type for that kind of living. Too prim and proper. This sanctuary was, in fact, my retirement gift for a life of service."

"But why this?"

"It's the complete opposite of the army sites that I'd gotten sick of."

Carna' shifted uncomfortably in her chair, but she wasn't exactly sure why. Maybe she should tell xem about what the Brigadier General had 'proposed' back at the military station.

"You don't seem happy," Mx. Hiraya remarked empathetically. "And my daughter mentioned that you weren't exactly excited about the 'promotion' that she offered you. I have no doubt she's baffled by that, but, in time, I think she'll grow up like the rest of us did."

"I am. It's just –"

"Have you considered heading back home?"

Carna' nodded.

"Me too."

"Why haven't you?"

"The same reason you haven't. Not that home was ever as nice."

Carna' thought for a moment about her option. Perhaps for the first time, but she came back to the same unsatisfying answer that had led her to this life in the first place.

"Maybe I should find somewhere in the universe to settle," she mused.

"You think?" Mx. Hiraya leaned in and tapped the table. "How about here, dear?"

Carna' blinked, bewildered, but Mx. Hiraya carried on as if it was the most casual invitation:

"GARISOL and I could always use more—"

"No." Carna' paused for a moment before adding with a nod, "And thank you."

Mx. Hiraya chuckled.

"That was the answer I was expecting." Xe rolled xeir eyes playfully. "Maybe not as promptly."

"But I know I can't keep going on like this with the UCS."

"How about striking out on your own?"

Carna' had never thought of that before, and why would she? It's not like it ever was or ever would be a feasible option.

"You mean as an independent courier? I've got no money for my own scooter, and it would take years for me to save up. I don't think I have the years in me to give to the Universal Courier Service."

"Ah, I had a feeling," Mx. Hiraya said, then told her — seeming quite assured of what xe was saying: "That's not something you need to worry about anymore."

"What do you mean?" she asked, just as GARISOL made its way back to the patio, then walked over to their table and gently placed some broken chips onto it.

"Are those —"

Mx. Hiraya nodded and chuckled.

"Yes, the tracer and a bunch of other 'restrictors' placed on UCS space-scooters." Xe then brushed the instruments of Carna's torment off the table as causally one would dust. "The last report sent to the UCS was that the parcel had finally been delivered to the Narra Harbor." Mx. Hiraya winked playfully. "We thought the UCS would prefer that the queue be completed before you hijack one of their scooters. It's all yours now, of course. No reason for the UCS to send someone here if there's nothing more to deliver. No way they could find you now or reason enough to waste the resources to try to recover one scooter out here."

Carna' was speechless.

All she could think to do was lunge and hug Mx. Hiraya, then GARISOL, who both managed to hug back in their own way.

"Thank you for this — for all of this."

"You know," Mx. Hiraya leaned back in xeir chair, pondering the possibilities. "We would have loved to have you here."

"I can always come back." Carna' took a deep breath. "Maybe someday."

"Will you?" Mx. Hiraya asked, amused — already knowing the answer.

But Carna' considered it seriously, for just a moment, before gazing up at the endless expanse beyond the clear blue sky.

Turkish Delights

OMAR FODA

"I'M THE PRIME MINISTER!" I SHOUTED AT RAGHIB PASHA.

"I'm eternally sorry, my lord," he said, head bowed. "I meant no offense. But I have overstepped on account of how important this Hamid Bey could be for us in the Delta."

"Yes, yes, you ignorant donkey. No one is that important."

"If he runs under our banner in the election, I'm assured the rest of the large landholders in his province will follow him. With his constituency, we will have every big landholder in the Delta and will have a stranglehold on the region. Coupled with our strength in the provinces of Upper Egypt, we will be able to quash the opposition. Their popularity is limited to Cairo, Alexandria and the surrounding provinces. This is especially important because free elections are so new in this country. What we do now could have an effect for generations. I want to repeat, pardon my rudeness, that I have been told to tread cautiously with him."

"Enough!" I yelled, hoping to peel the stupid off him. He skittered away. He was a sweet, foolish boy. I let him brief me before these meetings as part of my promise to his mother, my mother's sister. She was right to worry about him. I heard he wrote plays in his spare time. They would eat him alive. Because of my affection for my aunt, she would always sneak me some lokum when my mother wasn't looking, I suffered him telling me things I already knew. I drew the line, however, at warnings about peasants, no matter how rich.

He knew of my previous positions as the governor of Fayoum, Minya, Minufiyya, Sharqiyya, Gharbiyya, and Dakahliyya, but did not understand what that meant. I had planted generals throughout the provinces, so I was aware of this Hamid Bey and all the other farmers puffed-up by their fortunes drawn from the pitch-black land and their precious cotton. I knew this man did not even have banners up in his village declaring his candidacy for parliament. I also knew the extent of his wealth. My generals warned me about him, but they warned me about everyone. I'd never had a problem. I was well-versed in how to undercut the bluster they brought into my office, thinking my skin, not so darkened by the laboring sun — almost as white as the lokum that now sat on the tray in front of my desk — covered a soft middle that would allow them to leave an impression if they pressed hard enough.

The boy surely grasped my skill. He was at my inauguration as the Minster of Foreign Affairs. He saw the pomp and respect the King gave me. He also had witnessed bull-headed village headmen leaving my office domesticated and Brits exiting with their stiff upper lips quivering. He was even in the crowd when I gave an impassioned speech to our party leadership and our British allies. Not an eye looked away from me and my gesticulations. I remember the disorienting applause.

It may be time to let him sit in on these meetings. Then he wouldn't dare talk to me the way he just did. Meetings with the British were a good entry point. They had an innate ability to unsee any Egyptian who didn't matter to them. Egyptians would spot his weakness and use it to undermine me.

He had a good grasp of English and earnestly believed that elections were won with good policy and respect for voters' intelligence. The British loved to hear that, believing they had gifted us a wonderful form of government that brought out the best of man. All the while, they played the game of democracy just like us, relying on shows of power and personal charisma. By speaking their language of rights and representation, using names that rolled off my tongue with perfect pronunciation, I convinced the limeys that I was not so different from them. Like how the lokum, Turkish Delights as they called them, weren't so different from their Jelly Babies.

The lokum, or melban as the peasants called it, was part of my game. My guests would see it when they first entered my office, but I would only offer it to them after we had sat and talked for a bit and the coffee boy, Mahmoud, brought in the drinks. It let them see I could offer something sweet, if they decided to follow my rules.

But that offer was the intermediate step, a lifeline, if you will. I first had to show them where they stood, or rather sat. It was a rickety, cushionless wooden chair. I made sure to have it polished and presentable so that they were caught off guard when they sat and found the seat uncomfortably small. Even the smallest hipped would be left sitting with flaps of themselves hanging over the wooden rim. Any movement would also set the chair into spasms as it negotiated the uneven floor with its even more uneven legs. The dance was made more disconcerting by the chair's shortness, it was dwarfed by my heavy wooden desk and its palatial chair.

The third phase of attack was the cigar. If my message had reached them and they accepted the lokum and my offer, then I would offer them a cigar. I would pick up my cigar, which was always lit beforehand, and we would happily bathe in our thick, shared smoke. Our laughter and expressions of companionship pushing clouds between us. If they had plugged their ears to my message, then I would offer them only a cigarette. I would proceed to overpower them with words and the nimbuses billowing from my mouth. Their small little clouds being swallowed by mine. By that point, everyone understood. It was customary to be generous when guests arrived, both the Egyptians and the British expected it, but I did not let age-old habits prevent me from asserting myself.

The farmers and peasants wanted to see and feel power. Once they did, I could lead them to the ideas of votes and constituencies and rallies and compromise. The sons of Albion needed to see the Oriental's charisma. They believed that their superior fire power and advancements in technology, which we could not yet compete with, meant they were superior in all things. That's why these spindle thin half-men, with skin peeled by the unobscured desert sun, came into my office thinking they could ignore me. Pay lip service to the foolish savage.

They all left enthralled. I was a credit to my race, and they could all imagine working with me.

The meeting with Hamid Bey was a chance to see how my new chair could enhance my routine. It had a large dark mahogany frame and was upholstered with a merlot-colored leather. It sat upon a rod, also mahogany, that extend out into four wheels. The mechanism meant I could roll it back and forth between my desk and the wall, which was adorned with the picture of the King, and rotate a full three hundred and sixty degrees. It even allowed me to lean back. In the few days I had had it, I had come to rely on the backward bend to express my displeasure at the boy without scolding him. If I pelted him with too many insults, I would hear words from my aunt.

It was only when he suggested forcefully that I be careful with Hamid Bey, that I shot up from my chair and screamed at him.

Now that he had wisely left, I readjusted my suit, sliding my hands down the front to feel the wonderfully crafted fabric and eliminate any creases. I instinctively jumped into my grooming routine. Running my right forefinger and thumb in opposite directions over my mustache, and then my right and left forefingers over my eyebrows. I reached up and verified my tarboosh was properly sitting.

Why did he insist on warning me of this man, one who I had never met but had met a hundred times? Was it because of his training at al-Azhar? There was little doubt that I could not keep up if he aimed to discuss the dusty sciences of jurisprudence and moral philosophy. But those weren't relevant to our laws and our government. We had crafted a new advanced Islamic society which mixed the best the West had to offer with our morality. That meant I, who had studied in France and spent time in England and had not forgotten my roots, was the master of the knowledge needed for this world.

I was also royalty. A cousin of the King. What was he? Yes, he knew the dirt. But so did the worm. Like the ibis, I had flown across this whole country and feasted on worms. I picked up my cigar and let my throat and chest fill with smoke. I wanted to add something more theatrical to our introduction, so I blew a wall of smoke as the man walked in.

I could scarcely see his face behind the cloud, but I saw his freshly polished black shoes, visible in the penumbra, and heard the tapping of his cane on the tile. The elderly were even easier to sway to my cause, they had so little fight left. But as his face appeared through the smoke, he was not as aged as I imagined. His beard was shaped into a large white tuft below his chin with neatly manicured sides that hugged his jaw and upheld his powerful cheekbones. As he walked to the traitorous chair, it was clear he did not need the cane to walk. It was meant to punctuate. The smooth alabaster ball that sat at the top, the point of contact between the man and the stick, looked menacing. I thought I saw flecks of red on it, but when I blinked, they disappeared.

"My dear Hamid Bey, please sit. It is a great honor to have you visit me today. I assume that the trip was uneventful."

"Yes, your grace, it was. I thank you so kindly for hosting me today and honoring me with your invitation." If there was any emotion in the words, I could not find it.

He sat, with severe posture, which seemed to disarm the chair. If Raghib had come in at that moment and removed it, the Bey would have been undisturbed, maintaining his seat on an invisible chair. The poor little chair was perplexed.

I didn't need a chair to bend this village thug! Look at his dark skin, it was a shade darker than the mahogany of my chair. Look at how he was dressed! His white waistcoat sneaking out from under his black galabia. His white turban, the mark of an al-Azhar graduate, making the blackness of his dress and the brownness of his face even more stark.

"What would you like Hamid Bey?" I asked, ostensibly enquiring what he wanted to drink, but hoping, in the cold pit of my back, he would ask for more.

"You are too kind, your supremeness, I do not need anything."

He refused three times, using the same words and the same gesture. Each time bringing his darkened mahogany hand to his chest, to supplement his words of apology. The hand was thin, calloused, and brimming with the power to rip out a cotton boll.

The third time the hand came to his chest, I noticed how crisp white his waistcoat was. My eyes darted to his galabia, also spotless. No dried clods on the fringes. I found the fake modesty pretentious. Why not dress like a proper modern man? Who was he trying to fool?

He finally relented and asked for a coffee with no sugar. I matched him. I could just as easily display my abstemiousness. I should've known he would have turned down the Turkish Delight when I offered it after Mahmoud brought in the coffee.

"No thank you, your resplendence, I am not one for sweets."

His face carried the gauntness of forbearance. I was by no means portly, not like some of my kith and kin, but I carried the soft unwillingness to deny myself the joy of sweets and other finer things.

"I have brought you here so that we may discuss your membership in our party," I said.

"My advisers tell me you are planning to run for parliament."

"If God wills it, your grace."

"And they tell me you have yet to put up banners or posters. That is good! When we come to our agreement you can put them up in support of us."

"I will not put up anything. I trust God and the people of my village. They do not need cheap signs to understand my positions and how I will fight for them."

"Fair enough, the signs can be seen as intrusive, especially in a rural setting. Speeches and feasts do a better job anyway."

"I will not do those things either. The people know me, and I have earned their respect through fair and honest actions. My family's reputation is unimpeachable. If God has ordained my victory, then nothing I will do will change that. I will only have a feast afterwards to celebrate our good fortune and assure the villagers I will always stayed tied to them."

"Yes, of course, God has a Plan for all of us. I'm sure you know what is best for your constituents." I was at a loss for words. The man had no political sense, yet my general told me he would win easily.

"We, the party bosses and myself, believe you would find the party very much in line with your sensibilities. We think, inshallah, you can be the leader of our effort in Dakhaliyya for years to come."

"If God Wills it, your grace," he said softly with none of the eagerness I expected.

"You will find that we have access to the halls of power," I said, gesturing around my office, "And that we have the interests of the great landowners, like yourself, always in our minds. You are the backbone of this country, and we are committed to ensuring your prosperity for generations. Egypt will, inshallah, become an independent world power carried by men like you."

I did not even bother offering him something to smoke. I picked up my cigar and took a big, long drag. As I sat with it, his dark jasper eyes bored new holes into my forehead. I hadn't noticed until now, but even seated he looked down on me. If I had spent a moment looking at his shoulders, I would have seen, I was dealing with 'Ug ibn Anaq.

The inside of my cheeks burned, and I was forced to jerk my head to the right and blow out the smoke. Despite my cheeks' urgency to rid themselves of the acrid smoke, I maintained my sangfroid. I had been forged in the most intense negotiations. I had faced death and never shuddered or stammered.

"Raghib Pasha," I shouted. Now was the time to show the boy my power, to teach him who ran things, to make clear what democracy demanded, what this country demanded. I would slay this bogeyman, the frightful, duplicitous, pious, severe, unflinching, uncompromising, unsubtle peasant. I would do it with the third pillar of real democracy, favor. It was the failsafe when power and charisma were not enough. I would offer him the thing he could not abstain from. The thing he desired, even if he was not aware of it. A place besides those of fair complexion and noble lines, a title like my title. He would be a pasha, something his sow of a mother, who birthed him in some mud-floored hut, could never imagine.

I eased my chair away as I said, "Hamid Bey, to show how much we value your loyalty, I wanted to present you with . . . ," and then I pushed my right side into the chair, spinning it to the cabinet behind me. It was a technological marvel. I could only imagine what the future held for chairs. Maybe an engine would move you wherever you wanted with a pull of a lever. I unlocked the top drawer of my cabinet and sought paper with the official seal to write out the promise of his future pashadom. We would schedule his official investiture for a later date. I fumbled with the paper, and I looked for a pen, but remembered that it was, of course, on my desk. I was so out of sorts.

I pushed my jittery body back and to the left in the chair and successfully spun in a parabola that landed me nearly to the position I started. When I looked up, I saw Raghib Pasha standing behind the empty chair.

"Hamid Bey has left, your grace."

I threw the pen and paper at the ignoramus.

"Did you give him a drink?"

"Yes."

"Did you give him the lokum?"

"No, he wouldn't take it."

"Cigar?"

"No."

"Did you offer him pashadom?"

"I was just about to. I was turning around in my chair to get the papers."

"You turned around, while still seated in the chair? You didn't get up? You didn't say anything to him? If you pardon my saying, I told you he was a prideful man."

"And I told you, you dunce, not to worry. I know these men, his only other political option is the nationalists who hate landowners like him, he is bound to return to us."

"Yes, your grace, I'm sure he will return."

"Of course he will, I'm the goddamn Prime Minister," I screamed.

The Settlement

TARIQ MEHMOOD

SHE WAS SECURE IN THE STOREROOM OF THE FIRST SETTLE-
ment that had sprung up on top of Hill 21. The room had no windows
and the door was locked from the outside.

"I have a few questions for you," I said to her, but again she gave the
same answer, "What animal are you?"

Every now and then she banged on the door and screamed. A gut-
tural scream, which had changed over the past few hours, from one
filled with fear to a beastly groan.

Like everyone from the Settlement, I too was hated by the people
of her village, which was outside the security parameter. These were
squalid places, full of dark alleys with stubborn inhabitants who refused to move on with the times. In villages like these, it was always the
same: old men stopped whatever they were doing and stared coldly at
us when our patrols went past; young women, looked at us and spat on
the ground, and you had to have your eyes in the back of your head out
here, especially when schools finished. You never could be sure which
of the vicious bastards would lobv a rock at you.

I wasn't much liked in the Settlement either. Not only had I come
from the city to conduct the enquiry, but I was on the darker shade of
skin color to be a proper one of these zealots, all of whom had traveled thousands of miles to live in ultramodern houses, inside a barbed
wired enclosure.

"I should have shot her when she came screaming towards the
check-post. It was a clear shot," Private K said. "I don't know why I

hesitated. That's all it took for them to catch up to her, drag her down, throw her in the van and bring her into the Settlement."

He was on guard in front of the storeroom.

"Sometimes it is very difficult," I reassured him. He was in his early 20s but looked much younger, especially with his short hair and round glasses. "Did you see who set the tree alight?"

"I was detailed to protect them when they went to pray there, that's all," Private K ignored my question.

"Who set the tree on fire?" I repeated.

He looked away from me, shook his head and said, "I just saw her standing in the lower branches first. There were other soldiers from my unit, but she spat at me again and again. Once she pointed up in the tree and said, 'Beloved, so long as there is breath in my body, no one will step in your place,' And then she spat at me again and I brought her down."

I thought for a while, imagining the scene. The woman in the tree, a tree with which I was familiar. It had fist-sized frayed brown leaves, and its trunk was split into two enormous parts, which resembled a human figure leaning down on one knee, with the other leg going around it. It was claimed to be the tallest and oldest tree in the world, now partially burnt, with strange branches that sprouted in all directions, from what appeared to look like seven crafted platforms, each one rising out of the other. The leaves of the uppermost level seemed to melt into the sky.

My mobile vibrated and brought me back to the job at hand. I received some CCTV photographs. One showed the woman running towards the communal open-air swimming pool. Another showed frightened swimmers scrambling out. Another showed her being wrenched out of the water by two men. One showed her kicking one of the men.

I went into the living room to continue with my investigation. The room had a carved wooden bear dangling from the ceiling.

S., my next interviewee, was sitting at a table, her hands wrapped around a cup of tea, which was placed next to her Settlement-issue pistol. She had shoulder-length brown hair, and sharp blue eyes.

As soon as I entered, she looked up at me and said, "I want you to know how I deeply appreciate your investigation." Her voice was charged with emotion. "I am eternally grateful for the fact that the tree survived."

I nodded.

She continued, "I mean what has that tree not seen?"

"Who do you think actually set it on fire?" I asked.

She sighed, "I have long argued that the only way to save the tree is to bring it into the protective jurisdiction of the Settlement. If this had been done, then there would be no need for your investigation and all this waste of time and resources."

I wasn't making much progress with S. and said, "That will be all for today, but I may come back to you."

She pushed the cup away from her and stood up crying, "I am deeply disturbed by the way those men held her and did what they did to her inside the Settlement."

"Indeed," I concurred and then asked out of curiosity, "Surely you saw her running around in the playground, why didn't you apprehend her?"

"I was off duty at the time and was far more concerned about my daughter, who was terrified," S. replied calmly. She spoke with a stiff upper lip. She had warm brown eyes and a broad smile. She continued, "I had heard on the radio that a terrorist was running amok inside the Settlement. It was 3:15 p.m. I was on my way back here when my car cut out. I was about three kilometers away from the edge of the village, it's a notorious part of the road, hidden between two hills, where stone throwers often target us, but thank god, the car started, and I managed to get here."

S. left and I finally managed to get to B. and D., the main witnesses. They came into the room a few minutes later.

B. was a thin man, with long hennaed hair tied into a bun at the back of his head.

"A bit of straight talking would help," I said to B. "This investigation has dragged on already."

He looked at D., who scratched his tattooed neck and smirked.

"This is not a laughing matter," I said. "The tree is protected . . ."

"I was about to shoot her when she fell into the pool," D. said running a finger through one of the curls of his hair dangling by the side of his face, "but as I am the pool keeper, it would have meant a lot of cleaning."

"Is it wrong to assume, that as you two were the only ones by the tree, one of you, or both of you set it on fire . . ."

"*He* forgets he is not in the jungle anymore," B. laughed, tapping D. on the shoulder

I didn't rise to the bait and kept quiet.

D. added, "The tree is sitting on the temple of *our* ancestors."

"She could have set fire to the tree and then climbed it, for all we know," B. said.

"According to the report, there was no hint of petrol on her clothing or . . ." I changed the line of enquiry and asked, "Why were two of her fingers broken?"

"They can use them as weapons," D. said touching a fresh scar on his forehead.

I dismissed them with a wave of my hand. They stood up and left.

I finished writing my notes and was about to leave when S. came back. She was flustered.

"As a woman, I am really disturbed by what happened here. She is a woman, after all," she said. "I mean, when wolves get the taste for human flesh, they can never stop wanting it, can they?"

"No, I suppose not," I replied and went to the storeroom to check on the prisoner.

S. followed me.

"Who opened the door?" I asked pointing to the storeroom. The door was ajar.

"I did," Private K replied.

"Why?"

"She would not stop asking?"

"What?"

"'What animal are you?'" he replied. His arms dangled by his side. His weapon was leaning against the wall. "And I know why she asked me this and why she spat at me."

"Stand to attention, Private!" I ordered.

He didn't and said, "She knows who I am, I am sure of it."

"Stand to attention, Soldier!"

He raised his head, picked up his weapon and obeyed.

"Where is she now?" I asked.

'Still inside?" he replied.

I tuned my ear towards the storeroom. There was a rustle of leaves, and a moment later she stepped out. Matted earthy brown hair covered her face. Her open hands raised skywards.

By the time I unclipped my pistol holder, S. had shot her in the stomach. The captive fell down a few feet from Private K., first on her left knee, then the right slid behind her, all the while muttering something unintelligible. She threw her head back, her hair flicked off her face. Her blazing eyes stared unblinkingly at me, and then she smiled.

The Peacock

SAHAR MUSTAFAH

FERYAL SITS AT THE HOTEL BAR AND SIPS HER SUGARY COCK-tail. Annoyed with the cumbersome fresh fruit garnish, she removes the plastic spear of sliced pineapple and strawberry and watches their juices soak into a tiny napkin the bartender gave her. He was much more amiable when he'd mistaken her for a tourist. As soon as she opened her mouth and spoke perfect Arabic, he nodded coldly at her order and set about blending her frozen virgin drink, casting glances over his shoulder.

Feryal swivels around and watches the hotel patrons. A white European couple sits in the lounge area, a private conversation drawing their bodies close, shutting out the rest of the world. A small group of hijabi women in stylish abayas and lavish couture purses, laugh and chatter above each other. They sip from the same tropical drink as Feryal's. She's the only woman sitting alone. Her neck flushes and she swivels back to the bartender

In her peripheral vision, a man heads to the bar, his silhouette tall and slender. When he doesn't clear his throat or tap her on the shoulder, Feryal casually turns toward him and smiles. He glances at her then leans into the bar, his back to her. He thumbs his mobile and continually checks the entrance to the lounge until his pensive expression breaks. A beautiful woman appears at the man's side and they order champagne. The bartender offers them an expansive smile before pouring two glasses that nearly fizz over. Between sentences, the woman's laugh bubbles up like the champagne she's sipping. Not once does she look over at Feryal.

Feryal is disappointed. The man is handsome and fit – he doesn't have to pay for sex. She hopes, for her first time, her appointment is attractive. She measures every man against Othman, the only one she's been with. She misses his hard, muscled chest and dark features, in spite of his not loving her back. What a fool Feryal had been, believing he would leave his wife – even when Feryal lied about being pregnant

If you have the baby, it will destroy your family. Don't be stupid, he told her. *I will pay for you to pull it down.* The easy way Othman had said it, like he'd found himself in this situation before, still scalds Feryal's heart. How could he have professed to love her if he was perfectly willing to get rid of his child?

She took his money, told him she'd made an appointment at an Israeli hospital, bought herself a bus ticket, stuffed the leftover bills inside the compartment of her old messenger bag, and never looked back. To the undiscerning passengers seated across the aisle, she was a student attending university.

Feryal taps her sandal against the footrest of her stool until another man approaches. This time she keeps her gaze fixed straight ahead, fingers her plastic straw. Behind the bartender, she studies the reflection in the mirrored panel. A balding man with hunched shoulders shuffles toward the bar like someone about to deliver somber news. Feryal's stomach sinks.

Don't stray from the lounge. He'll find you, Ani had advised her earlier, standing naked in the kitchen of their flat, rifling through a basket of clean laundry. Her roommate's lack of inhibition shocked and impressed Feryal. Ani found a pair of panties and a loose summer dress, and slipped into them.

They met at a posh outdoor café in Ramallah. Feryal was sitting at a table by herself, newly arrived in town. She was anxiously calculating the cost of her meal before ordering, when she caught a stranger studying her from across the terrace. A woman with short fashionable hair, dark-tinted sunglasses that nearly swallowed her face, and a pair of golden hoops dangling from her earlobes. She flashed an amused grin at Feryal.

A server returned to her table. *The sister wants to treat you to a meal, Miss.* He pointed across the canopied terrace and the woman waved, summoning her over. Feryal's cheeks turned splotchy red: she felt bumpkin in her long tunic and mules.

The stranger removed her sunglasses and two cat eyes peered intently at Feryal. Long bangs swept her forehead and she tucked them behind her ear with manicured fingers until they fell loose again. Ani is half Armenian, half Palestinian, though she doesn't tell Feryal which side belongs to which parent, only that she's a *double tragedy of history.*

Where are you from, ya hilwa? She drew on a black vape stick and tipped her head to release smoke away from her face.

Ain al-Deeb, Feryal responded, a pang of fear and nostalgia rushing her lungs.

The only thing in al-Deeb is a factory, I believe.

A warehouse, Feryal says, surprised this elegant woman has heard of her village. *For textiles.* She sensed men and other women glancing Ani's way, catching their attention before they resumed their conversations and tea.

You're visiting alone? Her cat eyes roved down her face to her breasts.

I'm never going back, Feryal blurted, cheeks blazing.

You're a pretty girl, Bismillah, Ani told her appraisingly, nodding toward a basket of pocket bread cut into neat triangles and a small bowl of hummus. *Please.*

Self-conscious, but ravenous, Feryal dipped the bread, brought it carefully to her lips.

Ani watched her intently. *What will you do here?* Another deep intake of her vape stick, smoke snaking into the air.

An important question to which Feryal had no answer. She was at the head of her class in math and linguistics, earning one of the top tawjeehi scores in her neighborhood. Yet there was no celebration for her matriculation from secondary school. Sitti Rasmeah, her paternal grandmother, prepared a batch of ghraybeh, Feryal's favorite shortbread cookies. When she was a little girl, she had sat across from the old woman, eagerly waiting to offer her small contribution – a single thumbprint in the center of each, forming a tiny mound to be filled with ground pistachios or fresh-made apricot jam.

Now each cookie has your special mark, her grandmother winked at her. She cleaned the batter from her fingers with a dishrag and pull out a piece of hard candy from the breast pocket of her thobe. There seemed to be a wonderful surprise every time Sitti Rasmeah slid her hand inside the chest-panel of her embroidered dress: a silver shekel, a stick of gum, a sky-blue marble. It was a trove of delights. When she nestled in her grandmother's lap, she traced a row of opposite-facing peacocks, sewn in variegated purple and yellow thread, each cross-stich perfectly uniform.

After she sat for her matriculation exams, Feryal's mother announced her schooling was done.

It's a shame. The girl is smart enough to be a lawyer, mashallah, her Sitti Rasmeah had argued. *A doctor, even.*

She can marry a lawyer or a doctor, her mother had scoffed. *Until then she must pull her weight around here.*

Feryal went to work in Othman's warehouse, where a quarter of the villagers earned their wages. She expected to work the floor, pulling boards of fabric for orders, or standing on a wobbly ladder, dusting row upon row of crushed velvet, denim, and lace. She was grateful to be assigned to the office, and away from the prying eyes of the older women. Othman's previous assistant, a sympathetic hijabi woman in thick glasses named Salma, was finally getting married. She trained Feryal on the computer, explaining the application process between enthusiastic interjections about her khateeb. *He's from Nablus,* Salma told her.

He's prohibited from traveling north, but he promises I can see my family whenever I want. She patted Feryal's shoulder. *Azeem! You pick up very quickly – mashallah!*

At a small desk in the office, Othman drew the blinds after the workers went home and fucked Feryal in his swivel chair. He seemed utterly enamored with her, impressed at how quickly she learned and performed her duties, telling her how clever she was. She opened up to him like a crisp, new textbook, ready to be learned.

I hear you were first in your class, he said, zipping up his pants.

I could have gone to university, she told him, her chest flooding with pride.

But then you wouldn't be here. He pinched her bottom. *Did the invoice for the Husseini order get settled? Those bastards never pay on time.*

At the café in Ramallah, Feryal told Ani, *I wish to enroll at university.*

Ani's gold-speckled eyes glimmered and narrowed. *And how will you pay for it, ya hilwa?*

Feryal bashfully chomped at her expensive shawarma sandwich which Ani insisted she order. It wasn't as flavorful as the ones back home which were for half the price.

If you trust me, I can help you. Ani leaned conspiratorially. *Women like us need to stick together.*

Feryal wasn't sure what kind of women they were – or more importantly who she was – but Ani's easy laughter and the way she tenderly touched Feryal's hand across the small table were disarming. She was already missing her grandmother's kindness.

•

The bald man lingers a few stools down from her. In spite of what she can make of his looks and age, Feryal hopes he's the one so she won't feel obliged to order another drink in case her actual date is running late. Ani has been gracious since she's arrived, paying for Feryal's food and keep, welcoming her to a box of Kotex pads and her expensive shampoo. *You'll pay me back*, Ani smiled at her, *as soon as you get on your feet.*

He appears Arab – foreign-born, confirming what Ani has told her. She has a contact in the Palestinian Authority who arranges these things.

He's some kind of a scholar. A director of a museum in Belgium, Ani offered as she waved her wet glossy nails dry. *He's on a temporary visit. Acquiring something for a special exhibit, I think. I'd take him except*

Mario has been giving me shit lately. She paused to admire her nails — the color of slick eggplant skin — then batted her eyelashes at Feryal. *Do this for me, ya hilwa. I've already confirmed.*

The fact that he's affiliated with a museum makes it less egregious for Feryal to accept the proposition. And he certainly looks the part, she observes now.

"Good evening," the man tells the bartender, glancing sidelong at Feryal. "A Scotch, if you please." His Arabic is clipped as if he's not accustomed to speaking it often.

Basheer — another customer had called the bartender by name — heartily greets him, placing a small round coaster in front of the man. "Welcome, ya Ustaz."

Feryal notices a laminated badge on his lapel. Her heart beats wildly. For a moment, she thinks of leaving, hopping off her barstool and exiting as quickly as possible. But she waits, sipping the remainder of her cocktail until she hits ice cubes and is forced to stop slurping.

Wait until he addresses you first, Ani had instructed, zipping up Feryal's long, tight-fitting black dress. It has a high neck with a mesh bodice. It belongs to Ani, is not something Feryal would ever own. Though she's completely covered, the jersey fabric accentuates every part of her body and is uncomfortably tight around her bottom. *You don't want to stand out*, Ani says. *A wink, a smile. Nothing loud or crass. You want to appear as a quiet invitation.*

"Good evening, Miss," he finally says, his eyes darting nervously around the bar.

"Ahlan, ya Ustaz," she says a bit too hastily, swiveling her entire body toward him. "How are you, Professor?" Icy sweat trickles down her back.

He slips her a plastic room key. "Wait ten minutes. Room 405." He gulps the rest of his drink and abruptly stands, giving the bartender an overly jovial goodbye.

Feryal is stupefied. She expects dinner — something to break the ice. The hotel has an acclaimed Japanese fusion restaurant Ani raves about. She's eaten there several times with customers.

Basheer gives her a long look and his lips part as if he wants to say something to her. Feryal quickly settles her bill – which she'd also expected the professor to pick up – and finds a washroom. Her key allows her admission to a hotel toilet off the lobby. The cocktail syrup churns in her stomach and she begins to retch. She clutches both sides of the stall and breathes through her nose. At the sink, she palms cold water and gargles before reapplying gloss to her full lips. She fluffs her hair which Ani had spent a long time straightening. It looks dull, the ends like straw. The mirror reflects her pale face, brown eyes shiny. She checks the time on her mobile and finds a guest elevator. A hotel attendant presses a button and bids her a good evening.

Imagine it's someone you want, Ani had winked before Feryal heads out the flat. *Someone you once loved.*

She knocks on the door before waving her plastic key across the handle's "Hello?" she calls, tentatively stepping in.

The professor is already naked except for his undershirt and socks. He's laid a towel in the center of the bed, across crisp, white sheets. The fancy duvet is neatly peeled back to the foot of the bed. There's a pair of folded hand towels on his nightstand and a single condom.

"If you please," he says politely, gesturing to the bed.

She unzips her dress and pauses. He says nothing, studying her coolly, as if she's a new exhibit and he hasn't quite drawn a conclusion about her. She slips out of her panties, unclasps her bra. He's immediately on top of her, eyes clamped shut, and she stares into his nostrils, the long black hairs like the quills of a porcupine. Perspiration beads his bald head. As he struggles to enter her, she examines his face, wrinkles deepening in ecstasy and tries to imagine what he's like when giving a serious lecture. Do those same age lines contract in serious contemplation?

Ani chuckles at Feryal's shock, that a scholar would requisition sex. *All men have cocks, ya hilwa,* she says. *In the end, the only thing that separates them is which head they think with.*

The professor finally begins to rock back and forth on top of her. After a short time, he grunts and she knows he's close. He emanates a strange combination of menthol, camphor and lentil soup – not the crisp and spicy fragrance of Othman. Perhaps these are the natural odors of an older man. His body is no longer active, his brain becomes his major organ – besides his cock – until both begin to fail him. Feryal imagines the professor's biceps haven't always been so flabby. His paunch slaps against Feryal's stomach, an embarrassing sound that makes it difficult to think about anything else.

◆

Feryal's body has never really belonged to her. Not ever since she was nine years old and her maternal uncle coaxed her into his lap and pressed his erection against her. When her body transforms, the boys in the harra notice, even under her loose clothes, hungry wolf eyes penetrating through the fabric, imagining her small, hard breasts, her rounded bottom. The store clerk rubs the back of her hand when she exchanges money for groceries until she learns better, spreading the coins across the counter, keeping her eyes down. The opposite sex suddenly lay claims upon her body, one she barely feels in possession of herself. Her existence becomes an affirmation of their desires, their power to ravish her. She no longer belongs to herself.

Her mother grows harsh, as if Feryal's body is a liability, a precarious entity on the brink of catastrophe that will bring down their home. She stares while Feryal does her chores around their flat, sweeping floors, dusting the window frames. Her mother calls her away from the small veranda that overlooks a narrow street. *Do you wish to be on display for all the neighbors?*

Feryal's father is the only man who looked at her with love, not scrutiny. She was 13 years old the night their building was raided. Israel's occupation forces arrested her father, hauled him away on suspicion of conspiracy to commit acts of terrorism. Three soldiers threw a black sack over his head, so Feryal was unable to see his face for the last time, his pure adoration twinkling in his eyes every time he beheld her.

Sitti Rasmeah attempted to intervene, clawing at one soldier's body until he knocked her down with the butt of his rifle, shouting at her to stay put. Feryal ran to her side and was violently shoved backwards by another soldier. Her mother was on the floor, clutching her husband's leg and held on until a swift kick to her head finally released her father.

The next morning Feryal's first period arrived.

Her father languished for four years in prison before Israel ejected him into Jordan. Her mother was inconsolable, snapping at Feryal, their only child, calling her a "habla" and "good for nothing." She wondered what she was supposed to be good for, how in her father's absence she might ease her mother's pain. She moved around their bayt like a ghost, trying not to make a noise or disturb anything that would incite her mother. After her chores, she finished schoolwork and read a book her teacher Miss Basima had loaned her, a translation of *Anne of Green Gables*. Once a year, her mother traveled to a refugee camp on the other side of the border where her father took up shelter. Feryal pretended to be orphaned – not only of her father, but happily of her mother – and in her imagination, she embarked on new adventures like the red-haired, precocious Anne.

Sitti Rasmeah, who has lived with Feryal's family since she was born, gives daily du'aa for her son and the members of her family – including her daughter-in-law whom Feryal secretly believes unworthy of supplications. In her mother's absence, a calm settles over the flat, a gossamer happiness like the long white strands of her grandmother's hair. Feryal looked forward to two months free from her mother's cruelty, the horrible verbal lashings. Sometimes it was a hard slap across the face, or rough fingers snatching the soft flesh of her upper arm and twisting it awfully, making Feryal's eyes instantly water.

Pray to the Prophet, Sitti Rasmeah would admonish her daughter-in-law. Then she smiled at Feryal. *Come here, my dear,* Sitti Rasmeah smiled. *Help me with this.* And she'd set her to a task that made her feel useful and good for something. Her grandmother, on powerful and sturdy haunches, showed Feryal how to core squash without piercing the skin and how to mince parsley and onion for folding into freshly ground lamb.

You can still be book smart and a good cook for your children one day, Sitti Rasmeah had said with a wink, retying a white mandeela at the base of her neck, a few gray, straggly hairs escaping her temples.

Around her black thobe, bright green and yellow smudged her white apron, joining other faded stains.

One day, Feryal pointed to the row of peacocks prancing across her grandmother's bosom. *What kind of birds are those, Sitti?*

Al-tawoos, her grandmother smiled, trailing a craggly finger over one. *You see their feathers? They'll be in jannat illah when we arrive someday, by the Lord's will.*

They are regal creatures to Feryal, evoking respect and veneration. Among a dozen stitched by her grandmother, she loved this thobe best of all.

•

When the professor is finished, he rolls off Feryal's body, wraps the slimy condom in tissue paper and tosses it into a wastebasket. He lights a cigarette from a pack stamped in foreign words, not offering her one though she doesn't smoke. He shuts his eyes as he exhales, murmurs something to himself she can't make out. Then he writes in a tiny notebook on his nightstand, as if he's just worked out the answer to a problem in his head.

Feeling ignored, Feryal props herself up on one elbow. She hasn't properly taken in her surroundings. The hotel room is modern décor, finished in a muted white, black and royal blue palette. The professor's belongings — a single opened suitcase, a few paperback books scattered on a lacquered cherry wood desk, and several prescription bottles — disrupt the tidy space. Directly across from the bed is a television screen hidden behind the doors of an entertainment center. There's an oil painting on the same wall, the silhouette of a woman standing on a sandy shore, one hand clasping her straw hat against the wind. Frothy waves crash at her feet as she watches the last traces of the sun dipping below the horizon.

Feryal wished she could linger alone in the cool sheets of the bed, order room service — Ani told her about the late-night meals she orders on her dates and which Ani consumes naked beside her lover. Eating might help Feryal feel normal again. It's quiet inside this room, unlike the noise of their flat, cars honking below their steel-barred window, loud music pulsating from a barber shop below.

Sadness prickles her skin. She wants the professor to disappear along with all of his odors. She reaches for a water bottle on the nightstand beside her and gulps, trying to wash down her dejection, the same feeling she lugged home after an hour with Othman in his office. He'd kiss her cheek, examine his hair in a mirror hanging behind the door, and lock up.

Her eyes travel across the other side of the room. For the first time, Feryal notices a headless mannequin standing near the washroom. The figure is draped in a white thobe covered in a sheath of plastic.

"Who's that for?" she asks the professor.

His head shoots up from his notebook, his interest suddenly ignited. "It's a very important acquisition," he declares, springing from the bed. He stands beside the mannequin, producing an absurd juxtaposition of real and counterfeit bodies. His penis is deflated in a nest of graying pubic hair. He appears ready to give a lecture on the embroidered dress as he peels off the plastic sheath.

Feryal sits up against the headboard. "You came all the way from Belgium for a thobe?"

"Not any thobe," he says disdainfully before smiling in mock congeniality. "This belonged to a prominent family in Yaffa. My museum is acquiring it from the University. A pre-war relic like this will enjoy a much wider audience."

He delicately holds up one sleeve as if he's taking the arm of a beloved. "You see here," he says, his eyes shining. "There are idiosyncratic touches in the way the cross-stitches are . . ."

But Feryal has stopped listening. Sitti Rasmeah's face suddenly intrudes and her past tidal-waves into the hotel room. She's swept back to her family bayt, her grandmother brushing her hair when her mother has lost patience. Her grandmother's calloused palm, cradling a small luscious plum she's extracted from the breast pocket of her thobe. *Sweet like you, habibti.*

Feryal finds it hard to breathe, the ceiling suddenly collapsing, the professor blurring into the blue walls, his droning warped and distant. She squeezes her knees together and clutches the bedsheets until the hotel room regains its normal proportions.

The professor is pointing at the chest-panel, unperturbed. "The reflective nature of the peacocks reveals a perfect harmony."

"My grandmother loves peacocks," Feryal blurts out. "They roam in Paradise. That's what she told me when I was a young girl." She bites her lower lip to keep tears from falling.

He gives a mirthless laugh. "It's far more sophisticated than the eye can see." He lingers near the mannequin, brushes off a piece of lint before replacing the plastic sheath over the dress. He wraps a white terrycloth robe around his body and walks to the pair of trousers he was wearing earlier and withdraws a worn leather wallet from a back pocket. He extracts fewer bills than Ani had advised her to accept.

"I was told a thousand shekels," Feryal says.

"Perhaps a misunderstanding, my dear," the professor responds. "Take it or leave it. I'm having a shower. Please see yourself out." He slips his wallet inside the pocket of his bathrobe and locks the washroom door behind him.

The blood in Feryal's body runs white-hot. She can hear Ani's mocking laugh. *Demand what you're owed, ya hilwa. He'll give it to you in the end. No man will want a scene. Remember—you're in control of the situation,* Ani told her as Feryal slipped into a pair of silver strappy heels.

She rises from the bed, dampens a hand towel with her water bottle and wipes between her legs. It's not much different than her first time with Othman. He kissed her gently on her lips and neck before handing her a roll of rough paper towel he'd brought from the employee restroom at the warehouse. *You're still bleeding,* he'd said, and Feryal could hear a kind of pride and it made her feel special and proud, too, that he'd been her first.

She hears the shower running and finally climbs out of the bed, slipping into her bra and panties. Before she reaches for her black dress, she studies the thobe, touches the chest-panel over the plastic. She runs her hand under the protective layer and slips it inside the breast pocket. Once, Feryal had discovered a tiny bouquet of tiny jasmine flowers, the magical source of the delicate perfume that wafted from Sitti Rasmeah's body every time she drew Feryal close.

Unsurprisingly, the pocket of this thobe is empty. Whose grandmother had once worn it? What had she carried inside?

There was nothing technical or ancient about Sitti Rasmeah's thobe. Feryal had never regarded it in any deliberate way. It's how it made her feel – safe, loved – that lingered still. Such associations mean nothing to the professor, pose no real value in his important acquisition.

Feryal's heartbeat quickens. She quickly and carefully lifts the thobe from the mannequin. She pauses, listens for the shower and hears a faint singing coming from the washroom. She pulls the thobe over her head and cinches it at the waist with the professor's belt, which she removes from his trousers. A musty scent emanates from the linen fabric.

She gazes at her reflection in a full-length mirror mounted on a narrow wall between the bathroom and exit door. She touches the sparse, though recognizable plumage of the peacocks, then runs her fingertips along one triangular sleeve where a parade of rosettes are stitched.

Before quickly gathering her purse and sandals, Feryal drapes the naked, headless mannequin in her crumpled black dress – Ani's dress – its high collar drooping down one narrow shoulder without a neck to support it.

She leaves the money on the nightstand.

Foolish girl! Ani might tell her if she decides to ever return to the flat.

For Feryal, it's more than an even trade.

The Icarist

OMAR EL AKKAD

IN THE SUMMER OF THAT FINAL YEAR, SHEIKH HAMAD'S DAUGH-ter turned thirteen and they built her a private schoolhouse on the grounds of Doha College. That same summer, Mo'min Abdelwahad got braces.

He didn't know why he needed them. Something to do with curvature, a word his dentist used: They were not bad teeth, not hopeless, she'd said, but wouldn't he like a better smile? Mo'min had never considered the quality of his smile before.

He'd managed to keep his composure during the consultation but after they left the dentist's office, he started crying. The previous winter a classmate of his named Armand had gotten up to retrieve a math test from the teacher's desk without noticing a wayward erection. Someone had given him the nickname Kharmand and it had stuck. Mo'min was thirteen and these were bad years to be anything but anonymous. There was no surviving attention.

On the drive home, Mo'min's father said back where he grew up, in Shobra, your teeth did whatever they did and nobody did anything about it. Once when he was young he'd felt a tilapia bone go right through his gum, the pain so sharp he thought he'd throw up, and the only thing his aunt offered by way of remedy was a teabag to chew on. It's easier these days, he said, it's easier here.

It was noon on a Friday, the streets empty, the mosques filling. On QBS the Whigfield song cut out mid-note, a muezzin replacing it, and Mo'min felt, as he always did in moments such as these, a little guilty. Outside of Ramadan, when suddenly every breakfast was communal and came with the social obligation to perform the sundown prayer at whoever's house they were invited to that day, he only ever prayed on Friday — usually with his father at the mosque down the street from where they lived. It had been explained to him from early childhood that this prayer was special in some way, worth more in the grand accounting of things in part because it was done in such large groups, but in truth he'd only ever associated the Friday trip to the mosque with the end of the weekend. For the rest of his life, even after decades in the West, he'd always have a hard time associating Monday, not Saturday, with the start of the workweek.

His father said it was okay to skip prayer today. They went to Baskin-Robbins instead.

In early July Mo'min went back to the dentist's office for the procedure. The only part that hurt was when she inserted the wire. He felt the contours of his mouth tighten, and for a few days afterwards his jaw ached the way it did during those first few bites of breakfast on mornings when he slept in too late. He imagined it was the pain you felt when you got punched, but he'd never been punched before. In English class that year, they'd been forced to read a book about boys stranded on an island and he felt now a kinship with those boys, though he couldn't quite explain why.

*

Fall came. In early September, it rained for the first time that year and on the evening news the anchor led with thanks to the Emir for his fruitful supplications. At school, a few of the upper-year boys made fun of Mo'min but it wasn't as bad as he expected. Anders, who was two years older and lived in a suite in the Sheraton where his father was manager and normally wouldn't have wasted time on some kid in 7P, passed him in the hall one day and said it looks like the Bedouins up in Shamal are going back to their tents with scraped cocks tonight. Later, at first break, another boy in Mo'min's small orbit of friends choked a little on a bite of tuck shop brownie and Mo'min, seizing the opportunity, repeated the line Anders had said to him, and though or perhaps because it made no sense at all it got such a rousing response from the other boys that Mo'min briefly considered going to Anders and thanking him.

Months passed, and he disappeared as he'd hoped he would, happily avalanched under the school's endless supply of gossip. In October Miss Lordes and Mr. Polk ran off together to Australia and left that year's graduating class suddenly forced to do two years' worth of GCSE coursework in a semester and a half. Some parents complained, and one threatened to sue, but the chances of either teacher ever returning to the country were known by all to be, essentially, zero.

In November, it came out that Mr. Park, the graphic design teacher, had been sleeping with one of his students. For a while there was another rumor affixed to the first, a rumor of pictures that had been taken and possibly distributed, but this turned out to be a lie. Khalid, who was in 7P but had an older sister in one of Mr. Park's classes, said it didn't really matter either way: both teacher and student were British and the British don't care about stuff like that.

In December, Tamim and Lina started dating. Soon the teachers charged with patrolling the yard during first and second break learned never to go near the concrete alcoves round the back of the physics labs where the two spent all their free time. There were rules against physical contact between students, but no teacher was willing to risk their work permit to find out if those rules applied to the Emir's son.

Then in January, Tamim's sister came to school. She was Mo'min's age but he never learned her name.

For the better part of a year there'd been construction going on by the school's east-facing wall, hidden away behind plywood and canvas. Someone said it was a new technology building but nobody could figure out why Doha College needed yet another suite of sewing rooms and home economics kitchens to teach students the things their housemaids already knew how to do. And then in the new year Mo'min returned to find a small neighborhood of trailers, guarded by police officers along its streetside gate. In the morning, after the rest of the students had gone to first period, a parade of black-windowed

Mercedes sedans pulled up to the new construction, and the Emir's daughter walked into her own private schoolhouse.

By February, everyone had a story about how they'd seen her but almost no one really had. Someone said her name was Mozza or Manga, but someone else said it was her mother, not her, who was named after a fruit. She was stunning and hideous, useless at school and three grades ahead, and ranged in age from ten to nineteen. No one in Mo'min's orbit knew anything for certain or cared to find out. After school at basketball practice one day Anders said it was just her and Ms. Demitri in that compound all day, fingering each other dizzy. Mo'min had no idea why they'd be in there doing that, but the image of the school's biology teacher and the Emir's daughter sitting in a room pointing at one another until both keeled over struck him as funny in an absurdist way. The next day he repeated the joke to his friends at break. They found it funny too.

In March, it rained again and all the big streets flooded.

He had a few days off school. He spent most of them at Al Naseem, the compound where he lived. There was nothing to do. Sometimes his mother would tell him to go swim in the compound pool or play in the squash or tennis courts or go for a bike ride, but it was already getting too hot to do anything outside any time between noon and sundown. He spent the days watching *MacGyver* and *America's Most Wanted* on QTV and wondering about what kind of place America must be. He read his parents' copies of *Time* and *Newsweek*, holding the pages up against a lightbulb to try to see past the government censor's ubiquitous black ink, the smudged shapes of women in miniskirts or Israeli politicians all so tantalizingly close to visible. Toward the end of the month his father went to London on a business trip, and came back with a smuggled copy of *Sliver* on Laserdisk. The film was indecipherable to Mo'min even after the tenth time he watched it.

One morning his father took him for a drive out past the edge of Doha, into the desert, where clear of all other construction a single house stood seemingly without place or purpose, an aberrant thing. In the sanded clearing ahead of the house's front door were parked various breeds of Mercedes and Land Cruisers. His father parked near these cars and told Mo'min to wait. He went inside and when he returned a few minutes later, he carried a mango crate full of beer and liquor. Other men did the same, rushing out the door with their heads down, eager to leave the house and the desert that wielded its emptiness like an anvil on the chest.

In April, Mo'min went back to the dentist who said the treatment had worked much better than expected. After less than a year the wires came off and for a few days he felt the same fortifying pain in his jaw and believed now that yes he had been *through* something, had become tougher for it. He saw no difference in his smile, but his mother said it was straighter, more appealing.

Gone down the narrowing funnel of exam period, the students careened through late spring and into the hot glowing days that would forever mark Mo'min's memory of this place. There was less to do now but study for the end-of-year, finish up coursework. In early May he finally worked up the courage to ask a girl named Aysha if she'd go with him to the newly opened A&W but she said no. He went to the Dubai team try-outs and did all right in basketball, but Mr. Frome said they needed all-rounders since they could only take so many students on the trip. Still, it felt good to try for things, to build callouses against rejection.

The only person at school who'd noticed Mo'min's braces had come off was Anders. One day in the hall the two of them passed and Anders said I guess those Bedouins don't have to worry about getting their cocks all scraped. And Mo'min, before he caught himself, replied: I bet you'd know what that's like, which only later he realized was a non sequitur but still caused Anders to stop anyway and observe Mo'min not with anger so much as genuine surprise. And then Anders smiled and Mo'min, believing they'd shared a moment of something like camaraderie or mutual respect, smiled back and Anders gracefully, almost as though the motion were rehearsed, took two quick steps toward Mo'min and flicked the upper row of his newly realigned teeth. Fireworks shot up through Mo'min's gums, for a second he saw them as little white bursts against the field of his vision, and by the time the pain subsided, Anders was gone. The bell rang, sounding the end of second break.

All around him students began to return to their classes. For the first time, he experienced claustrophobia. The thought of sitting through another 80 minutes of tedium felt suddenly unbearable.

He had never skipped class before. He'd seen the upper-years jump the gate, hop in those boxy orange-and-white taxis and take off, but had never thought about doing it himself. Now, the pain in his mouth gone, he did. The day's last period was double science. Mr. Ballard never took attendance.

He waited out the bell by the east-facing wall, near the place where Tamim and Lina spent their time but far enough away from the physics lab windows so as not to be seen. In a few minutes the students had all returned to class. There was an ugly silence about the yard. In the distance he heard the Indians and Pakistanis and Filipinos working on the rugby club building, the sound of metal on metal, the occasional shout: *Yallah, rafik, yallah, no lazy, make work*.

Quietly he walked toward the school's front gate, unsure of whether he'd be able to get out unnoticed. Lacksman, the custodian, manned a small outbuilding by the front but someone said he spent most of the afternoon sleeping away the heat.

Before he got to the front gate, Mo'min heard a sound on the other side of the wall. It came from the new block of trailers, the hid-away place. It was a soft squeak, a repeating sound. Instantly he placed it as the chains on a poorly oiled swing.

Without thinking he climbed onto a stack of wooden crates, in which had recently been delivered a new set of sewing machines for the technology building. He peered over the edge of the concrete wall.

She was a small girl, her posture cashew-rounded as she sat rocking gently on the swing. In Doha College, the A-level students wore white dress shirts and black pants or skirts and everyone else wore shades of light and dark blue, but she wore neither. From the way she sat he couldn't tell if it was just another niqab or a black dress. She stared at her feet.

And then she looked up. She looked at him without expression, no hint of fear or shame or warmth or curiosity. It was not a poker face so much as a face that seemed unaccustomed to the mechanics of such interaction, the ways in which the muscles move to signal recognition of another, acknowledgement.

In the few seconds before he heard the sound of the teacher behind him, Mo'min stared at the Emir's daughter the way, years later, he'd stare at the grounded paintings in the basement of the National Gallery, the ones the curator let him inspect one night in a burst of indiscretion but which were otherwise locked away for reasons of suitability or fragility or internal politics, and which for the life of him Mo'min couldn't tell apart from all the paintings that hung in the gallery proper, one bowl of fruit no different than any other.

He smiled at her.

And then there was the voice of Miss Demetri behind him: "Are you out of your mind?"

He hopped down from the crates, half-stumbling. He apologized but Miss Demetri only said, over and over: "Are you out of your mind?" He had never seen a teacher behave that way before, so visibly, plainly afraid. She led him to the principal's office, walking three steps behind him the whole way there, as though he carried something contagious.

The next day he was marched again to the principal's office and told never to speak about what had happened, never to tell anyone. With great solemnity the principal said if word got out he risked expulsion and although the prospect did scare Mo'min he knew such things never really happened. Someone's father always knew someone else's father, phone calls were made, things got straightened out. Still, he told no one. The weeks passed.

In May, Mo'min went to a friend's birthday party in Al Misseilah. When his mother came to pick him up, it was clear she'd been crying. She did this sometimes, but not very often. It was something he'd simply taken as her way of being in the world. Less than pain or regret or the simple homesickness she only talked about indirectly every once in a while – going off unprompted about how artificial a place this was, how if the oil ever ran out it'd be a ghost town within a week – he associated it with boredom. He had no idea what his mother did with her days.

They drove home in silence. Just before they reached the compound, she turned at the lights and pulled into the parking lot of the Pizza Hut strip mall. They sat there a while, watching the young men drive in circles, yelling their phone numbers at the passing women. Occasionally a Land Cruiser drove by, its windows open, speakers blasting, the plastic covers still wrapped around the seats, as was the style.

Finally his mother said something had happened. That morning, the Sheikh whose sponsorship allowed Mo'min's family to remain in the country had called Mo'min's father and said his work permit had been revoked. There was no recourse, no process of appeal, and no matter how much Mo'min's father begged for an explanation, a clue to the infraction he'd committed to earn this punishment, the Sheikh would offer none.

We're going to have to leave, Mo'min's mother said, and then she broke down crying again. But the words made no sense to Mo'min. He'd known nowhere else. The Shobra of his father's youth was no more real than the made-up cities from which all those criminals on *America's Most Wanted* came, storybook places all of them. But when his mother regained her composure and drove them home, he entered to find the movers already packing.

•

In autumn, the Crédit Suisse Exhibition featured Lucian Freud. He had no idea who Lucian Freud was but he liked looking at the paintings, late at night after the crowds had dispersed and the gallery belonged to the janitors and the security guards – what his friend Melaku called the after-people. The bodies in the paintings seemed to be trying to shed themselves, break free. He liked paintings in which he could infer suffering.

All in all it was decent employment, given his circumstances. Elsewhere in London a man on the wrong side of forty, his immigration status irreparably illegal, couldn't hope for much more than a late-night gas station or Tesco's shift and a bedspread in the space beneath a staircase. But here he was, an agent of culture, cleaning up the floors of one of the finest art galleries in the world. Sometimes when the guards weren't looking he took pictures of the paintings and sent them back to his relatives in Shobra. Sometimes he made up stories about the painters, the lives they'd lived. Sometimes he said he'd met them personally. No one ever challenged or corrected him.

One day he arrived at work to find a row of black-windowed Mercedes sedans parked illegally outside, and an entire wing of the gallery closed.

Visiting dignitary, Melaku said. A collector too, big big money, make big donation, get private tour.

It had been more than a quarter-century since he'd last seen her, and he had long since stopped thinking about what he'd do if he saw her again. Against the flattening glass of years, his memory of the girl on the swing had become smeared past the point of recognition. It was only an artifact of sensation now, the faintest trace of blood rushing, falsely electric the way all youth is in rearview.

Through a small crack where the grand hall doors failed to meet, beyond the two-man security detail stationed there and the half-dozen more that surrounded her highness in the gallery, Mo'min caught a second glimpse of the Emir's daughter. She was taller – of course she was, they were only thirteen last time – and smiling, in conversation with the gallery director. She was flagpole-postured now, grown fully into the comfort of her fortressing.

Mo'min pushed his janitor's cart toward the towering doors. One of the men who guarded them put out his hand.

"Not today, mate."

But Mo'min didn't listen. He simply kept moving toward the door, and when the two men stepped in to stop him he rammed the cart into them and tried to carry his momentum through the doors, through the other guards, through the walls on which hung the paintings of old men who sought to escape from their own melting flesh, which as he saw the paintings again now and as if for the first time seeing them thinking, no, it was the flesh trying to escape the men. Through the streets and buildings, the sea and the sea. Through time.

He felt himself lifted. The marble floor came up to greet him and all the air left his lungs. He felt the oddest lightness. Even when the other guards, alerted, came running and pinned him further against the floor, the weight of them was nothing, less than nothing. The floor wrapped itself around him and through a phalanx of limbs he caught sight of her a last time and she was home.

The Devil's Waiting List

AHMED SALAH AL-MAHDI

Translated from the Arabic by Rana Asfour

MANSI WAS NERVOUS. HE SHIFTED IN HIS SEAT OPPOSITE A desk behind which sat an attractive woman. Her eyeglasses, he noted, seemed only to add to her allure. The unremarkable, even dilapidated desk, appeared as if straining to hold its form, ready to collapse at any moment under the weight of the piles of papers spread across almost every inch of its surface. In fact, now that he took a moment to survey his surroundings, he noticed that the entire office seemed rather shabby and unkempt. It felt suffocating.

Mansi reached up and slightly loosened his tie.

It was a stifling August day and the heat had followed him into the room along with a swarm of flies that flitted about haphazardly from one surface to another. Mansi was annoyed and tired from constantly having to swat away at the bloated ones that were keenly intent on gluing themselves to the sticky sweat running down his face.

The concerto of buzzing flies mixed in with the screeching hum of the whirling, ancient, and useless ceiling fan, succeeded in further rattling his nerves.

As he sat there, he wondered at the reasons that had possessed him to seek this place out, the impetus that had started this whole endeavor. He was an obscure, average writer, who'd managed to publish a few stories and poems, albeit in publications that hardly anyone seemed to read or care about. He longed to bask in the fame and glory that other writers, certainly with less talent than him, enjoyed. He wanted acclaim, recognition and for all to sing the praises of his work. It pained him that no one seemed interested in what he had to say.

Despite that, he always got a kick out of seeing his work printed along-side a photo of himself dressed up in his suit, the only one he owned.

Waiting for the woman to look up from her papers, his thoughts drifted back to the day he'd met with his friend at a coffee house in one of Cairo's oldest and most over-crowded quarters. He'd been observing the steam rising from the coffee placed on the dirty table in front of him as his lips puckered around the plastic nib of a hookah's pipe, drawing in a lungful of air so that the coal burned, and the water at the base of the contraption gurgled, after which he'd exhaled a satisfying breath of smoke out of his nose and mouth that rose into the sky in what seemed like interlacing circles.

"They say," he told his friend who was sipping quietly at his tea, "that all these famous writers and artists actually sold their souls to the devil for their fame and glory. I despair at the length of my failed state. If it's true, I'm willing to sell my soul in order to succeed."

His friend had laughed then. "Books have corrupted your mind," he said. "No one can sell his soul to the devil."

Back at home, the notion had kept playing round in Mansi's mind like a hallucination. Even as he'd sat at his computer, and typed in *how to sell your soul to the devil* in Google's search engine, he acknowledged the foolishness of his actions. Mansi trawled through websites on conspiracy theories, celebrity accounts, and all manner of weightless trivia, but seriously doubted he would ever find a concrete answer to his question.

After what seemed like half the night, there it was, a site that despite its need for an updated design was in all other respects the answer to what he was looking for. Spare with information, it nonetheless displayed a number for inquiries and an address. *Was this some kind of joke?* he'd thought to himself.

And so, this morning, he'd decided to check the authenticity of the address for himself. Joke or not, he reasoned, he couldn't allow the slimmest possibility of becoming a renowned writer slip away, even if the path he sought was based on a crazy, feckless idea that most likely would, in fact, turn out to be a full-blown hoax that he'd naively fallen for.

The address had brought him to a narrow alley lined with old, semi-dilapidated buildings. The street was filthy and rank with foul-smelling water. He could hear the sounds of people quarreling behind doors, children playing in the distance, hurling abusive language that burned at his ears. Dressed in his suit, his presence marked a stark contrast with his surroundings.

He'd finally found the office on the ground floor of a worn-out apartment building. Only a few stories high, the internal layout reminded him of the offices in government establishments. No sooner had he knocked on the door, than a female voice had asked him to enter and sit down, before she'd gone back to her pile of papers.

And, here he was, he noted, still awaiting his turn, his frustration and annoyance gathering momentum.

"... Your name?"

He flinched at the high-pitched voice that had pulled him out of his simmering stupor.

"Mansi," he replied. "My name is Mansi."

She jotted that down on a paper in front of her.

"How can I help you, Mr. Mansi?" she asked.

For a brief moment, he was reluctant to mention the advertisement that had brought him to her, worrying that she'd make fun of him, or worse, doubt his sanity. He thought of leaving, but something inside him was willing him to go through with what he had come to do, if only to bring a definite end to this insane situation he found himself in.

Finally, mustering up the courage, he said, "I'm here to sell my soul to the devil."

He waited for her to laugh at his words, to mock him, to chase him out of the place.

"Did you bring the required documents?" she said instead.

He looked at her, astonished beyond words. "What documents?" he finally managed to say.

She raised her eyebrows in irritation, as she scrutinized him from above her eyeglasses.

"A personal photo, a copy of your government ID card, and a written and signed affidavit that you consent to giving up your soul to the devil once your request has been fulfilled."

He couldn't tell at this point if he was confused, or disappointed, at the banal proceedings. But again, what had he been expecting? For the devil himself to be waiting in greeting? He handed her his ID and a personal photo he kept in his wallet for emergencies.

"I didn't know anything about a statement. Can I write that now?"

The woman reached her hand towards one of the desk drawers and retrieved a plain piece of paper and a pen, which she extended towards him.

He looked down at the white sheet and drew a blank. His mind felt porous, riddled with tiny holes, like a sieve through which his words leaked through until his mind was left empty. A slate clear and clean.

"What do I write?" he asked, his confusion palpable.

She sighed impatiently.

"Write what everyone usually does. I, so and so, pledge to give up my soul to Satan for such and such, and give my full consent to the transaction. Sign it at the bottom and that's that."

"But I'm not clearly sure I know what I want," he said.

"You want what all men want," she replied, sounding bored now. "Fame, fortune, clout. The phrasing of the request may vary but in the end you all desire the same thing. Just write down the real reason that pushed you to drag your own two feet into our office today."

"Honestly, I came here thinking this would turn out to be a joke. It seems I was mistaken. So be it, let me think."

He scratched his head with the tip of the pen.

"I want to be a best-selling author and for my books to fly off the shelf faster than hot cakes," he told her.

"See, it's exactly as I predicted. Nobody wants to sell their soul in exchange for world peace, or to bring an end to famines, or to find a cure for cancer. Everyone is here for purely selfish and personal ambition."

His emotions and facial expressions alternated between shame and anger at the woman's words. He wanted to explain to her that only desperate people, like him, sold out by everyone, abandoned, and left to wallow in misery and despair, would consider something as mad as selling their souls to the devil. Nobody was deserving of his sacrifice, for where were they when he had needed them most? Before he could formulate any of these thoughts into words, the woman was back to talking again.

"It's none of my concern what you write really, as long as you make sure to sign your name at the end of it."

Once he'd written and signed the affidavit and handed it back to the woman, she scanned his ID card, attached his photo to his statement, and tossed the application on top of the pile of papers scattered around her desk.

"Right. All that's left for you to do is to go home and wait your turn."

"Turn?" he repeated, incredulous. "My turn?" he repeated.

"Yes, Mr. Mansi, your *turn*," she repeated, slower, as if he were an imbecile. "You're not the only one who wants to sell his soul. These papers are all requests from customers. We run quite a complicated operation and it will take time."

The feeling returned to Mansi that he might yet be the victim of a ridiculous prank. After all, the whole situation hadn't lost any of its absurdity.

"I didn't know there'd be such a long waiting list," he said to the woman, his tone dripping with sarcasm.

"Did you really think you were the only one to come up with this ingenious solution to your troubles?" said the woman, matching his sarcasm with her own. "Do you not see all these papers? They're all applications submitted by writers like you, as well as actors, singers, footballers, and so many lottery hopefuls. As I said, the process is intricate, and requires your patience. We can't have everyone winning the jackpot at the same time now, can we? Do you understand what I'm saying?"

"Yes," he answered begrudgingly. "But . . ." he trailed, his bewilderment and distress getting the better of him. His tongue felt heavy all of a sudden, and the sweltering heat had intensified so that he felt like he was suffocating. He reached up and loosened his tie for the second time that day. And the flies, which seemed to have woken up from slumber, had returned with a frenzy that was driving him batty.

"So, I don't get to meet with the devil? I certainly didn't expect my business to be concluded with his assistant."

"No one can see the devil," she said, raising one eyebrow high, and pinning him with a piercing stare. "I thought you knew that, Mr. Mansi."

For an instant, he held her gaze before he bowed his head towards her in acquiescence.

Mansi stood up and headed toward the exit, leaving behind him the susurrant screech of the fan, the tormenting frenzy of the flies, and a paper bearing his signature in which, in his own handwriting, he had pledged his soul to the devil.

*

Mansi never told anyone about that day.

He lived his days in the hope that his turn would come soon and that his wish, as promised, would be fulfilled. And so, he waited.

Days, then months, passed and he went back to questioning whether his meeting with the woman had been nothing more than a prank he'd stupidly gone along with, one set up by evil, sick-minded individuals who got a kick out of preying on the desperation and desolation of the ill of mind and spirit. Soon the years began to go by, too, and he doubted whether the entire incident had happened at all. With each passing day he was more and more convinced that what he'd really experienced was nothing more than a fantastical nightmare. A hallucination.

In the meantime, Mansi worked on a new novel. Once it was published, he resigned himself that this one, just like all the other ones that had preceded it, would end up as fodder for the warehouse moths. However, this time was different. Critics hailed his novel, newspapers wrote about him, and readers rushed out to buy his book. Overnight, Mansi had become the toast of the town and the name on everyone's lips.

Initially, he felt a joy like none he had ever experienced. He relished every moment, basking in the warmth of the fame and glory he'd spent years waiting and hoping for.

It wasn't long, though, before fear crept up on him, setting up residence in his heart. As he recollected the details of the pact he'd made in the presence of that woman in that stifling office, the weight of what he had done began to gnaw on his conscience. Over the years he'd managed to convince himself that his sojourn into that alley had never really happened, the whole incident a mere figment of a troubled imagination. Every day he'd question himself whether anything was ever worth selling one's soul to the devil for.

As Mansi's fame and fortune increased, so did his depression deepen, and insomnia set in. Everyone wondered at the reasons behind his haggard and drawn appearance, the dark circles under his eyes, the misery that overwhelmed him. It ate at him that he couldn't tell anyone the truth, not even the psychiatrist he could now afford. Bit by bit, it dawned on Mansi that it wasn't fame, fortune, or glory that he needed most, but the soul he'd thoughtlessly given away on that day, which he now wanted back.

It had been years since he'd made his way to that alley, to that apartment building and to that office. It seemed as if time had unraveled back on itself to that same August day, with its stifling heat and suffocating warmth. The lane itself hadn't changed, its inhabitants regarding him with suspicion as he walked through. He stood out like a sore thumb in his luxurious new suit, one of several that he now owned.

He barged through the door without knocking and found the woman sitting at her desk, absorbed, just as she had been the first time he'd been there, with whatever it was she was always writing on those papers. His rude intrusion had ruffled her, for he noticed her eyeing him with a look of disapproval.

"Perhaps you don't remember me," he rushed to say before she could open her mouth. "I was here a few years ago."

She furrowed her brows in concentration.

"Yes, I remember you. You're that writer. Mr. Mansi if I recall correctly? What can I do for you today?" she said.

"I'm distraught and only you can help me," he said.

"Rest assured," she answered, "we can certainly ease any burden. However, you're still on the waiting list, and your turn hasn't come yet. You've waited this long, surely you can go a while longer."

Mansi was stunned. His legs felt wobbly and the room began to spin around him. His thoughts were jumbled as they raced through his mind. What was she talking about? He couldn't possibly be on the waiting list, he told himself, not after all the good fortune he'd enjoyed since his last visit to this place. The woman had to be mistaken. But what if she wasn't? he asked himself. Did he dare believe that his fame and fortune had had nothing to do with his pact with the devil? That it had been a success long overdue, one born out of hard work and persistence? Is that what all this meant?

"I'm here to withdraw my application," Mansi announced.

"Have you lost your mind?" asked the woman, incensed.

"That may be so," he said. "Although I've never felt more rational in my entire life."

"This is most unusual. I don't think we've had anyone dare to renege before. I'll have to consult the agency's guidebook on this one. Give me a moment, please."

His heart sank. What if the manual stated that he couldn't have his application back, or that a deal with the devil could never be rescinded? What was he to do then?

The suspense of the wait combined with the room's stifling heat was getting to him. Nauseous and dizzy, he sat down in the same chair he'd occupied that very first time he'd been to the office all those years ago. As the minutes crept by, it seemed to Mansi like he'd been waiting for an eternity. He shifted uncomfortably in his seat, silently willing the woman to put an end to his misery. The sooner he could put all this nonsense behind him, the better.

"Only a minute longer, and we'll have this solved one way or the other," the woman said, as if reading his mind.

Mansi desperately wished he could gauge from the tone of her voice which way his day was headed. By then, he knew he was clutching at straws but desperate times require desperate measures, he thought. Just as he was about to ask her another question, the woman cleared her throat.

"Well, it's as I thought," she said. "It seems that once an application has been received by the devil, backing out of the deal is no longer an option. In fact, doing so incurs rather unfortunate, by which I mean painful, consequences to the applicant. You must understand that we conduct a serious operation here. A pact with the devil is no trivial matter. Therefore, I'm sure you'll understand that the punishment should be deserving of the gravity of the deal at stake. This is the Devil, Satan, the Shaytan himself, and he does not appreciate any disrespect or waste of his precious time."

Mansi blanched. It was all over. The game was up. All he could think of was how a moment's insane lapse of judgment, fueled by a rabid desire for fame and glory, had reduced him to this infernal wretched state of affairs. He had no one to blame but himself.

"I'm asking you one more time, Mr. Mansi, are you sure you want to proceed with your request?"

Later, if anyone ever asked him why he had gone ahead with what he had done, his honest reply would be that he didn't know what had possessed him. All he'd been thinking of was a compelling need to set things right in the only way he knew how, even if it meant risking everything, including his life.

"Yes," he replied. He repeated his answer a second time, his tone more forceful and confident.

And just like that, for the first time that day, the woman smiled.

"It seems this is your lucky day, Mr. Mansi. It appears, as per the guidebook, that as your request is still pending on our waiting list, it hasn't been seen by the devil yet, which means you are free to withdraw your application with no strings attached."

With that, the woman moved a pile of yellowed papers behind which some old files appeared to be arranged in alphabetical order. She searched for Mansi's name, found his application, and placed it on the desk in front of him.

Mansi could hardly believe this incredible turn of events. But – just as he was about to reach forward to grab the paper – the woman raised her index finger in warning.

"Think carefully. If you go through with this, you'll lose your place in line. Should you decide to submit a new application, you'll be relegated to the bottom of the list again."

Delirious with relief and happiness, he snatched the paper off the desk, and held it in both hands.

"May your waiting list go to hell," he said, a manic laugh already bubbling its way out of his parted lips as he registered the absurdity of what he'd just said. By this point, Mansi was beyond caring. He'd got what he'd come for, and all he desired now was to put as much distance between himself and this place as he possibly could.

With his sworn statement in hand, Mansi stepped outside into the alley. He tore the damned thing into tiny little pieces that scattered everywhere, in a sudden gust of hot wind. For the last time, he turned on his heels and headed home, his hysterical guffaws bouncing off the walls of the alley's battered buildings.

About the Writers and Translators

SALAR ABDOH is a writer and translator who contributes to many publications, including *Guernica* and *The Atlantic*. He is the author of four novels, *Poet Game* (Picador, 2001), *Opium* (Faber and Faber, 2004), *Tehran At Twilight* (Akashic Books, 2014), and *Out of Mesopotamia* (Akashic Books, 2020). He is the editor and translator of the anthology *Tehran Noir* (Akashic Books, 2014). His fifth novel is *A Nearby Country Called Love* (Viking Books, 2023). He is based in New York and frequently travels the world.

Sudanese-born LEILA ABOULELA is the author of two short story collections and six novels, including the New York Times Editors' Choice and LA Review of Books–praised novel *River Spirit* (Saqi Books, 2023). She lives in Aberdeen, Scotland.

FARAH AHAMED's writing has been published in *The White Review*, *Ploughshares* and *The Massachusetts Review* amongst others. She is the editor of *Period Matters: Menstruation Experiences in South Asia* (Pan Macmillan India, 2022, periodmattersbook.com). You can read more of her work at farahahamed.com. She was born and raised in Kenya and now lives in London.

OMAR EL AKKAD is the author of the novels *American War* (Knopf, 2017) and *What Strange Paradise* (Knopf, 2021). Born in Egypt, he spent his youth in the Gulf, then moved to Canada, and now lives in Oregon.

SARAH ALKAHLY-MILLS is a Lebanese American writer living in Rome who was born in Burbank, California.

NEKTARIA ANASTASIADOU is the author of the novels *A Recipe for Daphne* (Hoopoe/AUC Press, 2021) and *Στα Πόδια της Αιώνιας Άνοιξης/ Beneath the Feet of Eternal Spring* (Papadopoulos, 2023). She is a Turkish citizen writing in Istanbul Greek and English.

RANA ASFOUR (translator), a native of Amman, Jordan, is a writer, book critic and translator whose work has appeared in such publications as *Madame* magazine, *The Guardian UK* and *The National*/UAE. She blogs at BookFabulous.com and chairs the TMR English-language Book Club, which reads literature of the greater Middle East and meets online the last Sunday of every month. She is the managing editor of *The Markaz Review*.

AMANY KAMAL ELDIN was born in Egypt. She received her MA from Columbia. Her short stories have appeared in diverse publications, including the anthology *Countries of the Heart* (Read It Again Books, 1997). She has lived in the United States, England, France, Austria, Kenya, Italy, Oman, Yemen and, for the last 20 years, in the United Arab Emirates.

JORDAN ELGRABLY is a Franco-American writer and translator of Moroccan heritage whose stories and creative nonfiction have appeared in numerous anthologies and reviews, including *Apulée*, *Salmagundi* and the *Paris Review*. The cofounder and former director of the Levantine Cultural Center/The Markaz (2001–2020), he was producer of the stand-up comedy series The Sultans of Satire (2005–2017), and the producer of hundreds of other public programs, including the play *Sarah's War*. He is the editor-in-chief and founder of *The Markaz Review*. He is the co-editor, with Malu Halasa, of the forthcoming anthology *Sumud: a New Palestinian Reader*. He divides his time between California and Montpellier, France.

OMAR FODA is a graduate of the PhD program in Near Eastern Languages and Civilizations at the University of Pennsylvania. He has published articles and a book on the history of Egypt including *Egypt's Beer: Stella, Identity and the Modern State* (University of Texas, 2019) and has taught at Towson University, Bryn Mawr College, and the University of Pennsylvania. He was born in Oklahoma City and lives in Syracuse, New York.

MAY HADDAD is an Arab American writer of speculative fiction whose work deals with the Levantine Arab experience across time and space and touches on themes of nostalgia, isolation, memory, and longing. With roots tracing all over Lebanon, Syria, and Palestine, they currently alternate their time between the U.S. and Lebanon. As of this publication, you can find their work in the SFWA Blog, *The Markaz Review*, and *Nightmare Magazine*.

DANIAL HAGHIGHI is a Tehran-based author of seven books and numerous essays in Persian. His work has appeared in the short story collection *Tehran Noir* (Akashic Books, 2014).

MALU HALASA is a Jordanian-Filipina American writer in London. She is the author of the novel *Mother of All Pigs* (Unnamed Press, 2017) and numerous non-fiction anthologies, including *Woman Life Freedom: Voices and Art from the Women's Protests in Iran* (Saqi Books, 2023); *Syria Speaks: Art and Culture from the Frontline* (Saqi Books, 2014); *Transit Tehran: Young Iran and Its Inspirations*, with Maziar Bahari (Garnet Press, 2010); and *The Secret Life of Syrian Lingerie: Intimacy and Design*, with Rana Salam (Chronicle Books, 2009). She is the literary editor of *The Markaz Review*.

MK HARB is a writer from Beirut who serves as editor-at-large for Lebanon at *Asymptote Journal*. His writings have been published in *The White Review*, *The Bombay Review*, *BOMB*, *The Times Literary Supplement*, *Hyperallergic*, *Art Review Asia*, *Asymptote*, *Scroope Journal* and *Jadaliyya*. He is currently working on a collection of short stories pertaining to the Arabian Peninsula. He lives in Dubai.

ALIREZA IRANMEHR was born in Mashhad, Iran. He has written extensively as a critic and scriptwriter, and his novels and short story collections have won several of Iran's major literary awards. His works include *The Pink Cloud* (Candle and Fog, 2013), *All the Men of Tehran Are Named Alireza*, and *Summer Snow,* both collections published in Persian. Presently he lives and works in the Gilan province near the Caspian Sea.

KARIM KATTAN is a Palestinian writer from Bethlehem who writes in French and English. He is the author most recently of the novel *Le Palais des deux collines* (elyzad, 2021). Kattan, awarded the Prix des Cinq Continents de la Francophonie in 2021, has been shortlisted for many other awards. His second novel, *L'Éden à l'aube*, is forthcoming in 2024.

HANIF KUREISHI is the author of the novels *The Buddha of Suburbia* (Faber and Faber, 2009), *The Last Word* (Faber and Faber, 2014), *Intimacy* (Faber and Faber, 2017) and *What Happened?* (Faber and Faber, 2019). He has published dozens of short stories, including in the collections *Love in a Blue Time*, *Midnight All Day* and *Love + Hate*, all from Faber and Faber. He lives in London.

AHMED SALAH AL-MAHDI is an Egyptian author, translator and literary critic in Cairo who specializes in fantasy, science fiction, and children's literature. He has five novels published in Arabic so far. Two of them – *Reem: Into the Unknown* and *Malaz: City of Resurrection* – have been translated into English. He has published many short stories, poems and articles in various languages.

DIARY MARIF is a Canadian Kurdish nonfiction writer and freelance journalist. He moved to Vancouver from Iraq in 2017, where he has been focusing on nonfiction writing and has recently written two book chapters for two different projects. He is an author at New Canadian Media focusing on immigrants' and newcomers' issues in Canada. He earned a master's degree in History from Pune University, in India, in 2013.

TARIQ MEHMOOD is a novelist and filmmaker. His first novel, *Hand On The Sun* (Penguin, 1983), on racism and resistance in the UK, has been republished by Daraja Press, 2023. His next novel, *Sing To The Western Wind, The Song It Understands*, is due out in Spring 2024 from Verso. He is making a British Film Institute–supported film on the case of the Bradford 12, in which he was a central defendant. He works at the American University of Beirut, Lebanon.

SAHAR MUSTAFAH's first novel, *The Beauty of Your Face* (W.W. Norton, 2020), was named a 2020 Notable Book and Editors' Choice by the *New York Times Book Review*, and one of *Marie Claire* magazine's 2020 Best Fiction by Women titles. It was long-listed for the Center for Fiction 2020 First Novel Prize, and was a finalist for the Palestine Book Awards. She was awarded a 2023 Jack Hazard Fellowship from New Literary Project and a literature grant from the Illinois Arts Council Agency. Mustafah is a native Chicagoan and currently resides in Orland Park, Illinois.

MOHAMMED AL-NAAS is a Libyan writer who is interested in alternative Libyan stories. He writes about gender roles, freedom of speech, social norms, cinema, and other marginalized aspects of life in Libya. His novel *Bread on Uncle Milad's Table* (HarperVia, 2024) won the 2022 International Prize for Arabic Fiction. He divides his time between Libya and Turkey.

AHMED NAJI is a writer, journalist, filmmaker, and criminal who was born in Menyet Sandoub, near Mansoura, Egypt, in 1985. He is the author of four novels in Arabic: *Rogers* (2007), *Using Life* (2014), *And*

Tigers to My Room (2020), and *Happy Endings* (2023). *Using Life* landed him a sentence in one of President Abdel Fattah al-Sisi's prisons for offending public morality, an experience he writes about in his memoir, *Rotten Evidence: Reading and Writing in Prison* (McSweeney's, 2023). His work has been translated into a number of languages and he has won several prizes, including a Dubai Press Club Award, a PEN/Barbey Freedom to Write Award, and an Open Eye Award. He was recently a City of Asylum Fellow at the Beverly Rogers, Carol C. Harter Black Mountain Institute. He lives in exile in Las Vegas.

MAI AL-NAKIB is the author of the novel *An Unlasting Home* (Mariner Books–HarperCollins, 2022) and the award-winning short story collection *The Hidden Light of Objects* (Bloomsbury Qatar Foundation Publishing, 2014). She was born in Kuwait and spent the first six years of her life in London, Edinburgh, and St. Louis, Missouri. She holds a Ph.D. in English from Brown University and is an associate professor of English and comparative literature at Kuwait University. Her fiction has appeared in *Ninth Letter*, *The First Line*, *After the Pause*, and *The Markaz Review*, and her occasional essays in, among others, *World Literature Today*, *BLARB: Blog of The LA Review of Books*, *New Lines Magazine*, *Index on Censorship*, and the BBC World Service. She divides her time between Kuwait and Greece.

ABDELLAH TAÏA was born in 1973 in the public library of Rabat, Morocco, where his father was the janitor and where his family lived until he was two years old. He is the first Arab author to come out as gay. He writes in French and has published nine novels (many translated into English and other languages), including *L'armée du salut* (2006), *Une mélancolie arabe* (2008), *Infidèles* (2012), *Un pays pour mourir* (2015), *Celui qui est digne d'être aimé* (2017), *La vie lente* (2019), and *Vivre à ta lumière* (2022). His novel *Le jour du Roi* was awarded the French Prix de Flore in 2010. *Salvation Army*, his first movie as a director, is adapted from his eponymous novel and won many international prizes. His novel *A Country for Dying*, translated into English by

Seven Stories Press, won the Pen America Literary Awards 2021. In the U.S., his novels are translated and published by Semiotext(e), among them *Salvation Army*, *An Arab Melancholia*, and *Another Morocco*; and by Seven Stories Press, including *Infidels* and *A Country for Dying*.

NASTASHA TYNES is a regular contributor to the *Washington Post*, *Nature* magazine, *Elle*, and *Esquire*, among other publications. Her short stories have appeared in *Geometry*, *The Timberline Review*, and *Fjords*. Her short story "Ustaz Ali" was a prize winner at the prestigious annual F. Scott Fitzgerald Literary Festival. She was born in Amman, Jordan, and lives in Rockville, Maryland. She is the author of the speculative literary novel *They Called Me Wyatt*.

Glossary

AHLAN WA SAHLAN — Arabic: Welcome; commonly used as a general greeting, like "hello" in English. Can be shortened to just *ahlan* (hi) in informal settings.

ALHAMDULILLAH — Arabic: Praise be to God; an Islamic term.

ALLAH YERHAMO — Arabic: May God have mercy on his soul.

AMREEKA — Arabic: America, the United States of.

ARAK — Arabic: strong clear-colored spirit, similar to Turkish *raki* and Greek *ouzo*.

ARGILEH — Arabic: a popular smoking device, aka *nargila*, *shisha*, waterpipe or hookah.

ATHAN *or* AZAAN — Arabic, Punjabi: the Muslim call to prayer.

BABA — Arabic, Persian and Turkish: father.

BARRA — Arabic: as in *la barra* — Get out of here.

BAYT — Arabic: house, or home.

BEEDI — Urdu, Hindi: a type of cheap cigarette made of unprocessed tobacco wrapped in leaves.

BESHARAM — Urdu: shameless; usually abusive slang.

BEY — Turkic: honorific title given dignitaries linked to the governor of a district or province in the Ottoman Empire that continued to be in use in Arab countries until the late 20th century.

BHENCHOD — Urdu, Hindi: motherfucker figuratively ("sisterfucker" literally); abusive slang.

BISMILLAH — Arabic, Islamic: In the name of God, the Most Gracious, the Most Merciful.

BRICOLAGE — French: handiwork, do-it-yourself, or in the Claude Lévi-Strauss lexicon, one's personal mosaic of identity, piecing your identity together from multiple parts.

CHADOR — Persian: head, veil and shawl covering that leaves only the face exposed, similar to the *niqab* in Arabic, which covers the face except for the eyes.

CHARPOY — Urdu: a type of bed made with a frame strung with tape or light rope.

CHUTIYAH — Urdu: asshole, idiot; abusive slang.

DUPATTA — Urdu, Hindi: a length of material, like a scarf, worn around the shoulders, typically with a *salwar kameez*.

ENSA — Arabic: Forget it.

FI QADIM AL-ZAMAN — Arabic: in the past.

FRANGI/FIRANGI — Arabic and Urdu: foreigner; usually a white person.

FOUL *or* FUL — fava beans, comfort food in Egypt, Palestine and beyond, often made with garlic, lemon, parsley.

GALABIA *or* DJELLABA — Arabic, French: a loose-fitting unisex robe, often worn by men, but also women in North Africa.

GORA — Urdu: foreigner; *franji* or *faranji* in Arabic.

GURDWARA — Punjabi: a Sikh place of communal worship.

HABERES BUENOS — Ladino: good news.

HABIBI/HABIBTI — Arabic: dear or darling; masculine or feminine, used with a family member, a friend and sometimes a lover.

HALAL — Arabic: Islamically sanctified meat, humanely butchered, akin to "kosher."

HANEM — Arabic: a lady or noblewoman.

HARAM — Arabic: un-Muslim, anything that is forbidden or taboo. Can be used humorously as well.

HARRAGA — Algerian Arabic: anyone who flees their country looking for a better life under questionable circumstances; an illegal immigrant, especially one who braves the dangerous Mediterranean.

HIJAB — Arabic: headscarf, usually worn by conservative Muslim women.

HILWA — Arabic: term of endearment to describe a beautiful woman.

INSHALLAH/ENSHALLAH — Islamic: If God wills it; the Spanish derivative is *ojalá*, "I hope so."

JAAN *or* JOON — Persian: a term of familiar endearment, equivalent to *aziz* or *aziza* in Arabic.

KALBE — Arabic: dog, also *kalbeh*, female dog; frequently used in insults. *Ya kleb*: You dogs.

KEFFIYEH *or* KUFIYYA — Arabic: traditional headdress, usually worn by Arab men and occasionally women, now a Western fashion statement. Yasser Arafat was rarely seen without his black-and-white-checkered headscarf, the symbol of the Palestinian people. Also known as the *ghutra*, *agal*, *hattah* and *shemagh*.

KHALAS — Arabic: That's it, that's enough.

KHARMAND — Arabic: horny.

KHATEEB — Arabic: the groom or the imam at the mosque.

KIBBEH NAYYEH — Arabic: raw meat mixed with bulgur and spices.

KUNEFE *or* KNAFE — Turkish, Arabic: traditional Palestinian dessert made from semolina, cheese, rose water and sugary syrup.

KURTA — Urdu, Persian: in Pakistan, a loose collarless shirt

KUTIYAA — Urdu: bitch, abusive slang.

LAHM B AJEEN — the Lebanese version of pizza or what is known as *man'oushe*, which consists of flatbread topped with oil and *za'atar*, plus toppings like cheese, pickles, veggies, labneh and meat; traditionally cooked over a wood fire.

LOKUM *or* LOUKUM — Turkish delight, confections made with cornstarch, sugar and flavorings.

MAGHREB — Arabic: the lands of the west, where the sun sets (Morocco, Algeria, Tunisia).

MAKTUB — Arabic: One's destiny is *maktub*, written by an invisible hand.

MANAKEESH — Arabic: breakfast flatbread with *za'atar*, cheese or both; also *man'ousheh*.

MARKAZ — Arabic, Hebrew, Persian, Turkish and Urdu: center, as in a gathering place.

MASHALLAH — Arabic: God willed or wills it.

MASHRABIYA — Arabic: traditional window coverings or shutters made of wood that allow one to see out but not in.

MASHRIQ — Arabic: the lands of the east, where the sun rises (from Libya and Egypt to the Levant, the Gulf and Iraq).

MOULOUKHIYA — Arabic: a type of regional herb stew, usually made with meat, popular in Egypt, with Palestinian and Lebanese variations, similar to the Persian stew *ghormeh sabzi*.

MUEZZIN — Arabic: the man who performs the *Athan* or *Azaan* (the Muslim call to prayer).

PASHA — Turkish: title of high rank in the Ottoman political and military system, typically granted to governors, generals, dignitaries; also used in Arabic as a term to show respect.

PEDAR SAG — Persian: dog father; an insult that is sometimes an endearment.

SAHARI *or* SUHOOR — Persian: pre-dawn Ramadan meal consumed before the start of the fast.

SALAFI — Arabic: an extremely puritanical creed of Islam.

SALAM — Arabic: a form of greeting, literally "peace"; the Hebrew equivalent is *shalom*.

SALAT — Arabic: mostly refers to the five-times-daily ritual prayer, one of the five Pillars of Islam.

SALAT AL MAGHRIB — Islamic: sunset prayer.

SALWAR KAMEEZ — Urdu: a long tunic and loose trouser worn by women.

SARDAR — Persian: chief or leader; amalgam of *sirr*, meaning head, and *dar* from *dashtan*, to hold.

SHARMOUTA — Arabic: bitch; derogatory, a prostitute.

SHISHA — Arabic: a hookah or argileh water pipe, used throughout the Markaz region.

SHLONAK — Arabic: How are you? (colloquial, used in the Gulf, Iraq and the Levant).

SHU FEE *or* FI — Arabic: What's up? informal; also *shu fi ma fi?* with the response *ma fi shi* (Nothing much).

SIBHA — Arabic: prayer beads with either 33 or 99 beads for the 99 names of Allah.

SITTI — Arabic: grandmother; also *teta*.

STEHEH! — Arabic: Mind your manners; exclamation at the start of a sentence.

SUNNAH RAK'AHS — Islamic: optional prayers, either two or four *rak`ahs* or *sunnah* before the *fard* or *Asr*, afternoon prayer.

TAKBEER — Islamic: the call to glorify Allah.

TARBOOSH — Arabic: a traditional Turkish headdress.

THOBE — Arabic: a traditional Palestinian ankle-length robe, usually with long sleeves.

TSOUREKI — Greek: sweet Easter bread (Turkish *çörek*).

USTAZ — Arabic: leader or teacher.

YA HEK YA BALA — Arabic : Either one does it this way or not at all.

YALLA — Arabic: Let's go!

YIH YIH — Arabic: an exclamation of surprise.

YALI — Turkish (Greek γιαλί): mansion on the Bosporus.

ZA'ATAR — Arabic: a traditional Palestinian, Jordanian or Lebanese dried herb mix with a native variety of thyme and/or oregano, sumac, marjoram and sesame seeds.

Acknowledgments

THIS COLLECTION IS THE RESULT OF MY LOVE OF THE SHORT story and the encouragement I received upon preparing to launch *The Markaz Review*. From my adolescent fascination with stories by Edgar Allan Poe, Arthur Conan Doyle, Mark Twain and Jack London, to reading as a young man the stories of Ghassan Kanafani, Isaac Bashevis Singer, Guy de Maupassant, Anton Chekhov, Vladimir Nabokov, James Baldwin, Doris Lessing and Nadine Gordimer, I fell in love with the form and continue to marvel at the power that a brief tale can have on our imaginations.

I might not have dared to start *The Markaz Review* in the midst of the pandemic had it not been for the encouragement of Tom Lutz, the founding editor of the Los Angeles Review of Books, nor my long-standing friendship with Ammiel Alcalay, both of whom urged me forward against long odds (support for the literary arts in the United States, a second cousin to the visual and performing arts, is the least generous in terms of individual philanthropy and foundation grants).

And the success of the review has largely depended on the stalwart camaraderie and creative ingenuity of my key collaborators—literary editor Malu Halasa, managing editor Rana Asfour, and contributing editor Salar Abdoh, as well as the members of the editorial board, among whom are writers Iason Athanasiadis, Jenine Abboushi, Melissa Chemam, Monique El-Faizy, Mischa Geracoulis, and Francisco Letelier. I would also like to thank Terence Ward for the many years of friendship and solidarity that have led to some surprising and unexpected results.

The Markaz Review would like to thank our generous supporters over the years, first and foremost Dr. Diane Shammas of the Shammas Family Trust, and Dr. Linda Jacobs of the Violet Jabara Charitable Trust, as well as Rowan Storm, Tony Litwinko, Mark Amin, India

Radfar and the A & A Fund, and Bana and Nabil Hilal, all of whom were the first people to understand what *The Markaz Review* could bring to the conversation about literary arts and the region we like to call the center of the world, from Afghanistan, Pakistan and Iran in the east, to Morocco, Algeria, Tunisia and Egypt in the west, including the Mediterranean and Levantine countries that have been so essential to the personality of the region, among them Turkey, Lebanon, Syria and Palestine, which, although it has been removed from the world map, is still very much on our minds, as we continue to hope for an outcome that will enable Palestinians and Israelis to become partners rather than combatants.

We also wish to acknowledge the visionary support we have received from the Open Society Foundation, Hawthornden Foundation, Andrew W. Mellon Foundation and the Community of Literary Magazines and Presses (CLMP), without which *The Markaz Review* would be a much hungrier and emaciated version of what it is today.